Land of Entrapment

Andi Marquette

Quest Books

Nederland, Texas

Copyright © 2008 by Andi Marquette

ISBN 1-935053-02-7
978-1-935053-02-6

First Printing 2008

9 8 7 6 5 4 3 2 1

Cover design by Mari SanGiovanni
Cover concept byDonna Pawlowski
Photograph: Adobe wall, New Mexico. Courtesy of the author.

Published by:

Regal Crest Enterprises, LLC
4700 Hwy 365, Suite A, PMB 210
Port Arthur, Texas 7764

Find us on the World Wide Web at
http://www.regalcrest.biz

Printed in the United States of America

Acknowledgments

This has been a hell of a journey and there have been a hell of a lot of people (and a few dogs) who have shared at least some of it with me. To all the people who have read this damn thing in various incarnations and offered excellent advice about plot and writing: A million thank you's for your work, patience, and humor. To my betas who went several rounds with K.C., Chris, Sage, Melissa, and Megan and me on top of all that, drinks on me when I see you next! You know who you are. And what the hell, even if you aren't, join us for a beverage anyway. And thanks to Fran, who rolled her eyes every time I pulled a southern belle with the vapors routine, convinced I couldn't write my way out of a bad adverb convention, and told me to ignore the inner critic and keep at it.

A big shout-out and massive thank you to Regal Crest Enterprises. Many thanks to Cathy LeNoir and the assessment team for reading the manuscript and offering me a contract (as opposed to putting a contract out on me). And special thanks to Cathy and Lori Lake, author liaison, for putting up with my seemingly incessant questions with astonishing patience and professionalism and thanks to Angel Grewe, for her gentle reminders and always pleasant responses. Thank you also to Donna Pawlowski for her patience, as well, and for her willingness to work with me on developing the initial concept (several times over) for the cover design. Big shout-out as well to Sylverre, who exhibited firm but gentle editing and guidance and whose advice I freakin' took because I knew it was good stuff.

A massive thank you to Mari SanGiovanni, who designed the version of the cover you see here. I have of course added several candles to my Mari shrine and may just start a petition for sainthood. "Saint Mari: patroness of flip-flops, cool pictures, awesome pasta, and generalized goofy mayhem." Thank you to Joan Opyr, who read this thing twice (at least) and STILL liked it. What the hell? Obviously, my evil spells are working! Thanks, Joan, for laughing at my jokes and for the encouragement when I was feeling like the lone urchin at a jellyfish squaredance. May the farce always be with you.

And of course, thanks to my muses, who cajoled, berated, and kicked my butt over the years to just sit down and get this thing written.

And many thanks to YOU, the reader, who opted to spend some time with K.C. and company. Hope you enjoy the trip.

To my parents, whose encouragement and support made me believe I could do this and to my sister, who keeps me focused and reminds me to laugh.

Chapter
One

"MAMAS, DON'T LET your daughters..." I sang, pulling the bale of alfalfa off the stack and hefting it into place in the back of the pick-up. "No, don't let 'em grow up to be scary-ass sociologists like me." Another bale, another impromptu verse. "Mamas, don't let your sociologists research neo-Nazis." A pause to rest in the central Texas heat, then I started bouncing up and down, the truck moving with me. "Mamas, don't let your daughters grow up to be college professors 'cause all they do is write boring books." Two-stepping in place now, turning a circle in the back of the truck. "Unless they're working on Grandpa's farm between semesters, oh, yeah. Hell, mamas! Don't let your daughters fry to death in a fucking Texas summer!" I hollered the last lyric and started laughing. "Sorry, Willie. It used to be a good song until now."

I stopped dancing and pushed the brim of my battered straw cowboy hat back and squinted in the sun, watching a cloud of dust that marked a vehicle's approach and waiting for the sound of its engine. Out here, neighbors know each other by the sound of car engines. The dust cloud slowed at Grandpa's quarter-mile driveway and hesitated before making the right-hand turn toward the house, picking its way slowly down the deeply rutted stretch.

Nope, didn't recognize the engine or the vehicle, a black SUV. Some rancher's kid from college stopping by, maybe. Or a tourist off the beaten path. Possibly a townie. Shrugging mentally, I continued loading bales of alfalfa into the pick-up from the monumental stack that last season's harvest had generated.

"Mamas, don't let your daughters stay out in the sun too long." I shoved another bale against the cab and the truck's bed shuddered. Ick. Even my hands were sweating. Prickly bits of alfalfa clung to my wrists and fingers inside my gloves. "Mamas, if your daughters say they want to research neo-Nazis, just say no. Because they'll end up in Texas!" I paused and stood watching as the newcomer pulled to a stop in front of the main house. *Nice rig.* Way too nice for these parts. Grandpa came out of the house, trying to calm Barb, who was on the verge of apoplexy as she ran circles around the vehicle. She was a dog of extreme moods. Dan and Perry tended to be the more methodical and thoughtful of the group and probably had already peed all over those nice new tires. Jane, the baby of the batch, stood on the porch's top step, watching Grandpa talk to the visitor through the driver's side window.

Sweat was collecting in the waistband of my jeans. I hate that. During a central Texas summer, the heat fogs your brain and wrings every drop of sweat from your pores. It hangs in the air like heavy clouds and follows you like Grandpa's heelers. You can sit inside and watch the heat sniff around your windows and doors or you can try to out-drive it, but it's always as fast or as slow as your vehicle and when you stop, it glares at you like a pissed off ex-girlfriend.

A central Texas summer isn't a season so much as a state of mind. I sighed heavily and hauled another bale off the stack. "Mamas, why'd you let your daughters leave New Mexico?" Two years since I'd left Albuquerque. God, I missed the dry heat. And the landscape. I shoved the bale into place. The Texas sun beat on my bare arms, which were already the color of topsoil. I tried not to think too much about the consequences of my UV exposure. Time to worry about that come fall. "Dammit, mamas, you know your daughters hate Texas," I sang, stomping my foot. "So why, mamas, didn't you get your daughters teaching fellowships in New Mexico?"

I grabbed the hem of my old white Indigo Girls concert tee and flapped it, trying to generate a breeze. I had cut the sleeves so that most of my biceps were exposed. The extra air flow was delicious when a breeze decided to stop by. Grandpa always expressed Puritan disapproval about my summer fashion. I told him that the cows didn't care what I wore as long as I fed them. That, plus threatening to lose the shirt entirely and just work in my jog-bra or half-naked, tended to win the argument with him.

The visitor hadn't gotten out of the SUV. Probably someone just needing directions. Grandpa would handle it. "Mamas, your daughters are scary in the heat," I said under my breath, grabbing another bale off the stack. "And your daughters would rather be back in New Mexico eating green chile." A shadow from the nearby silo crawled imperceptibly east. My work would be long done here before it offered any shade. I grunted and heaved another bale onto the truck's bed, maneuvering it into position. A rhythm developed, as I reached for another, looping my gloved fingers through the twine. Loop, lift, fling. Grunt for good measure. Loop...

"Howdy, Cowgirl."

There are times in people's lives when something so completely unexpected happens that their brains lose all ability to send messages to arms and legs. This was just such a time. And even if I'd wanted to turn toward the source of the voice, I was physically incapable of it. Instead, I chanted over and over in my head, *Please, please, please. It's a bad dream. A really, really bad dream. Please, please, please...*

"I always said nobody looked better in boots and jeans than you, Professor Fontero."

Against my will — it's truly amazing how your body can completely betray your best interests — my fingers untangled themselves from the twine and I turned to the woman I hoped so desperately was not really standing there. No deal. She spoke again.

"Hi, K.C."

The memories I had spent nearly three years filing carefully away in the warehouse of my heart suddenly appeared on the loading dock. I can speak, generally, but in this instant, it wasn't happening. "Melissa. I—"

"Didn't expect you," she finished gently. She smiled wanly, looked away, then looked back just as quickly. I could barely see her eyes behind her sunglasses. I felt shaky and cold, an odd sensation in the heat.

"I'm—" she started. Her voice broke and she looked at the ground. Teva sport sandals graced her feet and comfortably faded denim shorts hugged her still trim, athletic body much better than my memory served. A white T-shirt completed her ensemble. *Damn. Still gorgeous. How unfair.*

She regained control. "I'm sorry to interrupt you like this, but I need to talk to you."

What she meant was that she was sorry to invade what we both knew was a haven from the failed relationship whose bones I'd left back in Albuquerque. I shrugged, staring down at her from the truck. "You wouldn't have if it wasn't important," I finally offered, numb. All the bad memories I'd tried to sort through over the last three years hovered in the thick air between us.

I got down slowly, not realizing I was actually doing so, and joined her on the ground. I was still four inches taller than Melissa, though she seemed taller — time and my imagination hadn't diminished her. She brushed a strand of hair out of her face. Hair the color of Swiss chocolate, that my own hands once brushed away from her face.

We stood regarding each other. I noticed a silver chain around her neck. It looked like the chain I had bought her in Italy four years ago. She saw me staring at it.

"I never took it off," she said softly as she took a step toward me. More than anything, I wanted to hug her. And that scared me.

"Don't," I heard myself whisper. No matter how badly I wanted to, I couldn't have her touching me. I needed to maintain some sense of control, of pride. Her hands dropped to her sides. I abruptly pulled my gloves off and shoved them into a back pocket, trying to dispel the moment. "Well. You're here. So let's talk. Would you like something to drink?" I winced. My hostess mode always steps in when I'm having a problem with reality. I'm not sure if this is a good or bad thing. It might be inappropriate in certain situations. *Sir, before you kidnap me and make it look like I died in an accident, would you care for a sandwich?*

"Yes. That'd be great." She followed me as my steps automatically traced the tire-packed track back to the house fifty yards away. Dan and Perry left Grandpa's side and cautiously sniffed Melissa's feet as we neared the large covered porch where he sat in his favorite chair, a big wooden rocker. Barb lurked behind him, eying Melissa suspiciously. Jane leaned contentedly against Grandpa's leg, watching as we climbed the steps. My boots clunked on the wood.

"You want some tea, Grandpa?"

He shook his head in typical response.

"You sure?"

He nodded.

"I've got some business to attend to here. I'll finish the load afterward. Why don't you take a break, too?"

"Think I will," he said quietly, folding his hands across his stomach. It was a ritual we had. He would never admit how his arthritis pained him so I would give him the leeway he required to leave his work for a bit until his feet quit hurting. And he also wanted to make sure I was okay.

I opened the screen door and motioned Melissa through. The dogs all relaxed, evidently deciding that things were under control. They'd fly off the handle if necessary. Melissa followed me into the kitchen through the low-ceilinged, spacious living room — Grandpa called it "the parlor" — and the dining room. Time stopped in this house around 1942 and the furnishings reflected it. The kitchen, however, was an early twenty-first-century testament to technological innovation, courtesy of yours truly, my parents, two neighbor guys, and my cousin Luke. We'd lowered the cabinets, installed new countertops, tiled the floor midnight blue, and bought a refrigerator, microwave, new range, and dishwasher. I knew Grandpa found it easier to get to things he needed and he loved the microwave, though he complained the whole time the kitchen was under renovation.

I washed my hands and set two glasses on the counter before digging ice out of the freezer and taking the big jug of tea out of the fridge. Tea straight from the front porch. There's nothing quite like sun tea after you've been wrung out in a Texas summer day. I filled both glasses, feeling Melissa's eyes on me.

"Is your grandpa okay?"

"Yeah. His arthritis is a little worse, but he's doing all right." I put the tea back.

She picked up a glass and took her sunglasses off, exposing her blue-grey eyes. *Dang.* When she raised her eyebrows in a mute question, I motioned her to the screened back porch, where I had set up a yellow lawn table and chairs a month ago. Grandpa liked to sit out there in the evenings, watching sunsets splash the fields.

She and I sat down at the same time, Melissa across from me, and I tossed my hat onto an adjoining chair. I took a long pull from my glass, waiting, feeling raw and numb at the same time, like when an ornery horse dragged me a hundred feet down the driveway last fall. I limped the first two weeks of the new semester, earning some points with my students from ranching families.

"You really look wonderful, Kase."

A strange rapport occurs between ex-lovers. You can say things to each other without worrying about ramifications, repercussions, or social mores. After all, the worst that could happen – other than dying – already did. There's no need to impress and each statement is truthfully simple, uttered for no reason other than blunt observation. Had I looked like shit, on the other hand, Melissa would not have mentioned my appearance. But the implications would be clear: *"Woo-wee, Kase. These years have not been good to you. Lose some weight, girlfriend. Get a life."*

"Thanks. You're looking fantastic as ever yourself." I meant it.

"Texas has been good to you, then?"

I nodded. "Good enough, I guess." I swirled my tea and the ice clinked in the glass. "How did you know I'd be here at Grandpa's?"

"A feeling. And I found out you weren't teaching this summer."

I nodded again, for lack of anything else to do. Another silence descended. I heard, faintly, the creaking of Grandpa's rocker and the thump-thump-thump of a canine hind leg as one of the dogs scratched.

"K.C., I thought –"

I interrupted her. "Why are you here?" There was a hard edge to my voice. I could see its reflection in her expression. She dropped her gaze and her lower lip trembled slightly. *Dammit.* "I mean..." *Damn, damn, damn.* I took a deep breath. "I mean that I don't think we should talk about that. Later, maybe." Without thinking, I reached across the table for her hand. I suddenly realized what I was doing and jerked it back to my lap. She noticed.

"I'm sorry." Her voice was barely a whisper.

Of all the things she could have said, that was the one I didn't want to hear. It threatened to destroy my resolve. *Please don't let her see me cry.* I rubbed my eyes, intensely relieved that my fingers came away dry. "Just tell me why you're here."

She sighed, the old *you can be so stubborn but I'm usually right* sigh I remembered too well for my own emotional well-being. "Megan's gone." Melissa stared hard at the tabletop.

I sat back, caught somewhere between shock and anxiety. "What do you mean, gone?"

"She took off about a month ago. We haven't seen her since."

I didn't miss the *we.* "Did you call the police?"

Melissa jerked her gaze back to me. "They can't do anything. Megan's twenty-one. She's considered an adult. Besides, she's been calling."

I stared at her, perplexed. "So why are you saying she's gone? What's the problem?"

"She's calling from different numbers and she's not using her ATM card." Melissa looked pointedly at me. "And I think she's in questionable company."

Okay, I thought. So Melissa trucked herself out here to a broiling part of Texas because her younger sister ran off with a guy. I hadn't seen Melissa in nearly three years and the only reason she came calling was to tell me that Megan's keeping "questionable company." My skepticism must have been obvious because she continued, impatiently.

"I think her boyfriend is a neo-Nazi."

Now *that* was a different matter. I knew Megan had some issues growing up, but she seemed okay even after Melissa and I had parted ways. "Why would you think that?"

"His tattoos, for one. He only wears long-sleeved shirts around us, but a week before Megan disappeared, he showed up at a barbecue at our house and he had his sleeves unbuttoned but not rolled up. He reached for something and I saw that he's got a swastika on his left forearm."

"Oh, hell." I sighed and shifted into analytical mode, always a safe way for me to deal with my emotional shortcomings. "Well, maybe he's seen the light and hasn't had it removed yet. Does he know about you and Hillary?"

"Yes. When Megan first introduced him to us, she said that Hillary and I were partners."

"So has he done anything that would make you think he's still running with a bad crowd?"

"No. That's just it. He was always very polite and friendly to me and Hillary and he seemed to like Megan a lot. But when she disappeared, I went to her apartment and found all kinds of...of really horrible pamphlets, full of racist bullshit and stuff about the white race and...K.C., it made me physically sick. To think that

Megan might be getting into that."

It generated a physical reaction in me, as well. My stomach clenched. "Had she been saying anything strange, acting differently toward you? Maybe it was subtle and you didn't catch it. Think."

Melissa fell silent. "No." She paused. "Wait. She asked me about two months ago why I thought I was gay. She's never asked me that. She's always just... It's never even really been a topic of discussion."

"What did you say?"

"I told her I was born this way and she asked me why, if there's a genetic component, *she* wasn't gay. Never mind the fact that we only share one parent. But I told her that the latest studies — you know, trying to use science — suggest that whatever goes on *in utero* might have something to do with it. That the way hormones interact in the uterus — you know what I'm talking about, right?"

I nodded. I'd seen the latest studies, too.

"And then she asked if that was true, could I take hormones and change it?" Melissa stared at me, intense. "What the hell do you say to that?"

I didn't know. So I waited.

Melissa brushed hair out of her face. "I told her that nobody knew for sure what the hormone cocktail did or was made up of in the womb and that there was no way to alter the hard-wiring of your brain, which is what happens when you're *in utero* and when your hormones continue to work on you throughout your life."

"And what was her response?"

"She just kind of shrugged and said she had heard that you could change your sexual orientation and then Cody called — "

"Cody? That's the boyfriend?" I interrupted.

"Yes. And she took the call and said she had to go."

I chewed my lip, thinking. "Did she bring it up again after that?"

"No."

"Has she said anything about your grandma?"

Melissa shook her head, sad. "She stopped talking to her."

Oh, hell. Melissa's Nez Perce grandmother lived in Oregon. She had married a white man and their kids married other whites, as well. Still, Melissa was close to her grandmother and her Native roots. Megan was the child of Melissa's father and his second wife. Because of dad, Megan and Melissa shared their Native American grandmother. I sat back. "It sounds like this guy's not trying to leave the movement and that he's recruiting Megan."

Melissa watched me, lips drawn in a thin, tight line.

"Here's the hard part," I said gently. "She's an adult. And you can't really tell her what she can and cannot do. The police can't do anything about this unless one of them has committed a crime.

Belonging to a white supremacist group is not a crime in this country. I'm sorry." She looked at me and I could see tears in her eyes, which made me want to hug her. I refrained, with a mighty internal effort.

"But what if you think they *might* commit a crime?" she pressed.

I frowned. "What do you mean?"

"I don't think she really wants to be with Cody or his group. Not anymore, anyway. She calls about once a week and she's vague about where they are, but some of the stuff she says makes me think that she's waking up to what's happening here. And if she really did totally buy into Cody's message, why is she still calling her dyke sister?"

"What does she say to make you think she's not on board?" I leaned back in my chair, mentally calling up my research files.

"It's not so much what she says, it's how she says it. She'll say that she's fine and everything's fine and she doesn't want me to worry about her and then she'll say weird shit like if I think it's wrong to take money from corporations and give it to struggling Americans."

"What?" I furrowed my brows in thought.

"Remember I told you that back in the late eighties I was involved in ActUP! And QueerNation and all those groups that protested Reagan's response to AIDS?"

"Yeah." I had done that, too.

"Okay, Megan knows I did that stuff and she knows that I rag on corporate interests and I've told her that if you believe in something, you should fight for it. Except I never thought she'd believe in the supremacy of the white race, especially after knowing you and what you research." Melissa paused for a moment. "Anyway, she asked about belief and what it might take to make you believe something. I told her that belief was a really powerful thing but it could also work against you and it could make some people do bad things, things that hurt others. And she said she had to go and she hung up."

I tugged on my chin, listening.

"I asked her why she just doesn't come home and she said that she has something to do that's bigger than herself but something in her voice... I don't think she wants to be part of it anymore."

"Do you think she's being held against her will?"

"I don't know." Melissa sighed. "Pressure from a group..."

"Cult."

She looked at me, surprised. "Is this a cult?"

"What my research shows is, yes. White supremacist groups are like cults. There's usually a charismatic leader who convinces others to follow his—the leader's usually male—example and then the underlings perpetuate the message and actively recruit outsiders.

The group controls access to information through whatever means, whether peer pressure, threats to tell the leader, appeals to your convictions, things like that. You're indoctrinated with the beliefs of the group through constant repetition and constant reinforcement." *Jesus, I sound like a documentary.*

"The group controls information?"

"Yeah. And eventually, you come to think that any outside news or information is suspect and part of the larger conspiracy that the group's leaders and indoctrinated members are trying to convince you is real." I ran a hand through my hair. "See, not many people think of white supremacists as a cult so there isn't really a network of de-programmers."

"People who get you out of a cult." She reached for her iced tea, avoiding my eyes.

"Exactly. It's an approach to white supremacists that I've been digging around in for the past couple of years especially. Anyway, de-programmers help those who leave the groups adjust to real life outside the cult. However, even if you do manage to leave the movement, it takes a long time to let go of what it did to you."

Melissa's shoulders sagged. "So I can't do anything until Megan either commits a crime, comes home on her own, or winds up hurt or dead somewhere?"

I wasn't sure how to respond to that so I kept my mouth shut.

"That's total bullshit, K.C. That is total fucking bullshit."

"Megan's an adult."

"She's a hostage!"

"Maybe. Maybe not. Cults..." I paused, considering the ramifications of my words, decided to say it anyway. "They're like addictions."

She glared at me. "Megan's not using anymore."

"Hey, relax." I wanted to believe her. "One of the things many modern white supremacists espouse is absolutely no drug or alcohol use. So if Megan's with this crowd, chances are they're not allowing her access to anything. Which is a good thing because it keeps her from completely falling under their control. Think about it. Did you ever see Cody drinking?"

Melissa shook her head, realization in her eyes. "No. He always went for the Diet Coke."

"Did you see any names on the literature from Megan's apartment? Any group affiliations?"

"No. I was so disgusted and scared I didn't really read it."

"Did you save it?"

"Yes," she said with a *well, duh* tone. "I'm an attorney. It's evidence."

Before I could think about what I was saying, I said it anyway.

"Let me have a look at it." The relief in her eyes wouldn't allow me to change my mind. I kicked myself mentally from Grandpa's porch to Amarillo and back again.

"Thank you. It would mean so much to me. When can you come?" She leaned forward, hopeful.

"Um. Where? To Albuquerque?"

"That *is* where I live," she said snappishly.

"Whoa. Hold on. I don't think that's a good idea."

"How else are you going to see the stuff I found?"

Mail it? "Melissa..."

"You can stay at Megan's place," she continued. "I'm paying the rent and bills on it until..." She stopped and bit her lip.

I shook my head slowly. "Hold on. As much as I think it sucks what's going on with Megan, I don't know if I can help. Why don't you hire a private investigator?"

"I tried that," she said impatiently. "And most would have taken the case but they don't know anything about groups like this. I even tried contacting other people who research them and they all politely told me that it sounded like I needed the police or a PI."

I ran both hands through my hair, extremely uncomfortable with what she was asking of me. "Hey, I don't have any sort of affiliation with law enforcement. There's not a whole lot I can do. And besides, you're a lawyer. You deal with stuff like this all the time. Why can't you just—"

"Please, K.C.," she said, a slight sarcastic edge to her words. "Don't think I haven't considered that. It would make everything so much easier." I heard the unspoken "than having to deal with you." She looked at me, pleading. "You know Megan's history. You know *her*. She trusts you." Melissa watched me. "Remember what happened the last time?"

I did. Megan got strung out somewhere five years ago and Melissa didn't see her for a week. She hired a PI her firm used to track her down and he found her in some dive over in Albuquerque's War Zone. The police had to get involved because drug paraphernalia littered the apartment. Megan was arrested but Melissa managed to get her probation—Megan was a minor—and treatment.

"If Megan's caught up in something illegal, I might not be able to keep her out of prison this time." Melissa faltered and glanced away, clearing her throat.

"So you want to know exactly what she's doing with this guy," I said slowly, to make sure I understood what she wanted. "And you want it sort of 'unofficial.'"

Her gaze snapped back to mine. "Yes. If Megan is caught screwing up again, I have some decisions to make. I can either let it go, as much as that hurts, or report it. As much as *that* hurts. But if she's not with him of her own volition, then I might be able to cut a deal with the DA if Cody's doing anything illegal that Megan's privy to."

I saw Melissa's point, but I felt extremely uneasy. "What about Chris? Did you call her? Or think about calling her?" I was reaching here, knowing almost instinctively she hadn't, because Chris would've called and told me if Melissa contacted her. Chris tells me pretty much everything, unless it's something that'll compromise her investigations with the Albuquerque Police Department.

Melissa's eyes clouded. "I didn't feel right doing that. Especially since I haven't talked to her since you left. Besides, she would have told me to talk to you, too."

She was right. *Shit.*

"You've worked with groups like this," she continued. "You've talked to people who are still part of them. You've gone to meetings with them. You *know* these people. Maybe you can figure out which group it is and what they might be planning to do." She leaned forward. "And Megan knows you. She likes you. She's always liked you. Maybe she'll come back on her own."

Dammit. I chewed my lip, trying to find an excuse, any plausible reason, to avoid this situation.

"Believe me," she said, as if reading my thoughts. "If there was any other way to do this, I would have."

I watched her as she looked down at the table. She looked like she was going to cry again.

"I would do anything to have someone else do this, but I trust you with Megan's past."

In spite of our own, I finished for her. I could hear a slight catch in her voice.

"I'll pay you."

I stared at her as if she had just offered to pay me for sex.

"No," she said, realizing how it must have sounded. "I mean as a researcher. I know you've done that in the past. I'll pay your going rate for research."

I continued to stare at her. She might as well have just slapped me.

"Plus room and board? Please. It would mean a lot to me. You could use it for your next book. You're doing research this fall semester, anyway."

My stomach lurched. "How did you know that?"

She looked away.

"How did you know that?" I said again. She had been tracking me and it bothered me. Why didn't she just call? *Because she knows it'd be harder to say no to her in person.* I clenched my teeth, feeling used.

She stood, slightly flustered. "I checked. I needed to know where I could find you."

"It's not on my Web site," I said, testing her.

"I called the department."

I stood as well and stared out at the fields. By the sun, it must have been almost three o'clock. Somewhere in the heat and haze I heard a tractor. And somewhere further away than that I heard the engine of Melissa's Toyota Camry as she drove out of my life and into someone else's sunset. *Don't burn your bridges,* I heard someone saying. *'Cause you might have to cross the river again.*

"On the off-chance—" I started, keeping my eyes on the field, "that there *was* some other way for you to do this, would you have done it?"

"Yes." No hesitation.

I shifted my full attention back to her. "What exactly does this entail?"

"So you'll do it?"

"I didn't say that. I want to know what it is you're expecting."

She went into professional mode. "I want to know who Cody is, what group he's with, what they're planning to do, and where they might be."

"And?"

"Once you get that figured out, I'll take the next step myself. If she really does want to leave and he's forcing her to stay, I'll get the proper authorities involved."

I crossed my arms over my chest. "I don't want your money, Melissa."

"I'm hiring you to do research."

I wondered if Hillary had bought Melissa the same way she was trying to buy me. *Here ya go. Money'll fix it. I'll buy your heart and give you a new one.* A mouthful of bitterness accompanied my thoughts. *How much is your sister worth? How much am I worth?* I tugged my left earlobe, staring out across the fields again. "If I do this, I don't want your money," I said stubbornly.

"Will you at least let me provide the place to stay? And help with expenses?"

"If I do it." I sounded petulant.

"Thank you."

"I'm not sure. Let me think about it."

"Thanks for hearing me out." A faint smile lifted the edges of her mouth.

I nodded, feeling numb and cold inside, like I'd been left out in an early fall snow. The silence stretched between us until Melissa broke it when she opened the screen door. "Walk me to my car?" She raised her right eyebrow quizzically, almost playfully, like when she used to flirt with me. I guess I could still fall for it because I examined the outline of her back as she pulled the screen door open and stepped into the kitchen. Even underneath the T-shirt, I could envision her wiry muscles plunging below the waistline of her shorts. I quickly glanced away. Misdirected lechery, I attempted to convince myself as I grabbed my hat and followed her through the house.

Grandpa rocked slowly on the front porch, his eyes closed. The heat of the day weighed heavily on him and the dogs. Barb and Dan gave Melissa only a cursory once-over as she stopped to say goodbye to Grandpa, thought better of it, and quietly descended the five steps.

I took my time putting my hat back on, waiting for her to slide into the driver's seat and shut the door, saving me from any inadvertent physical contact. Sinking my hands into my pockets, I maintained a respectful two-foot distance from the Lexus. She twisted in her seat and fumbled through something on the floor in back. She must have found what she wanted because she resumed appropriate driving posture and fastened her seatbelt before directing her attention at me. Automatically, I stepped closer.

"It's good to see you," she said with what sounded like genuine pleasure, though tinged with sadness. She was holding a business card and she wrote something on the back with a black pen. "I know you might think differently, but I'd like to maybe talk sometime."

I shrugged.

She handed me the business card. "I know you'll think about this. And I know you'll call me either way."

I took the card, glanced at it and shoved it into a front pocket of my jeans. She started the engine. It purred smoothly, powerfully.

"Nice rig," I said softly. "You must be doing okay."

She smiled and slipped her shades on before resting her right hand on the steering wheel. I heard Bonnie Raitt issuing from the vehicle's sound system.

"K.C.," Melissa said firmly, over Bonnie's voice, "no matter what you decide, I'm glad I saw you." She smiled and shook her head in a "well, hell" motion. "I used to think you were a damn good-looking woman, and I didn't think it could get any better." Even through her shades, I could see her eyes sweep over me, from the toes of my boots to my hat. "I was wrong." And she was backing up before I could retort.

Damn her. Damn ex-girlfriends in general. Dammit. I watched the Lexus until it turned left onto the main road, heatwaves swallowing the sound of its engine.

She was gone again, leaving me staring after her. I guess there were a few ghosts that needed to be put to rest. Out of habit, I glanced skyward. Evening was coming on. I had to finish with the alfalfa.

Chapter
Two

MY EVENING RUN lasted longer than usual. When I returned to the house, darkness was forcing a reluctant sunset behind a gathering thunderstorm. Rain would be nice. Nights in the old house were nearly as oppressive as the days out of it. I thought I heard a quiet assurance from the distant clouds and I turned to study them. Grandpa's match scraped in the darkness behind me. He stood on the porch, leaning against the railing. The embers from his pipe glowed.

"I didn't see you," I said, searching the dark for his face. "I thought you'd be in bed by now."

I could almost hear him shrug. "A bit too hot yet."

I joined him on the porch, feeling a breeze ruffle the sweaty hair around my face. The breeze died as quickly as it had come. The evening felt stuffy. We might be in for some rain after all. "Luke'll be here in a few days. He's excited to be coming back."

Grandpa didn't reply, but I knew he liked the idea. Luke was his youngest and favorite grandson. I didn't mind my cousin, but he was a bit too Texas good ol' boy for my tastes. What was important was that he loved Grandpa and I knew that he'd take care of him.

"I'll be heading out in a couple of days," I said simply. I waited for him to say something. Instead, he nodded in the dark. I caught the motion because the embers in his pipe bowl bobbed.

"I asked Luke if he'd install an air conditioner for you. He'll pick one up at Home Depot and take care of that."

"Don't need it," he said in his gravelly baritone.

"Luke might. He gets used to it at school."

He didn't respond. I had let him off the hook with that and he didn't need to answer.

"I'll go check on the fences tomorrow," I added. I knew he needed to say something so I waited, perched on the railing.

"You going to call Melissa, then?"

I didn't say anything at first. We were a lot alike, he and I.

"Sounds like she needs some help."

"Yeah. It does." *What a sneak!*

"Long way to drive to ask you in person."

"Twelve hours, maybe." I picked at a splinter in the wood underneath my hand.

"She did you wrong," he said softly. I heard him take a pull on his pipe. He smoked tobacco that smelled like vanilla. "And she knows it."

Does she? Does she really? I stared up at the approaching storm, watching flashes of lightning in the roiling clouds.

"She made a mistake."

I looked at him, surprised. He couldn't see my expression in the dark. I tried to read the meaning between his words.

"Forgive and forget." He exhaled slowly and I caught a whiff of tobacco. "Or the past'll poison you."

I clenched my teeth.

"You'll do the right thing," he said. "Just remember who you are and where you came from. It'll get you by." It was the closest he would come to saying "take care of yourself," to saying that he was worried about me and please could I not get myself into a major loony-toon fuck-up situation.

"Yes, sir." He was old school and I often addressed him as such. I envisioned him smiling in the dark, looking up at the sky. I smelled the tinny, moist odor of rain. "C'mon," I urged him quietly. "Let's get in before it storms." Wordlessly, he entered the house ahead of me, Barb and Dan materializing simultaneously and darting around his legs into the parlor as the first discontented whispers of thunder caught my ear. I called Jane and Perry in and latched the screen door. I left the heavy inner door open, since Grandpa and I both liked to hear the rain. Lightning flashed in the distance, big electrical pogo sticks glancing off the plains, and I shivered. *God, I hope I do the right thing.*

THE MORNING ROLLED in on a stifling fog, residue of last night's monstrous storms. Leaving the house was like walking into a Swedish steam bath even this early. Muggy, moist, and threatening to get hotter. I hated days like these, when the sun swam in a thick, turgid sky and everything moved listlessly in a humid fishbowl.

Grandpa left the house at seven to check on a couple of fields. He'd said what he needed to say the night before and we both knew where we stood. Too bad every relationship couldn't be handled the same way. I went to saddle Ol' Jim up for today's fencing inspection. "Sorry, Jim," I muttered as I tightened the cinch and checked his bit. "We'll get done as fast as we can and come back."

He might have understood because he grunted softly. I swung into the saddle and coaxed him out into the heat, my legs already sweating underneath my jeans. Dan and Perry decided to accompany us, though after a half-hour, they gave up and headed home. I ended up walking most of the fence lines, Jim following along. We stopped at every watering tank for both our benefits. I drank from the spigots and soaked a bandanna that I tied around my neck. Nothing out of the ordinary, though I ended up ratcheting a few strands of fencing tighter.

By one o'clock I had nearly finished with the last stretch. Jim munched on some nearby grass while I adjusted the tension on a lower strand. I had spent most of the morning thinking about Melissa and what she had asked me to do. I hadn't heard from her since the break-up, and all of a sudden, here she was. Still, Melissa was pretty diligent about things. If she felt there was any other way to deal with this situation, she would have done so. I was sure of that. And she didn't call me or try to e-mail me. She drove down and talked to me in person, even though we had ended on bad terms.

I pulled my gloves off and clicked my tongue at Jim. "Let's get the hell outta here, buddy." I climbed aboard and steered him toward home. He didn't need any extra urging. At the barn, I removed his saddle and blanket and rubbed him down as he munched on what Grandpa called "horse chow." I made sure the saddle was clean and wiped off before I slung it over the sawhorse in the corner and then I stood and watched Jim eat for a while.

If Megan was mixed up with white supremacists—and from what Melissa told me, it sounded like she was—what were the options? Megan was twenty-one. She could run with any group she wanted as long as she wasn't doing anything illegal. Melissa, however, suspected that this group was on its way to doing something scary. Well, so what? Why was it *my* problem? I wasn't involved with Melissa anymore. I didn't owe her a damn thing. Not after the shit she pulled with Hillary. I sat on a bale of alfalfa and absently chewed a stalk while I tiptoed through that corner of my mind.

My cell phone rang. I stood so I could pull it out of my pocket and check the number. "Hey, Detective Gutierrez," I answered, rolling the r's with extra inflection. "*¿Como estás, mi amiga bellisima?*"

Chris laughed. "*Esa,* you crack me up. Spanish and Italian in one sentence. What the hell do you call that?"

"Italish."

"That's why I keep you around. Ten years and counting. Jesus. You're my longest relationship."

I laughed. "Holy hell, you're right. That's *my* longest, too. Why don't we just get married?"

"What, and ruin a perfectly good friendship?" she countered, though the warmth in her voice was palpable.

"Good point. Promise me you'll reserve a spot on your porch for me and my rocking chair."

"And a pan of green chile lasagna." Before I could respond, she continued. "Got your message last night but got in too late to call you. What's up?"

I exhaled slowly, settling into a more serious mode. "Melissa showed up yesterday."

Long pause. "There? At your grandpa's?"

"Yeah."

"What the hell for?" She sounded more puzzled than pissed. Chris didn't have much love for Melissa after the break-up, but she never directly insulted her.

I dug the toe of my boot into a bale of straw. "Megan's gone missing and Melissa thinks she's with her boyfriend."

"And you're supposed to care because—?"

"Her boyfriend seems to be a neo-Nazi."

Chris didn't respond for a while. When she did, she was using her "just the facts, ma'am" tone. "And Melissa wants you to come back to Albuquerque to help her find Megan."

"And that's why you're the detective," I said dryly.

"So presumably in the discussion she outlined why no other course of action would work."

"She's pretty thorough, as you know."

Chris remained quiet, but I knew she was thinking that Melissa was using any excuse to contact me.

"It's been three years," I pointed out. "She didn't contact me before this. I don't think it's about hooking up again."

"I'll leave that to your judgment, *esa*. What are your feelings about it?"

I paused, watching Jim munch. What exactly *were* my feelings? "She needs some help. And it took a lot for her to come down here." Though she hadn't brought shit up when we were together toward the end. I sighed.

"True," Chris said, cautious. "So—"

"Yes. I'll be coming to Albuquerque." Voicing that sent a little jolt of longing down my back. Going home. That's what I was doing, essentially.

"When?"

I heard Chris's grin, which triggered one of my own. "I guess...really soon. A couple of days?"

"*Mi mujer favorita vuelve a casa,*" Chris said, laughing. "This is some *good* news, Kase. Circumstances notwithstanding. I *knew* you'd come back."

"Your favorite woman?" I teased. "Really? And yeah, I suppose I am coming home in a lot of ways."

"Are you getting all mystical on me? Damn. I thought Texas might have baked that out of you by now."

"Yep. That's me. Mystic Chick. I'll go find my crystals and patchouli now." I rolled my eyes and stroked Jim's hide.

"Careful. Don't make fun of shit like that. *Abuelita* always says what you ridicule returns to haunt you."

I smiled. "I love your grandma. How is *Abuelita*, anyway?"

"She'll be much better now, after I call her and tell her that her favorite *gringita* is coming to town." Chris paused, then continued. "I am *so* excited to see you. It's been a while, *esa*."

"Don't get all excited just yet. I don't know what-all's involved here and I might not be in town too long."

"Oh, of course," Chris said with mock seriousness. "Nuevomexico is in your blood. I knew you'd come back."

"Chris, it's a visit."

"And isn't that how you ended up here in the first place?" she asked innocently. "Just checking out Albuquerque for grad school. Not sure you wanted to be here. Two days later, you'd found a place to live and accepted the department's offer."

I groaned. "All right, all right. But this is serious business and the last thing on my mind is moving back. I still have to finish out this damn post-doc, after all."

"Details," she retorted smugly. Then, "And fuck, I'm about to be really rude because I have to go put in some time *con la familia* and I'm late for dinner. Call me and tell me when you leave?" She voiced it as a question.

"Definitely. And say hi to your folks and your bros."

"Of course. Do you want to stay with me when you get here?"

"I'm not sure how that's going to work out. I'll probably end up at Megan's, since the shit I have to look at is there." I wasn't looking forward to that, either. Someone I considered a younger sister in a lot of ways, involved with racist crap. It made me kind of queasy.

"If you need a break from that, just go to my house."

"Will do. Thanks, *mujer*. I'll call you in a few."

"Damn right you will. *Buenas noches*."

"Yep. Catch you later." I hung up and thought a bit more about Melissa. She'd left me alone, like I asked. Until now. I sighed. "Jim, be glad you're a horse." He snorted. I watched my hand moving slowly over Jim's neck. I had the expertise to help Megan. She might not actually like me—God knows, her sister wasn't all that thrilled with me—and she might resent me for the rest of her natural-born life if I meddled. But I had knowledge that could help her. And not doing so did a disservice to her, the rest of her family, and to me. I thought about the researchers Melissa said she had contacted for advice. If it was true that they politely told her to go away, then why the hell did they ever pursue their fields in the first place? Aren't those of us who get advanced degrees and have all this excess crap floating around in our heads supposed to use it in *and* out of the classroom?

I couldn't *not* do this. And no matter what had happened between me and Melissa, ultimately it was irrelevant. It was in the past. Megan was in the *now* and she probably needed help. I patted Jim one last time and went back to the main house. On the porch, I stood holding my cell phone, staring blankly at the business card in my other hand. "Melissa T. Crown, Esq.," it read. I turned it over and carefully punched the numbers she had written on my keypad.

She picked up after the first ring. "K.C.?"

I winced at the hope I heard in her voice. "Yeah, it's me." I gripped the railing on the front porch. "I'll do it."

She didn't say anything for a while but I heard her breathing. "Thank you," she finally whispered.

"I'll drive up day after tomorrow. Where does Megan live? I'll meet you there."

"Over behind the Monte Vista Firehouse."

"I'll call you when I get into town. Give me the address then."

"I can't begin to tell you —"

"Later," I interrupted. "I'll talk to you in a couple of days. I'll time it so I arrive after you're done at work."

"That doesn't matter. I'll meet you whenever you get here."

I nodded to myself, feeling a little pang. Why hadn't she extended herself to me like that three years ago? "Okay. I guess I'll see you in a couple of days. Bye." I hung up, not wanting to keep the channel open between us. I stood staring at nothing, listening to the hum of summer insects and the rustling of dogs on the porch. I missed some things about her, but I wasn't able to remember how it had been. When I tried to think about what had attracted me to her, it was always overridden by the shock and pain I felt seeing her with Hillary that night in the parking lot. That night that triggered my leaving. I thought about the first time Melissa and I made love but I couldn't remember quite how it happened. I threw a glance over at Jane and Dan.

"Am I still in love with her?" I asked them. Jane looked at me with an expression that I would have sworn was canine pity. No, I decided, I wasn't. I did need some kind of closure, though. Maybe later, Melissa and I would have that talk she mentioned. I sighed. I had some more phone calls to make.

Chapter
Three

THE DRIVE FROM Central Texas to Albuquerque impresses upon the eyes how huge Texas is and how unrelentingly flat it can be. Perfect landscape for listening to music like Shawn Colvin and Catie Curtis, though I also secretly liked to listen to country when I had to cover long distances by car. I sang along to Trick Pony, watching the horizon retreat behind heat waves and rolling hills only to stretch itself flat along a series of high plains, no matter how fast I drove. I had already counted four dead armadillos, eight ground squirrels, and six rabbits on the asphalt. Summer was rough on people, but rougher still on animals.

Heat swam across Highway 84, which connected Lubbock to I-20 on the Texas side and Clovis, New Mexico on the other. I was just coming into Lubbock at one-thirty. I had left around four that morning to beat as much heat as possible. Granted, New Mexico isn't a slacker in the summer heat department. Desert natives will tell you, however, that "it's a dry heat." Which basically means it's the difference between a steam room and a dry sauna. I prefer a dry sauna because at least your clothing doesn't cling to you like wet sheets. Like sweat, it dries quickly. The closer I got to New Mexico, the dryer the air.

I pulled into a gas station and began filling up my Subaru. Chris sometimes teased me about my "sporty little dyke-mobile" and then she'd laugh and tell me I looked sexy in it. While my tank filled, I rummaged around in my car, picking up bits of trash to throw out. I had packed a couple of duffle bags and put them in the back. My laptop rested in its case on the passenger seat and a variety of books and pairs of shoes lay haphazardly in the back seat. Comfortable clutter. I reached for an empty cup that had held Starbucks coffee that morning. As I did so, my cell phone rang. I pulled it out of my pocket and checked the ID.

"Hey, Mom. What's up?" I balanced the phone on my shoulder as I walked to the trash can and emptied my hands.

"Hi, honey. Where are you?"

"The beautiful thriving metropolis of Lubbock." I leaned against the hood of my car, watching summer heat float above nearby fields. Semis roared past on the nearby interstate.

"Sounds wonderful. Did you call Kara?"

"I did. She's not still living in a redwood, thankfully." I scraped the concrete underfoot with the toe of my Birkenstock. "My kid sister. The eco-freak."

My mom ignored that. Instead, she said, "Okay, good. She worries about you, you know."

I pushed off my car and went to check the gas pump. It clicked off as I approached. I left the nozzle in the tank. "I'm not the one sitting in ten-story trees throwing sticks at loggers."

She chuckled. "Oh, and researching extremists is — what? A walk in the park?"

"Point taken," I said, laughing. "I e-mailed Joely, too, but you'll probably hear from her first."

"And she'll want to know what else Melissa had to say." Subtlety was not my mom's strong point. From staid New England stock, she managed to be both blunt and reserved in the same breath, a true counterpoint to my gregarious Italian father, to whom everything was larger than life.

I sighed. *What is it about sisters and moms all up in your business?* "I think she wants to talk."

Long pause that broadcast a hell of a lot more than words could. "And?" she said, voice tight.

"I don't know. It was weird seeing her and yeah, I'm kind of confused about it. But I know I'm doing the right thing and I know if Melissa thought she could resolve this issue without me, she would have." I watched a late model blue Ford truck with dualie tires on the back pull in at another pump and a kid in jeans, cowboy hat, and boots get out of the passenger side and head into the gas station while a man who was probably his father started fueling up.

"Are you sure?" Suspicion colored her tone.

"Yeah." I said it a little defensively, coming back to attention. "Tell Joely that, too."

"Well, what does she want to talk about? What could there possibly be to say after what she did?"

I stared blankly at my feet, another ripple of confusion in my chest. Why did I want to defend Melissa all of a sudden? "I don't know."

She made a *hmph* sound. "Just be careful."

"Geez, Mom. Don't you have a paper on some Latin American culture or something to write up for a lecture series? Or some world religions conference to go to with Dad?"

"I'm sorry," she said, a little more gently. "I just worry. I'm your mom. I don't want you to get hurt again."

"Shit, you think I *do*?" I ran a hand through my hair.

"Of course not. But sometimes you don't think too clearly about—" she stopped.

About the women I let into my life, I finished for her. "It's fine. I'm fine. I'm just going to see if I can track this group down and if I do, it's up to Melissa to take the next step. I have other work to do, after all."

"How long will you be there?"

"I don't know. A week or two, most likely. It depends on what I find. I might not be any help at all."

"I doubt that," she said in her "my daughter is the smartest thing on the face of God's green earth" tone. "Okay, honey, just check in with us when you can and drive carefully."

"Will do. Say hi to Dad."

"And you say hi to Chris."

I grinned. My mom thought Chris was the coolest thing since sliced bread. "She'll appreciate that. All right, I'm outta here. Talk to you later, Mom. Love you. Bye."

"Bye."

I hung up and put the phone back in the pocket of my cargo shorts. What was it about talking to my mom that made me feel sixteen all over again? I took the pump nozzle out of my tank and waited for my receipt to print out. That done, I drove a short distance away from the pumps and parked again so I could access my cooler and make a sandwich. Fifteen minutes later, I was back on the road and within about forty-five minutes I was coming into Clovis, a town just on the inside of the New Mexico border known for its meat-packing and Air Force base. I passed a battered Ford pick-up as the music switched to a different country mix.

Singing along as I-84 snaked north, I put an extra twang in the lyrics and watched out my windshield as the landscape morphed into Billy the Kid country, windswept grassy buttes speckled with cholla cactus and small hills that swelled from the soil like geographic pimples, some with bases carved into hidden arroyos, a few deep enough to hide a man on a horse. By four I was nearing the eastern edge of Albuquerque on I-40. The Sandia Mountains loomed out my windshield, the eastern plains lapping at their flanks like an ocean wave at a beach. The freeway wound through them via Tijeras Canyon, which opened slightly above the city and spilled travelers into a seemingly never-ending strip mall and hotel hell that served as oases for tourists and hang-outs for residents in some of the beaten-down neighborhoods in this part of town.

Albuquerque sprawled for miles across a high desert floodplain of the Rio Grande. Seeing my old stomping grounds made me grin like a kid. I mentally catalogued the parts of the city, ticking off the names like I was pointing out old friends at a reunion. The older neighborhoods lined the river and the newer ones — the 'burbs — pushed east until they rammed up against the base of the western side of the mountains. Residents refer to those areas as the Far Northeast Heights, though I dubbed them "The Frights" when I lived here.

The outline of downtown swam in the early evening haze, the highest building probably no more than thirty stories — nice because it didn't overwhelm the awesome expanse of landscape that surrounded the city. West of downtown sat Old Town, the site of the original Spanish Plaza. Older haciendas and estates occupied land north of Old Town, along the east side of the river while newer suburbs spread along the west side of the river — the poor cousins of the Northeast Heights though nicer neighborhoods lined the banks farther north. Developers were always busy ramming big tract homes into West Side enclaves then surrounding them with more strip malls and chain restaurants.

Melissa and I had rented a house near campus, just off the funky and occasionally monied area called Nob Hill. Central Avenue — what had been part of the original Route 66 — split off from I-40 and ran west all the way through the city. It crossed the river just past downtown and smacked into the West Side. I-40 then picked up the role of Route 66 and continued on to California. I exited I-40 onto Central just west of Tijeras Canyon. I wanted to see the city because I hadn't been back since last January, over a year ago.

I cruised west down Central, noting that things hadn't changed on the eastern edge, generally run-down and seedy. As I neared Nob Hill, the businesses began to appeal to a more upscale clientele, sporting galleries and groovy restaurants. I slowed, reminiscing about my years here. All sorts of people hang out in Nob Hill, from skate punks to college students, local hippies to yuppies. I smiled as I passed the Flying Star, a popular restaurant-coffee joint and then Kelly's, a local brewpub. On my right stood the Monte Vista Firehouse, a two-story adobe-like structure that really had been a firehouse once. The downstairs served as an upscale restaurant but the second-floor bar had a more casual ambiance. Patrons could hold onto the original brass pole as they went up and down the stairs. I found a parking space on the side street next to the Firehouse, which sat on a corner, and dialed Melissa's number. This time, she picked up on the second ring.

"Hi. Where are you?"

"Parked next to the Monte Vista across from Disco Display House."

"I'll be right there. Give me about fifteen minutes." She cleared her throat. "I was wondering—"

"Okay," I said, cutting her off. "See you when you get here. Bye." I knew she wanted to say more, but I wasn't ready to hear it. Not yet. Maybe not ever, but I still wasn't sure. I got out of my car and walked around to the sidewalk so I could lean against the passenger door. On this side of the Firehouse, big elms provided some nice shade. The air felt like hot parchment. I reveled in it as I opened my phone and speed-dialed Chris.

"Hey, *esa*! *¿Estás aquí?*"

"*Hola*, Detective Gutierrez. Or should it be *¿mujer caliente?*"

She laughed.

"Just got in. I'm waiting on Melissa."

"Girl, you'd better not be."

I grinned. "Not in the biblical sense."

"That's a relief. So when is it my turn to see you? And hopefully it's sooner rather than later."

"Let me get settled and see what the situation is. We've got some catching up to do."

"We do."

I had a thought. "Well, wait. How about dinner tonight? I'm dying for some chile."

She paused for a moment, probably checking her calendar. "I have time. A rare thing, but for you, Kase, I'd call in sick. The dead guys can wait, after all. Call me when you're done with Miss Thing. *Besas, amiga.*"

"Will do. Later."

I hung up and slid my phone into my pocket, still smiling to myself as I watched traffic crawl past on Central, part of the lingering rush hour. A group of goth teens wandered past, all in black trousers and tees. I wondered how they managed to do that during the summers here. *The price of fashion.* I smelled food from the Firehouse and my stomach rumbled. After Melissa took me to Megan's I'd give Chris a buzz and go in search of some New Mexican food. There was a restaurant off Rio Grande Boulevard near Old Town called Monica's. I had been thinking about it since Lubbock.

A black Lexus SUV turned left from Central. Melissa parked behind me and got out. She was still dressed for work, in a cream power suit and a dark blue blouse. Her hair was pulled back. She took her shades off as she approached. "Hi." She stood looking at me and I saw from her body language that she wanted to hug me but thought better of it. "Okay." She pointed down the street. "It's actually right around the corner, a little mother-in-law place behind a house just off Monte Vista on Berkeley. I'll show you."

"Sounds good." I got into my car and waited for her to pull out ahead of me. We turned immediately right behind the Firehouse onto a street that was barely a block long and cruised onto Monte Vista. Melissa turned left into one of the nicer older neighborhoods that made up Nob Hill. She stopped after half a block at a stucco house whose covered front porch required five steps to reach the two camp chairs positioned near the front door.

The main house, like so many others in this city, mimicked Spanish and Native American adobe style, sand-colored and flat-roofed. I call it "faux-dobe," a desert-colored stucco that imitates the rounded, organic lines of actual adobe. Whoever lived in the front house had xeriscaped the yard with native plants and cacti. A second concrete walk on the right probably led to the back house. It squeezed between the main house and the tall wooden fence next door. I touched both easily with my arms outstretched. This arrangement was typical of a lot of older neighborhoods here. Big main houses often harbored cottages in the back.

The two residences shared the back yard, hard-packed dirt surrounded by a six-foot wooden fence. Melissa motioned me to precede her down the walkway. Someone had cordoned off a small garden plot in the back against the fence. A few tomato and chile plants showed their bounty. Maybe I could have a couple of each later on. I'd check with the people in the front house. A barbecue grill—one of those four-legged affairs that still required charcoal—stood just off the roofed back porch of the main house, also accessible by five steps.

I turned my attention to the cottage's wooden front door, visible through the security door's black grill. Like the two windows that framed it, the door was painted turquoise. A plain white shade covered the small window in the door itself and dark blue curtains hung in the other windows. Melissa unlocked the security door and pulled it open, then unlocked the front door, which swung inward.

I stepped in. The entire place was saltillo-tiled and the smooth stucco walls glowed soft white. Megan had put a few colorful area rugs down, giving it a nice ambiance. The first room was a living area. A futon couch stood against the wall beneath a side window and a coffee table sat in front of it on which Megan had placed three red pillar candles. Bookshelves adorned the opposite wall, surrounding a compact entertainment center that included a television and stereo system. A small desk with a flat-screen computer monitor on it took up the far corner just beyond the couch. I noticed papers and pamphlets stacked next to the monitor.

A doorway on my right past the bookshelves led to the kitchen, small but bright. It sported a Mexican tile counter and 1940s-era cabinets painted white though the handles were red. A new sink and appliances and a bistro table in the corner gave it a cool retro look. I walked back into the living room. Beyond the living room—shotgun style — through an archway covered with a beaded curtain was obviously Megan's bedroom. I pushed the beads aside and surveyed the room. The door to the bathroom stood directly across from me. I entered the room, liking the vibe in this little house.

Megan's bed was made. A small closet occupied the left back corner. It was open and I glimpsed her clothes hanging neatly within. She was like Melissa in that respect — a place for everything. For a college student, Megan was a neat freak and her decorations indicated sophisticated tastes. Little pieces of folk art, nice lampshades, framed photographs of landscapes and European cafés. I peeked into the bathroom. Small sink, commode, shower stall. Two plants sat on the windowsill to the right. They seemed to be doing okay. Melissa must have been taking care of things.

I turned. Melissa was standing near Megan's bed, head bowed. Her arms were crossed over her chest. She looked like she might cry. She glanced up at me and managed a smile, her eyes clearing. "It's nice, huh?"

I nodded in agreement. "It's very nice. I won't mess it up," I added, a half-hearted attempt at humor.

"Here's a key." She handed it to me. I took it and put it in one of my front pockets. "I left the stuff I found next to her computer," she added.

"Is it okay if I check her bookshelves?"

"K.C.," Melissa said with a gentle remonstration, "make yourself at home while you're here."

"Yeah, but..." I let the question hang between us.

"She hasn't been using in a while. Over two years now." Melissa's tone was distant.

I hoped I didn't find anything to suggest otherwise. Megan's history was such that I worried about another relapse and if I found anything that would indicate that she had, I'd have to let Melissa know. And I didn't think either of us was up to dealing with that. "Okay. Let me unload my stuff and I'll check in with you tomorrow — oh, do the people in the front house know I'll be here?"

She nodded. "I told them Megan was enrolled in a school program out of state and that a friend would be here for a while. Their names are Jeff and Sage. Nice people."

"Well, I won't pee on their cacti, then."

She stared at me, not sure what I meant.

I cocked my head. "You can laugh. It was a joke."

She smiled then. "Sorry."

I shrugged. "I know. This is weird. I don't know what else to tell you." I held the key up. "I'm going to unload."

"Kase —"

The way she said it made me pause.

"Can we..." she stopped. "Never mind. I'll talk to you tomorrow. Call if you need anything." She left and I followed at a distance, watching as she got into her car. *It's just residue. That's all it is.* The black Lexus pulled away from the curb as I opened the hatchback of my car and hauled my duffle bags out and slung them over my shoulders. After dumping my stuff on the bed in Megan's room I poked around in her kitchen. Melissa had apparently emptied it of all perishables. *God, that must've been hard.* I found coffee in a container on the counter by the sink and a coffee maker in a cabinet. That was good news. I returned to the living room and decided not to start looking at racist crap just yet. I locked up and went back to my car.

I BIT INTO my chicken enchiladas, served "Christmas," with both red chile and green chile sauces poured over the top.

"As good as you remember, huh?" Chris had ordered a burrito, also smothered Christmas.

"Better." I took a sip of my Negra Modelo. "Is it just me? Or is this truly some of the best chile ever? Or is it that I just haven't had it in a while?" I took another bite, savoring.

"Could be. Bet you can't get it in Texas."

"Of course not. New Mexico is the chile capital, *mujer.*"

"I'm glad you remember your loyalties." She winked at me.

"Always." I cut a piece of enchilada off with my fork and worked it around my plate to get both red and green on it. The low murmur of conversation drifted from neighboring tables, all heavy Mexican-style wood. Monica's was always cheery, the tile floor and windows always spotless, and entering was like coming into your favorite aunt's kitchen. Great food, made with lots of love. I chewed and swallowed, enjoying the food, the energy, and the company.

Chris set her beer down. She was off this evening and didn't have to be at work until the next day at nine. "Do you have this kid's name? Megan's boyfriend?"

I looked up. "Damn. I forgot to ask Melissa what his last name is. So far, all I know about him is that his first name is Cody, he drinks Diet Coke, and he has a swastika tattoo on his left forearm."

"Sounds nice," Chris said sarcastically. "See if you can find a photo of him at Megan's and maybe his full name and I'll run a check for you. If he's violating probation or anything, then we'll have a reason to find him and bring him in."

"That'd be great. I have to go through the stuff Melissa found to see if I can get a sense of what type of group this is and how many people we might be talking about. Thank God Megan has high-speed Internet there. I'll be doing some poking around online, too." I looked across the table at her, and felt a familiar stirring in the air between us.

Chris ordered another Dos Equis from the server, a nice middle-aged woman who was probably part of Monica's family. "So how are your folks?" Chris smiled. "Still running wild in Tucson?"

I laughed. "On both sides of the border, lately. They just got back from Central America a few days ago. Mom says hi, by the way." I reached for my beer. "What about yours? Anything new to report that you didn't have time to tell me two days ago?"

"Nope. Same shit, different day. As usual, Dad wishes I had stayed a counselor and Mom hopes to get me married off some day, police thing notwithstanding. And you and I both know that has as much chance of happening as the moon falling." She grinned.

"Well, it depends. Married to a man or a woman?" I waggled my eyebrows at her.

"Either." Chris took one of the chips from the basket, dipped it in salsa, and took a bite.

"Oh, ye of little faith! How are the boys?" I used my favorite term of endearment for Chris's three brothers.

"Working their asses off for the company. At least my dad has nice, big, strong sons to carry on at Gutierrez and Sons Construction. With the possible exception of John. He's not as into the business as Pete and Mike are."

I cut another piece of enchilada. "Oh? Is he on the verge of finally coming out?"

"No, dammit, and it's so obvious. Why won't he talk to me about it?"

I chewed and swallowed before answering. "Maybe because he's the youngest, and he's trying to make his own way."

Chris made a noncommittal noise and reached for a chip. "I don't want to push him. I just want him to be happy with himself."

"We should all be happy like that. But even if John decided to go his own way, there's always *you* to take over the business and show those big, strapping men how it's done," I teased.

Chris threw a piece of chip at me. "Nah. I love building things and I love that I learned all that growing up, but I did my time there. Every damn summer from high school through college. I definitely don't want to do it full-time."

"But you look so damn sexy when you're running around with power tools," I teased. "Way sexier than your brothers."

She kicked me lightly under the table. "Speaking of siblings, how are your sisters?" Chris looked at me expectantly after swallowing a bite of her burrito.

"Kara's probably sitting in another tree in northern California to protest logging and Joely is probably running guns in Estonia."

"Kara's still working for that wilderness group?" Chris grinned at my eyeroll.

"Yeah. She seems to like it, so I should probably quit making fun of it. And I'm kidding about Joely. She likes Germany and she enjoys teaching, so it's all good."

"Oh? When will she be back in the States?"

"She decided May, last we heard. She's doing a full year of teaching at the university there."

"Sounds cool."

"She'd like to end up teaching at some small liberal arts college in the States, and it'll be a professor package deal, her and the hubby." I took a chip out of the basket. "And *Abuelita*? Did you tell her I was going to be in town?"

"Of course. And she's ornery but funny as ever," Chris said dryly though she was grinning again. "She's told me to tell you to come by. She's got some damn herbs she'll give you to help deal with your demons."

"I'm sure it's a delightful powder I'm supposed to mix in some freaky tea."

Chris laughed. "Hey, that shit's worked on you in the past. It helped get you focused after Melissa. She's good with everybody's aches and pains in the 'hood, mental and physical. Still driving Mom crazy, who throws up her hands in dramatic Mexican fashion and demands to know how she ever came to be born of *esa loca*." Chris smiled. "I'm actually going over this weekend to put some more shelves up in her pantry. When I told her you were coming she said, and I repeat, '¿*Cuando volve mi K.C. para siempre?*'"

I laughed. "She thinks I should move back for good, huh?"

Chris raised one shoulder in a shrug. "She misses you. Maybe almost as much as I do." She regarded me with an expression in her dark eyes I knew very well. "It's good to see you, *esa*. I *have* really missed you."

"Oh? In what sense?" I baited her, my beer bottle poised at my lips.

"All." She flashed me a smile and picked up her glass. "Since you went to Texas, I don't see you or talk to you enough." She pretended to pout.

She had a point. Since I'd moved, we talked maybe once every two weeks or so. Sometimes less. "You're right," I agreed. "And as of right now, I don't like that. So let's talk more often."

"I have a better idea." She took a sip from her glass.

"And that would be?"

"Move back."

I sighed and started fiddling with my fork. "I don't know."

"C'mon," she coaxed. "You know Texas isn't you. Nuevomexico, *that's* you."

"High compliment from you, *mujer*." I nudged her leg under the table with my foot.

"It's true. You know you miss it. For the chile, if nothing else." She focused on her burrito again.

"I do," I conceded. "A lot. And I miss you. But I have another two semesters on this post-doc."

"So? This fall you're researching and writing and then you teach in the spring and then you could be back here in May. Or June." She took another bite, watching me hopefully.

"Tempting." I smiled as she gave me her "pretty please?" grin. "I'm leaving my options open. I have to think about gainful employment, you know."

"You can live with me until you find it."

"We'd get sick of each other. I love you, but I think I'd drive you crazy in your house."

Chris tossed another chip at me. "The offer stands. We've been friends for ten years. If you haven't driven me crazy yet, you probably won't. Speaking of — are you okay at Megan's?"

I slumped. "Yeah. It is a little weird, though."

"I thought it might be." Chris kept her tone neutral.

"Melissa wants to talk." I stared at the tabletop then lifted my gaze to Chris's.

"Oh?"

"I don't know how I feel about that."

Chris didn't respond, giving me space to continue.

"I think I probably will but I'm not ready right now."

"It might help."

I shrugged and Chris regarded me for a long moment, assessing. She changed the subject, as I knew she would when she saw I wasn't ready to talk about it.

"All right. So how are you since I saw you last year? Anybody new and exciting down there in Texas, whose identity you're hiding from me? Though somehow I doubt it."

"No. Not seeing anyone. I'm actually enjoying being single. Besides, I can't keep stuff like that from you."

"True." The server dropped a beer off and Chris poured it into the fresh glass. She squeezed the lime into the beer and dropped it in. Bubbles caressed it as it sank. "I'm surprised you don't have the entire lesbian population after you there, as good as you still look." She offered me one of her slow grins and a familiar heat coursed through my abdomen.

"You're one to talk," I shot back as I studied her face. The years I'd known her had enhanced her physically. Her angular features had softened only slightly, and though a few streaks of grey showed in her black hair, which she allowed to fall around her shoulders now, she was still the Chris I remembered at that house party near the University of New Mexico where we'd met, grinning at me from across the room, brown eyes sparkling then as now. We'd been in our mid-twenties then, and neither of us had any idea the kind of friendship we'd be able to build.

"I can do a lot more than that," she coaxed. "So if you have any time this trip, maybe we could..." The thought settled on the table.

"I think you might be able to persuade me." I picked up my beer bottle and clinked it against her glass.

She took a sip, regarded me with a certain expression. "So how much persuasion would it take to get you to follow me home tonight?"

I laughed, flattered. "You always did move fast."

"I miss you, Kase. I miss our talks. The phone just doesn't do it justice." She sighed. "I miss hanging out. And I miss the *other* part of our relationship. It's been a year, after all." She had a "woe is me" tone in her voice that I knew was part of how she teased me.

"That is a while." I considered my energy level after the drive and decided I was more than up to a romp with Chris.

"A long while." She took another swallow of beer and then finished her burrito. I watched her, let my gaze linger on her strong hands. What I liked most about Chris was her easy demeanor and the frank way she approached life. A week after I had met her, she asked me to dinner and told me she thought I was sexy and she'd sure like to find out how much. She also said she wasn't interested in a commitment along those lines, but if we could be friends, it would be great. I wasn't seeing anyone at the time and neither was she so I took her up on her offer and discovered that sex between us was a lot of fun. There were never any strings attached to that part of our friendship on the occasions it happened. Sometimes the sex was rebound-oriented. Sometimes it was comfort sex. Sometimes it wasn't about anything except sex.

Tonight, I knew, it was about reconnecting. "Not much persuasion at all because that sounds really good. You want me to bring anything?"

"Hell, no," she said, laughing at my inner hostess. "Just your libido."

"Not a problem," I answered, feeling a comfortable pleasure in my gut as I met her eyes. We finished dinner and I picked up the check. A few minutes after that, I followed her home.

Chapter
Four

I ARRIVED AT Megan's place around eight the next morning, needing a shower and breakfast before dealing with the "situation," as I dubbed it. Fortunately, her house seemed to stay fairly cool inside, a much-appreciated quality, as the Albuquerque heat would be at full strength in a couple of hours. I stripped my clothes off on the way to the shower and stood under the water, feeling relaxed.

Chris had cut loose on me the night before and we had been up late. A delicious chill lingered between my thighs thinking about it. She was as free and easygoing in bed as out. She knew what she wanted and she gave me what I needed. Last night was no exception and as I was leaving that morning, she hugged me for a long time and told me again she had really missed me and please, would I at least think about moving back. Then she sent me to Megan's with a large mug of coffee.

The water coursed over my shoulders and down my back. Maybe I should really think about returning to Albuquerque. I turned off the water and opened the shower stall door so I could grab the towel off the sink. I smiled to myself. Commitment-phobic Chris. We'd never be girlfriends, but that was okay. More than okay. I liked the friendship we had and the occasional forays we took into more intimate physical territory when neither of us was seeing anyone. Instead of making things weird between us, it served somehow to strengthen the other aspects of our bond.

I finished drying off and hung my towel on the hook on the back of the door before padding into the bedroom to rummage in one of my duffle bags for clean clothes. Another pair of cargo shorts, faded tee, and Birkenstocks. I'd grab something to eat at the Flying Star and then I'd be ready, at least physically, to see what Megan might be into.

An hour later I was sitting at Megan's desk looking through the stack of flyers and pamphlets Melissa had found. Sinking into research mode, I set my legal pad next to the monitor, prepared to take my plethora of notes and to log times and dates in addition to complete citations of things I examined, whether online or in real life.

What Melissa had found was pretty standard racist stuff. I read a flyer apparently downloaded from the National Alliance Web site and started writing notes, mostly in case Melissa wanted to read through them, but also to help me remember things. Writing something down cemented details in my head. "National Alliance, based in West Virginia, chapters all over country." I tapped the butt of my pen against my teeth and wrote some more. "Organized 1970, slick and professional." Another flyer honored the group's founder, a former Oregon physics professor. "Founder William Pierce, died 2002, wrote *The Turner Diaries*, under name Andrew MacDonald."

Did Megan have a copy of it on her shelves? After fifteen minutes, I hadn't found one and for that, I was grateful. Underneath my "Pierce" entry, I added a few sentences about how *Turner* allegedly served as a blueprint for Timothy McVeigh, the man who blew up the Murrah Federal Building in Oklahoma City in 1995. I sat back, pondering. There were rumors that McVeigh used to carry multiple copies of the book and sell them for five bucks each at gun shows. I imagined him, pockets of his camouflage pants stuffed with books, trolling the aisles, surreptitiously trying to sell the damn thing with dark whispers about how the government was coming to get us all, and take our guns, too.

I wrote "NA, recruitment" on my legal pad and scribbled a few notations. Even after Pierce's death, the NA still actively recruited young people, appealing to them with a classy Web site, easy downloads, and an online bookstore. I checked in with them probably once a month, to see what issues were pissing them off. Like other right-wing extremist groups, the NA had tried to downplay the more violent rhetoric that characterized it during the 1980s and 1990s. The leadership started using phrases like "be proud of your heritage" and "we don't hate non-whites. We just love the white race." *Not very catchy for T-shirts,* I thought as I read over another sheet of paper Megan had downloaded.

The other flyers called on Aryan warriors to take a stand against "mud people," a term I wrote down along with its definition, "non-white people." Some flyers also mentioned "ZOG" — "Zionist Occupied Government" — part of the anti-Semitism that riddled the white supremacist right. Those in the movement believed that a secret cabal of Jews had been running world events for thousands of years and that this group controlled global finances and all major governments on the planet. I shook my head at the next paragraph, which said that Jews weren't really God's chosen people. Rather, the white race was actually the chosen people and Jews had spent hundreds of years keeping this fact secret from European and later

American whites. *Zog. Sounds like something off a PlayStation game.*

I stood up and stretched. Though it was nothing new for me, I was having a difficult time reading through this stuff knowing that Megan might believe it, especially since she had known me for six years prior to the break-up and she knew what I researched. *What were you thinking?* I silently asked her, wishing she'd just come home and that this was just a mistake she'd made on relationship road and that she'd be okay and still clean and would just go back to school and finish up her degree and get on with her life.

My eyes fell on a reference to "Identity." I sighed heavily and picked the paper up so I could read it more thoroughly. I added some notes about "Christian Identity" to my legal pad: "belief forms core of white supremacist groups, based on obscure school of thought that claims that one of the ten lost tribes of Israel was progenitor of white English people, who eventually ended up in U.S." I thought about that for a bit, too. Eventually, in the hands of a core of racist preachers just before and then after World War II, "Identity" took on anti-Semitic overtones. I set the paper aside and studied another National Alliance flyer, my brow furrowing. *All it takes is some guy with an audience and an axe to grind.* It makes it a lot easier to hate people if you think they'd been purposefully hiding shit from you since Biblical times.

I started dividing the piles into categories on Megan's couch, recognizing all of the groups. Klan chapters, some neo-Nazi stuff out of Pennsylvania, National Alliance, Aryan Nations. Somebody had underlined certain phrases on some of the pamphlets, especially references to the role of white women in the coming race war — referred to as "RAHOWA," or Racial Holy War — and how to prepare for doomsday, which for these people generally meant a government takeover. *Oh, look. A handy diagram showing you what kind of bomb shelter to build.* I turned the pamphlet over. Nothing to indicate what group it came from. That got its own stack. I had seen a lot of "how to" stuff like this at gun shows. Y2K had come and gone, but many of these groups still prepared for an apocalypse and in this country, a lot of them were eying the Pacific Northwest as a place for an Aryan homeland. Which would be a major bummer, as I happen to be a big fan of Portland and Seattle.

I stood looking at my stacks of leaflets and then sat down at Megan's computer. Maybe she had some photos on her desktop or in her files and if her Web access wasn't password-protected, I would be able to check the Web sites she'd been frequenting. I turned it on, waiting as the familiar Windows icon unfolded across the screen, then clicked on the Explorer icon and it opened up onto AOL. I wouldn't be able to access her e-mail accounts, but Melissa might know what her passwords were. I clicked Favorites to see what came up. Amazon, University of New Mexico, MapQuest. And, unfortunately, Stormfront, a hub site for white supremacists with a variety of views, and the site for the National Alliance.

The other favorites included a link to an ex-gay ministry, ultra-fundamentalist Focus on the Family, Aryan Nations, and one to a "Free the Order" site. "Shit," I muttered aloud, and I clicked on it just to satisfy my morbid curiosity. The Order was the group responsible for assassinating Jewish talk show host Alan Berg in Denver in 1984. I wrote that down. The last time I had checked, most of the members were serving prison sentences and had continually been denied parole. The leader, Robert Mathews, died in an FBI and ATF stand-off in 1984 on Whidbey Island, Washington. I scrolled through the site, which wanted all whites concerned with the future of America to help get the members out of prison. How was a concerned white person supposed to do this? Ah. Letter-writing campaigns and sure, it was fine to send money to "our imprisoned brothers." *How special.* I wondered if Cody sent money to them.

The stuff about The Order worried me. If the group that Cody ran with was interested in re-creating some of The Order's exploits, that could mean trouble. The original chapter was based in Washington State, where Mathews had settled. They had been into theft, counterfeiting, and other illegal ways to fund the movement, including an armored car hijacking in California. If Cody and company were planning things like that, Megan was in a world of hurt and there wasn't much Melissa could do for her, especially if Megan was with Cody of her own volition. The guys in the photos of incarcerated Order member stared at me. *Shit.*

I checked her document files next. Megan was meticulous in her organization, a bad idea if she was hoping to keep things secret. She had folders for every class and in each were assignments and papers. I read through them, finding nothing beyond the usual analyses and argument papers that all college students had to write. The white supremacist right liked to recruit college students because they couched racist arguments in more palatable terms. Some recruits deliberately researched white supremacy for school papers, pretending they were nothing more than research topics. Megan apparently hadn't gotten to that point, thankfully. Yet.

I slogged through every class folder, of which there were twenty, since Megan had just finished her sophomore year at UNM. She was a bit older than most juniors-to-be, but that wasn't unusual these days. I eyed her "photographs" folder and opened it. Thanks to her anal streak, she had labeled all her pictures with names, time, and date.

And *voila.* here was Mr. Cody Sorrell. I opened the earliest images first. On the label of the first photo she had included "cute guy I met last night!" The image was dated June 10th of last year. He looked to be about six feet tall. Broad-shouldered, dark hair, blue eyes. He was handsome in an all-American way and he had a nice smile. I could see why Megan might have been into him.

The next few pictures, taken about a month after their initial meeting, showed the two of them, arms around each other, smiling and staring at the camera. Those pictures creeped me out a little. The photos dated two months after June 10th were a little more revealing, in many senses of the word. Cody with his shirt off, flexing his muscles. Showing off his tattoos. On his left pectoral was the double lightning bolt of Hitler's SS while on his right pectoral was the number "88." I saw the swastika that Melissa had noticed on his left forearm in these images.

I clicked on another image. In this one, Cody's bare back was to the camera. I tried not to think about Megan taking the photo and hoped that one of his friends did. My eyes were drawn to a huge Nazi Third Reich-style eagle tattooed across his upper back. The swastika in the eagle's claws dangled to his mid-back. I clicked on the image to enhance it. Grudgingly, I had to admit that the work was very good. The artist had captured minute details on the raptor and the perspective was excellent. Maybe Chris had a line on local artists who might have done the piece. I noticed another tat on Cody's left bicep that I didn't recognize. It looked like a pissed-off rat clutching a Nazi iron cross. Above the rat's head in gothic script were etched the letters ADR.

I went through the rest of the photos. There must have been fifty. The most recent date was June 5th of this year, about six weeks ago. Cody figured in about half. Some of the photos depicted other young men and women. Probably some of Megan's other friends. Two guys in a few of the other images looked like they might be friends of Cody's. I'd have Chris check them out, as well. Megan had included names of everyone in her photos, little control freak that she was.

I webbed over to Gmail, which handles my personal e-mail accounts, and zipped three photos of Cody to Chris. I included two others that pictured guys I thought might be part of his group. Maybe Chris would get some hits on them as well. I also asked her if she recognized the tattoos and if she knew of any local artists who did that kind of stuff. If not, I'd have to suck it up and visit local shops myself.

Finishing that up, I glanced at my watch. Three o'clock. No wonder I was hungry. I closed all the windows and stood up, stretching. Melissa probably wanted to hear from me. As I reached for my cell phone, it rang and I glanced at the ID. Speak of the devil.

"Hey. I was just going to call you." Too late, I realized how that sounded. She didn't say anything right away and I fumbled. "Uh, I finished some stuff up and I wondered if you wanted to come over and have a look. It might upset you, but—"

"I don't care. I need to know. I'll come by after work. Five-thirty okay?"

"Yeah, that's fine. I'll be here. See you then."

"Thanks." She hung up.

I closed the phone and stood staring blankly at Megan's computer screen. Melissa used to rush home like that after work until Megan's relapse. Then she started coming home later and later. The waves of my past slid over the beach of my present as I thought about the last time I had seen Melissa before she showed up in Texas, when she was standing ten feet from me, saying she loved me and asking me if we could talk. I'd slammed that door shut. Well, why not? She was having an affair, for chrissakes. That's not something you forget. And it makes everything past that suspect. What was there to talk about? She was doing Hillary. She'd betrayed the relationship she had with me.

What the hell? *Why am I trying to excuse her?* The image of Melissa in Hillary's Mercedes was burned into my brain. But as I focused on it and waited for the pain that accompanied it, only sadness came up. Shoving it out of my head, I decided to walk the four blocks to La Montanita, a local cooperative health food store. I locked up and headed toward Central in the late afternoon heat.

Chapter
Five

I LEFT THE outer security door unlocked and the inner door open. When Melissa showed up, she called softly through the wire mesh, announcing her presence before she came in. I had just finished putting my groceries away when I heard the door open.

"Kase?" she said again.

"Yeah." I emerged from the kitchen. "You want something to drink? I got some Tazo at the Co-op." I assumed Melissa still drank the stuff. I did.

"No. But thanks."

"Okay. Hold on." I returned to the kitchen and retrieved one of the small chairs from the table. I brought it over to the computer and set it down next to the chair that I had been using most of the day. I sat down and opened up Megan's photograph file. Melissa took her suit jacket off and tossed it carelessly onto the couch before she sat down next to me. She smelled faintly of citrus. I was careful not to touch her and instead opened Megan's photo file. We clicked through together. She recognized a couple of Megan's non-racist friends, but that was all. I clicked on the images of Cody without his shirt on.

"What do his tattoos mean?" Melissa's voice sounded tight.

I pointed at the double lightning bolts on his left pectoral. "That's a tribute to Hitler's secret police, the SS." I moved my finger to his right pectoral, where the number "88" was etched. "That means 'heil, Hitler.' 'H' is the eighth letter of the alphabet. Hence, eighty-eight."

Melissa looked at me, a hard expression in her eyes. She commandeered the mouse and clicked on the next image.

"That's the eagle of the Nazi Third Reich," I explained. "If the artist is local, I'll see if I can find him." I kept my tone gentle, since it was obvious that this was hard for her. She didn't say anything and her jaw muscles remained clenched. I then explained some of the things about the flyers that I had discovered. "So basically, given the tattoos and the other stuff, I think Cody's probably neo-Nazi. KKK tats are different. They like the Confederate flag and hangman's nooses and stuff like that. Or a stylized cross with a blood drop in the middle."

"Why a blood drop?"

"It represents the oh-so-pure blood of the white race."

Melissa stared at me. "You're shitting me."

"No. For real. They take that 'blood' stuff really seriously." I retrieved a Klan flyer from the couch and pointed out a paragraph that went on about "pure white men" and "fighting for the pure blood" of the white race.

Melissa shook her head. "How the hell do you manage to look at this all day?"

"Not really thinking about it." I caught her eye and smiled wryly. "Yeah. I'm compartmentalizing. If I don't, I can't do it."

"You know, it's funny, but I guess I never—I guess I wasn't really paying attention to your research when we—when you were here."

We sat in silence for a few seconds before I responded. "Shit was happening. I, um, might have kept a lot to myself."

She handed the flyer back, expression unreadable. "So do you know what the group's name is?"

I relaxed. This I could talk about. "No, but I'll check in with a colleague at the local chapter of the ADL."

Melissa waited.

"Judy. You know. I met her in grad school."

Melissa looked puzzled.

"I know I must have mentioned her when I was dissertating. Didn't I? Judy at the Anti-Defamation League?"

She pursed her lips, thinking. "Maybe." She kept her eyes on the monitor. "I e-mailed over there to see if anyone would help me but somebody—not Judy—wrote back and said they were basically a non-profit watchdog organization and didn't have the resources to conduct private investigations. I offered to pay for research, but they said they couldn't accept the funds."

I moved to put my hand on her shoulder but stopped. I instead ran my hand through my hair.

"So is he a skinhead?" Melissa was staring at the photo.

"No, though his tats are definitely neo-Nazi leaning. Except for this one." I reached over and clicked on the one that showed the pissed-off rat. "This could be skinhead, since skins like to put some Nazi stuff in their body art. And that is the Nazi iron cross. But skins like to have lots of tats signaling their allegiance. So I think Cody's probably more neo-Nazi."

"Okay," Melissa said thoughtfully, "skinheads tend to be neo-Nazi but not all neo-Nazis are skinheads."

"Bingo. I also think that Cody's part of the recruiting arm of whatever group he's in, which might be a local chapter of a larger one. Local chapters sometimes name themselves something other than the parent organization."

"How do they recruit?"

"Lately, the Internet and, especially within the last few years, college campuses. They'll flyer cars in parking lots there, but some are already students. They *want* educated, articulate people for the movement. Think guys like David Duke."

"Wait. You're saying that they actually manage to get college kids in these groups?"

"Remember your college days? College is really freaky for some. It's a time for trying on new identities and new ideas. And if you're in a vulnerable place at home or with your family or for whatever reasons, these guys make you feel welcome."

"Guys?"

"Yeah. The movement is mostly male. When women join, it's generally through a guy. It's rare to find a woman who goes and signs up all on her own."

"Jesus, Kase," Melissa said softly, staring at the photo of Cody on the monitor. "He recruited her."

"Yes. He did. He's probably very good at finding weak spots and manipulating them. And Megan's history..." I allowed my voice to trail off. I didn't need to go there. Melissa knew what I was talking about. I cleared my throat instead. "I haven't gone through all of her files yet," I managed, changing the subject.

"I have her e-mail password." She didn't look at me.

I didn't really want to know how Melissa had that information. I assumed it had something to do with Megan's rehab years. Melissa probably had one of her IT friends figure it out.

"Is it recent?"

"Yes."

"Okay. Do you want to open it now?"

She reached past me to the legal pad I'd been writing notes on. I handed her a pen and Melissa wrote down the log-in information.

"Has she been e-mailing you too, or just calling since she left?" I looked at what Melissa had written and went to the AOL log-in site.

"Just calling." I watched her out of the corner of my eye. Melissa kept her hands in her lap, palms pressed against her thighs. She was wearing another power suit, this one olive green linen. The color looked good against her skin. I glanced away and quickly typed Megan's log-in and password into the blanks. Her account opened.

"When was the last time you checked it?" I asked, still not looking at Melissa.

"Last week."

"Did you see anything that seemed out of the ordinary?"

"No. She's kept a lot of the e-mails from Cody but I haven't read them."

That did make me look at her. "Why not?"

She shook her head and sighed. "Here's the thing. I got her password and log-in because I was worried that she might fall in with the wrong crowd after her last rehab. But I promised myself I wouldn't use it unless I had a reason to. So I actually didn't use it until she left." She chose the euphemism carefully, pausing slightly before she said it. "I feel really guilty about it."

"Don't," I said gently. "I mean, you had a good reason to do it. She's not where she should be and because of her history, well..." I shrugged and turned my attention back to the screen. There were five new e-mails. Three were from Amazon — updates about books she might want to read for her psychology classes. One was spam about paying off your mortgage that had made its way past AOL's filters and the other was from one of her friends whose name I recognized from the photos. Allison. I clicked on that one. It was barely three sentences long. She was just checking in because she hadn't heard from Megan in a while and wanted to know how things were going.

"Do you know Allison?" I glanced over at Melissa.

"Yes. She's local."

"Do you have her number?"

"No."

"Then e-mail her back from your account and CC me. Tell her you need to talk to her about Megan and you'd appreciate it if she'd call you." I wrote Allison's account address down on the legal pad.

Together, we scrolled through Megan's e-mail from the past month. Almost all of it was junk mail. Amazon, Barnes and Noble, UNM student events and news. I clicked on the Amazon and Barnes and Noble. Just innocuous updates. Three others from Allison, two from another friend named Bill who was home in California for the summer. Melissa vaguely recalled him. Fifteen from other friends who were just saying they'd see her in the fall. I hoped fervently that they would. I printed out all the personal e-mails.

"Does Megan have a MySpace page or anything on Facebook?"

Melissa thought for a bit. "She did say she was going to set up a MySpace page and she was working on some of the graphics for it. She said she'd let me know. I don't know if she ever finished it."

"When did she start?"

"Toward the end of May, I think."

"I'll check her files and see if I find anything like that. Ask Allison about it. She'd probably know if Megan has a page."

Melissa seemed to relax. She looked at me and managed a tired smile. "You should have been a cop."

"I'll take that as a compliment."

"I meant it as one." She stood then. "I already feel better knowing that you're here." She said it quietly, without looking at me.

I logged out of AOL and shut down the various applications. My heart was beating a bit faster than it should have. "I'll call you tomorrow and let you know what Chris finds out. I'm going to try to see Judy at the ADL, see if she's heard anything. Let me know what Allison says." I stood up and ran my fingers through my hair. I tend to do that when I'm nervous and Melissa obviously recognized the gesture.

"Do you think — that is — "

I interrupted her. "Yeah. I think maybe we should talk. Just not right now, okay? I don't think I'm quite ready."

She nodded and managed a tight smile. "Are you all right for dinner?" She made it sound like she was just checking on my welfare, like she would do with an acquaintance or a coworker.

"Fine. Thanks. I'll call you tomorrow." I forced an answering smile and watched her leave. As an afterthought, I moved to the door and watched her as she walked to her car, which was just visible from my vantage point. She got in and pulled away from the curb. I felt strangely empty.

"YOU OKAY, *CHICA*?" Chris was worried about me. I switched the phone to my right ear and checked my watch. Nearly nine. Melissa had left around seven-thirty and I had gone for a run at eight, appreciating the evening cool, and then did my requisite push-ups and sit-ups. I was just opening Megan's door when Chris called.

"Yeah. This thing with Megan has me kinda worried."

"And?" Chris's tone was patient.

"And yeah, it's weird being around Melissa."

"I thought it might be. You wanna come and stay here?" There was only concern in her voice.

"No, being at Megan's isn't the problem. It's the — "

"Past," Chris said wryly. "So why don't you talk to her? Get shit out in the open?"

"What do you mean?" I said cautiously.

"Come on, Kase. When things ended with her, you pretty much slammed the door."

"Well, what the hell else was I supposed to do? I busted her going at it with Hillary."

"Hey, I'm not saying what Melissa did wasn't shitty. But leaving the way you did — I'm saying that maybe you need some closure. For your own sanity if nothing else. Put those ghosts to rest."

I didn't respond. Chris was right, but I didn't really want to talk about Melissa.

"Think about it. It's not healthy to hold on to things like that." She paused, then continued. "Okay, next topic. About your Mister Sorrell. Turns out he does have a record. Basic stupid juvie shit. He's from Denver originally and got into trouble there while he was in high school. Vandalism of school property—I'm waiting on the incident reports—petty theft. Sounds like your garden-variety candy bars and beer from the convenience store stuff. Comes from a broken home and grew up with his dad. No word on where his mom went. He moved here in 2003 after completing his GED and enrolled in a few classes through UNM continuing ed. He does have an aunt here in town, whose address is the same as what's listed for his. You might want to have a chat with her."

Chris provided the aunt's address, which was on Albuquerque's east side. I had an image of what the neighborhood looked like. Run-down suburbia, filled with bored teenagers who sat on front stoops at night smoking and drinking cheap beer, talking about who was doing whom, who was pregnant, and who might be running with gangs.

"Thanks, Chris. That's a *huge* help."

"*No hay problema.* I'm working on the others and should have some more info about Cody in the next couple of days. I can also get you in with our gang division. They've got files on tattoos and for the past few years at least, they've been tracking racist groups, too. They might have a line on the artist who worked on Cody's back."

"Jesus, Chris. You are a total godsend."

"That's a lot of spiritual talk for one sentence, *esa*," she said teasingly. "Let me call somebody down there to see if they'll let you have a look. I'll let you know tomorrow."

"I so owe you."

"And I will so collect." She laughed. "You're a good friend and it's the least I can do. You okay tonight?"

"Yeah. I'm tired. I'll crash here and check in with you tomorrow."

"Sounds good. *Buenas noches.*"

"'Night." I hung up and used the remote to turn the TV on. With some inane reality show on in the background, I made a list of all the angles I wanted to pursue. Tomorrow, I'd finish going through Megan's files and if I had time, I'd cruise over to Cody's aunt's place and see what I could scare up over there. I'd also call Judy. I put the tablet down and closed the inner front door and opened a window in the bedroom a crack. The place stayed fairly cool, but I still flipped the switches for the swamp cooler to drive the rest of the heat out of the house. I turned the TV off and put on a pair of boxers and a clean tee, then went to the bathroom, where I washed up and spent some time flossing and brushing my teeth.

I was pretty tired and didn't feel much like reading, so I called Grandpa to check in with him. Luke answered. He said everything was fine. We chatted a bit and then signed off. I called my folks as well. They didn't answer so I left a message, telling them I'd call back in the next day or so. I then turned out the light and climbed into bed, staring into the dark and listening to the hum of the cooler.

I thought about Cody and Megan, and about what might draw her to a guy like that. He was good-looking, and he was probably charming and had that "aw, shucks" thing that attracted people to James Dean. He was kind of a bad boy and Megan had flirted with that sort of lifestyle for a while. She was still trying to figure out who she was and Cody probably flattered the hell out of her, telling her how proud he was of her for getting off drugs and for trying to make something of herself. If he was Megan's primary recruiter, chances were that he figured out pretty quickly what she needed to hear to draw her to him.

I'd have to go through her e-mail files to see how they interacted. I was not looking forward to that so I thought instead about Melissa and what Chris had said about closure. I definitely could use some of that, especially since we were working together to find Megan. It struck me, suddenly, how jarring it was to go from no contact to daily contact with an ex over the course of just a few days. I put my hands behind my head and continued to stare into the dark. My eyes were adjusting to the dim light in the room and I could just make out the shapes of Megan's dresser and shelves near her bed, which held little art objects and a few books. Photos, too, but I hadn't really looked at them. I'd check those out in the morning.

I did want to talk to Melissa about what had happened. I wasn't sure why, exactly, but Chris was right, even if Melissa said things I didn't want to hear. What had gone wrong between us? Besides the obvious? I remembered things getting tense when Megan went into rehab again, but I'd figured we'd work through it, like we had the first time. I sighed heavily, thinking about Melissa and Hillary. Usually an affair means that someone can't communicate effectively or doesn't want to. Sometimes it means the person having the affair wants the other person to make the first move and end the relationship. Either of those could have described what happened.

I turned onto my side. I didn't recall talking about much of anything with Melissa when Megan went back into rehab. I had been working so hard to finish up my dissertation that I sometimes only spent a few minutes a day talking to Melissa or Megan. I clenched my teeth. No, I hadn't been around much. *So? I didn't have an affair.*

But a twinge of guilt zipped through my thoughts. I remembered how much I had loved Melissa and how right it had felt to be with her, even when her family chickens came home to roost. We had some good times and I knew she had loved me, too. But dammit, I just couldn't get past Hillary. Fortunately, I fell asleep.

SOMETHING GRATED AGAINST the pleasant, soothing hum and burble of the swamp cooler. A sound that didn't fit, that worked its way into my skull and tugged me into wakefulness. My eyes shot open. Adrenaline whipped through my body but I lay perfectly still in the bed, listening to the rattle at the front door. Someone was messing with the security door, trying to get in. I sat up and reached for my cell phone, ready to call 911. Gripping my phone in my right hand, I eased out from under the covers and tried to find something I could use as a weapon. There was a broom in the kitchen. It would have to do.

I listened again. The rattling had stopped. No, there it was again. I padded quickly into the kitchen to the corner by the table and grabbed the broom, then went back into the living room. My heart hammered my rib cage like a pro boxer and I was sure whoever was messing with the door heard it. Every nerve stood at attention, prepared to send me flying down the street either fighting or fleeing. I saw a silhouette through the shade that covered the window of the interior door. Just one person, from the looks of it.

I moved quickly to the light switch on the front wall and without really thinking about what I was doing, I flipped the outside light on. The rattling stopped and I watched as the silhouette disappeared. I unlocked the inner door and threw it open and saw what looked like a man dressed in jeans and a dark T-shirt running at full speed down the walk toward the street. I flipped the lock on the security door and ran after him, obviously leaving my sanity and shoes inside.

I made it to the sidewalk and started to follow but he had a head start, running toward Central, and the bottoms of my feet hurt. I started to shout after him, but clamped my mouth shut, opting not to scare the entire neighborhood. I jogged back to the house and slid my tennis shoes on. That done, I grabbed my keys and locked the inner door, leaving the security door slightly ajar.

I'd cruise Central. Maybe I'd find him. I flipped a U-turn and headed down the street. My car clock glowed the time. Two thirty-four AM. Lovely. I worked an eight-block radius east and west on Central then cruised some of the neighborhoods nearby. I didn't expect to find him, but you never know. At three I headed back to Megan's and spent the next ten minutes studying the lock on the security door. If he had a key, wouldn't he just have used it and come in? He was doing something at the front that caused the door to rattle. Was he trying to pick the lock? Or was it too dark for him to find the right key? Maybe he had a bunch of keys and he was trying to figure out which one it was. I carefully opened the security door, using my foot. Chris might be able to get a print off the handle. The interior door was still locked. If he was inside, he probably would not have locked himself in.

I pulled the security door closed. I'd definitely get that lock changed tomorrow. Chris was on duty at nine, so I'd see if she had time to swing by beforehand. I picked the broom up from the living room floor, but decided I might need it after all so I didn't return it to the kitchen. I pulled the comforter off Megan's bed and stretched out on the couch in the living room, my cell phone on the coffee table. I positioned my head so I was facing the door. I didn't think the guy would come back, but that didn't ease my frame of mind and I didn't sleep much after that.

CHRIS FINISHED WORKING on the security door and looked up at me. "Give me your prints so I can rule you out."

"Melissa's will be on there, too."

"If I don't get a hit on anybody else, I'll check and see if she's on file and rule her out." She stood regarding me, looking extremely professional in her pressed khaki trousers and white button-down shirt. Her badge was clipped to her belt. "What else?"

I shook my head. "Not a hell of a lot. I'm pretty sure he was male. It was dark and all I saw was his back but his body shape was male and he was at least six feet tall. Short hair. Jeans and a black tee. I don't know if I actually thought to look at his shoes."

"That's all right. Hopefully I'll get something from the prints on the door." She followed me into the house and I waited as she peeled an inking strip open. I pressed all my fingers onto the ink. Chris then slipped it into a small paper envelope on which she had written my name. She put the envelope in her kit. She gathered her gear and looked at me again. A grim expression crossed her face. "What the hell is going on?"

"I don't know. I don't think it's random. Maybe it has something to do with Megan. Could have been Cody. Same height, roughly."

"Yeah. I'm not discounting that." Chris noticed the comforter on the couch and the broom on the floor. "Why don't you stay at my place tonight?"

I considered her offer but decided against it. "I think it's a better idea for me to stay here. He might come back."

Chris looked at me as if monkeys had suddenly flown out of my butt. "Exactly. I would prefer that you're safe with me than fighting some crazy racist in a small space like this."

"I'm getting the locks changed today. And if he comes back, I can find out who he is and maybe even get some info about Megan."

"So you're going to ask some perp breaking in whether he's seen your ex-girlfriend's younger sister? How is *that* conversation going to go down?" Chris grimaced at me, frustrated. "And will that be before or after you smack him with the broom?"

I ran my hands through my hair. "Chris, see it my way for a minute. I think he has a key, which means he knows Megan. And he might have been coming here to get something for her. So if he comes back, it's because he thinks he's still able to get in."

"You are psycho." Chris was glaring down at me. She's about five-eight and can be really intimidating. I'm maybe two inches shorter, but when Chris gets her cop look, I feel about two inches tall, period. "That is a bullshit plan," she said in a tone of voice that left little room for argument, but I tried anyway.

"C'mon, Chris. What if Megan comes back with him? For all we know, she's been stopping by her place for clothes." *Shit. Why didn't I think of that?* I'd have Melissa check Megan's closet to see what might be missing.

Chris relaxed, but only slightly. Her eyes glinted steel. In cop mode, she could scare the crap out of most people. "Here's the deal. I'm going to work. I'm taking a day off tomorrow. I'm going to stay with you here tonight and I don't want to hear anything from you about it. I'll drive my own car and I'll park it up the street. And if this *cabrón* comes back to fuck with you..."

I leaned forward and kissed her on the cheek. "You're really hot when you talk dirty like that," I teased, trying to lighten the mood.

Her jaw tensed and then she laughed softly. "Promise me you'll get the locks changed."

"I'm calling Melissa as soon as you leave."

"All right. I'll see you tonight." She smiled, though I saw the concern in her eyes before she headed out the door.

"Hey, Chris—"

She turned, halfway down the walk.

"Thanks."

"Kase, I love you. I care about you. And if anything happens to you, I and the wrath of my ancestors will find whoever messed with you." She threw a wave with her free hand and returned to her unmarked car, its front end just visible on the street. I let out a sigh and shut the security door, then called Melissa. Fortunately, she answered and I told her what had happened.

"What? Someone tried to break in?" She was obviously upset.

"I don't know if that's what he was doing. I get the feeling that he had a key and he was trying to open the door that way."

"Well, who the hell would do that?"

"I don't know. Maybe Cody? Maybe one of his friends? When you stop by, have a look in Megan's closet and see if you notice anything that's gone missing since she left."

"Jesus. I—"

She was thinking she had put me needlessly in danger. I headed her off. "It's okay. I chased him off and Chris already came by. She might have gotten a print she can use. If he's got a prior, we'll be able to find out who it is."

"Dammit!" Melissa seemed to be struggling with words. "I'll put you up in a hotel—"

"Look, all we need to do is get the locks changed."

She hesitated before responding. "Call Heights Lock and Key. Give them the address. The landlord is on file. He's a friend of mine—Rob Tanner—and we have an arrangement when things need to get done. I'll let him know about it. Just make a couple of extra copies of the new key."

"Will do."

"Oh, and save the receipt for me so I can give it to him." She sounded frustrated.

"Yep."

"Are you sure you don't want to go to a hotel? What if he comes back and tries to break in through a window?"

"I don't think he will because he knows someone's here now and he won't want to risk drawing attention to himself."

"I don't want you there by yourself tonight," she pressed.

"Not to worry. Chris is staying over after she gets off duty."

Long pause. Melissa knew that Chris and I'd had more than a friendship sometimes, though she also knew that Chris and I never slept together when one or both of us was seeing someone. I knew that Melissa wanted to ask about present circumstances between Chris and me, but on the other hand, she really didn't want details. I heard an almost imperceptible sigh. "All right. Call me if you need anything. I'll talk to you later."

"Will do. Bye." I hung up and put my phone in my pocket, glad for Megan's little neat streak. She kept her phone books stacked on the shelves in her living room. I called Heights and explained my situation. No problem, the man said, after they looked up the address in their system. They'd be there in about an hour. That was actually pretty good for Albuquerque, so I set to brewing coffee and toasting a bagel.

As the coffee finished brewing, I heard a male voice at the security door. It had only been ten minutes, so it couldn't be the locksmith.

"Hello? Anybody home?"

I stuck my head out of the kitchen. A guy about my height stood outside. He looked to be in his mid-twenties.

"Yeah?"

"Hi. I'm Jeff, from the front house."

"Oh, yeah. Melissa told me. Come on in. It's open. You want some coffee?"

He pulled the door open and stepped in. "That'd be nice, thanks."

I returned to the kitchen and poured coffee into my cup and got another one out of the cabinet near the sink. "You want some cream?"

"No, thanks. Black is fine."

I handed him the cup. "I'm K.C., an—" I stopped, then continued, "an old friend of Melissa's."

"Cool. Melissa said you'd be hangin' here for a while." He blew on his coffee and took a sip. I studied him. Straight black hair and stocky build. He wore tattered black shorts and a plain gray tee. Flip-flops graced his feet. He looked like the quintessential young college student type. I got a good vibe from him.

"So. A cop?" He looked at me, not wanting to pry but clearly needing to know what an officer of the law was doing near his house early in the morning. Chris's unmarked squad car still screamed "police."

"Oh, Chris. She's a friend of mine and stopped by on her way to work. Sorry about that. Didn't mean to freak you out."

He smiled. "I'm actually glad. I haven't told Melissa this, but there's been some weird stuff happening around here since Megan's been gone."

I looked at him, gauging what I could and could not tell him and it occurred to me that I was still in my boxers and thin white tee without a bra. I set my coffee down on the counter and crossed my arms over my chest. "Like what?"

He took a tentative sip from his cup, maybe debating what to say. "Well, last week some guy was messing around back here. It was late—like, eleven or something—and he went back to Megan's and tried the door handle. We were up watching a movie and I was in the kitchen getting something to drink and I just happened to look through the back door and saw him. I shouted at him and he bailed, but it was weird."

"Did you get a look at him?"

"Not really. About all I could tell was he was wearing jeans and a dark shirt. I didn't see his face."

"Was it Cody?"

"No, I don't think so. Cody was coming around a lot the last few months and he always said hi to me or Sage if he saw us. Though Sage never said hi back." Jeff smiled and shook his head.

I sipped my coffee. "Huh. Weird. Well, thanks for letting me know. I'll tell Chris and she'll swing by a little more."

"That'd be great." He smiled again. "Good coffee."

"Thanks. So what else have you noticed?"

"Sage saw a couple of creepy dudes hanging out by the curb a couple of weeks ago."

"Creepy how?"

"I didn't see them. I was at work. But Sage'll tell you. She said they were wearing jeans and white tees and they had scary tattoos on their arms and necks."

"Really?"

"Yeah. Sage says the tats were swastikas and shit like that. Couple of skinheads, sounds like."

"That *is* creepy." I took another sip of my coffee and changed the subject. Sort of. "So what do you think about Cody?"

Jeff shrugged. "He seems nice. He's always polite and Megan seems to really like him. Sage hates him, though."

"How come?" This Sage already sounded like a damn smart cookie and I should probably have a chat with her.

"She says he's a racist, but I haven't seen or heard anything like that from him. But Sage is pretty good at reading people, so if she says he is, he probably is. Still, he's always polite to me."

"Have you seen him recently?" I tried to keep my tone conversational.

"No. I figured he's just waiting for Megan to finish the summer term she's doing and then they'll just pick up where they left off."

"Huh. Well, maybe I'll get to meet him."

"Maybe." Jeff finished his coffee and reached to put his cup on the counter.

"You want more?"

"No, thanks. Hey, why don't you stop by later? We're having some friends over and we'll be grilling out tonight."

"Sounds good. I might do that. Thanks for the invite."

"Sure. Gotta stick together in the 'hood," he said, slipping into a strong New Mexico *cholo* accent. I laughed as I followed him to the door.

"Take it easy," I said as he left. He waved and loped to the steps of the main house's back porch. I returned to the kitchen and ate my bagel, which was cool but still yummy after I slathered cream cheese all over it. I finished and cleaned up and poured myself another cup of coffee and was just about to take a drink when I heard another knock at the door. *Damn. Grand Central Station.*

"Hello? Heights Lock and Key."

An older guy wearing a work shirt stood outside. I let him in, noting that the name "Joe" was emblazoned on a patch on his left pectoral. He set to work and within thirty minutes had changed out both locks. He set them to open with one key but he handed me two. "One plus a copy," he said in his gruff but friendly voice.

"Thanks a bunch." I paid him with a credit card and included a nice tip. "Thank you, sir," I said, falling into my Texas respect-for-my-elders mode. He looked at me funny. He'd probably never been called "sir" here. New Mexico is pretty informal.

"Let us know if there're any problems with these."

"Definitely. Thanks again."

He gathered his tools and hefted them down the walk to his truck. I breathed easier and locked the security door. Time to shower and then get some copies of the new key made. After that, I'd go back to work on Megan's e-mail files.

Chapter
Six

I FINISHED READING through the e-mails from Cody that Megan had saved. Some were pretty mushy, but nothing really graphic. Thank God. I had been dreading reading about Megan's sex life with a white supremacist recruiter. The e-mails she saved often included what she had written in response to something he had said and vice versa. So I actually ended up with a good record of their relationship.

They had met last June, as I had already surmised from the photos. Within a week, he asked her out and a week after that they were getting physical because he wrote that he really enjoyed dinner with her and he hoped she wasn't "freaked out" when he kissed her. *Aw, how sweet. Mr. Hitler Youth wants to make sure she's okay.* The thought of him kissing Megan pissed me off. I stopped reading for a minute, then continued. Their messages the first month they were dating were mostly like that, usually with "I can't wait to see you" notations in them and silly, goofy things you say to that special someone you've just started seeing.

By month two, however, Cody had started to work his campaign. He asked Megan if she'd like to go to a barbecue with him. Yes, she would. I clicked on the next set of e-mails. Megan was uneasy here. She was confused about his friends. Why did they talk about pride in the white race? And why were they so hateful toward gay people? After all, Megan pointed out, her sister was gay.

Cody's response was masterful. He said that some of them were just assholes but most of them just wanted the same rights as everybody else. He said he didn't have a problem with Melissa—he used her name—but, he added, Megan had to admit that homosexuality was a little weird. It didn't make sense biologically, since people are supposed to reproduce and you need a man and a woman for that. He apologized to her for freaking her out and could he make it up to her? I had to admit, the kid was smooth.

Megan tried a half-hearted defense of Melissa and told him that homosexuality existed even among animals and just because someone was gay didn't mean they couldn't have kids. Cody agreed with her in his response, but said that he was raised Christian and it just wasn't considered "normal" but he certainly didn't think it made any sense to run around hating. He included a Web site to an ex-gay ministry. I recognized it as the site Megan had bookmarked in her Web browser.

In the e-mails they sent to each other over the course of the next couple of weeks, the barbecue did not come up again. The third week Cody invited her to go dancing. That reminded me. I needed to check her MP3 files and her CDs to see if she was also listening to racist music. Well, one heinous task at a time.

Another week of mushy sweet nothings. Finally, month four rolled around. Cody asked Megan if she had read the book he had given her. She had, she responded, but she wasn't sure she believed it. The next e-mail from him was a standard explanation of Christian Identity. He provided another link—this one for a book that was advertised on the National Alliance Web site. After that, the e-mails between them were filled with more and more of Cody's recruiting, offset with his professions of love for her and how she was the best thing that had ever happened to him. His anti-Semitism began to show up.

By month six, Megan was starting to agree with him. I felt slightly sick and had to stop again. I stood up and went into the kitchen, pacing. *Megan, what the hell? How could you believe his bullshit?* I rubbed my forehead. I'd been researching this crap while Melissa and I were together. Megan *knew* that. She *knew* what I did. She'd talked to me a little bit about it and she'd expressed profound disgust about it And here she was, sucked in, preyed on. *Why? What was it about him?* Was she replacing drug addiction with another kind of addiction? Was she filling some kind of empty hole she thought she had in her soul? *What the fuck?*

I thought then about the years I'd known her, about the serious expression she'd get on her adolescent features when she and I had talked about her crushes on boys at school, and about college and how hard it was to be around her dad sometimes. She'd stay with Melissa and me for a few days every now and again, and the lines of worry around her eyes would always dissipate, even with Melissa's anxiety about Megan going back to their father's house, with its hidden rage and pain. But Melissa wasn't ready to confront him, wasn't ready to tell him that Megan would live with us because she'd tried challenging him, years ago, and he exacted payment with his fists.

So Melissa made herself scarce, like Megan later learned to do, but I knew she blamed herself for Megan's addiction and I knew that she made a pact with herself that she'd be the parent to Megan that neither of them had. But Megan's demons proved hard to handle, harder than either of us could have imagined.

I bit back tears, remembering the way Megan could look like she was fifty and fifteen all at the same time, trying to stay clear of her parents, trying not to be noticed, and I remembered her first stint in rehab, and how she cried on my shoulder during the initial visits Melissa and I made because she felt like she'd let me down. Me. Not Melissa. Me. And I would tell her that she was strong enough to kick it, she could get through this and I loved her anyway and no matter what happened, I'd always love her. I told her that when she went into rehab the second time, too, but not as often and she looked haunted those months, surviving along the knife edge between hope and despair.

And then I let *her* down because when I left Melissa, I left Megan, too. If I had stayed in contact with her, would this have happened? Would she have hooked up with a guy like Cody? Or would she have remembered who she was, and how much she had overcome? If I had called her every once in a while, would that have been enough to keep her out of a group like Cody's? I stared at my past, at the decisions I'd made, and the cold hands of guilt and regret squeezed the breath out of my lungs until I couldn't even cry and I ached all over like I'd been beaten.

I swallowed past the lump in my throat. I'd get her out of this. I had to. No way was I going to let some asshole suck the soul from her body. Not without a hell of a fight. *Hang in there, Megan. I'll find you.* I finally managed a deep breath and returned to the computer, sinking back into analytical mode. Megan was depending on me. So was Melissa. I had to make this right. I owed it to Megan. And in a roundabout way, I owed it to Melissa, too. I jiggled the mouse to bring the e-mail back onto the screen and started reading again.

Month six, I reminded myself. Megan asked Cody if he thought Melissa could be cured. He responded in the affirmative, but she had to *want* to be cured. He said that being gay was like being addicted to something and then he said that he knew she knew something about that and she knew how hard it was to break an addiction. I stopped again for a little bit, needing to clear my head again. I threw a sandwich together with stuff I had bought the day before and looked over Megan's bookshelves while I ate. I turned the radio on and tuned to my favorite public radio station, KUNM. Their afternoon music show reminded me to see what Megan listened to.

I checked the spines of the CDs in the living room, chewing another bite of my sandwich. Megan had a few, but nothing like the collections of people who were into music before digital downloading. Standard pop. A few hip-hop CDs. I didn't see anything out of the ordinary. I hadn't found an iPod, so if she had one or some comparable MP3 player, she probably had it with her.

I went back to her computer and opened up the file in her documents division called "Music." More standard pop. Some country and even a few salsa tunes. Hip-hop and punk. Okay. I scrolled down. Yep, here were some racist groups. Final Solution, Oi Boys, and White Terror. These were harder-edged than punk and probably sounded like speed metal. I didn't listen. I didn't need to. She had one album of each on her hard drive. I wiped my hands on my shorts and went back to her e-mail files and by the end of month six, she was talking about that music with Cody.

I slogged through months seven and eight, sadness, anger, and fear twisting around in my stomach as she was drawn in to the movement. In month nine, Cody said that he could see himself marrying her and would she maybe consider that with him? He also started talking about "preparing." That was a buzz word for the end of the world through a race war. He clarified in subsequent messages, saying that he needed a strong woman by his side in order to further the cause. He said that "something big" was going to happen soon and he had chosen her to weather the storm with him.

I sat back, trying to sort through all the emotions and thoughts running through my heart and head. Cody Sorrell had the makings of a charismatic leader. The rhetoric he used, the manipulation of Megan's feelings through flattery and appeals to her strength, references to how strong she was to kick her addiction and find a path of righteousness — Megan had been sucked right in. He found her weaknesses and he exploited them, convincing her that she belonged with him, that her "friends" were in the movement. These were tactics, I knew, that abusive partners used in relationships. Flattery, manipulation, then isolation from outside support networks, and finally, control. Was Cody abusive, as well? Most likely. The thought tore at me, dug its teeth into my psyche.

I took a deep breath and forced myself back into research mode, paying extra attention to the e-mail messages from month ten to eleven. Cody had started saying that he had to leave soon and would she come with him? He started talking about buying a place out in the country somewhere where they could live without having to worry about minority crime or drugs. He said that they should get married and raise their children on a farm, making sure they had good things to eat and wouldn't grow up influenced by "corrupt Jew culture." But he also said that he needed to get some money together for the down payment on the land. He was going to go to work for a couple of his friends, he said, and within a few months, they'd have enough. He signed off with "for blood and future." That was a new one. Oddly, he made no reference to any particular group with which he might be affiliated. *Damn.*

Megan's responses to these overtures were at first noncommittal. So she hadn't bought it completely. Still, the last e-mail she sent to him said that she was really looking forward to being with him forever and she had packed up a few things and was waiting for him. She sent that message the week before she disappeared. I stood, gritting my teeth. The whole relationship detailed right there. I'd tell Melissa about the e-mails, but I didn't think she'd want to read them.

I went to the bedroom and got my address book out of my "college bag." I flipped to Judy Hansford and dialed the number on my cell. I got her voice mail and left her a brief message along with my number and asked her to please give me a call when she had a chance. Almost five. I'd better check in with Melissa.

I dialed her number, thinking I'd probably better program it into my phone. She answered on the second ring.

"Hi."

"Hey. I went through Megan's e-mail files. She saved everything she got from him. It's—" I paused. "Well, it's how he recruited her."

Melissa was silent for a moment. Then, "Do I want to read them?"

"I don't know. Some of it's hard to take. He worked on convincing her that being gay is like an addiction and if you would just get into treatment, you wouldn't be gay anymore."

"Oh, God..."

"Maybe you shouldn't," I said. "Let me deal with it."

"Thanks." She paused. "Is it okay if I swing by now?"

"Sure. I need to give you a new key, anyway."

"Give me a half-hour. See you soon."

I hung up and started poking around on Megan's bookshelves, trying to fill the time before Melissa arrived. I found three paperbacks with inscriptions from Cody within. He loved her and was so glad she was taking an interest in his life. I flipped through the pages, noting what was underlined. Megan liked blue highlighter. I had checked the textbooks on her shelves. The underlining in these books was in black pen. Cody had given her his personal copies. I checked the shelves in her bedroom. Nothing racist here, thank God. One shelf was devoted to three framed photos, including one of Megan with Cody—I recognized it from her hard drive—and one of her with Melissa.

I remembered the trip. I had taken this photo. The three of us had gone to the Grand Canyon about eight months before Megan started using the second time. Though they only shared one parent, they had similar facial features. Both had dark hair though Melissa's had a sort of auburn sheen to it. Where Melissa's eyes were a mixture of blue and gray, Megan's were a clear blue. Both women enjoyed those high cheekbones that straight women would kill for and lesbians would die for. I stared at it for a long time, thinking that Megan had seemed happy on that trip. We all had. I put the photo down and picked up the third.

Melissa again, alone and smiling. I didn't recognize it, so it was probably taken after I had left. Idly, I opened Megan's jewelry box, which sat on the top shelf. I didn't know what I expected to see in it and I was still nervous about finding drug paraphernalia. Fortunately, only earrings and bracelets inhabited the top tray. Underneath that I found another framed photo. I almost dropped it when I looked at it. Melissa with me. We were standing near Taos Pueblo and she had her arms around my waist while my right arm was over her shoulders. We were both smiling. I remembered that trip vividly because we were celebrating the first anniversary of our official relationship.

It was late summer so we went camping in the mountains above Taos and spent a couple of days wandering the town and pueblo, inseparable. Enjoying each other's company and the landscape. The sky had been impossibly blue. New Mexico blue. So clear you could see the edges of time. The pueblo's architecture flowed from the earth, matching the color of the soil. Windows and doorways appeared like magic in its walls. I remembered the residents going about their business, laughing and talking. I almost smelled the bread from the *hornos*. Pueblo dogs ran free across the dirt pathways that served as streets.

I remembered how much I loved her then and another lump formed in my throat. I remembered who had taken that picture. A local Indian man, charmed by Melissa's smile. *What happened? Where did you go, Melissa? Where did we go?* I heard the security door open and hastily slid the photo back into the jewelry box and set it on the shelf before returning to the living room. Melissa stood near the door, wearing black cotton pleated slacks and a loose white blouse. She had the two top buttons undone. The silver chain glinted around her neck. She took her shades off when she saw me and propped them on her head.

"Hi." She offered me a smile and it made me think of that photo at Taos Pueblo.

I ran a hand through my hair. "Hey. Thanks for coming by." I looked around, almost desperate. Where had I put the key? Oh, on the coffee table. "Here. It opens the security door and the front door."

She took it and stood looking at me. "Kase, I'm really worried."

"Look, I'm making progress. I'll get this figured out and hopefully you'll at least know where Megan is."

"I know that. I'm worried about *you*. I shouldn't have asked you to come."

I shifted my weight from foot to foot, extremely uneasy and a bit overwhelmed by memories. "I'll be okay. If I think anything's really freaky, I'll let you know."

She stood watching me. I read things unspoken in her eyes. "I'm sorry," she said quietly. "This whole thing has been kind of stressful." She chewed her lower lip, then glanced over at the computer. "What else can I do? I haven't heard from Megan's friend yet."

"Keep checking. If I think of anything, I'll ask. How's that?"

She nodded, but she wasn't completely appeased. "I can't believe someone's been trying to break in."

"Oh, that reminds me," I interrupted. "Can you check her closet? See if you notice anything missing that maybe wasn't missing before?"

"Okay. But I don't really know what she wears except maybe stuff she liked a lot."

"It can't hurt." I waited for her to move past me and then I followed her into the bedroom. She stood in the closet with the light on, concentrating. She stepped back, puzzled, and looked around again.

"That's strange," she muttered. She looked up at me. "There's a sweatshirt missing."

"Really? Which one?"

"UNM. It was her favorite and when she left, it was here. I know because I hung it up. It's not here now."

"Are you sure?"

"Definitely. I remember it because..." her voice trailed off. "It was that one you got her when she was accepted."

I felt like I had swallowed several large stones and they were sitting in the pit of my stomach. "And it's gone?"

"Yes." She had her right hand on the door jamb and she was studying Megan's carefully organized clothing. She looked at me. "So maybe she's still in town?"

"Possibly. Or nearby, at the very least." Or Cody was coming by with his friends. But I doubted that. The sweatshirt had sentimental value. That was something Megan would fetch herself. It also told me something else. If she was still in New Mexico, she was somewhere that required a sweatshirt, at least on occasion. New Mexico summers were hot. At the lower elevations, even with the heat escaping in the dry night air, you didn't need a sweatshirt after dark. But at the higher elevations, like in the East Mountain area and up toward Santa Fe, you might. The middle region near Ruidoso probably required a sweatshirt in the evenings, as did the western Gila wilderness. If they were still in the state, they were somewhere that required a sweatshirt. I told Melissa what I suspected and I also told her what Chris had discovered about Cody.

"But it could mean that they're out of state, too," Melissa said slowly. But from her tone, she didn't quite believe it. After all, she told me that when Megan called, the area code was always 505. Though that might have been a cell phone. But my gut told me otherwise.

"I'm not quite there yet. I have a feeling that she's still in the state. Let me follow this up a bit and see what we can see. Chris is trying to get me in with the gang unit to look at photos of tattoos. If we can figure out who the artist is, then he or she might have a lead on other members of Cody's group."

Melissa sat down on the bed. She seemed physically drained. Faint dark circles showed under her eyes and creases marred her forehead.

"You need some sleep." I stood studying her.

"I'm all right. I just really want to know where Megan is and that she's all right."

"Are you sleeping at night?"

Melissa's jaw clenched. She rubbed her forehead with her right hand.

"You've got to get some rest, Meliss'. You've got to stay alert on this."

She sighed.

"Has she called?"

"No. Not for almost two weeks this time. That's got me worried."

"It might not mean anything. When she does call, let me know. Try to write down things she says."

"I keep a log." Melissa sounded deflated. "I'll bring it by so you can look at it."

"Thanks. That might be helpful. You want something to drink? You're not taking care of yourself and that's not doing Megan any good."

She looked up at me. "You sound like old times." She said it kindly.

My breath caught in my throat. "Shit, you're right. Sorry."

Melissa stood. "For what?" She shrugged and went back into the living room. "I couldn't help her then and I wonder if maybe I should just let her go now." She stood staring at Megan's computer.

"This is different. She's with people who might actually—well, it's different. If you're using, you're doing it to yourself. It's different when others do things to you." I didn't bring up my suspicions about the possibility of abuse. Melissa had enough to worry about.

"But it's her boyfriend. People get involved all the time with people their families don't approve of. If there were an intervention for every partner a family didn't like, nobody would ever get together. Maybe I should just back the fuck off."

I chose my words carefully. "It's your decision. If you think that's the right course of action."

"I don't *know* what the right course of action is." She turned and regarded me. I felt an echo in my heart and attempted to ignore it. She watched me. "What do *you* think?"

"Well—" I shifted. "Okay, here's the deal. From what Cody was telling her in the e-mails leading up to her leaving, it sounds like he's getting involved with potentially illegal activities. And that takes this out of the realm of simply a partner the family doesn't like. When you cross that line, it becomes everybody's business whether you want it to or not. I think he and his groupies are doing stuff that's not legal. And I have a feeling that they might be headed down a road that requires a Butch and Sundance kind of scenario."

Melissa's eyes narrowed. "You mean like a martyr thing?"

"Maybe. It's not unknown among groups like this."

She crossed her arms over her chest and we stared at each other for a while until she broke the silence. "Why are you here?"

"Excuse me?" The question caught me off guard.

"You didn't have to come. We haven't seen each other since you left and you're still angry in some ways. So why did you come?"

I looked at the floor, looked back up at her. I tried to latch onto a coherent thought and failed. "Honestly, I don't know. I haven't figured it out yet."

"Please believe me when I tell you that if I thought there was any other way to do this, I would have done it."

"I do. It took a lot for you to come to Texas. And I guess I got to thinking that here I have this, oh, so *useful* knowledge—" I rolled my eyes in a weak attempt at humor. "It makes no sense not to try to help you and Megan."

She smiled. It seemed genuine. "Ever the logical one. Sometimes that side of you drove me crazy."

"Me, too. It's hard being so good at what I do." I paused and then grinned. "Joke. Ha ha?"

She managed a chuckle. Her body language was still tense. I envisioned her with giant porcupine quills all over her skin. That must've been what it was like for her trying to deal with me in the past. And now this shit with Megan was wearing her down and I really didn't know what else was going on in her life.

"I have to get going," she announced.

"Sure. Don't worry. I'll keep you posted, okay?"

"I know."

I wasn't quite sure what that meant so I just followed her to the door. "Try to get some sleep. Really. I'm going to need your help and so is Megan. I need you to be able to kick ass if it's required."

She caught my eyes with hers. "Please don't think you need to see this through. If this gets more dangerous..." She let that float between us.

"Hey, we'll think about that when we get there. If we get there. Keep an ear open for your phone. Check your e-mail. And get some damn sleep," I chided her gently. "I'll talk to you later."

She waved half-heartedly as she turned and headed toward the street. I watched her go, feeling ungrounded. I thought about seeing her in the Mercedes with Hillary that night three years ago and I felt nothing. Nothing except maybe the beginning of a headache. My phone rang so I went back inside and checked the screen. A local number. Ah. Judy.

"Hey, stranger!"

"K.C., it's been too long. I got your message. Do you have some time tomorrow?"

"Yep. What time?"

"Swing by around ten. Do you have pictures?

"Yep again. I'll bring them and pick your brain. How about this—I'll meet you for a late breakfast. Flying Star in the Heights?"

"I like that even better. See you there at ten. I'm looking forward to it. Bye."

"Bye." I closed my phone. Good. Judy might have something. Then I'd swing over to Cody's aunt's house. I'd have to think of a good cover story for that. Almost six-thirty. I'd go buy some beer for Jeff and Sage's barbecue. After today, I definitely needed one.

Chapter
Seven

I GOT BACK to Megan's around seven-fifteen with two six-packs of beer. One was Rio Grande Desert Pilsner, a local beer, and the other was Fat Tire, a Colorado brew. As I got out of my car, I heard voices, laughter, and music coming from the back yard and I smelled burgers grilling. A few people stood on the front porch chatting. I went around back, carrying the beer.

"Hey," Jeff called when he saw me. "Grab a burger!"

"Don't mind if I do," I said.

Jeff flipped one of the patties, checking it. "Oops. Not quite ready. How about a beer instead?"

I held up the two six-packs and he grinned. "Excellent. There's a cooler on the porch and you can stash some in the fridge." He motioned with his spatula at the back door. Two young men were standing near the grill, holding bottles of Tecate. Jeff motioned from them to me. "Guys, this is K.C. She's chillin' at Megan's while she's out of town."

They smiled and tipped their beers toward me. One introduced himself as Rob and the other as Mike. I climbed the steps onto the porch and opened the cooler. There was room for one six-pack. I stuffed the six bottles of Fat Tire into the ice and then entered the house. The doors stood wide open and I heard voices inside. I stepped into a mud room/laundry room. The kitchen was just beyond, and through that, I glimpsed what was probably a living-dining room, where a few people were chatting.

The kitchen was a funky 1940s-looking place but it had new appliances. The linoleum was clean but needed updating and the countertops looked like the original ones, edged in chrome. A man and woman stood near the kitchen sink, engaged in some kind of intense conversation. I smiled politely and focused my attention on the fridge as I took the bottles out of the carrier and slid them on their sides onto the bottom shelf.

"Hi."

I looked up. A woman who I gauged to be about Jeff's age if not younger stood watching me. Even from my angle, I could tell she was athletic and toned, exuding youthful health and enthusiasm. She wore baggy khaki shorts, a blue sleeveless tee, and sport sandals. Chaco brand, by the looks of them. Wavy light brown hair hung loose to her shoulders and her soft brown eyes seemed to twinkle when she smiled, little laugh lines appearing at their corners. I labeled her "nature girl." Typical New Mexico gearhead. I'd probably find mountain bikes and backpacks in the living room.

"You're K.C." Her eyes sparkled. "I'm Sage." She stuck her right hand out. I stood up and wiped my right hand on my shorts before taking hers. A nice, firm handshake. Nice, firm hands attached to nice, firm arms.

I looked at her, surprised. "Good to meet you. Thanks for the invite." I stared into her eyes for what seemed an inappropriate amount of time for a first meeting, holding a bottle of Rio Grande in my left hand. *So this is Sage. A perfect name for her.* I tried to bury the thought that bubbled to the front of my brain. Major hottie. *And there's something beyond the physical here. Yikes. Don't go there.* I shut the fridge to interrupt my train of thought.

"No problem. So what's the K stand for?"

I looked at her, a little confused.

"Megan said your name is spelled with a K and a C. What does the K stand for? Megan said it didn't stand for anything, but she always thought you might be teasing her." Sage reached behind her to the counter space next to the fridge and picked up a bottle opener.

"No, I wasn't pulling her leg. It doesn't stand for anything."

She took the bottle of beer out of my hand and opened it and then handed it back. "Nothing?"

She had me slightly unbalanced. "Nope. My mom has a weird sense of humor. It says K period C period on my birth certificate. She figured I could fill in the blanks later if I wanted."

Sage giggled. "That's really cool. Where's your mom now?"

"My folks are in Arizona."

"Well, let me think of something for your name."

I took a sip of beer, looked down into Sage's eyes. She was about two inches shorter. I grinned. "Don't worry about it. Many have tried. Letters have served me well this long, they'll keep it up."

She grinned back. Sage was *super* cute. I shut that thought down immediately. She was also roughly ten years younger and probably straight. Jesus. I was lusting after Jeff's girlfriend. *Live-in* girlfriend.

"Jeff said you were asking about Cody."

Well. Doesn't waste much time.

She reached around me and opened the fridge. She pulled a bottle of Rio Grande out and opened it. "I like this stuff," she said after she took a drink. "I tried it for the first time last month." She tossed the bottle cap onto the counter next to mine. "Jeff doesn't have a problem with Cody but I do."

"Oh?" I moved away from the refrigerator as another guest opened it, smiling apologetically.

"He has bad energy. I saw it a mile off. I told Megan to be careful with him, but she didn't listen." Sage's brow furrowed and I quickly took a swallow of beer because she looked adorable.

"What did you think was bad about him?"

"Melissa said you're a professor." I must have had a bewildered expression on my face because she elaborated, patiently. "And I can tell you are because you ask questions that try to get me to be more specific within the context of analysis rather than judgment." Her eyes seemed to spark mischievously.

I chuckled nervously. "All right, yes. I am and I do. It's a habit. So what's the deal?" I was still off-kilter. But I didn't mind.

"He's an asshole and a racist fuck."

I was taken slightly aback but I found her frankness appealing. I waited for her to continue.

"I saw his freakin' tattoos. He thought he was being all discreet, wearing those stupid long-sleeved shirts all the time. I saw him outside Megan's one morning a couple of months after they met. He was on the phone and he had his shirt off. When he saw me watching him from that window—" she gestured at a window that overlooked the back porch, "—he went back inside fast. Asshole." She took another sip of beer. "And his loser friends came around a lot, too. They didn't even try to cover their tats."

"All guys?"

"Yeah. White. Of course." She shook her head with disgust. "Megan fell for their bullshit. I could see it happening. She used to hang with me all the time but after Cody, that stopped."

"Did she stop on her own or did Cody tell her to?"

Sage thought about that. "Both, probably. They were having some kind of argument last fall. He was really yelling at her about Melissa—called her 'that fucking dyke sister' of hers." Sage's eyes registered anger. "I was gonna go over there and kick his ass, talking about Melissa like that. Then he said something else and she said something like 'but Sage's my friend,' and he started yelling about dykes corrupting white women or some asinine shit like that. Please." She made a disgusted noise before continuing. "I think *all* women could use a little lezzie corruption, thank you very much." She grinned wickedly. My heart fluttered. So Sage was, at the very least, bi. Or maybe she just didn't care about labels. Still, she was with Jeff. Maybe she was just letting me know that she was okay with the whole "gay thing." Why the hell did I care, anyway?

"So how long have you lived here?" I asked, trying to shift the conversation.

"Two years. Same as Megan." Sage looked sad, then. "I thought we had gotten to be pretty good friends. She told me about her addiction problems and I told her if she needed to talk, just let me know. But she seemed okay. She hadn't used the whole time she's been here, as far as I can tell, and she didn't seem to have a problem around other people if they were drinking. And then Cody showed up and she started getting weird."

"Jeff said about a week ago you saw a couple of Cody's friends hanging around."

She grimaced, distaste clear on her features. "Roy and...what's the other guy? Timmy or something juvenile like that. Total losers."

"What do they look like?"

"Roy's about thirty. A little too old to be playing white man rising, if you ask me. He's blond and he has blue eyes. He's probably all proud that he looks like some little Aryan youth. He's about six feet tall. The other guy is about your height. He has dark hair and dark eyes. Oh, and a really nice beer gut. A fine example of manhood." She snorted then and grinned.

I had to smile back. Her demeanor was infectious. "What were they doing here? Has Cody been coming around?"

"Nuh-uh. Not that I've seen. I told them to get the hell out of here or I'd call the cops."

"Really? You said that?"

"Hell, yes. Assholes. Timmy or whatever his name is smokes and he was throwing his damn butts into the yard."

"What'd they do?"

"What they usually do. Called me a bitch and left."

"So you've had dealings with them before?" The thought of someone calling Sage a bitch rankled me, though she could clearly take care of herself.

"Well, *duh*," she said, laughing. "I told Cody to fuck off, too. I told him to leave Megan alone, that she was too good for him."

"When?" *Holy shit.*

"About the time Megan left."

"What'd he do?" I found myself admiring her and worrying about her at the same time.

"He thought he was all menacing and shit, getting into my face. I know his type. My dad was like that and when he tried shit with me, I told him the same thing. My dad backed down and so did Cody." She shrugged. "He told me if I wasn't a woman, he'd knock my teeth out and I told him to fucking try it. I'd kick his ass into next year." She giggled, but I saw a flash of anger in her eyes. "Bastard. He tried to stare me down but he blinked first." She stopped then, thinking. "Megan left the next day." She looked at me, intense. "Megan's not really taking classes, is she."

It wasn't a question. I debated how much to tell Sage and decided she wasn't the type to accept BS from anyone. I shook my head.

"She's with him." Sage said it quietly and her fingers tightened around her beer bottle.

"Yeah. Melissa asked me to help find her."

"Fuck," Sage said softly. "Megan told me after I first met her that you research racist assholes."

"She talked about me?"

"A lot. She said after you and Melissa broke up, she almost started using again."

Oh, that hurt.

Sage must've seen the expression on my face. "Oh, no. She understood why you left and she told me she didn't blame you. Don't feel guilty." She squeezed my right forearm with her left hand. "I'm sorry, I didn't mean to make you feel bad."

"It's okay. I'm just a little..." I rubbed the back of my neck. "Surprised, I guess. I didn't realize that Megan—"

"She missed you really bad. And she was really pissed at Melissa for months. They had some knock-down arguments about it, too."

I tapped my half-full beer bottle against my thigh. "Look, Sage, I appreciate all this info, but there's some stuff that I really don't need to hear."

She looked at me, a trace of embarrassment and concern in her eyes. "Sorry. That was really shitty of me. Sometimes I just talk and—"

"No, no. Don't worry about it." I changed the subject quickly to minimize her discomfort. "So Jeff mentioned that he saw someone poking around back there, too."

Sage's brow furrowed in thought. "Yeah. I remember. It was about eleven and I heard him yell something out the back. He wasn't sure who it was. I think it was probably one of Cody's asshead friends."

I debated whether to tell her what had happened the night before. I decided I'd better for safety's sake, if nothing else. "Someone was messing with the place last night, too."

Her eyes narrowed. "When?"

"I was in my car trying to find him at two thirty-four AM, according to my car clock."

She stared at me. "What the hell?"

"I think he had a key and he was trying to get it to work in the door. I don't think he knew I was inside."

"Holy shit. What'd you do?"

"I scared him off and then tried to find him."

Sage's eyebrows lifted.

"It's okay. My friend Chris came by this morning to take fingerprints. She's a cop."

She relaxed. "That's a relief. Do you want to stay here tonight?"

Nice offer. I felt a little thrill. "Thanks, but no. I had the locks changed. And Chris is staying over tonight. I'll be okay."

Her eyes searched mine. The effect was wholly unnerving. "Any time you need anything while you're here, come by. I don't care what time it is."

I smiled, unable to look away. "I will. Thanks. So what else about those two guys—"

"Later. Let's eat." She grinned, grabbed my arm, and pulled me toward the back porch where we joined Jeff at the grill. She fixed a burger for me, asking what I wanted on it. I watched her, bemused. She was a force of nature, this Sage. And a font of data. Hopefully I'd get a chance to pick her brain a bit more. She went back into the kitchen and loaded my plate with pasta salad and some sliced vegetables. Red peppers, carrots, and celery. "Do you want green chile on your burger?"

"Please."

She handed me the plate and placed a plastic fork on it. I grabbed a paper napkin from the stack on the counter. "Make yourself at home." She went back outside. I wandered into the living room where six people were already sitting around on a variety of chairs eating. Bowls of chips and other snacks sat on the table, which stood just to the right of the kitchen doorway as I entered the living room. I found a spot on the couch and took a bite of the burger. The tangy, earthy taste of fresh roasted green chile exploded in my mouth. I savored it, then introduced myself after which those of us in the living room chatted amicably about local politics, and what everybody was doing that summer, among other small talk. Sage reappeared and plopped down onto the couch next to me. Her thigh bumped mine and I wondered at the spark I felt shoot up my leg. She had two fresh beers and she handed me one.

"Thanks." I took the bottle and clinked it against hers, trying not to think about the fact that she hadn't moved her thigh away from mine. She smiled enigmatically and ate her burger in silence. I finished and was about to stand up but she beat me to it.

"I'll take it. Just hang out."

I handed her my plate and watched as she bounced into the kitchen. She had a nice ass. Probably as toned and muscular as the rest of her. *God, I'm like a dirty old man. And how fucked up would that be to seduce a friend of Megan's? And somebody else's girlfriend?* The thoughts so disturbed me that I shuddered but I couldn't shake the entirely pleasurable chills bubbling around in my stomach. I checked my watch. Almost eight-thirty. Chris had called earlier and said she'd be in around ten. So I had another hour or so to hang out with Sage. I liked that thought.

Jeff came in and cranked the music louder. The living room's comfortably worn hardwood floor looked like it lent itself to lots of dancing. Mike rolled up the rug and moved the various furnishings out of the way and sure enough, some people availed themselves of the space to do just that. I eased into the kitchen where Sage was busy cleaning up.

I helped her, ignoring her protests. "Whatever," I said. "You feed me, I help clean up. That's the deal."

She laughed. "Fine." She patiently directed me around the kitchen to various plastic and glass containers for leftovers. She made up two separate plates and covered them with plastic wrap. "Is Megan's place open?" She asked.

I looked at her, puzzled. "Yeah."

"Be right back." She left quickly, carrying the plates.

"Hey, Sage, you don't have to — "

"I'm not listening," she called back in a sing-song voice as she balanced both plates on one arm and headed down the porch steps toward Megan's front door. She reappeared a few moments later and crossed the yard to join me on the back porch of the big house. "No reason for food to go to waste. Besides, I know how you bachelors are."

"Oh, really?" I cocked an eyebrow, wondering how she knew I was single.

"Nobody eats shitty food when I'm around."

I laughed. Sage was like nobody I had ever met. My mom would call her a "free spirit."

We went back inside and Sage soon engaged in animated conversation with Rob and a woman who had introduced herself as Jenny, bringing me into the dialogue. I didn't know how long we chatted, but after a while, Sage excused herself to go to the kitchen and a heterosexual couple that was about my age left. I heard Jeff out on the front porch talking to three other people. Most people had already left and cigar smoke wafted into the house through the open front door. The music blared in an empty room. Time to go, I thought reluctantly. Maybe I'd be able to talk more to Sage later. I turned back toward the kitchen just as the music switched to a popular salsa number.

Sage appeared in the doorway to the kitchen. "Oh, my God. I *love* this song. Can you salsa dance?" She looked at me pleadingly. "Jeff denies his heritage and refuses to do any kind of Latin American dancing. Please tell me you can dance."

I gauged the situation. Chris had taught me and said I was

pretty good for a *gringa*. Well, what could it hurt? It wasn't like Sage was dissing Jeff. He was right outside and it was possible to see us through the front window. "Sure. I'll dance."

She bounded across the floor. "And I'll bet you lead, right?" she asked mischievously as she held her hands out in the correct position for this particular tune.

I smiled and placed my right hand carefully against the small of her back and took her right in my left. She placed her left hand on my right shoulder. "Ready?" I bobbed my head in time and began moving. It had been a while since I had done this, but like riding a bike, once you know, it sticks. This particular beat called for a modified box step that was easy to follow. Step, step, slide...

A good leader instills confidence in a partner and someone who follows well can pick up on the rhythms of the leader. Sage clearly knew what she was doing. She followed me easily and gracefully, teeth flashing as she grinned. Her eyes were half-closed. Step, step, slide. Turn. Arm extension. Bring her back... She eased closer to me so that her pelvis was nearly touching mine. My palm at the small of her back felt like it was burning. *Oh, God*, I thought. *This might not have been a good idea.*

"You've got that hip thing *down*," she said appreciatively, watching my waist. I was glad the lighting was dim beneath the low ceilings. She couldn't see me blush.

"Practice, practice, practice," I said with a mock long-suffering undertone. "You know how *gringos* are—takes them a bit longer." I caught her eye.

"Whatever," she laughed as I guided her over the floor. "You were *born* with it."

I led her into another turn and arm extension as the music ended. With a quick flick, I pulled her back, snapping her into my arms, like old-fashioned tango dancers. Too late, I realized it might have been a mistake. I was all too aware of her breasts against mine and the heat I felt rolling over me in waves didn't have much to do with exertion, though we were both breathing heavily. Dancing's a workout. Among other things.

"Damn," she breathed, staring into my eyes a little too long. "Thanks."

"My pleasure. Thanks for dinner." I managed to break the moment and poked my head out the front door. "Hey, Jeff. Thanks for the invite. I'm heading home. It's a long way, you know."

Laughter. "No problem. Catch you later." He waved at me from the darkened porch.

I made my way to the back porch, smiling and nodding at the people I had met. Sage had apparently gone to the bathroom or something because I didn't see her. I decided I needed to get back to

Megan's before I started to enjoy being around her a little too much.
A few of the people who remained made nice comments about my
dancing. I murmured my thanks and finally made it to the back
porch. I was almost to Megan's front door when I heard Sage from
the big house.

"Hey!"

I turned, glad to see her again in spite of myself. "Thanks
again," I said, waving at her as I stood under Megan's porch light.

She leaned against one of the pillars that supported the porch
roof. "I figured out what K.C. stands for."

"Oh?" Given our interaction that evening and my assessment of
her personality, I figured she'd tell me.

"Killer Cute," she announced. "Good night." And she turned
and went back inside.

Shit. I watched her close the door behind her. *No. No way in hell
am I following up on this.* I exhaled and entered Megan's place. I shut
the security door. *And hold on, but she's with Jeff. Isn't she? Or is she?
Kids today!* I turned on the TV to distract myself and went to put my
sleep wear on.

I was sitting on the couch watching the ten o'clock news when
Chris arrived, which made everything feel better. She came in and
dropped her duffle bag on the floor. She had changed into shorts and
tee before she left work. I got her an iced tea from the fridge. Chris
didn't like to drink alcohol this late. We talked about her day and
mine. She was glad I got the locks changed and she was still waiting
to hear about the prints. The day after tomorrow I'd hang out with
the gang unit. That was good news. I told her what Sage had said
about Cody and his friends. I also told her about Sage.

Chris grinned. "So she's an omnisexual hottie, huh?"

"They should name hurricanes after her."

She laughed. "Sounds like she might be a lot of fun, *esa.*"

"No. I mean, yes. I'm sure she's a blast. But I am not hooking up
with Megan's friends. There's something really wrong about that."

"What? She's of legal age."

"Barely! There's got to be at least ten years between us."

She shrugged. "I'm not talking about marriage, *amiga.* Maybe a
summer fling is what you need."

I was sitting on one end of Megan's couch. Chris had her long
legs stretched out and her bare feet on the coffee table. I'm sure
Megan would've had a cow if she saw that. "No. Nope. She's with
Jeff, for chrissakes. And I'm not here to hook up with anybody. I'm
here to do a job."

Chris laughed softly and turned her head to regard me. "So how
are things going with Melissa?"

I groaned. "Damn, you sure know how to ruin a mood." I

sighed. "It's weird, being here." Chris waited for me to elaborate, as I knew she would. "I feel guilty," I said with a sigh.

"About what?"

"I was thinking today that maybe if I had at least stayed in touch with Megan, maybe she wouldn't have hooked up with somebody like Cody."

"I thought you might guilt-trip yourself about that."

"Shit, do I have *any* secrets from you?" I reached for my own bottle of tea.

"That's just how you are. Sometimes you think you're Superwoman, and you should be able to save the damn world." She reached over and squeezed my knee. "I'm here to remind you that you are an awesome human being, but you are not omnipotent."

I looked at her in mock horror. "You are really bursting my bubble here."

She rolled her eyes then became serious. "Megan made a choice. It was a bad one. We don't know for sure why she made it or what she was feeling or why she thought Cody was the guy for her. There's nothing you can do about that. Maybe it would've been different if you'd kept in touch with her. Maybe not. You know her history. Megan has a hard time making healthy choices and to suggest that you might have been the person to change her is arrogant, *esa.*" She regarded me for a moment. "Make sure that helping her now is about *her* and not necessarily *you*. Though I know you're tangled up in this." She took a swallow of tea.

"I hate it when you're right." I pretended to pout.

Chris smiled and pulled at the wrapper on her bottle. "Are you feeling guilty about Melissa?"

"No, really," I grumbled. "I totally hate it when you're right."

Chris sat back and crossed her arms over her chest. It was her "well?" expression.

"Yes," I said, exasperated. "I don't know why."

"Maybe because three years has allowed you a little space to see a bigger picture."

I nodded, thinking about that. Had I let Melissa into my apartment that day she came by to try to talk to me, would Megan be in the position she was in now?

"Don't second-guess," Chris interrupted my ruminations. "The past is done. But maybe you'll learn something from it."

"I keep wondering what would have happened if I'd tried to work it out with her."

Chris shrugged. "Nobody can say. You did what you thought you had to do, based on the information you had at the time. You know what they say about hindsight."

I drummed my fingers on my thigh, thinking about the picture of me with Melissa at Taos Pueblo.

"Are you feeling anything for her?"

I glanced up at her. Chris always knew how to nail me to a wall. "I don't know. I mean, there've been a couple of times that I thought maybe I did, but then when I think about getting together with her, I don't feel anything. I think it's just the past coming up."

"If she asks you, would you get back with her?"

I shook my head. "Right now, I'm going to say no. I haven't talked to her but my gut's telling me no."

Chris leaned forward and picked her bottle up off the coffee table. "*Esa*, I'm going to tell you something that I think you need to hear."

I looked at her, a twinge of anxiety in my stomach. When Chris said stuff like that, it usually meant it was something I didn't want to hear though it most likely was true.

True to form, she launched right into it. "Melissa's not good for you. In the beginning, I thought I'd give her a chance because she loved you and you loved her. But as time went on, it didn't feel to me that she was trying to move beyond her demons, especially where Megan's concerned."

"I'm not perfect, either." I said it defensively and I knew she heard it in my voice.

"I know that." Her tone was gentle. "But Melissa didn't give you the opportunities to grow into yourself or in the relationship. You both got stuck."

"Well, maybe I'm not very good at communicating, either."

She shrugged, clearly unconvinced. "You've never had that problem with me."

She was right. I kept my mouth shut.

"And I know how you are. You started working a lot when Megan went into rehab before Melissa had the affair."

"Maybe my working was a cause for Melissa." I said the words before I considered them. I hadn't really addressed that angle before and here it was, breaking the surface of old anger.

"All she had to do was talk to you."

"I could've talked to *her*. I didn't." I crossed my arms over my chest protectively.

"Maybe you didn't feel welcome to. Don't get me wrong here. There are two people in a relationship and even in situations like this, fallout comes from both sides. But I never felt you two were a good match."

"Why are you telling me this now? Why didn't you tell me then?"

"It wasn't my place. Melissa isn't abusive and she's not an asshole. She loved you and treated you well. But it wasn't something

I felt was right for either of you. Now, it's been three years and both of you are in different places in your lives. So if you do go down that road with her again, I'll suspend judgment again. But I'm telling you my feelings on the matter, because I care about you and because you deserve someone who's in it with you, who can work through the hard stuff, and, frankly, who forces you to deal with things. That is, someone who keeps you from going off the deep end into your work."

Chris's words dug into the inner spaces of my past. I hated that, though I knew she was right and my reaction demonstrated that on some level, I recognized it. "Dammit," I sighed, mock distress in my tone. "Why don't *you* just hook up with me? It would be so much easier. I wouldn't have to negotiate all this bullshit."

She laughed. "You know I'm not that type. I'm not the marrying kind. But if I was, you'd be at the top of the list." She reached for her tea. "Except you'd have to live in your own damn place."

"Well, *yeah*. You'd drive me crazy if we tried to play house. And I know *I'd* drive *you* insane. I get really anal about stupid shit."

"Yes, you do."

"Hey!" I leaned over and punched her lightly on the arm. "So what's your perfect type, Detective Hard-to-get?"

"She's got to have her own house." She smiled at me. Chris had a really nice endearing smile that always pushed the right side of her mouth up first. It gave her a sheepish look. She was...well, not beautiful. Handsome might be a better word for her. Plus, she had a quiet confidence that lots of women seemed to find really attractive. Objectively, as a whole, Chris was pretty damn sexy.

"And?"

"And what? Kase, you know I don't look for relationships. Sometimes they find me. But I'm not interested in that. I don't think I'm destined for it."

"We've been together for ten years." I waggled my eyebrows suggestively.

She smiled and playfully smacked my arm. "Shit, you're right. But you know what I mean. That relationship intimacy stuff just doesn't work for me."

"Have you really tried it?"

She took a sip of her tea. That was Chris's way of avoiding an answer.

"Ah, I see. Detective I'm-a-cop-and-not-relationship-material hasn't really gone down that road." I was surprised.

"Maybe. Maybe not. You know how I am." She looked at me. "I don't need a relationship. I like my work, I have my friends, I've got my family. Relationships bring complications and require work that I'm not willing to do."

"So Trish —"

"Don't go there." Her voice had a clipped edge.

"Hey, I'm your friend. That was the closest I've seen you come to really liking someone."

She shrugged. "She didn't like the cop stuff."

"So she wasn't the right one."

"Whatever." She took another drink. "I'm in law enforcement. I have fucked-up hours, dangerous shifts, and I deal with the worst of people every day. That leaves a residue on your aura, whether you want it to or not. You think I have walls to protect me from getting hurt? Well, they're also there to keep my personal shit off the people in my life. And here's the *loco* part. I love what I do." She sighed. "And the price I pay for that is accepting that intimate relationships probably aren't going to work out for me."

I stared at her. "Chris, that is the saddest thing I've ever heard you say." I moved closer and impulsively wrapped her in a bear hug. "And I don't believe it. You just haven't met her yet."

She put her arms around me and kissed me on the cheek. "You're the incurable romantic. Thank God the world still has people like you."

"Don't let that be a self-fulfilling prophecy." I released her. "Because I've seen you at your best and your worst and dammit, you're a hell of a woman. But if you insist on keeping that attitude, fine. When you're old, cranky, and decrepit I'll keep a room made up for you."

"Oh, yeah. I'm sure that'll go well with whatever woman latches onto you."

"She'll love you, too, and we'll treat you like the crazy sister we both wish we had."

"Thanks," she said sarcastically though I knew she was teasing. She stood up and took her empty bottle into the kitchen. "I'm beat. Okay if I sleep in the bed with you?"

"Duh. But if you start sprawling, I'm shoving your ass over."

"How romantic."

"That's me." Yep. Romantic. I headed to the bathroom.

Chapter
Eight

I ARRIVED AT the Flying Star at nine forty-five and got in line for counter service, looking longingly at the pastry case as I stood there. When it was my turn, I ordered the breakfast scramble, a mixture of tofu, green chile, potatoes, and a variety of other vegetarian-type things. I also bought a large café mocha and carried my beverage and my number, clipped to its little stand, to an empty table, waiting for both Judy and my food. Like its sister stores in the city, the interior here was an oddly harmonious mix of bright colors, earth tones, and post-modern sensibilities. Call it Jetsons meets Swedish design.

I sat waiting for my food and for Judy, reading through a copy of the *Albuquerque Journal*, the local paper. I was feeling amazingly relaxed after a great night's sleep. At eight Chris had gotten up and made coffee. She checked around outside and didn't find anything that looked out of order. She was due at her grandmother's to take care of some repairs around the house so she showered and left by nine. Chris would call me later to let me know more about the gang unit. When I left the house that morning, I didn't see any activity at Sage and Jeff's. They were either at work or sleeping a good time off. I caught myself as I got into my car, thinking that I was hoping to see Sage. Total eye candy if nothing else.

I set the newspaper down and looked up in time to see Judy enter the restaurant and get in line. I waved at her. She smiled and waved back. Another granola-type, Judy's long blond hair hung most often in a braid down her back. She wore wire-rimmed glasses and baggy cotton capri trousers. More often than not, Birkenstocks adorned her feet. I checked. Yep. She wore a pair today. Her faded blue T-shirt had a yin/yang symbol above her left breast. The line moved quickly and soon she was joining me at the table holding a cup of coffee. I stood after she put her coffee on the table and gave her a hug.

"Good to see you, Kase," she said as she sat down.

A young hippie chick with a pierced eyebrow brought my food

out. I looked apologetically at Judy, who smiled. "Go ahead. I just ordered a bagel."

"Thanks." I was really hungry and dug in as Judy sipped her coffee.

"So what's going on?"

Between bites, I briefly outlined the situation with Megan. Judy did know about my relationship with Melissa though they'd never met. I first contacted Judy when I was in grad school and we maintained a professional research relationship. Though I was open about Melissa, Judy didn't know about Megan's addiction problems and I didn't bring them up. I stopped eating and retrieved a manila folder from one of the other chairs at the table and handed it to her. "Do you recognize these guys or these tattoos?"

Judy's bagel arrived and she took a bite as she looked at the photos I had printed out from Megan's hard drive. "I do recognize this guy." She pointed to the man I had decided was Roy, based on Sage's description. "Roy Whistler," Judy confirmed. "Hardcore. He's been on our radar for a couple of years now."

"Is he from here?"

"No. But I'm not sure where he's from. He's had some contact with Matt Hale's group. You know. World Church of the Creator."

"When did he come here?"

"That I don't know. At least two years ago, which is when he started showing up on our watch lists."

"So is he still doing Creator crap?"

"No, he started a chapter of Hammerskins but it's not very well-organized. Not like in other states."

"Does he have a criminal record?"

"Probably." Judy took a sip of her coffee. "We just try to track them locally and maybe find out where they came from if they're not from here. We don't have the resources to get more extensive than that."

I nodded and reached for my coffee. I'd have Chris check him out, now that I had a name for him. "Any other kind of group?"

"Not that I know of, but the tattoos on this young man look neo-Nazi. Nothing about the Hammerskins, though."

"Do you recognize him?"

Judy was looking at the photos of Cody. "He does look familiar. Maybe because he hangs out with Whistler. What's his name?"

"Cody Sorrell."

Judy shook her head. "Doesn't ring a bell. But that doesn't mean anything. He might use a different name for different things that he does."

"Have you heard anything about any local groups preparing for the end?"

"Aren't they all?" She laughed, though not necessarily because it was funny.

"True." I smiled wryly. "Anything along the lines of what The Order did?"

She thought about it. "Hold on. Whistler's Skins were having some kind of meetings last year. We found a couple of flyers of theirs and they did mention buying some land in the East Mountains to get ready for 'the big one.' " She took another bite of her bagel.

"The big one? You think it's the usual apocalypse crap or is this Whistler a little more action-oriented?"

Judy regarded me over the lip of her cup. "I honestly don't know. But he is a charismatic leader-type and I can see people following him no matter what kind of schemes he puts together."

"Charismatic like Bob Mathews was with The Order?"

Judy paused, thinking. "He does have that way about him. He's very soft-spoken and because he's older, younger guys seem to really gravitate toward him as an older-brother type. And, like Mathews, Whistler leads by example. He's one of those who will start digging the ditch, showing that he's one of the guys."

"Then he'll Tom Sawyer you into painting the fence."

She laughed. "Exactly."

"So have you heard of any new groups that might have moved into the area?"

"Since last year, there have been three neo-Nazi groups. One is an offshoot of Butler's Aryan Nations. They had maybe ten members and haven't had a meeting since December last year. The other is home-grown. They call themselves the Aryan Desert Rats. I'd never heard of them and they don't seem to be affiliated with any parent organization. This one I'm uneasy about. We can't figure out how many members there are but they have meetings at least once a month, according to APD. From their reports, there are at least twenty members at any one meeting."

"Is Whistler part of that group?" *Desert Rats, huh?*

"I don't know. You might check with APD."

I flipped through the pictures and found the one of Cody that showed the tattoo I didn't recognize on his bicep, showed the picture to Judy. "Is this their logo?"

"Yep."

"What about the third group?"

"It seems to be an offshoot of Hale's group. There's Creator literature associated with that one and they haven't had a meeting since March of this year. Last we heard, they were calling themselves Blood of the Creator."

"How special." I slipped the print-outs back into the manila folder. "What else can you tell me about the Desert Rats?"

She sat back. "We started finding flyers about a year ago. What's interesting is that they don't specifically say who they are, though they'll use the logo. They refer to cornered rats and fighting to the death quite a bit. They talk about that standard Aryan pride stuff and taking a stand for the white race. You know, the usual."

"So how do you know they call themselves the Desert Rats?"

"APD raided one of their meetings. One of the members had a parole violation and APD got a tip and did a bust. The officers heard them say that the meeting of the Aryan Desert Rats was about to come to order. Now it's official, as everybody there was fingerprinted and checked."

I thought for a bit. Cody was part of this group. It had neo-Nazi overtones, seemed fairly well-organized, and might be planning to buy some land. If Roy Whistler was hanging around Megan's place, chances were he and Cody ran in the same groups, which meant that Whistler might be part of the Rats as well. He might be on file at APD and I might be able to find some pictures of his tattoos. If I found Whistler, maybe I'd find Cody. And if I found *him*, Megan might not be far. "Any idea when their next meeting is?" I glanced over at Judy.

"No. They move times and locations quite a bit. And dates. It was luck that APD tracked them in February. We're hoping to get a handle on their patterns."

"How do you know they're still active?"

"Internet activity. Chat rooms. We've got a couple of interns who have infiltrated. But they use a code of some kind to schedule meetings and we can't figure out what it is, yet. Our interns claim they're in Texas, so nobody wonders why they're not coming to the meetings."

"Do the Rats have their own Web site?"

"No. But they frequent a local link through a Klan chapter based in Missouri."

Which made it hard to track individual users. I thought back to Megan's bookmarks. I'd have to check and see if any of them were that Klan chapter.

Judy checked her watch. "Sweetie, I have to go. Call me if you need anything else. And if you find anything out..."

"Definitely. I'll update you." I stood and hugged her.

"It's good to see you, Kase. Next time get me caught up on your personal life."

"Please." I laughed. "*What* personal life?"

She smiled and waved as she left. Almost eleven-thirty. I'd swing by Cody's aunt's house.

I CRUISED SOUTH on Juan Tabo, a main boulevard that paralleled the base of the Sandias in the Far Northeast Heights. I turned right on Claremont and left on Tippet and slowed down, watching the addresses on the houses until I found 11593. It looked like it had never seen better days, not even when it was built sometime in the 1970s, by the looks of it. What little grass made up the front lawn was yellowed and probably gasping for help. A battered lawn chair stood on the covered front stoop, strips of plastic hanging off the frame, and a raggedy Chinese elm tree stood near the street, looking as forlorn as the chair. One of the front windows had a crack in it and dingy, once-white drapes hid the inside from the outside. I caught a glimpse of a chain link fence in the back, surrounding a yard that looked like it hadn't been visited in months. A few weeds that stood about three feet tall lined the gate that led into the back.

I shut my car door and locked it. Half the houses on this stretch of Tippet looked like Aunt Terry's. The other half seemed well-kept. I noticed a beat-up blue Ford Taurus in the driveway. Would Terry be home? I stepped onto the porch and pressed the doorbell. I heard it echo inside, setting off a chorus of small-dog yaps. Somebody yelled at the dogs to shut up but it didn't do much good. I heard motion within, along with what sounded like dog claws on the door. Lovely. The door opened a crack. "Yeah?"

Stale cigarette smoke wafted to my nostrils. Could this be any more stereotypical?

"Hi, I'm lookin' for Cody. He around?" I affected a thick Texas drawl, the kind my cousin Luke had.

She opened the door a little more. "Who the hell are you?" She wore a tattered robe and dirty slippers. She looked to be about forty-five, but maybe a life hard-lived had wrung extra years from her. She glared at me with watery red-rimmed eyes. A beat-up New York Yankees baseball cap clutched her head.

Nice. "I'm Sandy, from Dallas. My cousin went to high school with Cody and I met him a few years back. We kep' in touch and he told me to stop by if'n I was ever around." I tried a smile. "So here I am."

"He ain't here."

I tried to look downcast. "Will he be back later? I really would like to see him. My brother and him got along real good and Jimmy's gonna go huntin' up here and he'd like to see Cody."

"Huntin'?"

"Yeah. Didn't Cody talk about Jimmy? He an' Cody went huntin' up in Colorado a coupla times. Didn't get nothin' but had a good time."

She opened the door a little wider. "What'd you say your name was?" Three pairs of buggy chihuahua eyes stared at me from just above her ankles.

"Sandy. You must be his Aunt Terry."

She held a cigarette in her right hand. She took a drag, blew it out. I fought an urge to cough. "Cody done skipped out on me two months ago. Little shit never paid no damn rent, never paid no damn bills. I told his sorry ass to get a job, but he wanted to go play fuckin' war games with his damn friends."

"War games?" I tried to look confused.

She made a disgusted noise. "Loser skinheads. Sit around and do nothin' but talk big and watch TV. And drink alla my goddamn beer." She took another drag, then looked thoughtful. "I'll give him that," she said grudgingly. "Cody never touched the stuff. But he didn't do nothin' 'round here. Hooked up with some pretty little thing and didn't come home most of the time."

"I didn't know he had a girlfriend. Jimmy didn't say nothin' about that."

"Oh, she's a looker. And sweet. What she sees in him I'll never know. Lazy sumbitch." She sucked on her cigarette again and the smoke oozed out around her words. "I ain't seen him. You might check over at that Roy's house. Roy what's-his-name. Whistle or something faggy like that."

"Roy Whistler?"

"Yeah, that's it. He's over on San Pedro and Coal. Those shithole apartments. 'Cause he's a loser like the rest. Me, I own my home." She dared me to challenge her.

"Well, I sure am sorry I bothered you. I was hopin' to get his number so's Jimmy could call him."

"Hell, I can give you that. Hold on."

I waited as she moved away from the door, leaving it mostly shut. One of the dogs shoved its nose into the gap and sniffed noisily. A couple of minutes later she returned. "Here. He figgered hisself some big man, got hisself some fancy cards." She opened the screen door just a bit and slid the card to me. I took it.

"Thank you, ma'am. Do you want me to tell him anythin' if I can get a hold of him? Maybe tell him he shouldn't be disrespectin' his aunt?" Validation always built rapport.

She studied me for a moment before replying. "Yeah. You tell that sorry-ass sumbitch he owes me money and he'd better not come showin' up lookin' for a handout without it. And my advice to you, Sarah—" I didn't bother to correct her—"you steer clear of Cody. He ain't right. Bad temper on that boy." And with that she closed the door and locked it.

I returned to my car and looked at what she had given me. A standard-sized business card. On the front Cody had listed his name, phone number, and e-mail address, which I already had. The back was blank. I turned the card over and read his name again. Underneath his name was the title Lieutenant-at-Arms. His rank in the Rats, however they figured it. Or he might just be blowing his own horn.

I pulled away from the curb and headed back to Megan's. As I drove, Melissa called.

"Hey," she said. "Allison e-mailed me back. She gave me her number and told me to call her tonight at eight when she's off work. Can you be around when I do that? I think you should talk to her."

Melissa was right. I probably should. "Sure. Why don't you come by around seven-thirty?"

"I can't. I have a meeting until six-thirty and then I have to get home to meet a handyman. Can you meet me at my place? I told Allison to call me there."

A cold chill wrapped around my guts. "I don't think that's a good idea—"

"She's out of town until tomorrow." Melissa's tone was as cold as my innards.

"Uh," I scrambled for a save. "Sure. Where's the house?"

She told me the address and the main streets. She was in a ritzy part of Albuquerque, where the old money lived. North on Rio Grande Boulevard about ten miles outside of town. An area where horse ranches and low-slung adobe hacienda-style homes recalled a Spanish past.

"Thanks. Come by around seven. I'll call you if anything comes up."

"Okay. Bye."

She hung up and I groaned. "Fuck." What now? It was probably best not to go by San Pedro and Coal looking for Roy, since I didn't know who he might have hanging out at his place and if he was the guy who tried to break in the other night, he might recognize my car. Besides, meeting Aunt Terry had left a bad feeling in my stomach. I opted instead to go back to Megan's and write down my findings, get something to eat, and maybe look through more of her files, which would help me not think about tonight as well. I turned left onto Comanche, which would take me west, away from the Heights, and the bad vibes at Aunt Terry's.

Chapter
Nine

"HEY – ANYBODY HOME?"

I emerged from the kitchen, wiping my hands on a towel. "Hi, Sage. C'mon in. Door's open."

She tried, using her elbow to knock the handle on the security door. Too late I realized she had a beer bottle in each hand. I rushed to open the door. "Geez, sorry. I didn't realize you came bearing gifts."

She laughed and held up two bottles of Fat Tire. "It's five o' clock somewhere," she said, quirking an eyebrow. I glanced at the clock on the wall above the kitchen doorway. Three-thirty. I took one of the bottles.

"True enough. Thanks. Have a seat."

She flopped onto the couch. It must've been a ritual with Megan when Sage visited. That was nice, I thought, that Sage had cultivated a friendship with Megan. I tried not to let my gaze hang on her more than what might be considered normal, but I knew I was going to fail a few times. Today Sage wore baggy grey shorts, a white tee, and her sport sandals. She was even more attractive in the daylight. *Damn.*

"It's nice having you here," she said. "I miss Megan and all, but I like you more."

I nearly choked on the beer, barely able to swallow, and managed a weak laugh. It probably sounded forced. "Oh, really. You don't even know me."

Sage flashed me one of her little smiles. "I feel like I do, from what Megan told me."

I took a nervous swig of my beer. "So what's *your* story?" I asked, desperate to change the subject. I must have been obvious. She humored me.

"I'm from Sheridan, Wyoming. I grew up like the singer Jewel. You know who that is, right?"

"I ain't *that* old," I retorted good-naturedly.

She shrugged and continued. "Sheridan's up near the Montana border."

"It's pretty. I've driven through."

She looked at me appreciatively. "Well, my dad wanted to be like Grizzly Adams or some shit and we lived in a freakin' cabin with an outhouse and no indoor water."

"Whoa. What about your mom?"

"She was into the pioneer crap. I didn't know you could have an indoor toilet 'til I started school. That was the *shit*. Literally!" She started giggling. "My dad's a roughneck." She meant that he worked the oil and gas fields here in the West. "I didn't see him all that much and when I did, he was a major prick to my mom and me and my brother. When I turned sixteen, my mom moved us into town and told him not to come around anymore. He drank too much." Sage shrugged and took a sip of her beer. "I worked my ass off in high school for a scholarship. I got one and went to the University of Wyoming, where I majored in journalism and photography."

"So are those your photos in your house?" I had noticed some beautiful shots of Yosemite, Yellowstone, and Chaco Canyon in their living room the evening before.

She looked surprised and pleased. "Yes. Did you like them?"

"They're beautiful," I said, completely serious. "You have a good eye for that. So how'd you end up in New Mexico?"

"I visited here my senior year in college and loved it. I traveled around a while, working and taking photos. And then I applied to grad school. I'm working on my thesis. I'm supposed to defend in December."

"Congratulations. Photography?" I was becoming more intrigued.

"Yep." She took another sip of her beer.

"That's great. Do you sell your work?"

"Oh, yeah. I've got stuff in *New Mexico Magazine*, *Arizona Highways*, and *National Geographic*. Plus some other mags."

I stared at her. "Wow. Here I am in the presence of greatness and I had no idea. I'll look for your stuff. What's your last name?"

"Crandall. Two L's. But I don't use it that often. I generally just sign as 'Sage.' "

"That's definitely cool."

"Megan said you teach in Austin."

I wasn't surprised at her change in topic. Though it seemed as if she couldn't stay focused, I had decided that Sage Crandall knew exactly what she was doing when she redirected a conversation. I just wasn't sure what information she was collecting. "Yep. Been there since I left Albuquerque after the break-up. Scored a post-doc fellowship and they've managed to keep me on." There was no sense dancing around the issues with her. She was far too perceptive.

"Austin is fucking cool. I've taken pictures there for their

Chamber of Commerce. It's a little too humid, though."

"You have no idea. I really miss New Mexico."

"So come back." She tossed me a smile.

"I'd need a job."

"Details. If you miss it, you should come back."

"I might."

She was quiet for a moment then brought up another subject entirely. "What's going on with Megan?"

I was actually relieved she switched topics. I was starting to really like the little bits and pieces of herself that she was showing me and it made me nervous. "Well, you're right about Cody. He's bad news. He's a recruiter for a white supremacist group that calls itself the Aryan Desert Rats."

She snorted. "Desert Rats? Yeah, that sounds really menacing."

I laughed. "You know. Cornered rat and all."

"Please. There are so many better names than that."

"All taken. Check the Web, if you're interested."

She grinned and set her beer bottle on the coffee table, careful to move a coaster underneath. It was automatic, an old habit. She had respected Megan's hang-ups. That warmed my heart.

"Anyway," I continued, "what I think is going on is that Cody and whatever assholes he's running with are looking to buy some land in the East Mountains so they can build a compound."

"Like those nut-jobs in Idaho. Aryan Nations."

I looked at her, surprised. "Yeah."

At my expression, she explained. "I went up there to take pictures of it after the leader—Butler, right? After he lost the compound in that lawsuit. I gave 'em to the ADL and the Southern Poverty Law Center. We had some dealings with freaks like that in Sheridan. A couple of families out on the land, stashing guns and shit waiting for some fucked-up race war. Mom wouldn't let us play with their kids. Thank God."

"I'll be damned," I said softly.

"So you think Megan is with Cody of her own free will?"

"I don't know. He sucked her in and..." I looked at her. "C'mon. Who are we kidding? You know how Megan is. He's a nice-looking guy. He said what she wanted to hear. She may have been in a weak place. Melissa thinks she doesn't want to be with him anymore but she's not sure how to get away. I talked to his aunt today and I think he's also abusive."

"That piece of shit," Sage said with pronounced venom. "I will so rip his arms off the next time I see him."

I had no doubt that she was capable of such. She looked at me then. "Do you think she's using again?"

"I don't know. I haven't talked to her in almost three years.

You're in a better place to gauge that. Do you think she is?"

She paused for a long moment before answering. "Well, I don't think Cody uses. He's, like, Mr. Puritan. You should have heard him go off on her when she took a drag on one of her friend's cigarettes. Shit, it was just one puff. You'd think she'd shot his dog. So even if she wanted to, he wouldn't let her. I guess that's a good thing. Or not." She finished her beer and took the empty bottle to the kitchen. I heard her rinse it out in the sink. She returned with it and set it back on the coaster. I looked at it questioningly.

"Recycling. I'll save you the trouble."

"Thanks. Appreciate that."

"So what's *your* story?"

I cleared my throat nervously. I couldn't avoid the question gracefully. "What do you want to know?"

"Why didn't you keep in touch with Megan after you left?"

Whoa. "I can't answer that. I was in a very bad place. Partially of my own making, maybe. And then I thought it might be hypocritical if I contacted Megan and not Melissa." I studied my bottle. "I feel pretty badly about it, actually."

"I can see that. Did you miss them?"

"Uh, in what sense?"

"Any sense. What happened, anyway? Megan said that Melissa was having an affair."

"She was. I busted them together."

Sage grimaced. "That totally sucks. I would never do that to anyone."

"You never know what you're going to do in a situation until you're in it." I shrugged. "It was a rough time for all of us. Megan was in rehab, Melissa was freaking out. I was freaking out. Hillary was available."

"That's bullshit. Melissa was weak. She needs to own it."

I stared at her. *Who the hell is this woman?* "Okay, I agree. But it's her shit, not mine. And I didn't handle it the best, I guess."

"You did what you thought you had to do. Megan told me that. But she did really miss you."

"Well, I fucked up there, I think. I left her a card when I moved—"

"She still has it. She showed it to me."

I felt a lump in my throat and I was out of beer.

"You didn't say one bad thing about Melissa in it."

I didn't remember what I said.

"You told Megan to stay strong because Melissa needed her and you told her that what had happened between you and Melissa was not Megan's fault and you didn't want her to ever feel that she couldn't come to you in the future."

Wow. I said that?

"It was the nicest thing I've ever seen in a goodbye card. And all that even though Melissa was fucking around."

"So you make it a habit to read people's goodbye cards?" I asked lightly.

Sage shrugged. "Megan showed it to me. She said you were the coolest person she knew and she wished Melissa hadn't been so stupid."

"Well, that's really nice. But keep in mind I'm an actual person with actual flaws and I was part of that situation and — well, I fucked up, too."

"You're genuine," Sage announced as she abruptly stood. "Genuinely human. You don't pretend to be something you're not and you try to own your shit, even when you screw up. I think that's hot."

She reached over and took my empty beer bottle from its coaster. I didn't know what to say. My breath caught in my chest and I watched her, the muscles in her arms sliding underneath her skin. Another wave of heat raced down my back, reminding me of last night when we danced.

She looked at me. "Melissa was an idiot. I wouldn't kick you out of bed, let alone my life. And I mean it. Stop by any time," she finished, flashing me an absolutely wicked grin. She turned and headed for the door. I watched her leave. *Okay, I'm pretty sure she's flirting with me.* I felt another stirring at my core. *No. No way. She's a friend of Megan's and young enough to be my student. Besides, she's with Jeff. This is so confusing.* I went back to checking the files on Megan's computer, trying not to think about Sage anymore. My phone rang. I checked the ID.

"Hey, Detective Hottie. What's up?"

"Nothing." Chris laughed. "I just finished at *Abuelita*'s and I'm on my way home. I heard from Mark in the gang unit and he said come on by tomorrow at eleven. Bring photos so you can compare tats."

"Cool." I gave her a quick run-down of what I had found out that day.

"And you've got Cody's number now?"

"I don't know if it still works. I'm going to call it from a pay phone. See what happens."

"Good idea. I'll check on the prints tomorrow. Do you need me tonight?"

"I *always* need you," I teased. "Nah, don't worry. Go home and have your space. I'll talk to you later."

"Are you sure?" She sounded worried.

"Yeah. Seriously, I don't think he'll come back knowing

someone's here."

"Okay," she said, hesitation in her tone.

"Chris, I know you're on shift early and I also know you haven't had any time to yourself in a while. If I need you, I'll call. Really."

"All right. Promise you'll call if anything is weird? I don't care what time it is."

"Promise."

"Good."

"You are the best, Detective Supergirl."

"No, you."

"No, *you.*"

"Yeah, don't forget it," she said, laughing. "Call me if you need anything."

"Will do. Thanks. Bye."

"Later."

I decided I wanted pizza for dinner. Il Vicino, known for its wood-oven pizza and funky Euro-style interior, was about five blocks away. I debated asking Sage to join me but decided since I was going to Melissa's afterward, I wouldn't. I'd much rather not have something like that hanging over my head should I ever ask Sage to go to dinner with me. I walked over to the restaurant in the early evening heat and indulged. When I finished it was just past six. It would take me at least thirty minutes to get to Melissa's and I was dreading it. Oh, well. *Face your demons.* Besides, Hillary wasn't there. I returned to my car, got in, and pulled away from the curb.

MELISSA CALLED WHEN I was halfway to her house. She was running about a half-hour late. No problem, I told her, I'd just grab some coffee at the North Valley Flying Star and continue on my merry way. I did just that. By the time I got to Melissa's house, it was almost seven. She lived in a Spanish-style hacienda, massive vigas jutting from the roofline. It looked historic, like it had been around a long time and updated a bit. It sat not a hundred feet from the Rio Grande bosque, amidst huge cottonwoods. It looked like it was equipped for horses but I didn't see any. I pulled into the circular dirt drive, admiring the architecture and grounds. A pale blue Jaguar sat in front of the house. So Hillary had switched to something even more pretentious. I admonished myself, trying not to let the past run roughshod through the present.

I parked and got out so I could stand in the driveway and appreciate the terrain. I inhaled deeply, smelling the rich, heavy odor of the river and the crisp tang of cottonwood. This was great. Too bad Hillary lived here. I laughed under my breath at that and went up onto the covered front porch, admiring the saltillo tile. A rustic bench crouched against the front wall beneath a picture window. A red chile ristra about three feet long hung from one of the vigas. Pure New Mexico. I moved to the bench, thinking I'd chill until Melissa got here. That's when I noticed the front door was partially open. *Okay, that's weird. Nobody's supposed to be here.* I looked around, saw only my car and the Jag. I pushed the door open more.

"Hello?" I called inside, nervous. Who the hell would be here? I heard a thump and what sounded like a crash from the back. I pushed the door open a bit more. "Hello?"

"Melissa?" Came a voice from somewhere in the back.

Fuck. Hillary. I heard the clink of glass and then an even louder crash and another thump. I pushed the door open and entered. Had I not been so freaked out about Hillary, I probably would have oh'ed and ah'ed over the Spanish colonial interior. As it was, I followed Hillary's swearing into the back of the house to the kitchen. She was lying face-up on the tile. I smelled liquor — whisky, maybe. Broken glass littered the floor and Hillary was sprawled right in the middle of it, in her expensive powder blue suit and ultra-blond glory. She struggled to get up. I saw blood on her left palm and also on her cream-colored shirt.

"God fucking dammit," she slurred as she half-heartedly tried to get to her feet. Liquor drenched her shirt and pants. Her right hand clutched an intact glass. I stepped gingerly around bottle fragments and took the glass from her, setting it on a nearby counter.

She managed to sit up and stare at me with an expression bordering on bewilderment and awe. Blood oozed sluggishly out of her palm but she seemed completely unaware of it. "I know you," she mumbled, frowning. She stopped trying to stand on her own.

I eased carefully behind her and grasped her beneath the armpits so I could lift her to her feet. She sagged against me, breathing heavily. *Jesus.* She reeked of alcohol. God, how had she made it home? Unless she had been home for a while. I looked around, found a small table and chairs positioned under a nearby window. I maneuvered Hillary over to it and eased her into a seat. "Don't move, okay?"

She nodded, too drunk to really do anything. I left the kitchen and found a bathroom with a linen closet. I took what looked like an older washcloth and wet it, then squirted soap onto it from the dispenser. I also found some gauze, bandaging tape, and Neosporin. I returned to the kitchen. Hillary hadn't moved, but I doubted my instructions had anything to do with that. She was slumped against the table, holding her cut hand palm up.

"I think I'm bleeding," she announced slowly.

"Yep." I carefully dabbed at the slice, which was about an inch long, with the washcloth. She barely flinched. Probably too drunk. It was a clean, shallow cut that wouldn't require stitches. I washed it thoroughly and then dabbed her hand dry. Hillary remained completely compliant throughout my ministrations. When her hand dried sufficiently, I slathered Neosporin on the cut and placed a gauze pad on her palm. I then wrapped gauze around her hand, not so tight to be uncomfortable and not so loose to be ineffective, and taped the gauze down.

Hillary had her head back against the wall, her eyes closed. She probably felt sick. "Melissa never holds my hand anymore," she stated.

I glanced at her. *Can this get any more fucked up?* "I'm sorry. How come?"

Hillary was quiet for so long that I had to look at her to make sure she hadn't passed out. To my surprise and discomfort, she was crying silently.

"I'm a drunk." She leaned forward suddenly and put her head against my shoulder, which seriously freaked me out. She quickly sat back, as if she had located some kind of resolve in that motion. It passed and she sagged again.

"I think you should go to a doctor when you're feeling better. Have that looked at." I didn't expect her to register what I told her. It was just something for me to do in this most surreal moment.

"Melissa hates me," she said softly.

I looked at her, startled. Her eyes were green. I never knew that. "Why would she hate you?" I asked, trying to be conversational. Melissa was going to have a total shit-fit when she got home and I dreaded that even more than sitting here with the woman she had an affair with three years ago.

Hillary's gaze was surprisingly direct for her condition. "Because I'm not you."

It felt like Hillary had reached into my chest and squeezed my heart until it stopped beating. We stared at each other for a long time before I straightened. "I think you need some rest." I kept my tone neutral as I helped her to her feet. She didn't say anything else as I eased her out of the kitchen into the dining room. *Master bedroom. Shit.*

"No," she slurred, beckoning with her bandaged hand. "Over there." We crossed the living room, Hillary's feet dragging on the brick floor, and entered a hallway. "The one on the end," she muttered. I turned left, walked her carefully down the hall to the room she mentioned. The door stood half-open. I helped her through and eased her onto a king-sized bed. She collapsed on it. This room had a bathroom and I retrieved the wastebasket—plastic, fortunately—and placed it next to the bed. Hillary had passed out cold. The lines across her forehead disappeared as she relaxed and she looked kind of like a cherub. That's probably part of why Melissa was attracted to her. She loved taking care of people. And I hadn't necessarily let her do that with me the way she was used to.

I left the room, making sure the door was open in case anything happened. I went back to the kitchen and found the utility closet, hoping I could clean up the glass before Melissa got home. I found some de-stain chemicals and poured them into a bowl along with some water so I could soak the bloody washcloth in the mixture. I had just finished wringing out the mop and putting it on the back porch to dry when I heard a car in the driveway. *Shit. Here we go.*

I returned to the living room just as Melissa burst into the house. From the expression on her face, she was both angry and flipped out. "Where is she?"

"Asleep," I said, keeping my tone level. Melissa brushed past me, headed for the hallway that led to the bedrooms. I reached out, grabbed her arm. It was the first time I had touched her in three years. "Melissa." She stopped, looked at my hand on her arm, then at me. "Come and sit down," I entreated quietly.

She gently pulled out of my grasp and went to look in on Hillary. When she came back to the living room, the expression on her face scared me. Numb. Lifeless. "What happened to her hand?" Melissa said dully.

"She cut it. I happened to be here at the right time. I helped her with it."

"So now you know."

I didn't say anything.

"My dad. Megan. Hillary. I'm into addicts. Kinky, huh?"

I really wanted to run. I wanted to jump right out the nearest window and start running, right up the face of the Sandias and down the other side. Instead, I did the only other thing that seemed to make any sense. I pulled Melissa into my arms. She stiffened. I continued to hold her until she relaxed then started to shake as she cried. She grabbed onto me and let it out. She sobbed so hard I worried she might choke. I held on to her, rocking her a little bit, remembering the last time she'd cried like that around me, when Megan called from the rehab facility after her relapse and told Melissa where she was and after Melissa hung up, she collapsed against me and cried for an hour.

After about twenty minutes she stopped crying but she didn't let go. She continued to sniffle a bit against my shoulder. My shirt was wet with her tears but it didn't bother me. I felt so sad for her, so sad for us, for what had happened between us. And I felt sad for what was happening with Hillary.

She finally pulled away. "Sorry," she mumbled. She went into the kitchen and I heard water running in the sink. I glanced at my watch. Almost eight. I joined Melissa in the kitchen, where she was sitting in the chair Hillary had so recently occupied. I opened the fridge and saw a bottle of Tazo tea. So Melissa still drank it, too. I shook it up, opened it, and handed it to her. She took it and sat staring at the label. Then she started to laugh. I looked at her, worried, wondering if she was about to have a breakdown. She managed a smile.

"You want to hear something really funny?"

I watched her, not sure what to say.

"I really wanted to talk to you tonight. I wanted to get things out in the open. I'm not sure why, but I think it would help both of us. So you show up and..." she shook her head and took a sip of tea.

"Yeah," I said softly. "This might be a bad time."

She looked at me and started laughing again. "K.C. Fontero. Mistress of understatement. God, I miss that." She sighed and glanced at her watch. "Well, here we go." She pulled a scrap of paper out of her pants pocket and crossed the floor to a counter on the opposite side of the room. She picked the wireless phone up off its cradle and dialed a local number. Allison must've been waiting because Melissa was talking to her right away. I relaxed. This I could handle. An interview and research-related information. Melissa explained to Allison what was going on and she said she was going to put me on. She handed the phone to me.

"Hello?"

"Hi. K.C.?"

"Yep." Allison had a nice timbre to her voice.

"Megan's mentioned you."

Jesus. "Good stuff, I hope. So have you heard from her?"

No. Not since the middle of June. She called me and said she was going out of town for a few days with Cody."

I sat down at the table. Melissa placed a notepad and a pen next to me. "Did she say where?"

"No. She said that Cody had friends in the East Mountains and they were going to stop by. She said they might go to Colorado to visit some other friends."

"Did you meet Cody?"

"Yeah."

"What'd you think?"

"Creepy."

"How come?" *Interesting.*

"He watched her all the time. And not in that nice 'I love you' way. In that freaky stalker way. Possessive. And the longer she hung out with him, the weirder she got. She started going off on gay people. I mean, how lame is that? Her sister's gay. I told her she needed to pull her head out of her ass and dump Cody. She didn't call me for a while after that."

"When did you tell her that?"

"Oh, around the middle of April. After about a week she seemed to get over it a little."

"Does she have a Web site? Like on MySpace or Facebook or something?"

"No. She was trying to get one together and she told me in May she was all psyched about the graphics she'd been collecting but then she left town."

Okay, well, that was good. One less thing to check out. "What else did you notice about Cody? Anything that stands out?"

Allison snorted. "He's one of those loser racist guys. I couldn't figure out why the hell Megan would want to hang out with someone like that. I mean, she's so pretty and sweet. She could have any guy she wants. And she goes for that one."

"So you know he's racist."

"Oh, yeah. At first it was just little things he would say, like he was testing Megan and her friends. Stuff like we need to be proud of our heritage and affirmative action should extend to poor whites, too. And after a while, she stopped hanging with her old crowd."

Classic abusive relationship. Isolate her from her friends and family, then start indoctrinating her with his own belief system. I was really, really pissed at Cody Sorrell and I wanted to rip his arms off as well. Sage would have to take a number.

"Have you seen her since she called you last?"

"No. I've tried to call her cell phone but she doesn't answer and her voice-mail is full. So I tried e-mailing her. And I still haven't heard from her. Do you think she's okay?"

I hesitated before responding. "Here's the deal. Cody sounds like he's—" I glanced at Melissa and changed my wording—"like he might be controlling and he runs with some people who may or may not be dangerous. Hopefully, he'll want to keep Megan with him as a girlfriend, whatever that means to him, and we'll find him and get her away from him. So if she calls you, please tell her to contact me. Here's my number." I gave her my cell. "That goes for you, too. If you think of anything else or if you see anyone, call me."

"Definitely. I really hope you find her. Thanks." She hung up. I handed the phone back to Melissa, who set it on the counter. She stood looking at it for a while.

"How do you feel about talking?" She turned to look at me.

"I think it's a good idea. But I don't think here and now is a good idea."

"Neutral territory?"

I nodded automatically, feeling really drained. "I'd appreciate that."

"Meet me for dinner tomorrow?"

Not a good idea. She caught my expression. "Just dinner," she repeated. "We all have to eat. Please don't read anything into it. I just really want to talk to you."

I relaxed at the tone of her voice. "Okay. Where?"

"How about Old Town? La Hacienda?"

I mulled that for a moment. Okay food, some privacy. "Sure. What time?"

"Six?"

"Sounds good. I'll see you then." I stood and tore the sheet of paper off the tablet I had been using to scribble notes during my conversation with Allison. I handed the notepad back to Melissa. "Are you okay?"

She smiled, tired. The dark circles under her eyes were more pronounced than they were the day before. "I'll be all right."

"Don't give up. You've got to hang in there. Get some sleep and if you need anything, call me." I suddenly realized what I had said. I hoped Melissa didn't think I'd meant anything but that. We walked through the living room. I opened the door and was out on the porch before she spoke.

"Kase?"

I turned, waiting.

"Thank you."

I nodded. We stared at each other for a bit longer and then she quietly shut the door. I got into my car. It took me a very long time to get back to Megan's.

Chapter
Ten

I SLEPT LIKE a dead woman, crashing as soon as I got back to Megan's. Rolling out of bed at eight-thirty, I decided I needed some exercise so I stumbled into my running clothes and headed out. A half-hour later I felt better. While the coffee brewed I did sit-ups and push-ups, then poured a cup and headed into the bathroom. Emotionally, everything still felt freaky after what had happened the night before at Melissa's, but getting all that sleep had helped quite a bit. I opted not to think about Melissa and Hillary for a while.

I finished showering and towel-dried my hair. In the mirror, I saw an older version of my sister Kara, whose dark hair also lightened like mine a bit during the summer months. My sister Kara and I got our dad's hair color. Mine, though, is naturally wavy and I wear it short. Here in the dry air, I don't need to "shape and style" like I do in Texas. It tends to look "endearingly mussed," as my mom says. My sister Joely says it looks like squirrels nest in it. Whatever. Better squirrels than rats. I threw on yet another pair of grey cargo shorts and a red tee, poured another cup of coffee and toasted a bagel, which I slathered with cream cheese. More coffee for the road, my school bag, photos and print-outs — finally ready. I turned off the coffee machine, slid my feet into my Birkenstocks, and headed out.

I arrived at the police department with about ten minutes to spare. The main complex was located in the North Valley, up Second Street, about two miles from downtown. I pulled in and parked in the visitors' section, appraising. The building was a relatively new structure, sort of administrative-looking but with lots of windows. An open, airy lobby greeted me when I entered, scuffed but clean linoleum underfoot. The white walls featured photos of graduating police academy classes spaced at intervals. An information desk hunkered across from a carpeted area decorated with several tables and chairs. Vending machines near the carpeted area offered a variety of snacks from junk food to soup. And there was always coffee available. Through Chris, I had met a few cops and somehow always ended up with free coffee when I came here.

I approached the information desk. To my left a corridor led to a gym. Slightly to my right and behind the information desk another corridor behind grey metal doors led to the administrative offices. Visitors had to be buzzed in and out of that hallway. A woman in a police-type uniform looked up as I approached. She was probably in her early fifties. "Hi. I'm K.C. Fontero. I have an eleven o'clock with Mark Aragon." I pronounced Aragon with an accent on the long "o." The woman checked a list.

"Ah. Here you are. You're that friend of Chris Gutierrez?"

"Yes, ma'am."

She smiled. *Good. She likes Chris.* Although it was hard not to like Chris. I worried about people who didn't.

"Hold on. Let me page him."

"Thanks." I stepped back and watched as recruits wandered through. Some were on their way to the gym. A couple of admin types had arrived and they were drinking coffee at one of the tables, talking about dispatch.

"He'll be right out," the information clerk announced.

"Thanks." I idly scanned the premises while I waited. Within about five minutes, I heard the metal door that led down the corridor to administration click open.

"Ms. Fontero?" A big burly guy wearing jeans, cowboy boots, and a button-down denim shirt stood regarding me with that *other* cop look. Not really judgmental. More a sizing-you-up kind of way.

"Yessir. K.C."

"Excellent. I'm Mark. C'mon in." He motioned me to precede him down the hall. He moved lightly for a big man. "Chris says you're in town doing some research on assholes."

I grinned. "That about sums it up. I track white supremacists in the West and I got word that there might be some new groups setting up shop in Albuquerque. I'm on sabbatical in the fall and I need to finish up a book, so here I am." He led me to an office near the end of the corridor on the left and he opened the door into a big room divided into cubicles. Skylights provided some nice natural light, but it was still a cubicle labyrinth. He led me to the right and entered the last cubicle down.

"Technically," he said as he eased his frame into the chair behind his comfortably cluttered desk while motioning to the one in front of it, "I'm with the gang unit. But in the last few years, we've started including racist groups in our gang classification because in many ways, they behave similarly. As you probably know."

I opened my satchel and took the manila folder out that had the photos of Cody's tattoos. I handed them to Mark. He looked through them, nodding his head now and again. "I've seen this ADR one. That's the Aryan Desert Rats. They're new on the scene. About a year ago. I think they're actually home-grown."

"So they're not affiliated with any larger group?"

"No. They network through UNM and as of May, they had twenty-three known members. Including this *pendejo*." He motioned with his lips at a picture of Cody flexing. "I'd like to nail this little shit for something. He's real mouthy. But he's been clean since he got here."

"So you know about him."

"Chris gave me some data. She'll have the Colorado reports in probably today. They're supposed to fax 'em. The Rats have meetings but they're pretty good about staying a few steps ahead. Text messaging, online chat rooms. They don't announce time, date, or location until the day of. We've been trying to get someone on the inside, but these are hard nuts to crack. They're way more serious than some of the other clowns running around."

"Did he have that tat done here?" I pointed to the eagle on Cody's back.

Mark picked up the image, studied it. "I've seen that. Hold on." He opened a file on his desk and shuffled through a stack of photos. "Ah. Here it is." He handed me a photo. Different guy, same tattoo across his back. "This is Justin Marquez. Because he's in denial about his Mexican roots, he pronounces his last name Mar-kay, like he's French or some shit. But he was born in the South Valley."

"Is he with the Desert Rats?"

"Yep, last time we checked. He knows he's on our shit list, though, so he's kept his nose clean. Hold on." Mark sifted through another folder, pulled out four more photos. Two different guys, same tattoo across their backs. The other two photos showed the guys' left arms. Both sported the ADR logo on the bicep. "David Jordan and William Stein. I hauled Stein in last month for auto theft. He's in juvie right now. He'll be seventeen in November. Jordan, on the other hand, is into a little harder stuff. Armed robbery and assault. He's nineteen so he's doing time. He was convicted last year."

"Nice," I muttered sarcastically. "So these are all guys who are from here? Or at least lived here awhile?"

He nodded. "Chris tells me you're looking for the artist who's willing to put that shit on people."

"Yeah. I thought I might get a line on this group."

"Good angle. This guy is an equal-opportunity tattooist. He's up on east Central, just past Wyoming. Kind of a sleazy-looking shop on the outside, but it's pretty clean inside. He takes his work seriously. He'll do Aryans, gang-bangers, ex-cons. You go in there and you'll see some skinhead showing his tats to some Mexican gang-banger." Mark shook his head. "Crazy shit." Mark looked at the tats in the photos again. "Guy's name is—" He thought for a moment. "They call him Dragon. The shop is Eight Ball. Can't miss it. There's a giant eight ball painted on its front window."

"Do other artists work out of that shop?"

"Yeah. Three. Sometimes a piercer comes in. They keep their permits up and they pass inspection all the time." He shrugged. "And we've never had trouble there, so they must be doing something right."

"What else do you know about the Rats?"

Mark sat looking at me for a minute, assessing. "You want some coffee?"

"Love some."

"I'll be right back." He got up and I watched his head and shoulders bob above the cubicle wall to the door. He exited into the hallway. While he was gone, I looked through more of the photos. Standard neo-Nazi tats and a few skinhead affiliations. Three Klan. I stopped at another photo. A front shot, showing the guy's face. He had a huge swastika tattooed on his chest. *That must've hurt.* I looked at the guy closer. Roy Whistler. Had to be.

I looked through the rest of the photos. The last one gave me a very bad feeling. In it, a man lay shirtless face-down on asphalt. He had apparently been going to Dragon to get the Nazi eagle tattooed across his back, but it was only half-finished. He was positioned in such a way that I could just make out the ADR tattoo on his left bicep. His head was resting in what was most likely a puddle of blood. I looked up as Mark returned with two large paper cups of coffee and a few packets of sugar. He handed me a cup and sat down. Then he opened one of his desk drawers and pulled out a jar of fake creamer.

"I've got my own stash," he said conspiratorially, grinning.

"Thanks." I doctored my coffee. "What happened here?" I held the photo up.

Mark looked at it and shook his head. "Found him around the end of May down near Kirtland Air Force Base. You know where Wyoming dead-ends at the Base?"

"Yeah."

"There're some bad news apartments down there and one of the residents found him in the parking lot. He didn't live there, but a friend of his did. The friend has an alibi."

"What do you think happened?"

Mark shrugged. "I can't tell you a whole lot because the case is still open. He was shot with a thirty-eight. Probably a Glock."

"Can you tell me who he was?"

"Sure. It was in the papers. John Talbot, originally from Phoenix. We know he ran with the Rats for about three months after the meeting we busted up in February. Then he ended up dead. No evidence of drugs."

"His tattoo wasn't finished," I pointed out.

"Might've run out of money. Or maybe he didn't want to play anymore. Whatever happened, he pissed somebody off."

I picked up the photo of the man I suspected was Roy Whistler. "How about this guy?"

Marc looked at the photo. "Roy Whistler. In gang-banger terms, he's what you call an OG. Original Gangster. He's pushing thirty-three, which is old for gang-banging. Don't know if that's considered old for haters."

"Not really, but neo-Nazi movements do tend to favor the young. He's the oldest I've seen affiliated with the Rats."

"Yep. Rumor has it that he's responsible for the Rats. He tried to do a Skin chapter but nobody was buying it. So he decided to try something with a more local flavor and came up with the Desert Rats. This guy is slick. I'm waiting to nail him, too, but so far he's managed to avoid getting caught. I know he does shit, though." Mark stirred his coffee and took a sip. "Mmmm. fuckin' terrible," he announced as he smiled contentedly.

I liked this guy.

He put the cup down. "Okay. Here's the deal on the Rats. In February, we managed to bust up one of their little meetings. We got one for parole violation and he's in juvie now. We also got most of them on file. I can tell you that Whistler was there and so was Sorrell, who was Whistler's right-hand man at the time. Now, I can't tell you this for sure, but my feeling is that Whistler's one of those guys who wants to go out in a blaze of glory. He's a hard-core dude. Doesn't give a shit about anyone or anything but he can make you jump off a cliff for him." He took another sip of coffee. "My sources tell me that Whistler's trying to buy some land in the East Mountains. Like he's gonna put a bunker or something up there."

"Where's he getting the money?"

"Ah, therein lies the mystery. He's doing *something* to get it. I think he's got his little minions bilking relatives, friends, old ladies at the grocery store. Whoever. They're digging for gold, basically."

"Where in the East Mountains?"

"Couldn't tell you. Whistler's got friends in Edgewood so there's speculation that they might be looking on that side. It's cheaper, that's for sure."

"You think the Rats are based in Edgewood?"

He shrugged. "I doubt they really have a base. They move around a lot. And most of the guys I know of in the group use each other's houses as crash pads. Whistler might be the only one with a permanent address, though he's never there. It's a crap-pad in the

War Zone over on Coal and San Pedro. We keep an eye on it, but so far the bills are paid, the mail's picked up, and nobody seems to hang out there."

Good. That saved me a trip. Unless nothing panned out with Eight Ball. If that was the case, then I'd have to drive over to Whistler's and stake it out for a bit. "So what do you think Whistler's blaze of glory is?"

"He's a weird dude." Marc looked at the photo on his desk. "I could see him pissing somebody off and starting an ATF show-down. Or pulling some crazy Waco shit. He's got a chip on his shoulder the size of Texas and he pretty much hates everybody. He's one of those racial holy war believers, except I can see him pulling some shit to actually start the damn thing."

"What about Sorrell?"

"My personal opinion is that there's a little power struggle going on between him and Whistler. Just a feeling I got from watching them when we busted up that meeting. We're trying to get someone in there and play that card, see if we can cause a split."

I tugged on my earlobe. "That's a good idea. In the meantime, what's the most recent thing you've got on Sorrell and Whistler?"

He sat back. "Whistler actually has a steady job. He works at one of those Grease Monkey joints up in the Heights. Quickie oil change. Sorrell — he's a couch crasher. Last we heard, which was last month, he was hanging out with a couple of guys from a militia group that folded and they're in Edgewood."

"So he's not even really with Whistler?"

"Can't be sure. I think they might be on the outs. Or maybe not." He sighed and shrugged. "That's about all I know."

"I really appreciate your time. If I find anything, I'll send it along to you."

"Nice. Here." He reached across his desk and moved a stack of paper over to reveal a business card holder. I took a couple and put them in one of the zipper pockets of my bag. I took one of my cards out and wrote my cell phone number on the back before I handed it to him.

"Thanks for the coffee." I stood up with the cup.

"No problem." He stood with me to usher me out in standard procedure. At the door back into the lobby, he looked down at me. "These are some bad dudes. Don't try and be all Jane Bond and shit, okay? Watch yourself."

"I know. Thanks again." He waved and closed the door behind me. I smiled and waved at the information clerk and exited into the midday dry sauna that was Albuquerque in late July. *Where are the damn monsoons?* I opened my car and got in, placing my bag on the passenger side. Time to go look up a particular tattoo artist. Eight

Ball was on the other side of town so it'd take me forty-five minutes to get there. Plus, I was hungry. I'd have lunch and continue on my scavenger hunt.

AT ONE-THIRTY I pulled into the beat-up East Central strip mall that harbored Eight Ball Tattoos. A lurid neon sign in the window declared that the place was open. Over lunch I had consolidated my notes into a column system, one for Cody, one for Roy, and another for Megan. I'd also added a John Talbot column. Maybe I could get Cody and Roy into even more trouble if I made a connection from them to Talbot. From each source I added the bits of the puzzle to each column, seeing where they intersected. I didn't have a specific rhyme or reason to how I did things. It just helped me organize my thoughts to go about it this way.

I chose a parking space about a hundred feet away from the shop. If the guy who tried to get in the other night — and I was leaning toward Cody or Roy — was here by some weird coincidence, I didn't want him to see my car right off. I rolled up the print-out I had of the tattoo on Cody's back and stuck it into my right-hand cargo pocket. I locked up and crossed the asphalt to the crumbling sidewalk in front of the tattoo shop. As I opened the front door, a blast of cool air ruffled my hair. The place reeked of bleach and incense. Since it was still fairly early in the day, I was the only person in the waiting area. A bored-looking woman stood behind the counter. She had at least ten studs in her right ear in addition to a nose ring. Her arms were tattooed from wrists up. She looked me over.

"Hi. I'm looking for an artist named Dragon."

She pointed at one of the small rooms down the hall past the counter. "He's busy. You wanna wait?"

"How long?"

She shrugged, a faint smile on her lips. "Not very. Frat boy getting his first one. They can't take too much pain."

I smiled in return. "Gotcha. I'll just hang out." The place had lots of light, at least. Photos and artwork depicting all manner of tattoos in all manner of places covered the dingy paneling. Some were absolutely gorgeous. Others weren't really my thing. I actually would like to get another tat. I had one already, on my left shoulder blade. I thought a big pirate ship across my back would be cool. Or something for *Día de los Muertos*. One of Posada's *calaveras,* maybe. I didn't see anything like that here, but if Dragon was as good as I thought, he'd be able to create something from scratch.

After about thirty minutes, I heard people emerging from the back. One, I guessed, was the frat boy. Polo shorts, flip-flops, and a tee proclaiming his affiliation with Sigma Alpha Epsilon. He seemed a little green around the gills. The man I assumed to be Dragon followed him up to the front, instructing him on the "proper care and feeding" of his new tattoo, which was probably one of those passé tribal things around his upper arm, since he had his right sleeve shoved up around his shoulder and a large gauze bandage wrapped all the way around the circumference of his bicep.

The goth clerk rang up Frat Boy's tattoo. Dragon was going through some paperwork when he looked up at me and smiled. He was not at all what I was expecting. I had this image of him as some big scary biker dude with massive hairy arms and a goatee. He was supposed to have major piercings in his ears and chin (and probably nipples) and wear sleeveless leather Harley vests and chaps. And he was supposed to have big clunky biker boots and a massive beer gut. Instead, Dragon stood about my height and if he was thirty, I'd be surprised. He looked Hispanic and he was thin and wiry and balding on top so he kept the rest of his hair shaved close to his skull. He wore silver wire-rimmed glasses, baggy jeans, a button-down plaid short-sleeved shirt, and Adidas sneakers. The only thing about him that was even remotely close to what I had envisioned was his goatee.

"Hi there. Come on back."

I followed him and turned left into his little studio. He had some nice tapestries hanging on the walls that depicted busty women and guys with massive musculature — stuff like Conan the Barbarian — and a couple of religious candles lit on his counter next to the tools of his trade. A small speaker system designed for an MP3 player sat on a chair in the corner. The soft sounds of African chill emanated from it. This was definitely blowing my stereotype.

"I'm Tom, but people call me Dragon."

"So I've heard. Where'd you get the nickname?"

He grinned and lifted his shirt up, exposing his back. "I had that done in Japan by a guy who tats Yakuza." A stunning Japanese-style dragon curved down his back, its tail looping over his left shoulder so that it probably started on his pectoral. The dragon's front claws rested on his kidneys. Dragon's entire back was the landscape in which the tattoo dragon stood.

"Wow," I breathed appreciatively. "That is gorgeous work. Did you train in Japan?"

"I did." He lowered his shirt, pleased at my reaction.

"Are you working on the bodysuit?"

"Not yet. My thighs are tatted, but I'm not quite ready to go that route yet. So what can I do for you?"

I pulled the print-out from my pocket and unrolled it. "Actually, I'm not here for myself. Though I'll tell you what, if I get another one, I'll have you do it." I handed him the picture of Cody's back. "Is this your work?"

He looked at it, then nervously glanced at me. "Are you FBI or something?"

"No, no. Nothing like that. And it's not illegal to tat that kind of stuff, so don't worry. I'm trying to find this guy."

He studied it for a while. "Yeah, that's mine. It's not like I believe in this bullshit, you know." He looked up at me, troubled.

"I know. How much does something like that cost?"

"I charged this guy four hundred. And that was a deal. Look at the detail on the feathers. I cut him some slack because he seemed like a nice guy when he came in." Dragon shook his head, looking at the photo. "One of those guys who could sell sand to an Arab. Halfway through, I knew I hadn't charged him enough. But it was too late. I'd already bargained with him and I don't hedge on that."

"How long ago was this?"

"Uh." Dragon looked at the ceiling, thinking. "Maybe April last year? It was spring, I remember that. One of those windy days that's not quite warm enough for shorts."

"Did you do it in one sitting?"

"No. Four. So it took about two months. He paid me half up front and the other half later. Cash."

"How about the tat on his left arm? You can just see it. The pissed-off rat?"

Dragon laughed. "That's not mine. That's Eddie's. He's the other guy who works here. His specialty is cartoonie shit like that. He does a lot of gang-bangers, too, 'cause he's really good at those gothic letters. Learned it in prison." Dragon shrugged and handed the photo back to me.

"Is he the only guy you tatted with this?"

"No. I've done five of those. And a few basic swastikas. One guy came in—big blond dude—quiet but a real prick. He wanted a big swastika on his chest but he was such an ass that I didn't want to do it. Eddie took him on. He doesn't mind dealing with pricks as long as they pay." Dragon started chuckling. "But he actually managed to piss Eddie off so Eddie tatted it hard and slow."

I laughed. "What'd he do?"

Dragon leaned against his counter and grinned. "Oh, he whimpered a lot and had to take 'cigarette breaks' every few minutes."

I chuckled at that. "So did you catch this guy's name?" I gestured with the picture.

"Cody something or other. I remember it 'cause it's one of those cowboy names and I thought it was kinda strange, tatting Nazi shit on a cowboy."

"How about a guy named John Talbot?"

Dragon looked at me, suddenly suspicious. "I started to tat him. He paid me for the first part but didn't show up for other sessions. And yeah, I read about it in the paper."

"Look, I'm not with law enforcement and I don't think you had anything to do with Talbot. I'm just trying to find Cody. Did Talbot hang out with this Cody guy?"

Dragon thought about it for a bit. "When Talbot came in for the first part, Cody was with him. But I only saw them together that once."

"When was that?"

"Talbot started his this past March. I did two sessions with him then he quit coming around."

"Has Cody been in recently?"

"Once since he came in with Talbot. I think that was in May. Oh, and he had a girl with him. Cute. Looked kind of scared. I remember *that* because she seemed really nice and I wondered what she was doing with this loser guy. He did ask me if I'd seen that other guy. The one with the chest swastika."

"Why'd he come here looking for him?"

Dragon shrugged. "We get a lot of regulars. They'll come in not necessarily for a new image, but to have touch-ups. And we're like an ol' school barber shop. People hang out here. It's a peace zone. You can chill as long as you don't diss anybody while you're here. There's like a truce thing going on, which is why we have gang-bangers and Nazis hanging out in the same place. They know they can and if they don't screw around, they're welcome to come back. It's even funnier during gay pride, when all these chicks come in for rainbow whatevers or those paw prints on their chests and they're hanging out in the lobby with Skins and *cholos*." He grinned. "I should write a book. Anyway, Cody asked about that guy. I can't remember his name. Ron or something."

"Roy. Is he a regular?"

"He'll come in maybe two or three times in a month. Because we are the kind of shop we are, we're sort of a hub for a lot of people. There's an understanding among them — and this is true of the *cholos* and other gang-bangers — that they can't come here to make trouble with rivals."

"What happens if they do?"

"Nobody here will tat 'em and trust me, it's hard to find people who do good work and are willing to put some of the shit on people that they want. You wanna be a bad-ass mother-fucker gangster with shitty tattoos? No way. They know not to press their luck here."

I thought about that a moment. Tattoos as social currency. "So you don't have any trouble?"

"Nope. I've been here three years and we've had no problems with shit like that."

"So when was the last time this Roy guy was in?"

Dragon pursed his lips, thinking. "Maybe two weeks ago? He came in looking for that Cody dude."

"Did he find him?"

"Not that day. I mean, it's possible that Cody's come in since May but I might not have known about it."

True. Dragon might've been working on someone or eating lunch or any number of things. I smiled. "Thanks a bunch for your time. If Cody comes in again, would you call me and let me know? Like, within the next week or two?" I took a slip of paper out with my first name and cell phone number. I always had a couple of these on me when I was doing research. Business cards had way too much information on them and when you're dealing with extremist movements, it's generally not a good idea for people to know too much about you.

"Sure. What's this about?" He took the slip of paper.

"That girl who came in with him in April is my stepsister and I haven't heard from her in a while. I'm a little worried because of the crowd Cody runs with and I was hoping to talk to her."

He raised his eyebrows, suddenly looking sympathetic. "Oh, wow. That's heavy. So she's not taking your calls, huh?"

"No. And her family thinks that Cody might be a bit..."

"Abusive. Yeah. I could see that." He shook his head empathetically. "Man. That's tough. 'Cause she's an adult and you can't force her to get out of a bad situation. Good luck."

"Thanks. And thanks again for your time."

"No problem. And seriously, if you want another tat, stop by."

"Definitely." I shook his hand and left. A skinny guy wearing the low-slung jeans, long sleeveless tee, and hairnet of a *cholo* sat in the lobby, nervously tapping his foot. His skin appeared unmarred. A virgin. I waved at the clerk as I exited into the heat. An informative day thus far. Still no Cody, but at least I got the sense that he was in the Albuquerque area.

Now would probably be a good time to try the number on his business card. I got in my car and drove to a nearby gas station, where I pulled up to the pay phones, relegated to the back near the air hose. I took two quarters out of the little tray in my dashboard and pulled Cody's card out of my wallet. I got out and inserted the quarters into the slot, waited, then dialed the number. One ring. Two. Three. Four. Bump to voice-mail.

"Hey, this is Cody. Leave a message. Eighty-eight!"

I hung up before the beep. So the number was still good. I'd try again later. If he answered, I was going to pretend to be interested in the movement and see if he'd meet me, hopefully at Eight Ball. I'd ask Chris if she could go, though it was probably an unnecessary precaution. If he started trouble, he'd lose his Eight Ball privileges. I got back in my car and headed for Megan's, needing some time to consolidate my thoughts and prepare for dinner with Melissa, which I wasn't really looking forward to. Yes, Melissa moved me on some levels still, but the thought of patching things up with her and trying again was too weird. There was just too much of the past to unravel. I therefore decided to think about it as if it was a dinner with in-laws. I just had to get through it.

Chapter
Eleven

I WAS IN the process of getting my stuff out of my car in front of Jeff and Sage's when I heard the front door of the main house slam open. I looked up. Sage was standing on the porch. "Hey! Get in here," she ordered. From anybody else, that tone would have irritated me. On Sage, it was endearing.

"Hold on — let me get my stuff."

She watched me, obviously impatient. I grabbed my bag, made sure I had everything, locked up, then climbed the steps to the main house. "What's up?"

"Inside." She pulled me into the living room, agitated. "Cody was here."

I stared at her. "What? How do you know?"

"He was poking around Megan's about an hour ago."

"Shit. Why didn't you —"

"Call you? I don't have your number. Hello!"

"Oh, yeah. Sorry. Let me fix that right now." I pulled my wallet out of my pocket and removed a business card. I got a pen out of my bag and wrote my cell phone number on the back. Sage took the card and looked at it. She slid it into the front pocket of her shorts.

"Okay. What was he doing?"

"Looking in the damn windows. He probably tried to get in through the front and he couldn't because you had the locks changed. I wish I was here to see *that*." She smiled grimly.

"All right. From the beginning."

She rolled her eyes and sat down on the couch. I sat next to her, setting my bag on the floor.

"I got home around two and went in through the front. I went into the kitchen and checked out that back window that looks through the laundry room and then through that other window — it's a habit. I always look to see if Megan's home. Lately, I look to see if you're home."

I ignored that, though it gave me a little buzz.

"And I saw this guy looking in the side windows. I could not believe it. I went to the window and holy shit, it was that assmuncher Cody."

"Assmuncher?"

"Prick. Is that better?"

"Yeah, I think so."

"Listen to me!"

I shut up.

"I decided to watch him for a while. You know, play detective and shit. Like you do."

I shot her a look that she ignored.

"It looked like he was pushing on the windows, like he was trying to figure out if he could break in without making a big scene. Then he went back to the front door and he stood looking at it. I wanted to yell 'open, sesame' for him, 'cause he looked so lame standing there like the door was just going to fling open."

I struggled not to laugh. "What was he wearing?"

"Jeans and a black T-shirt. I thought that was stupid. I hope he fucking sweats to death. Anyway, he stood there for about ten years like he was conjuring secret powers. And the longer he stood there, the more pissed he got. He totally tried to smack the door."

"He hit the door?"

"Yeah. Took his fist and *pow!*" She mimicked him throwing a punch. She was laughing. "This part's funny," she explained though I was pretty sure it was going to be. "So he punches the door and then he starts shaking his hand because it hurt so bad. He looked at it, to see if there were bone fragments flying out of it or something, and he shook it some more. Then he *kicked* the door. He was wearing work boots so I guess he thought those steel toes could take down a New Mexico security door. Nope. And the whole time he's shaking his hand because it hurt so bad to punch the door. What a fucking moron."

"He kicked the door," I repeated, envisioning the scene. It gave me pleasure to do so. "What'd he do then?"

"He stood around looking really pissed off and then he left. I decided since I was being all secret, I wouldn't tell him to get the fuck off the property and I watched him through the windows as he left."

"Was he driving?"

"No. I thought that was weird. I mean, Megan's car is gone and since he's such a prick, you'd think he would've taken it."

"Unless he didn't want, say, *you* to see her car and think she was back."

Sage hesitated. "Huh. Good point. Anyway, he went toward Central and I checked on Megan's. The windows are fine and that door doesn't even have paint chipped from him." She sat back, satisfied.

"Sage, thank you so much for coming home at two."

She looked at me, trying to decide whether I was teasing her or not.

"And thank you for not yelling at him. He's a loose cannon and I know you could kick his ass into next year, but he might carry weapons and that would really suck if I came back and found you all messed up in your kitchen."

Her brow furrowed. "That *would* really suck." Then she flashed her devilish grin. "If you saw me like that, would you give me mouth-to-mouth?" Her tone was teasing.

My voice caught in my throat. *Okay, she is* definitely *flirting with me.* "Um."

She was enjoying my discomfiture. "Would you?"

"Uh, I don't think that would be a good idea," I managed, scrambling to find words for this most uncomfortable situation.

Her smile broadened. "You didn't answer the question."

Shit. She had me backed into a corner here and she knew it. I reached down and grabbed my bag and stood. "Look, Sage..."

She stood as well, no longer smiling. Her whole demeanor shifted. "Too forward?" She asked quietly.

"Look," I said, backing slowly to the door, "I'm really flattered. Believe me. But..."

"It's because of Megan, isn't it?"

I stopped. "Sort of. Megan is like a little sister to me and it's just kind of weird to, well, to consider dating her friends." I was totally tongue-tied.

"You think I'm too young."

"It's the context. Megan's way younger than I am and dating her friends would be—I'm sorry," I finished lamely. I continued backing toward the door.

"How old do you think I am?" She wasn't following me, thank God.

"I'm not going to answer that. I'll fuck up no matter what I say."

"Your honesty is refreshing." She said it without a trace of sarcasm.

"And besides, what about Jeff?"

"What about him?" She looked at me, visibly perplexed.

"Aren't you and him —" My hand was on the door handle.

She stared at me, realization dawning. "Oh, hell no. Jeff's, like, been my best friend since I moved here. He's like a brother. Oh, my God. He will so die laughing when I tell him you thought we were together."

I opened my mouth to say something, thought better of it. "I have to go. I'll talk to you later." *This is so nuts.*

"K.C., hold on. I'm sorry. I didn't mean to put you on the spot."

She moved closer.

I waited, holding the door partially open.

"It's just that—" She stopped and regarded me, a little smile on her lips. "I am *really* attracted to you."

I swallowed. "You don't even know me." *Oh, my God. This can't get any worse.*

She shook her head slowly. "I think I do."

I couldn't look away from her gaze. I had nowhere to hide. "Through Megan? That's—I mean, everybody has blinders on when they talk about somebody they like. You've only got a tiny bit of the picture through her. I'm not what she thinks and I'm certainly not what you think."

"I don't believe that." Her tone was intractable. I knew I couldn't argue with it.

"I'm sorry. It's just not a good idea." I slipped out onto the porch, feeling really shitty, slightly rattled, but also extremely flattered. And as much as it pained me, I had done a mature thing and said "no." I shut the door quietly and went around to Megan's. I checked my watch. Four-fifteen. I had to meet Melissa soon. *God, this day is starting to really suck.* I went inside, leaving the interior door open, and turned on some music as I organized. I knew this wasn't a date with Melissa but it seemed sort of disrespectful to wear rumpled shorts and a tee to a dinner that would most likely involve flaying open my soul. And then there was Sage. Why did she have to be so... *Damn*. Smart. Funny. Attractive. *Young.*

I put on a pair of lightweight khakis and a short-sleeved button-down shirt. This color always brought out the flecks of green in my eyes and for some reason, I really wanted Melissa to see that. Maybe that was petty. I wasn't entirely sure about my motives. I worked on my hair a little bit and put on some cologne with a nice citrus undertone. As I finished I heard a soft knock at the front door. I left the bathroom and walked through the bedroom.

"Door's open," I called, knowing it was probably Sage.

"Hey," she said as she came in.

I stopped near the kitchen doorway, waiting.

"I'm sorry," she said. "That was wrong of me to push you like that. I sometimes don't really think about stuff before I say it."

"I noticed that." *Why can't I be ten years younger?*

"Jeff's leaving tomorrow for Las Cruces. Will you come over for dinner?"

"Sage—" I felt my guts clench.

"Please? Just to hang out. And talk. And eat. Just dinner." She cocked an eyebrow. "You know how I am about food and bachelors."

I laughed, a little nervous. "Just to hang out?"

"And talk."

"I can do that." I don't know where the words came from. But as soon as I said them, I knew I might as well have thrown myself into a den of ravenous lions.

She grinned. "Anything you can't or won't eat?"

"Nope. Well, wait. I don't like—"

"Liver. Bleu cheese. Anchovies or escargot. Or fruitcake. Oh, and gorgonzola."

"How—"

She lifted her left shoulder in a shrug.

"Never mind," I said, flustered. "Do you drink wine?"

She brightened. "Definitely. And don't worry about matching it to the food. All wine is good."

"All right. When?"

"I don't get home until six. So how about seven-thirty?"

"Sounds good. Just dinner. And talking." I looked at her for confirmation.

She smiled angelically. "Yep." She appraised me then. "Hmm. Do I have competition?"

"Sage—"

"Kidding." She put her hands up.

"I'm having dinner with my past tonight. Honest opinion. How do I look? Wait—before you say *anything*. You're the old lady at Dillard's and I'm just asking you how I look."

She laughed. "Honestly, that's a great color on you." She paused, then continued. "So you're meeting Melissa. I think that's a really good thing."

"You should hang out a sign and read people's tarot."

"I already do." She flashed that damn grin. "Have a nice time. If you want to talk when it's done, stop by." She waved and left. I stood at the door, watching her cross the twenty paces or so between Megan's and the main house and climb the back steps. I really needed to move because if she turned and saw me watching her, she'd know that under different circumstances, I'd be all over her like a rez dog on a fresh bone. *Move away,* I repeated to myself. I couldn't. I didn't. I stared. Sage pulled the security door on her house open and, yep, she turned and caught me watching her. She stood for a few seconds, eyes locked on mine. I swore I saw a trace of that grin on her lips. And then she went inside.

"Oh, fuck," I muttered under my breath. *Dinner tomorrow is going to suck, too.*

I PARKED IN the structure north of Old Town on Mountain Street. It was free after five and I didn't mind walking the block or two extra. I locked up and crossed Mountain, which brought me right to the edge of the Plaza. I walked down San Felipe past the various galleries and "Indian Trading Companies." Roughly two blocks from the corner of San Felipe and Mountain sat La Hacienda, a sprawling restaurant complex in a one-story adobe, vigas jutting from the front, following the line of the roof. The restaurant's entrance faced the small square in the center of the plaza that served as a park. A gazebo stood in the square's center and people occupied most of the square's wrought iron benches.

I stood watching pedestrians wander past the gazebo. To my right stood San Felipe de Neri, the double-steepled Spanish-style church that Chris's *Abuelita* attended. She liked the early service, because it was conducted in Spanish. Stores, galleries, and shops selling little tourist doodads flanked the other two sides of the square and most were doing pretty good business, from the foot traffic entering and exiting.

I arrived about fifteen minutes early, but since it was Friday, I probably needed to get a table. I went inside the restaurant and waited in the dim lobby behind a group of tourists. The interior evoked heavy, dark Spanish colonial style. To my right a gift shop offered all kinds of things, from cheesy stereotypical rubber tomahawks to colorful jackets made out of Pendleton blankets.

The hostess, like other female servers here, was wearing a kitschy Mexican-style outfit that included a frilly red skirt and a low-cut white blouse with big puffy short sleeves. It evoked those 1940s movies that supposedly took place south of the border. She seated me at a four-top in a corner next to a window. The table, like the rest of the furniture here, was fashioned from heavy dark wood, as were the chairs.

A server came by within a couple of minutes. She asked if I wanted anything to drink. I ordered a margarita on the rocks, higher-grade tequila, no salt. It's almost mandatory to have a margarita with Mexican or New Mexican food. I looked over the menu, which hadn't changed much since the last time I was here. I had my back to the entrance and I was looking out the window when I heard Melissa's voice behind me.

"Hi."

I stood and acknowledged her. She wore a black power suit, which looked really good on her, along with a cream-colored blouse. She slid out of her blazer and hung it on the chair to my right. She took the seat to my left, her back to the window, and she set a small notebook on the table next to me. "My phone log."

"Thanks." I moved it to my right, out of the way.

The server returned with my margarita and Melissa ordered a Diet Coke. She glanced at the menu. She was generally pretty quick about what she wanted in a restaurant.

"Maybe the molé." Melissa started.

"No, not that. Remember that one time...?"

She shot a glance at me. "Kase, that was about four years ago."

I shifted uncomfortably in my chair. How easily I fell into old habits. "Sorry," I said, sheepish.

"Don't worry about it." She smiled.

The server returned with Melissa's drink and took our orders. Melissa chose the blue corn chicken enchiladas and I went for chicken fajitas. When the server left, I filled Melissa in on what I had been doing all day. The only mention I made of Sage was that she told me that Cody had been sniffing around Megan's that day.

"Cody? He was at Megan's?"

"So Sage says."

"She didn't try to kick his ass or anything, did she?"

I laughed. "Oh, so you *do* know her."

"She's quite a—" She broke off.

"Pistol, I think, is the word you're looking for."

Melissa smiled. "I can only take her in small doses. She'd give you the shirt off her back but she's extremely intense." She paused. "Although I think she was good for Megan in a lot of ways."

"I get that impression." *And I'd sure like to take the shirt off her back.* I took a sip of my margarita, trying to get my brain back on track. *Yum.* The higher-grade tequila made a big difference.

"What do you think he was doing?"

"I don't know. Maybe he wanted to access Megan's computer. Maybe she's got money stashed in there. Whatever it was, his key doesn't work anymore and Sage said it seemed to really piss him off."

"What do you think it means?"

"I think they're still in town. Or the East Mountains, but not much farther than that. And I've got his phone number now so I'm going to try to talk to him."

She stared at me as if I had suddenly sprouted antennae and extra arms.

"I'll pretend I'm interested in the movement. I'll set something up with him, see if he'll meet me. And Sage will kick his ass when he shows up," I finished with a feeble attempt at humor.

Melissa rolled her eyes, then got serious. "Are you sure that's a good idea?"

"I'm going to talk to Chris about it. She might come. And the guy at the gang unit would *love* to nail him for something. So hopefully—well, anyway. I don't even know if he's answering his phone. I'll call again tomorrow and see if I can get a response. If I can't, I'll get one of those temporary cell phones and leave him a message."

"Let me know how much it costs. I'll reimburse you."

I didn't argue with that. After interacting with her the past few days, I wasn't as uncomfortable anymore with the idea of her picking up a few of my expenses. I sat back when the server brought our food. My fajitas were snapping and popping on the skillet.

"I don't think I need to tell you this is hot," the server said as she placed it on the bamboo pad.

"No, but thanks," I acknowledged. She set everything down and retreated. I reached into the plastic tortilla warmer and took out a tortilla that I slathered with guacamole, sour cream, and pico de gallo before stacking it with grilled peppers, onions, tomatoes, and chicken from the skillet. I tried to close the tortilla to make it more like a burrito but I'd overloaded it.

Melissa laughed. "You always do that. Maybe order a regular-size tortilla next time."

"If I wanted a burrito..." I started.

She shook her head, smiling. "You would have ordered a burrito." She took a bite of her enchiladas and chewed, and I caught myself watching her, knowing that she'd lower her fork to her plate and move her garnish around a little before she took another bite. Funny, the things that stayed with me.

We ate and talked about inane things like the people at Melissa's office and some of the cases she'd been working on. Very superficial but at least I didn't feel like I was freaking out. We finished and I ordered another margarita when the server cleared our plates. I glanced at Melissa. It was time. She started.

"Thanks for meeting with me."

"Sure." I cleared my throat. "I don't really know what to say."

"So ask me something, then." She regarded me with an expression I recognized, triggering some pleasant memories. I thought about all the people I knew who had sex with their exes and I understood why, in that moment. But for some reason, Sage bounded into my head and my past with Melissa remained in my memories. I took a sip of my drink and remembered driving to Arizona on that awful night three years ago, when I saw Melissa with Hillary.

"Why did you do it?" The words were out of my mouth before I thought about them and she started as if I had physically slapped her. I backpedaled a bit, trying to soften the blow. "I mean, I guess I've always wondered. Why didn't you come to me and tell me you were having thoughts? Or whatever. Maybe we could've seen somebody about it."

Her jaw clenched and her lower lip trembled. "I was weak."

Sage had said the same thing. I nervously sucked on an ice cube from my margarita glass.

"I felt like I was losing my mind," Melissa continued. "Megan in rehab, me feeling like I couldn't keep it together. You struggling not to get caught up in Megan's shit—rightfully so. I know that. Addiction is so fucked up and I know I was enabling her. It felt like you pulled away and I didn't know how to ask for help. I didn't know how to talk to you."

The server came by with my second margarita. She took my empty glass and moved away. I considered Melissa's words. True, I had shut down to a certain extent. I hadn't wanted to get caught up in what I knew was an unhealthy cycle that Melissa sometimes got stuck in with Megan. So I'd done what I usually did to avoid contact, to avoid dealing with something. I worked. Constantly. The revelation hit me like a train. Chris was right.

"And I wasn't really around." I said it thoughtfully, analytically. "I wasn't there."

Melissa dropped her gaze. She folded her hands on the table in front of her. "It didn't feel like it."

"I wish you had said something."

"I wish I had, too."

I took a sip from the fresh margarita.

She studied the tabletop. "When I realized what I was losing, I hoped so much that you'd give me another chance, that you'd maybe work with me on things."

I slowly shook my head. "Think about it from my perspective. You violated a level of trust that I thought we had. I don't know if I could ever have gotten to that point with you again. I'd always wonder what you were doing if you called and said you were running late. Or if you said you had to go on a business trip. Or anything like that. I was afraid I'd wonder and then I'd feel guilty for *not* trusting you if you were telling the truth. That's the kind of damage an affair does." *And maybe I wasn't really strong enough to do damage control.*

She sighed. "I loved you so much. I couldn't believe what I had done. I wanted so much to rewind time and make different decisions." She shook her head. "Sometimes I still want that."

I had my elbows on the table and my lips braced against my hands. I lowered my hands carefully to the table's surface. "So Hillary offered what you felt you weren't getting from me." *Attention. A shoulder. Time.*

She nodded in response.

"Why didn't you come to me? Why didn't you just tell me to pull my head out of my ass and talk to you?"

"I didn't know how. And you seemed to be working so hard at just staying afloat, given what Megan and I were going through."

I felt like somebody was sandblasting scar tissue off my heart.

"But you knew me. You knew you could talk to me about anything." I ran a hand through my hair, frustrated.

"I got trapped in my own projections."

I sighed heavily. "On the other hand, I could've asked *you* how *you* were doing."

She managed a small shrug. "You didn't have the affair."

At least she owned it. Oddly, that made me feel better. Freer, somehow. "Did you love her?"

Melissa regarded me. I couldn't read what she was thinking in her eyes. "No." She leaned forward slightly. Her voice was soft. "I didn't see her for a good six months after you left."

That caught me by surprise.

"And then I started dating her, I guess you'd call it. We did have some things in common. A year after that, I moved in with her."

"So — wait a minute. You've only lived with her..."

"A little over a year."

I didn't know what to say so I took another drink.

"And no, it's not working out." She rubbed the back of her neck with her right hand. "I broke up with her about four months ago."

I stared at her. "Wait."

"I know. It's one of those fucked-up lesbian situations. And I'm feeling guilty about leaving an addict. So I'm still there at the house. And she just drinks more."

My heart sank. I automatically reached out and covered her right hand with my left. "Melissa, get the hell out of there. Don't repeat a pattern."

She moved her hand out from under mine and then took my hand in hers. "I'm waiting to hear from my realtor about another place in the North Valley. About half the size of Hillary's. It's really nice. It's on Candelaria between Rio Grande and Fourth. One of those old Spanish-style places with an inner courtyard and a wall around the whole thing. I have the down payment and it looks like it'll be okay. I'm just waiting to hear whether I get approval or not."

"That's great," I said, relieved. "When do you find out?"

"Monday or Tuesday probably."

"Does Hillary know?"

"Yes. She came home yesterday — as you know — and told the repairman who was supposed to come by to reschedule. I don't know. Maybe she wanted to have it out with me. But she gets to drinking and there's nothing you can say to her."

"Do you love her now?" I was still holding on to Melissa's hand and it felt okay. No charge, no spark. Just warmth.

She looked at me and smiled sadly. "No. I don't think I ever did. But because I had screwed around with her and hurt you so badly, I guess I thought — well, I thought here I had made my bed, so I'd better lie in it."

"You didn't have to start seeing her after I left."

"I didn't have to do a lot of things. I'm still sorting it all out." Before I knew what she was doing, she had pulled my hand to her lips and kissed my knuckles. She lowered my hand just as quickly, before I had time to do anything. The gesture surprised me and scared me at the same time.

"Thank you for coming to help me with Megan."

Whew. It was about Megan and not us.

"And I'll bet you're feeling guilty," she added.

I clenched my jaw. "Yeah. I am."

"Because you didn't keep in touch with her?"

I nodded. "I'm sorry," I said, not sure what else to offer.

"Don't, K.C."

I lowered my gaze to the table.

"Don't do this to yourself. It's not your fault."

"I know that here—" I tapped my forehead. "But I don't feel it here." I placed my free hand over my heart. "Seeing you now—I've been wondering why I was such an asshole to you that last day I saw you. If I had just talked to you..." I trailed off, remembering how the wound between us echoed in Melissa's eyes and tore through my heart as I shut her out completely. I might have winced, because this time the memory revealed what I refused to see then, revealed the chance I chose not to take.

She bit her lip and a tear coursed down her cheek. "You had every right to act that way. I know it was coming from a place of pain and I know I caused that. I don't blame you, though I do wonder sometimes if we could have made it work."

"I'm sorry," I said again. "I'm sorry for the past, and for what I wasn't strong enough to do." I knew I was about to cry but I didn't fight it.

She used a corner of her napkin to wipe her tears. "I'm sorry, too. I've said that to you more times than I can count for the past three years." She handed me a clean napkin from the stack the server had left with dinner.

I took it and chuckled. "God, you'd think we were breaking up again, from this." I wiped my face and drew a shaky breath.

"Please, no," she said, rolling her eyes in an attempt to lighten the mood. "I can't take that again." She smiled at me then. "So what have you been doing since you left?"

I had to laugh. "What do *you* think? Working my ass off."

She shook her head, concerned. "Kase, you have got to break *that* pattern too. It might get in the way of—" She paused. "Future things." She still held my hand. "So you're not seeing anyone?"

"Please, Melissa. You came to Texas. You saw what I was doing.

Did it look like I was involved with anyone?" I lifted a shoulder in a shrug. "I've dated here and there, but nothing serious. I did realize something, though."

She looked at me expectantly.

"I love my work. I love what I do, as difficult as it can sometimes be. I'm getting better about doing other things, too. Like traveling and outdoor stuff. Except in the summer. Texas is too damn hot for that," I joked. "Anyway, I do okay by myself. I do very well, actually. And I'm content with that."

"Do you think maybe you're afraid of a relationship?"

"Hell, yes. After what happened between us, I'm scared shitless. I can't go through that again. It's the worst feeling in the world." I squeezed her hand. "I'm not telling you that to make you feel bad. I think you've already made yourself feel totally shitty for three years. I'm just being honest." I regarded her for a moment and continued. "I know I have to deal with it. I'm not blaming you for my own failings. I mean, it's stupid for me to drag a dead horse around and say shit like 'oh, woe is me. Melissa dissed me so I'll never get involved again so I don't ever have to feel that pain.' " I rolled my eyes. "It's not something I'm looking for right now. I'll just say that." She smiled again and I changed the subject. "All right. So you're going to get yourself out of Hillary's house, right? How about out of her life?"

"Yes," she said emphatically. "I'm so tired of this. I can't tell you how tired I am of dealing with addicts. And now Megan's pulling all of this shit—"

"Let me just say something about that, okay?"

She waited.

"If I'm able to find her, you need to understand that she might not want to come back to your reality. And you're going to have to make some choices for her and for yourself. There's no reason for you to continue paying rent on her place if she's not going to use it. There's no reason for you to lose sleep because she's hooked up with an asshole. She needs to find her own way and if you constantly bail her out, that won't happen." It stung a little to say that because I didn't want to think of Megan living in the white supremacist underground much longer than she already had, but I also wanted Melissa to think about her role in Megan's life.

"I know," she readily agreed. "I just want to see if I can find out where she is and what she's planning to do so that I *can* make those decisions."

I sat with that for a little bit. The vibe I was picking up from Melissa indicated that she was trying to rearrange and move ahead.

"And I'm really glad you came to help," she continued. "You'll never know what this means to me. I just don't have the words for it." She pressed the back of my hand to her face, rubbed her cheek against it. I felt an old stirring as my past collided head-on with the present. *It would be easy,* I thought. So easy to overstep this tenuous rapport, but I knew deep down the right course of action and I had a feeling that she knew, too.

"I don't know if I'll ever be able to make this up to you."

I watched her as she held my hand to her cheek. "I think maybe this trip is reward enough," I said quietly.

"Thank you. Thanks for talking."

"Thanks for asking." I paused. Then, "So back to some business now."

She lowered my hand to the table but she didn't release it and I didn't pull away.

"I'm going to try to get in contact with Cody this weekend. I don't know if I'll be able to. I'll also stick close to Megan's because I want to see if anybody shows up. Chris will have the reports on Cody's run-ins with the law in Colorado. Maybe we can get him on parole violation or something. She'll also know more about the fingerprints from the other night. So just hang loose and I'll keep in touch. Where are you going to be?"

"Packing up."

"Really?"

"Yes. I can't stand it anymore. She's staying away most of the time and this weekend she says she has to be in Los Angeles. I don't really know and I don't really care. Isn't that sad?"

That *was* pretty sad. "Are you okay by yourself?"

"The existential question. We'll find out, won't we?"

"I'm serious."

She smiled. "Yes, I am. I actually really enjoy it when she's not around and when I have time and space to myself."

"Okay, but if you need anything or want to talk or whatever, just call me." *Holy shit.* If someone had said a couple of weeks ago that I'd be sitting in Albuquerque with my ex, whom I hadn't spoken with in three years, telling her to call me, I would've thought that person had smoked a bagful of supreme Mexican weed. But here I was. And it felt okay. It felt good, actually.

Her eyes filled with tears again. She released my hand and hastily wiped at her face. The server returned with the check and Melissa handed her a credit card before I was able to say anything. The server retreated. "I asked *you*," she said. "And I know you didn't really want to come."

I gave her a wry smile. "True. Thanks."

The server returned and Melissa signed off on the receipts.

"I'll walk you to your car. Where are you parked?"

"The garage across Mountain."

"Cool. Same here." I picked up the notebook she had brought as I stood and waited for her to squeeze out from her chair. I removed her blazer from the back of the chair and handed it to her. We exited the restaurant, sharing a comfortable silence as we walked down San Felipe. The best part of Albuquerque summers was like right now, when nightfall nudged evening and the temperature along that boundary was just right. Not hot, but not cool. Traffic was fairly heavy since it was a Friday night so we had to wait to get across Mountain. I heard laughing and shouting from somewhere on the Plaza. To my right—east—the jagged outlines of the Sandias hung in the dusk. I did miss New Mexico. Maybe Sage was right. I stopped thinking about her. *Shit.* That was another problem I had to deal with.

As we neared Melissa's car her phone rang. She pulled it out of her blazer pocket and looked at the screen. "I don't recognize the number," she said.

"Is it local?"

"Yes."

"Answer it."

She did so. "Hello?" A few seconds later she brought her free hand to her mouth as tears started rolling down her cheeks. I stood nearby, watching. "Where are you? Oh, God. Are you okay? When—"

I caught Melissa's eye and shook my head vehemently. *Don't ask her that.*

"Listen, I have someone here who wants to talk to you."

My eyebrows shot up to my hairline.

"Hold on." Melissa handed me the phone. There was no getting out of it now.

"Hey," I said, trying to stay calm.

"K.C.?" Megan's voice was low, like she was trying not to be detected.

"Yep. How are you holding up?"

"What are you doing in New Mexico?"

I debated what to tell her and opted for something relatively innocuous, since I guessed telling her that Melissa asked me to find her would piss her off, maybe drive her further away emotionally. "Visiting your sister. Doing some research. And I missed Albuquerque but I find out that you're not around and I can't catch up with you. So what's going on?"

"I can't really talk," she said tightly.

"Are you at a pay phone?"

"Yes."

"Are you still in Albuquerque?" I pushed a little because from her voice, she sounded like she might be ready to tell me some things. I recognized the tone from all the conversations we'd had in the past.

"Sort of."

"Edgewood?"

Pause. "Yeah." She said it with slight relief, like she'd been keeping a secret that she no longer wanted to hide.

"Can I see you?"

Longer pause. "I don't think that's a good idea."

I tried a different tack. "Remember when Melissa and I went through the bad time? I left you a card."

I heard her breathing.

"I told you no matter what, you could always call me. No matter what happened. I meant that."

"I guess I didn't believe it," she said so softly I wasn't sure I heard her right.

"I wouldn't say something like that unless I meant it."

"I have to go," she said. She sounded scared.

"Is he hurting you?" I said it and then immediately kicked myself because Melissa was standing right there, listening, and I didn't want her to worry about that, too.

"I really have to go."

"No matter what. You can call me."

"Bye." She hung up. I pulled the phone away from my ear. Melissa was watching me, tears in her eyes.

I closed the phone and handed it to her. "Write that number down. I'll have Chris find out which pay phone it is." I handed the notebook back to her.

"Is she in Edgewood?"

"She says she is."

"Is he hurting her?" The dread in Melissa's voice was palpable.

"She didn't say. Don't go there right now, okay?"

"I've been thinking it for a while now." She exhaled and I worried she would collapse so I walked her slowly to the driver's side door of her SUV. Her hands trembled as she checked her cell phone and copied the number into the notebook with a pen from her glove compartment. She handed the notebook back to me.

"All right," I said, trying to make her feel a little better. "Here's the good news. She's close. She's still checking in, which I'm thinking means she wants to come home. If she didn't, she wouldn't bother calling you. She knows I'm here now, which means she knows we're offering to help her if she's ready. She knows now that she has a way out. You need to focus on that and make sure you keep your phone with you."

She nodded, jaw clenched. She stared straight out the windshield.

"Are you okay going home?"

She nodded again.

"Are you okay by yourself?" It felt strange, taking this caretaker role with her. Melissa had always tried to do that with me in the past. And with Megan. Never any room for herself. I hoped that changed.

"I think I actually prefer it." She turned to look at me. "I'm really glad you're here."

"Me, too. Drive carefully. Call me if you need to." I stepped back and she shut her car door and started the engine. I watched her back out of the parking space then drive toward the exit. I walked to my car and got in. I headed for Megan's, feeling drained but somehow liberated as several different things careened through my head. Chris was right. So was Melissa. We had needed to talk. And I'd been able to talk to Megan, which might help us get her away from that rat-bastard Cody. Though she was scared, she sounded like herself, like Megan. There was nothing more I could do right now until I gave the number to Chris and she pinpointed the location of the phone. I called Chris and left her a message, letting her know that Megan had phoned and to give me a call when she had a chance.

My thoughts veered to Sage. I wasn't sure what to do about that so I instead focused on the fact that Cody had been by earlier. And extremely pissed off that he couldn't get in. Caught in the slow crawl of Friday traffic on Central, I had even more time to think about the incident. Maybe there was something in Megan's house that he wanted. Maybe it wasn't about Megan after all. And whatever it was he was looking for, it might have something to do with the incident earlier that week, when somebody else had tried to get in. I'd better go through Megan's stuff again the next day. Maybe I'd find something I overlooked.

Chapter
Twelve

I WAS UP around seven Saturday morning and decided to head up to the Sandias and do a trail run before the summer heat kicked in. I ran there all the time when I lived here and it really helped clear my head. I pulled my "skinnies" on—my runner's underwear. They're made of some ungodly chemical mixture and they hug my body like a second skin. Over those I put a pair of cargo shorts so I had pockets to carry my keys, band-aids, and cell phone. I then donned a sports bra and a muscle tee, filled my CamelBak, and laced my shoes up.

Twenty minutes later I pulled into the dirt parking area at the end of Montgomery, a major east-west street that narrows as it enters the ritzy residential area along the base of the Sandias until it dead-ends here, the open space area riddled with dirt trails for running, hiking, biking, and walking. I put my Camelbak on, adjusted the straps, and headed out, starting at a light jog. Soon I was loping along one of the wide main trails headed east into the mountains. I wanted to take it easy because I was running at altitude and I hadn't been here in a while. So I did a three-mile loop at a leisurely pace then jogged a half-mile to cool down.

The rich odors of dirt, sage, and piñon followed me along the trail. I passed a few other runners and we smiled and waved, commiserating in our shared pain. A few people were out with their dogs and I saw three people who had to be in their seventies hiking up a steep incline. I slowed to a walk and by the time I got back to the car it was eight-thirty. I headed down into the city and stopped at a gas station to call Cody. Four rings and voice-mail. I didn't leave a message, deciding that I'd probably have to get a temporary cell phone with a local number.

I drove to Megan's and parked in front of Sage and Jeff's. Both of their cars were gone. I sat thinking for a minute and then decided to park on the next block. If Cody or any of his associates were going to come around, seeing my car there might scare them off. I walked the block back to Megan's and found a note taped to the door:

Good morning, neighbor! I thought you might want to hang out in the big house today in case assmuncher decides to show up and spar with the door again. You could catch him in the act! Just go on in. Back door's open and there's a key on the kitchen counter. See you tonight.
Sage.
P.S. my cell is 332-4535.

She had drawn a little cartoon of Cody with boxing gloves on. I laughed. *Assmuncher.* I wondered if she made that up. I read it again, thinking that she had delightful handwriting. I didn't know what other word to use. If it were pictures, it would look like little nymphs bouncing around in an enchanted forest. I groaned inwardly. Definitely a messy situation, and the more I tried *not* to think about it, the more I did. I unlocked the doors and went inside, making sure to lock the security door from the inside. I stripped on my way to the shower, tossing Sage's note onto the bed.

I stood in the shower for a long time. For the first time in three years, I felt a sense of peace about Melissa. I guess I'd never really understand why she crossed the line and had the affair, but maybe now I had a better explanation for it, at least. And I recognized my unavailability. Which doesn't necessarily excuse what she did, but it did make me see a bigger picture. I thought about Melissa leaving Hillary and the messed-up relationship she'd had with her over the last three years. I thought about holding Melissa's hand in the restaurant the night before and how it was like a time warp, how it had made me feel. *Do I miss her?* The water poured over my neck and shoulders. Yeah, in some ways. *Would I get back with her?* No. Not now. I couldn't honestly say if that would change in the future, but right now, I was pretty happy with who I was and what I was doing. I missed New Mexico, and maybe I'd come back, but right now, this was how things were and I was okay with that.

My mind wandered to Sage. I had no doubt that she intrigued me, no doubt that I was attracted to her on several levels. I'd never met anyone so uninhibited, so unfettered. She eschewed conventional thinking but she wasn't a flake or an airhead. She simply *was*. She owned the space she occupied. She reveled in it. She said what was on her mind and she accepted the consequences of her honesty. *God, why can't I be ten years younger?* I was leery about seeing younger women. Maybe that was biased, but in my thinking, there was a world of difference between twenty-four and thirty-four. Not only that, but I could see myself being interested in more than dating with someone like Sage, but at twenty-four—which was what I estimated her age to be—the novelty of playing house can wear a little thin after a while. Different priorities, different paths.

I thought then about dancing with her. She had let me lead, no doubt about that, but she made it clear that my leading was contingent on her following. I liked that she claimed her space, and that she wasn't afraid to ask questions or talk about things. "Shit," I said to myself. *Who am I kidding? She's hot.* And she moved me in some strange and inviting way. I shut the water off. *Well, whatever. I've acknowledged it and now I can move on.* I simply would not go there. *Shit. I'm living an episode of* The L Word. *Here I am, acting like my ex's best friend, lusting after a woman young enough to be my student, and trying to corral a bunch of white supremacists. What the hell kind of reality show is this?*

I dried off and threw on clean clothes before I started the coffee, then spent the next couple of hours organizing my notes. I checked Megan's e-mail again, but saw nothing but spam. I then checked mine. Junk mail, a couple of notices about upcoming lectures at UT, one from a colleague in Boston. I e-mailed him and told him I was in New Mexico doing research. I checked in with my department. I wouldn't hear anything until Monday or Tuesday, but that was okay. I then did a search on "Aryan Desert Rats." Nope. No formal Web site. I was hoping to at least get a line on the plans they might have. I sat back, tugging on my chin and pondering my next move when my phone rang. I picked it up and looked at the ID. Good. Maybe Chris had some more information.

"*Hola, mujer*," I answered.

"Hey, I've got a couple of minutes. I got those reports in from Colorado and I got a match to the prints."

"Yeah? Our buddy Cody?"

"Negative. Raymond Watkins. He's got a couple of priors. I think you'll be interested to see who this guy is. You might know him as Roy Whistler."

Holy shit! "Chris, you're a goddess among all us mere mortals."

She laughed. "Takes one to know one. So what's going on with Megan?"

"She called Melissa last night. Do you have a pen and paper?"

"Yep."

"I talked to her. She called Melissa's cell from a phone in Edgewood. Can you do a trace and find out where the phone is?"

"Sure. Give me the number."

I did and she repeated it back to me. She paused for a moment, then continued, in typical Chris fashion, to another major issue in my life. "So," she started. "Melissa?"

"No, not what you think. Remember you told me a few days ago that maybe I should talk to her? Get stuff out in the open? Well, we did. We had dinner in Old Town yesterday. And you're right. It felt really good."

"And?"

"That's it. It felt good. I'm glad I did it and I'm really glad I'm where I am." I knew what she wanted to ask. I answered before she did. "No. I don't want to get back with her. I mean, there's still some stuff I need to work out with regard to what happened, but I don't want to go there. Down the line, I don't know. I never say never, as you know, but for now, things are where they need to be."

"I'm glad, Kase. I just don't want you to get hurt again. I know, I know. I sound like your mom or something. But you're pretty special and you deserve someone who sees that."

"Geez, you're making me wanna grab a tissue here," I said, only half-teasing.

"Yeah, whatever. Listen, I'm working this weekend to get caught up but I have time tomorrow evening. Can I swing by?"

"That'd be awesome. Oh, before I forget—Cody was poking around here yesterday around two. Sage saw him. No, she didn't run out there and open a can on his ass, but she said he was really pissed that he couldn't get in."

"Keep me posted on that. Do you want me to spend the night tonight? I have a training seminar I have to deal with that ends at ten so I can be there around eleven."

"Jesus. No, don't worry. Go home and have your space, you big ol' detective, you. You need your rest to keep us civilians safe."

She laughed again. "I'm so glad you're in town. All right, I'll check in with you later."

"Thanks. Bye."

We hung up and I sat for a bit, staring blankly at the computer. So Roy was Raymond. And he had a criminal past. I wondered if that meant anything with regard to John Talbot. My legal pad was lying next to the computer. I flipped to my organizational columns and wrote "Raymond Watkins" in the Roy column. I added "criminal record" and then wrote "Talbot" and a question mark. I tapped the pen against the paper, trying to see if there was any definitive connection. I added "called" under the Megan column and yesterday's date and time along with the place and the number from which she had called. I added "probably abused." I wrote "asshole abuser" in Cody's column. That reminded me. I needed to look at Melissa's log of Megan's calls, which I'd left in the car.

I stood and retrieved a half-full bottle of Tazo from the fridge and walked to my car to get the notebook. Once back at the computer, I set my tea on a nearby coaster and stared at the notebook, but I Googled Sage instead and her Web site popped up. I ended up perusing it for a good half-hour. Nicely designed, it included some stunning flash images of landscapes that I figured she had taken. A small recent shot of her graced the upper right-hand corner of her homepage. From what I could tell, it might have been taken on top of a mesa somewhere. She was grinning broadly, gazing past the camera, a mischievous faraway expression in her eyes. Her arms were folded casually over her chest. I stared at the photo for a long time. *God help me. She's absolutely gorgeous.*

I clicked through her site, savoring it like a rare liqueur. Her portfolio was unbelievable. She had already traveled all over the world, including Europe, India, Latin America, and Turkey. I clicked on her biography and my jaw dropped. She would be thirty-one in early February. Had I thought to do this sooner, I would have known she wasn't as young as I had assumed. This threw a whole other song into the mix.

The biography portion of her site included a couple of photos of her as a little cowgirl. Even as a child, she'd had that damn grin. The Wyoming landscape stretched for miles behind her in each image. Another photo showed her sitting in a downpour in what looked like a Central American jungle. She huddled amidst indigenous peoples beneath a leaky roof, laughing with them. My heart lurched and my breathing sped up. *This is either really good or really bad. Shit.*

The text provided just enough information without going into too much detail. She had been born in Wyoming and got interested in images and art as a child. From there, it was just a matter of getting her hands on a camera. Her mom gave her a used Kodak when she was five. After that, Sage said in the biography, there was no going back.

I clicked on another page of her Web site labeled "exhibitions." She had already had several over the years. University of Wyoming, University of New Mexico, a couple of galleries in Los Angeles, one in Austin, and two in Boston. Those featured European images. "Wow," I said out loud. Upcoming exhibitions included an installation on the UNM campus—Sage had already mentioned that one. But she also had an opening coming up in Santa Fe on Canyon Road, which was *the* place to get your art shown there. I was blown away. I clicked on "galleries" and found out that her work was currently on display at two here in Albuquerque. One was in Old Town.

Another page on her site featured several photographs that had been published in magazines. A few I actually recalled seeing somewhere. The last page I viewed was called "upcoming projects." According to this, in February she was scheduled to do a photo essay down in the Everglades after which she was going to document local fishing along the Gulf Coast. She thanked the Aaron Siskind Foundation underneath the description of the Everglades shoot. The Fifty Crows Foundation out of San Francisco was helping fund the Gulf Coast project.

I sat back. Her work was amazing. She captured not just the image, but the *essence* of whatever or whomever she photographed. Sage was not only talented, she was gifted. She was born with an ability to see into people and to draw out of them their innermost thoughts and dreams. She did the same with landscapes. I was spellbound. *So many layers.* Here she was, one of the up-and-coming talents in documentary photography and she was so understated. Humble. Real. I wanted to know more. In every conceivable way. And that thought both excited and scared the hell out of me. *She's not as young as I thought. This could be dangerous.*

I stood and stretched. Time to get my mind off Sage for a bit and do the job I was asked to do. There was nothing in Melissa's notebook that she hadn't already told me. But she had logged the three numbers from which Megan had called. The most recent number matched the last three times she had called. So she was staying put somewhere. Megan called Melissa at least once every eight days, it seemed, as I flipped through the pages and checked the dates. The longest stretch was the most recent.

I put the notebook down and went back through Megan's bookshelves, paying particular attention to the books Cody had given her. For all I knew, something he had underlined was some kind of secret code, in which case, I'd probably not ever know what he was looking for. But I might have missed something. I went through Megan's books again as well. School texts and some fiction that included Tony Hillerman and Nevada Barr. I could totally visualize Megan as a forest ranger. I hoped Nevada Barr was that kind of influence on her.

I moved to her bedroom, where Megan kept her addiction recovery books. Nothing in them beyond notebook paper on which she had written what looked like affirmations and a few thoughts. I was glad to see that the books looked like they got a lot of use. I finished in the bedroom and went back to the computer. Had I missed something in her files?

An hour later, I was stumped. I had gone through all of her files again. Maybe Cody and Roy wanted the photos. That seemed logical. But there wasn't anything that would get them arrested in those photos, which were all fairly benign. I looked through the two drawers of Megan's computer desk. I had already checked all the CDs but I decided I'd check them again.

Ten CDs later, I sat back, glaring at the screen. What was I missing? The CDs were just back-ups of files on her hard drive. I opened the drawer to put the disks back. A folded manila envelope rested on the bottom. The CDs had been sitting on top of it and it hadn't registered with me earlier. I took it out and knew immediately there was a CD in it from the way it felt in my hand. The envelope was sealed and addressed to Cody. No return address but the postmark date was July 8, after Megan had left. Did Cody hide it here?

I opened it carefully with my pocketknife and pulled the case out so I could remove the disk. I inserted it into the CD drive and clicked the mouse through the steps to open it. The only thing on this was one file—a photo. I clicked on it and waited for the appropriate software to open it. As it took shape, I felt my stomach clench. It was a picture of John Talbot's body lying in the parking lot. The angle was different than the photo that Mark had shown me at the station. Raymond Watkins stood over Talbot, looking down at him with a smirk. Cody stood to Raymond's right, glaring at whoever was taking the picture.

"Oh, my God," I said softly. I shouldn't e-mail this to anyone. I had to take it to Mark right away, so it could be admitted to evidence. Plus, I really didn't want anything like this traceable to my e-mail address. Should I copy it? *Fuck.* Then it'd be on Megan's computer and that might look incriminating. Better to just get the damn thing to Mark. I ejected the disk and put it back in its case before sliding it into the envelope, figuring that my fingerprints were all over it anyway. I quickly shut everything down and checked to make sure I had Mark's card. A gallon-sized plastic Ziploc bag I found in one of Megan's kitchen drawers worked for an envelope once I folded it over. No sense getting any more fingerprints on it. Halfway down the walk to my car, I remembered that Sage's house was open and I turned around so that I could retrieve the key from inside and lock up. The key sat on the counter, like she said, next to a plate covered with plastic wrap. A note rested next to the plate. "Banana bread. Come on, bachelor. Have a slice."

I smiled and lifted the plastic wrap for a piece and took a bite. "Oh, my God." It was the best I had ever tasted. I carefully re-wrapped it and glanced at my watch. One-thirty. I found a pen on the kitchen counter next to a phone and wrote on the piece of paper, "Thanks! Freakin' DEE-LISH-US!" I placed a copy of the key to Megan's on the piece of paper and wrote right next to it, "Just in case."

I locked up then headed to the next block to retrieve my car, which was only a couple blocks from Carlisle, a main drag that cuts north-south through the heart of Nob Hill. On the way to the police station, I called Mark and left a message telling him that I was on my way with a photo on a CD I'd found at Megan's that pertained to the Talbot case.

When I got to the station, the receptionist said that Mark wasn't in and was there something she could do? I left the envelope with her after writing a long note explaining the circumstances in which I'd found it and admitting that my fingerprints were thus all over it. I told him to call me for further information. I was hesitant to leave it with the receptionist, but it was a police station, after all. From the car, I called Chris and left a message telling her I'd found a photo at Megan's and she needed to check in with Mark. Then I called Melissa. Geez, nobody was answering their phones. I left a message with her as well, telling her to call me.

Two-thirty. I got back into my car and re-traced my route to Carlisle. An American Furniture store dominated the parking lot on the corner of Menaul, a major east-west route, and Carlisle. I turned left before the store into the shopping center and parked. The afternoon heat scraped against my skin as I walked toward Cost Plus Imports. Sculptures made out of rebar and car parts decorated a small grassy area in front, one a dinosaur or maybe a dragon and another a crane. I entered the store, trying really hard not to think about the fact that I found that picture in Megan's house. I hoped to God she didn't know what had been in that envelope.

I headed directly to the wine section and selected a dry sweet rosé from New Mexico's Blue Teal Vineyard, located in the Mesilla Valley near the Mexican border, and a darker red called Coyote, from Black Mesa, a northern vineyard near Taos. The Blue Teal needed to be chilled, but the Black Mesa was better at room temperature. I knew I was on autopilot, trying to do little stupid shit to keep myself on track, keep myself focused on here and now. There was nothing I could do about John Talbot or the picture. I'd done what I was supposed to. So why did I feel so damn helpless?

On my way back to Megan's I stopped at a gas station and called Cody's number from the pay phone. Four rings and voice-mail again. I hung up. Fuck this. Time for a disposable cell phone so I could actually leave him a message and get something going here with him. Maybe since Megan knew I was in town, she'd take the opportunity to bail on him if I could get him away long enough. I clenched my teeth and hoped Mark would call soon. Gripped by a sudden weird urge, I steered west again toward Old Town and the gallery where Sage's work was on display. I wanted to not think about Megan for a while longer.

I parked just off the Plaza, on Romero and walked a half-block to the main square. I walked another block to Amapola Gallery. An electronic sensor beeped as I entered. Loads of art graced every conceivable space. Gallery personnel had added display cases for smaller objects, including jewelry. Everything was arranged nicely so traffic could flow easily around objects. A man behind the counter near the back wall looked up. I guessed he was Navajo. "Hi," he said. "Looking for anything in particular?" He spoke in a pleasant baritone.

"Actually, yes." I approached the counter. "Sage Crandall's

work. She's — "

"Right over here," he replied, grinning. He came around the counter and crossed the room to a series of framed photographs on the wall. His cowboy boots thudded heavily on the wooden floor. He wore jeans and a red button-down shirt. The design on his bolo tie struck me as Puebloan. He gestured at the wall. Ten photographs, all landscape shots. Four looked as if she'd taken them in Central America. Two of those were marked "sold." Chaco Canyon's Pueblo Bonito at sunrise and sunset graced two more, both sold. Two others depicted the Great Stupa in Sanchi, India. One was marked "sold." But the last two were the ones that really caught my eye.

Slot canyons, probably in Utah. She'd been in these canyons and I wondered how she'd managed to bring her gear with her. Both photos captured the undulating but immutable nature of the narrow walls, splotched white and sandstone red. Soft sunlight filtered down through an opening high above the canyon floors. Sage had managed to capture a pictograph in each image. In one, the design looked like an animal of some sort. She had framed it in the lower left. In the other, the pictograph looked more like a human. It was about midway up, on the right. "Wow," I breathed.

"Her work is excellent."

I turned my head to look at him. "I'm not sure that word captures it."

He smiled. "I'd have to agree. Anyone who comes in here and sees her photographs is usually sucked right in."

I looked again at the slot canyons. There was something deeply intimate about the two images. Paired, they were like lovers, at once reflecting the other but also staking out their individuality. Complementary but solitary. Five hundred dollars for both, framed.

"The canyons. I'll buy them both." They spoke to me. No, that wasn't a strong enough word. They reached out and grabbed me by the throat. I found myself thinking that whatever happened with Sage, I would have these mementos of her and for some reason, that was comforting.

He grinned. "Ah. So she spoke to you."

I looked at him sharply. He motioned me over to the counter. "I'll write up a receipt. If it's okay, they're on display for another month or so."

"No problem. I'll check back." *And I'll check with Sage,* I found myself thinking as a weird light-headedness suddenly washed over me. Sage was in those images. She wasn't visible, but there was a part of her in each one. And I wanted to have her near, no matter what form. The thought shocked me with its intensity. I took a credit card out of my wallet as he wrote up a ticket.

"Don't lose this. It's proof of purchase." He handed the form to me, took my card, and slid it through the machine. "How did you discover her work?" He gave my card back.

"I met her."

He nodded slowly. "She has that effect on people."

"Compelling," I said wryly.

"Sage carries a rare spirit," he continued, keeping his eyes on mine. If he was Navajo, he had clearly adopted some white ways. "Uninhibited, I think, might capture it in English." He handed me the proof of purchase and the credit card receipt for my signature. I signed it and handed it back.

"Thank you so much." I wasn't sure how traditional he was so I hesitated about extending my hand. He noticed.

"Joe Montoya." He offered his right hand. I clasped it, relieved.

"K.C. Fontero. Thanks again."

He handed me one of his business cards, which he kept in the pocket of his shirt. I took it and slid it into one of the cargo pockets of my shorts. "See you in a month or so," he said.

"Definitely." I left and returned to my car.

By the time I got back to Megan's and parked just around the corner, it was nearly five. I grabbed the wine and crossed the street, doing a quick scan as I approached, in case Cody had come back today. He probably hadn't. He probably went back to Edgewood and bitched Megan out because the locks had been changed on her door. Or he'd blame her for giving him the wrong key. Maybe he didn't realize the locks had been changed. I let myself in and put the Blue Teal in the fridge, then turned some music on and stretched out on the couch, listening to the hum of the swamp cooler and the sounds of Central in the distance. My phone rang. I didn't recognize the number but figured it might be Mark, calling from work.

"Hello?"

"Hi, K.C. This is Mark Aragon, with APD."

"Oh, thanks for calling. I guess you got the CD."

"I did. This is some serious shit. I'm guessing the photo was taken right after Talbot was shot. I don't see a gun, but the fact that these two guys were there at the scene of a murder without informing authorities looks mighty suspicious. Where'd you find it, again?"

I went through the story again and this time, I explained what my relationship was to Megan and Melissa Crown. I included Cody's relationship to Megan. It took about fifteen minutes. When I was done, Mark was quiet for a bit. Then he spoke. "So what were you planning to do when you located Sorrell?"

"Nothing. Tell Melissa. She said she would then hire a PI to deal with it. Probably follow him around or something."

"Why didn't she do that initially?"

"She couldn't find one who was entirely comfortable dealing with white supremacists. And she couldn't really gum up APD with it because Megan's an adult. Plus, she can't prove that Sorrell's done anything illegal."

"True." His tone was thoughtful. "This changes that, though. We now have probable cause to get involved. I'm going to check this photo out and see if we can find Watkins and put a tail on him. We might get lucky and find Sorrell, too."

"So what does this mean with regard to Megan? I mean, I found the photo here, at her house. The envelope wasn't open, though. And it's dated after she left."

"We're dusting it for prints. Hopefully, hers won't be on it. I'll have Chris swing by to dust some of Megan's things that only she might have touched so we can run a comparison if necessary. We'll be checking the envelope for trace as well. I'm really hoping that she has nothing to do with this and that Sorrell hid it there without her knowing about it. In the meantime, stick around. This is getting complicated."

"Yessir." We hung up and I groaned, trying not to stress out just yet. I sank back into the couch and was staring moodily at the blank TV screen when Melissa called. Quickly, I told her what I had found. She was quiet for a bit before speaking. When she did, her tone was subdued.

"What do you think?"

"I don't think she knows about it. But they're checking the prints. They'll find mine and hopefully Cody's. Maybe Raymond's."

"I can't—I can't think about this right now."

"Don't. There's nothing we can do until the results come back. I'll let you know as soon as possible. Just finish your day and do some packing. Maybe get some sleep." I paused for a moment. "I'm sorry about this, Meliss'."

"It's not your fault. Thanks for telling me, even though it's really shitty news." She sighed. "All right. Let me know what they find out. Bye."

"Bye." I hung up and continued staring at nothing. For some reason, I believed that Megan didn't know about the photo. I clung to that and tried to focus on dinner with Sage.

Chapter
Thirteen

"HELLO? SAGE?" I entered her kitchen and noticed a couple of pots on the stove. *Damn, it smells like Indian food.* Music emanated from the stereo in the living room. Alana Davis. Nice. Sage was probably in the bathroom or something, so I'd open a bottle of wine. I pulled a couple of drawers open, found a corkscrew on my second attempt, and set to work on the Blue Teal, sniffing it when I pulled the cork out. *Oh, yeah. Good stuff.* Sage might actually have glasses on the table, since she seemed like such an organized hostess. Sure enough, when I poked my head into the living-dining room, the table was already set. I retrieved the two wine glasses and took them to the kitchen, pouring them each three-quarters full. I didn't hear her approach.

"Hi." She stood in the doorway that led into the living room and oh, my God, she was radiant. I never really understood how that word worked when you applied it to women until that moment. She had tied her hair back, which unfortunately for me exposed her most excellent cheekbones and the unbelievable planes of her face. She wore a loose faded red tee and a black wraparound skirt stamped with African-style fish and gazelles in cream and light blue. A leather anklet with small cowrie shells graced one of her legs. She was barefooted. God, even her feet were gorgeous. I needed to think about something else. Right now.

"Hi. Sorry. I kind of made myself at home." I handed her a glass of wine.

"I wanted you to make yourself at home." She smiled and took the glass, clinking it gently against mine. "Thanks for coming."

"The amazing smells lured me out of my cave. You look really nice," I added.

She flashed a grin and took a sip of wine. "Thanks. You're not so bad yourself." She gestured with her glass. "Hey, this is really good."

I pointed at the open bottle. "I like to drink local."

She peeked under the lids of the pots. "Your timing is perfect.

Go sit down."

"Yes, ma'am." I mock-saluted and headed for the living room, giving her a wide berth. *What the hell is* wrong *with me? I barely know her!* I took one of the seats that had a plate in front of it and stared at the candle in the center of the table. The room was awash in gentle, muted light from a lamp on an end table near the front door and several other candles, all lit. *God help me.* On the plus side, I had a feeling Sage just liked candles. From the looks of these, she fired them up fairly often. She emerged from the kitchen and picked up the plates.

"Be right back," she said softly.

She's going to kill me. Or maybe I'll just die. I took a swallow of wine. She reappeared with the two plates, loaded with food. She set one down in front of me and the other at the place to my right. I was facing the kitchen doorway. She went back to the kitchen only to appear seconds later with a basket full of nan. *I am in such deep shit right now.*

"I hope you like Indian," she said, obviously reading my thoughts.

"I love it. I cannot believe you can cook this stuff. Amazing." I mixed my chana with the rice, into which she had stirred cardamom pods. *I'm in the deepest shit ever.* Chicken tikka masala, nan, and raita. I was in heaven. At least I'd die well-fed. "This is unbelievable. Thank you so much. Wow." I relaxed, letting go of the day.

She smiled and dropped her gaze to her plate, shy. How many layers were there to this little mystic? I stood. "More wine?"

"Please."

"I'll just bring the bottle. How's that?"

"Good idea."

I returned and refilled her glass, asking her about her day. She was teaching a photo workshop that would meet for the last time the following week. She had me laughing at her descriptions of some of the students, two of whom she said had talent. I liked the kindness I heard in her voice.

"And you? How'd it go last night?"

I gave her a brief run-down of my dinner with Melissa. It didn't bother me that Sage asked. I didn't mention the gallery visit, however. I needed to keep that close for a while longer, maybe because I wasn't sure what this *thing* between us was all about.

"So overall, how do you feel about dinner with your past?" she said, watching me.

I hesitated, trying to find the right word. "Peaceful."

"Sometimes you need to debride a wound before it can heal." She took a bite of nan and looked at me. "Are you still angry with her?"

I shook my head slowly. "No. I thought I was, but I guess I haven't been for a long time. I guess I just wanted to hear what her reasons were for doing it." I took a sip of wine. "I'm part of the equation and I'm not entirely sure how that plays out, but it's done. I can't change it."

"You should let things go. Otherwise they build up and when they spill out, it can be ugly."

"Yeah," I softly agreed. I then told her that Megan had called and that I had talked to her. Sage looked at me sharply. I told her how the conversation went.

"She's in Edgewood?"

"She says she is. I don't think she'd have a reason to lie about that. I think she wants to get away from Cody and the group but she's afraid."

"I will so remove his arms from his body," Sage said firmly. "What's your next step?"

"Actually, I have a cell phone number for our door-bustin' buddy and I've been calling him. He's not answering and if he doesn't tomorrow, I'll leave a message. I'm going to get a temporary cell phone. I'll tell him I'm interested in the movement and find out if he'll meet me somewhere." I decided not to tell her about the photo I had found in Megan's desk. Not yet.

Sage's eyes widened. "And that's a good idea because?"

"If I can get him away from Megan, I might be able to use him as an informant or something. My friend Chris can help with that, since she's hooked into law enforcement."

Sage took another sip of wine. "She was here the other night." She sounded thoughtful. "She has good energy."

I looked at her, debating what that might mean.

"I can tell through you. She cares about you and you've known her for a while."

I decided not to go there. Sage was either really perceptive or part of some other-worldly group that used ESP to lure unsuspecting researchers like myself to awesome home-cooked meals. I finished every bit of food on my plate. She did as well. "More?"

"I'm great right now. Just right."

"Good. It's not healthy to stuff yourself." She picked up the plates and returned to the kitchen and reappeared just as quickly. She wasn't going to clean up just yet. I poured more wine and we continued to chat, sitting at the table companionably.

"Where did you learn to cook like that?"

"I've always had a knack for it. I started working with Asian cuisines when I moved to Albuquerque. Much easier to get ingredients."

I wondered at this other side to her. A much softer, introspective side. "Tell me about Sheridan."

She arched an eyebrow. "Let's see—I was born there, actually. I'll be thirty-one in a few months." She pinned me with her gaze though a smile pulled at the corners of her mouth. I kept my expression neutral. "My brother was born two years later."

I didn't tell her that I'd Googled her. I wasn't ready to admit that I could very easily find myself in a compromising situation with her. I wasn't sure what was happening here, but I was both excited and scared.

She regaled me with a variety of tales, including descriptions of running out to the outhouse in the dead of the Wyoming winters. "Hell, sometimes we had to roll burning logs from the stove through the snow to melt a path." Her eyes sparkled when she teased. She talked about how hard her mom had worked to make her father's paychecks last as long as possible. She spoke of the wind that howled across the grasslands. She told stories about antelope and elk, hawks and eagles. She and her brother learned how to hunt and fish. "I'm still a damn good shot. That's why I know I could kick Cody's ass," she said matter-of-factly.

She talked about her realization that she was different. Not like the other girls. At ten, she'd made up stories about rescuing a classmate from dragons, about rescuing her. In high school she kissed her first girl. At the University of Wyoming she started dating women seriously. Her longest relationship was three years with an older student. It ended two years ago. It bothered me a bit that I might be part of a pattern. On the other hand, maybe she was just a lot more mature than many of her peers. I changed the subject.

"What happened to your dad?"

She was quiet for a while, sipping her wine.

"I'm sorry. You don't need to talk about that if you don't want to."

"No, it's not that," she assured me. "I really don't know what happened to him. When Mom moved River and me into town, he didn't come around anymore. I saw him maybe once after that. He was sober, for once, and he told me I look like his mom. Whatever the hell that means. I never saw him again."

I shifted in my chair. "Where's your mom?"

"She lives in Cheyenne. She's an LPN now and she works in a hospital. She wants to be an RN so she's taking classes."

"That's great. And River?"

She grinned. "He's a hunting guide in Montana. He freakin' *loves* it. He calls once a week to check on me. He's supposed to be my baby brother but he worries about me all the time."

I returned her grin and reached for the bottle of wine. "Uh-oh. Empty," I announced.

She raised an eyebrow. The gesture made me weak. "So open the other one. That'll be your hourglass. When it's done, time for you to leave. We don't want you turning into a pumpkin, after all."

I laughed and went to the kitchen where I opened the second bottle and returned to the living room. She had moved to the couch with both wine glasses. *Uh-oh again.*

I sat down and finished what was left at the bottom of my glass then poured from the new bottle. I handed my glass to her. "First dibs. Try it."

She took it, her fingers brushing mine. *Shit.* I ignored it the best I could. She sipped and nodded, handing my glass back. "This is really good, too. Another local?"

"Of course. I'm kinda weird like that." I placed the open bottle on the coffee table.

"I like weirdness. So why are you still a bachelor?" She had an unnerving way of getting right to something, usually without an obvious segue.

"Excuse me?"

She sat facing me, both knees drawn up to her chest, her right arm lying along the back of the couch.

"You say that to buy yourself time for your answers. I think I must make you nervous." She flashed another grin.

And then some. "You're right. I do. And yes, you do."

"How come?"

"Like you said earlier—sometimes you say things before you think about them." I hoped I didn't sound as stupid as I felt.

She laughed. "And it does get me into trouble. You're really polite about it, at least. And you tell me if it makes you uncomfortable. So did that last question make you uncomfortable? Or are you reading meanings into it?" She cocked an eyebrow and looked at me above the rim of her own wineglass, her lips resting against it. I really wanted to be that glass. And the realization almost knocked me off the couch.

"Yes and probably. The short answer is, I don't know why I'm still a bachelor. I guess I like it."

"Or you work too much."

"Yes. But I like the work that I do. And after Melissa, I was pretty messed up for a little bit."

"That wasn't really about you." Her tone was surprisingly gentle.

I waited for her to continue.

"That was about Melissa not telling you she needed you. And rather than deal with it, she got sucked into something else."

"I worked a lot during those months that Megan was in rehab, Sage. I wasn't available emotionally. I'm not excusing what Melissa did. But I was part of that relationship, too. For whatever reasons, neither of us really handled it the best way."

She handed me her empty glass. I filled it and handed it back.

"Megan told me about you right after we met," she said. "She told me about Melissa and about what happened with you. She said she was really messed up before you left and didn't know what precipitated you leaving until later." Sage took a sip of wine. "And she described you. She said you're laid-back and really, really nice. You're not judgmental and you're funny. Those are fairly simplistic, superficial characteristics." She watched me. "But sometimes the simplest things tell the most complex stories."

I quickly took a sip of wine as she continued talking.

"I went over one day and I noticed Megan had some photos out on her coffee table in the living room." She smiled. "I notice things like photos. Anyway, there was one of you with Melissa at Taos Pueblo. Megan had never told me what you look like but I knew it had to be you in that picture. I could see that it was you in your eyes before Megan told me it was you. She said it was her favorite photo of you and Melissa but she didn't like to have it out. She put that one away somewhere and I didn't ask about it."

I poured more wine into my glass. I knew I should get out of there right away. If I didn't want this to go any further, I needed to leave. But I couldn't move. My feet felt like they were glued to the floor.

She sat regarding me and I swear I saw fireflies dancing in her eyes. "And when I met you, you were everything Megan had said but so much more."

"Sage—"

"I'm not trying to weird you out. I'm just telling you my thoughts and feelings on the matter. So relax. I don't go where I'm not invited." She took another sip of her wine. "And stop fighting yourself."

I stared at her. "What do you mean?" I was painfully aware of the music, a slow and extremely sexy groove.

She sighed patiently but smiled. "Have you ever gone swimming in a river?"

Another one of her side trips. I followed. "Yeah. Quite a bit."

"Well, the Poudre River flows through this canyon in northern Colorado, outside Fort Collins. Along the way are some really great swimming holes after the spring run-off. There's this one place where you can jump into a pool from a cliff above. It's, like, twenty feet down and in June and July, that pool must be thirty feet deep."

I waited. I was getting used to Sage's digressions, since she always had a point to make.

"But in August, the drop is more like forty feet and you might really fuck yourself up if you jump." She held me in her gaze. I had nowhere to hide. "In other words, yes, sometimes it's not a good idea to jump off a cliff. But there are other times when it's the best possible thing you could do."

I lost the ability to breathe, think, and speak. All at once.

She leaned over and set her glass on the coffee table. "I'm sorry, K.C., but I think it's a good idea for you to go, even though we still have wine left. I know I said I'd like you to come over for dinner and we'd just talk and hang out." She stood. "But I can't. I can't be this close to you and not want more."

I couldn't form a coherent thought, let alone a sentence. I felt completely out of control but in a strangely good way. I tried to run through the list of why I shouldn't pursue anything with Sage, tried to remember all the bullet points I had made in that internal PowerPoint. And for the life of me, I didn't come up with any.

She offered an apologetic smile. "Thank you for coming to dinner."

I stood as well, on autopilot. "Thank *you* for cooking. That was a really, really nice thing to do." *Oh, God.* My internal hostess again. I wanted to kick myself for sounding so stupid. She bent to retrieve the wineglasses.

"Sage." She looked up at me and I was useless in her gaze. Helen of Troy had nothing on Sage of Sheridan. "Will you dance with me?" I blurted. *What am I doing? Where did that come from?*

"I'd love to." She set the wineglasses back down.

I reached out with my left hand and she took it with her right. I refused to think about how that felt because when I pulled her gently into my arms it was as if all the secrets of the universe were soon to be revealed. I carefully positioned my right hand against the small of her back and pulled her against my body. I held her right hand against my chest. She rested her left arm on my shoulder, her fingers centimeters from my neck. She was looking into my eyes as we moved and I felt like I had eaten live coals. *A force of nature. Hurricane Sage.*

We fit very well together. Too well. Like we were supposed to be doing this. I hugged her closer and she lowered her head to my shoulder so that her forehead brushed my neck. I released her hand then and slid my arm around her. I had no idea how I had the gumption to do that. She let her free hand drop to my waist and I felt the fingers of her other hand teasing my hair where it hit the back of my neck. Her fingertips brushed the skin at the nape of my neck and every nerve ending in my body screamed. I was surprised she didn't hear it. Or maybe she did because she tightened her hold around me with her right hand and shifted her head slightly. The heat of her breath brushed my neck and it sent crazy shivers down my spine.

She's got to have some kind of magical powers, I thought. *Because I have never felt anything like this. Ever. But this can't be a good idea. Can it?*

"What are you afraid of?" Her voice, low against my neck.

"I don't know."

Her right hand glided up my back, pressed gently on my shoulder blade. I swear heat emanated from her palm. Worse, her breasts were pressed against mine and the sensation was unbelievable. I was afraid I might hyperventilate and I hoped Sage couldn't tell.

"Is it me?" The warmth of her breath caressed my neck and ear. I don't know how I remained standing.

"Yes."

She was quiet for a bit, absorbing that, I supposed. "Explain," she finally said. She raised her head and I was forced to look again into her eyes, reflecting mysteries on the verge of unveiling.

"I don't know if I can."

"Try."

I nodded, still caught in her eyes. Somehow, the words came out. "I've never met anyone like you. I've never felt so completely beyond any kind of rational thought around anyone before this. And honestly, I don't know what to do with that."

The fingers of her left hand stroked the line of my jaw from my chin to my ear. She studied my innermost thoughts through my eyes, unnerving and arousing me at the same time. I wanted to run up the Sandias again, run down the backside, keep running to Texas, and sling a few bales of hay. But deeper than that, I wanted to stay. I watched a very gentle smile lift the corners of her mouth.

"You're afraid of possibility," she said softly. "You're a worst-case scenario type. So you think of reasons not to do something rather than just seeing how things play out." She moved against me as the music changed. I thought I saw a path in her eyes and I wanted to see where it led.

"I think you might be right." My voice sounded steadier than I felt.

"And maybe you're worried about a repeat of the past."

"That's a definite."

The fingers of her left hand stroked my neck along the line of my shirt collar. "It's not me, then." Her fingers lifted my chin, forcing me to look at her. "You're afraid of you."

"Maybe," I finally managed.

She was right and she knew it. She lowered her head to my shoulder again and hugged me closer. I felt her completely relax against me and when I adjusted the position of my head to look at her, her eyes were closed though that damn smile continued to light up her face. *This is either really bad or really good.* I tried to think, tried to access the logical part of my brain as we swayed to the music. *I should go.* But for the life of me, I couldn't think of a reason to do so. My feelings had completely overridden my analytical streak. I was helpless. And somewhere within, that was okay. She felt amazing against me. I thought about what Joe Montoya had said earlier that day. "A rare spirit." And here she was, dancing with me. Setting my soul ablaze.

I adjusted my arms and stroked her back with my hands. *Jesus. How am I able to do this?* I heard her exhale with a low "Mmm." I closed my eyes and carefully allowed my lips to graze her forehead before resting my cheek there, astonishing myself with my newfound bravery. She started playing with my hair again, her fingers burrowing deeper into it. She kept brushing the back of my neck with her thumb.

"Give me your list of cons," she said, lips against my neck.

Oh, please don't do that, I begged silently. *Not my neck. Please.* I was completely in her power. "Your age was," I admitted. "Though now that I know what it is, I guess that's not a factor anymore." *Did she just kiss my neck?* "A friend of Megan's — that struck me as kind of weird. But it doesn't anymore."

"And?"

"I live in Texas. You live here."

"The only reason geography becomes a problem is if you make it one."

Oh, she is definitely kissing my neck. I tried to focus.

"You're about all out of ideas, aren't you?" She was teasing the hell out of me.

The grin that eased across my face must've looked as goofy as I felt because she laughed. I shrugged sheepishly. "Yep. I am."

She stopped dancing then and gently pushed away. "I had a wonderful time tonight. I need you to leave now," she said, promises of secret places smoldering in her eyes.

Her statement took me aback. She saw it immediately. "I know what I want." She pressed her palm against my cheek and I leaned into it, feeling my heart race. "But I'm patient. When you're ready — when your heart reaches an agreement with your head and you sort things out — I'll show you how I feel about you." And she pulled my head down closer to hers. She kissed me gently on the cheek, let her lips linger on my skin. "Sleep well." She released me and gathered the wine glasses from the coffee table. How I remained standing was completely beyond me.

I ran a hand through my hair, trying desperately not to sound as bumbling as I felt. "Can I help you clean up?"

She looked up at me, still smiling. "No. Tonight, it's my job. Next time, I might put you to work." She allowed that damn devilish smile to spark across her face.

I smiled back at her. "Thanks, Sage. Dinner was amazing. And you—I don't have words for how I feel about you." I didn't have words for much of anything at the moment.

"I know," she said as she moved past me into the kitchen.

I followed her. "I'll see you later," I said softly. She set the glasses on the counter and I took her hands in mine, brought one to my lips. I kissed her knuckles before I could stop myself and before she could react and then I headed out the back door into the cool night air.

Chapter
Fourteen

I WOKE UP with thoughts of Sage and memories of how she felt against me. I had no uncertainty about how she felt about me. But where the hell would I go with this? I lived in freakin' Texas. She based in New Mexico. Did I really want a relationship? I liked being single. But I also enjoyed relationships and with someone like Sage, I'd probably learn a hell of a lot.

I started some coffee in the kitchen. *Besides, what's the worst that'd happen?* It might not work out and then we'd break up and I'd go through an emotional rollercoaster that sent me right through purgatory, hell, and the arctic reaches of my heart. Well, so what? I'd been there already and here I was, still living. Still making coffee. Still enjoying myself. I stared at the coffeemaker as it gurgled and spewed. The room filled with the smell of a really good blend. I got a cup down from the cabinet and poured and heard the back door of the main house open. Like an over-eager puppy, I went to the front door, hoping for a glimpse of Sage.

I got better than that. She was on her way down the steps carrying a plate of something. I unlocked the security door and opened it. "Good morning, stranger," I teased.

She grinned back. She was so damn cute. Baggy khaki shorts, sleeveless green tee, and Birkenstocks. Her hair was down. "Cinnamon rolls?"

"That guarantees you entrance here much faster than 'open sesame.'" I stepped aside. She paused in the doorway and brushed a kiss across my right cheek, surprising me and causing my nerve endings to scream again. "You want some coffee?" I asked, trying to fill the space between my reactions.

She went directly to the kitchen. "Love some." She set the rolls on the counter and went right to the cabinet where Megan kept her plates. She got two down, placed them on the counter, and opened the cabinet with the cups, picking one. She placed a roll on each plate and set them on the bistro table before she filled her cup.

"Stuff's in the fridge if you want to doctor it," I said as I took a seat at the table. I wanted to run my fingers through her tousled hair. She retrieved the half-and-half and splashed a bit into her cup. She replaced it, shut the fridge, and joined me at the table. I took a bite of the roll, which was still warm. "Oh, my God. Did you just make these?"

"Well, *duh*."

"So you use food to get to me." I took another bite. "Dammit, it's working."

She laughed and took a sip of her coffee. I watched her gaze fall to my chest, linger, then return to mine. I coughed.

"I'm jealous," she said, a lascivious glint in her eyes.

"Of what?"

"Your shirt."

I almost spit out my roll. She took a bite and chewed, angelic. "So what's on the agenda today?"

Besides lusting after you? Focus, dammit. "I guess I'm going to try to reach Cody and around five, and Chris is swinging by with some information. She's probably traced the number of the pay phone Megan was using when she last called and I may go to Edgewood to see where that is."

"Will she go with you?"

"I don't know. She might have stuff to do."

"If she doesn't go, I will." Sage's tone was nonnegotiable.

I decided not to argue and hoped fervently that Chris could go. Sage was watching me.

"You're worried about me," she said quietly. "That's sweet." She reached over and squeezed my hand before she stood up. She brought the rolls to the table and put another one on my plate. I shook my head, bewildered. She bit into another roll.

"Sage," I started.

"Mmm hmm?" She was chewing.

"Shit, never mind." I took a drink from my cup.

"What?" She was waiting.

"This is..." I hesitated. What was it? "Crazy but really cool." I sighed. "And I am so fucking articulate. Thanks for everything."

A strangely tender expression crossed her face. "The definition of crazy is that you keep doing the same thing over and over expecting the results to be different. In which case, I'm one of the sane things in your life." She popped the rest of the cinnamon roll into her mouth and washed it down with coffee. "I have to run errands and work in the lab today. As much as I'd like to spend it looking at you, I can't." She smiled and stood, picking up the now-empty plate she had brought from the house. "I'll see you later. Be careful, okay?"

I stood as well and followed her to the door. She turned and watched me. I wanted to kiss her. Desperately. I absolutely ached to kiss her. "All in good time," she said softly. "Have a good day."

I watched her as she crossed to the big house, climbed the steps, and opened the back door. She turned. "Keep the key. I'd like you to make yourself at home whenever you want." And with that, she went inside.

This is bad. No, it's good. Bad? Good? I ran a hand through my hair, still watching the big house. I needed to get my shit together. But somewhere deep, deep within, I knew I needed to follow Sage down that path I had seen in her eyes the night before. The thought wasn't ready to surface completely just yet. I pulled the door shut and locked it so I could take a shower. Cold.

THE VERIZON GUY at the counter patiently walked me through the activation process of my new "pay-as-you-go" cell phone, basically what people call a "disposable" cell phone. He then showed me how to set up my voice-mail box. I decided that Cody wasn't going to answer any calls right off. He was too careful. But I bet he checked his messages.

After I activated the thing, I pre-paid fifty minutes and saved the receipts for everything for Melissa's reimbursement. I stood outside next to my car, watching traffic on San Mateo, a north-south route that practically ran the length of the city, and Montgomery.

I dialed Cody's number and waited for his voice-mail. It beeped. I left a message, using a thick Texas accent. "Hi. My name's Sandy and I'm from Dallas. I just moved here to beanerville and I'm looking for NA, NSM, or anyone who can help me out along those lines. I talked to a guy at Eight Ball who said you're a good person to call. He had your card. Please call me back. Five-oh-five, four-four-two, nine-six-three-eight. SWP, brother." I hung up then. What I had indicated to Cody, besides my anti-Hispanic sentiment, was that I was looking for a National Alliance chapter or National Socialist Movement members. "SWP" was the acronym for "Supreme White Power." I didn't want him to think I was just parroting the sign-off on his voice-mail. Cody was probably suspicious about law enforcement trying to infiltrate the movement. I watched the traffic for a few more minutes. The only thing to do now was wait.

Or not. Maybe I'd pay another visit to Eight Ball. I headed south on San Mateo to Central and turned left. I pulled into the parking lot around eleven-thirty and like the last time, I parked far enough away from the shop that unless you were specifically looking for my car, you wouldn't notice it. I walked the hundred feet to the door and entered. The same woman was at the counter. She recognized me.

"Dragon's in the back."

"Is he busy?"

"Nope. But he probably will be later. Sundays can get kinda crazy."

"Thanks." I passed her and went to Dragon's studio. "Hey," I said, poking my head in.

He was sitting in his chair, reading the latest edition of *Wired*. He looked up. "Oh, hi. Your boys haven't been in since I saw you last. Sorry."

"I figured. Can you do temporary tats?"

His brow furrowed.

"I'm working on a different angle here. Could you ink me with something temporary?"

Comprehension dawned in his eyes. "You're trying to infiltrate?"

"Kinda sorta. If I bring a logo in, can you temp it?"

He grinned. "Sure. I've had success with Sharpies, actually. That'll get you through a couple of days before fading too much as long as you don't rub it in the shower too hard or sweat a lot."

"Just a couple of simple things. To be convincing. I'm trying to set up a meeting with Cody in the next couple of days. How are you at last-minute? Think you can squeeze me in?"

"Hell, if I can't, Eddie will. He's good with Sharpies, too. Either way, we've got you covered."

"That'd be great. I might show up later today or I might show up tomorrow or Tuesday."

"No problem." His eyes glittered behind his glasses. "This is like some undercover shit. Cool."

I laughed. "Well, hopefully there'll be a happy ending."

"No doubt. Take it easy."

"You, too." I left, waved at the goth girl as I exited the shop, and got back in my car. I'd go to Megan's and print out the logos for my temporary tattoos. Since I was hungry, I headed back toward Nob Hill to pop in at Kelly's, a local brewpub with college ambiance so I could grab a sandwich. I kept my new phone with me, though Cody didn't call.

Around two I headed back to Megan's, watching for any suspicious visitors. I parked around the corner again and hoofed it back to the house. I didn't see anyone lurking, so I went in and checked Megan's e-mail and mine again. Nothing of note. I then jetted over to a couple of white power sites and printed out some sample logos. I picked a couple of simple ones, to save time for the artists, and shut down the computer so I could go hang out at the big house, just in case someone wanted to come around. I happened to glance at the answering machine that Megan kept on the living room bookshelf next to her landline phone. The message light was blinking. That was odd. I was pretty sure it hadn't blinked the whole time I was here. I grabbed a pen and pad and pressed the playback button. A mechanical voice announced that the message was left that day at twelve thirty-two PM.

"K.C.? Are you there?"

Oh, my God. Megan.

"It's me. I didn't think you'd be staying with Melissa. I'm scared, K.C. I don't know how to get in touch with you. I'll try again later. I have to go."

The message ended. I saved it and immediately picked the machine up, trying to figure out how to record a new message. I found the appropriate button and pressed it.

"Hey, it's me. Try me at four-four-two, nine-six-three-eight." I made sure to speak the numbers slowly and as clearly as possible. If Megan really did try her home phone again, she'd be able to call my temporary local cell. Since she was probably using a pay phone, a local number was a better bet for her than my Texas cell phone number. I decided to stick around Megan's after all, in case she called again. It was two forty-five and Chris wouldn't be here for another couple of hours. I perched on the couch, feeling restless but not really able to do anything at the moment. I went to the fridge to get a bottle of iced tea. My new phone rang from the other room. Cody, most likely.

I waited for it to ring again before I answered in my Texas accent. "Hello?"

"Sandy? This is Cody. You called earlier." He had a nice voice for an asshole. Sort of mellow. Not too deep. Too bad I wanted to rip his heart out and feed it to crocodiles.

"Oh, hey, thanks for calling me back. I was hoping to hook up with someone."

"Who gave you my card?"

"A guy at Eight Ball. I met somebody at a meeting in Texas who said to go there when I got to Albuquerque."

"Eight Ball? Who?"

"He didn't say his name but he noticed one of my tats and we got to talking and he said I might be interested in ADR. He said you're in charge of that and that you could help me out."

"I think I might be able to. Can you meet?" He was clearly flattered that someone had said he was in charge.

Oh, this is almost too easy. "Definitely. I don't know this place very well yet, so I'll need directions."

"How about Tuesday at Eight Ball? You've already been there. It'll have to be around four because I have some stuff to take care of."

I hesitated but only for a second. "That would be great. Um, do you accept females in ADR? It sounds like something I'd be into."

"All white women who are willing and able to advance the cause are welcome," he said in a smooth sales-pitch tone.

"Great. There weren't many in my home groups and I was hoping to find more here."

"I think you'll like what you see."

"Sounds like it. I'm tired of talk. I want action. I don't want my kids in school with a buncha muds or queers." I hoped I sounded vehement.

"We're the group for you," he said. He sounded pleased. "Courage, sister. Until Tuesday." He hung up.

I flipped the phone shut. Well, I was getting a meeting with him but Eight Ball was a problem. I didn't want to start shit there with this prick and get the place into trouble or upset the truce between various groups. I'd see what Chris thought about the whole thing. If she couldn't make it, maybe Mark could. I tried Melissa's phone but her voice-mail picked up. I left her a brief message outlining some of the latest developments and told her I'd check back later. I hung up and paced around the house, feeling like I was spinning my wheels. I got Megan's phone book off the shelf and found the number for Eight Ball. I called and asked for Dragon.

"I'm sorry, he's with a client right now."

"Would you please have him give me a call? Tell him it's K.C. He's got my number. It's about what we discussed earlier today." I signed off and stared moodily at the computer screen. Megan's home phone rang. It didn't register at first and then I was lunging for it as it dawned on me who it might be.

"Hello?"

"K.C.?" Megan said, tentative.

"You okay?"

"Oh, my God. I'm so glad it's you. I'm really scared and I don't know what to do."

"Can you talk for a few minutes?"

"Yeah. But not too long."

"Are you at the same phone you were the other night?"

"Yes."

I thought I heard cars in the background. "Can you tell me what's going on?"

"He took my car keys, my house keys, my cell phone. He gives me a few dollars for an allowance. They're planning something big. I'm not sure what. There're guns here. Lots. I'm scared." She was almost whispering the last part.

"Are you staying with him somewhere?"

"Yes. A place in Edgewood. There's always somebody there. Four fifty-seven Partridge. I have to go. If I'm gone too long they send somebody after me."

"Okay, listen. I know where that pay phone is. I'm going to leave a phone number there for you tonight. Memorize it and do not repeat it to anyone. I'll write it where you can see it."

"I have to go. I'll try to call you back as soon as I can."

She hung up and I swore. *That bastard.* But I had an address for Chris to check now and we might be able to pull something off. I was ready to look up the address in MapQuest and just drive over there and drag Megan out of the house. It was all I could do not to. I gritted my teeth. If they were stockpiling weapons, I'd just endanger Megan doing that. And myself. And it might drive Cody and Ray deeper underground. That would make them more dangerous because they'd be even more careful. No, Megan had to stay put for now, as much as I hated that. "Fucking prick," I muttered, for more emphasis. Sage would definitely have to take a number to rip this guy's arms off.

"GOOD NEWS, *ESA*," Chris said when she arrived. "Megan's prints aren't anywhere on that envelope or the disk."

I wanted to cry with relief.

"We found Cody's prints and Watkins's prints. And yours, of course. But we're ruling you out." She smiled and smacked me lightly on the arm.

I let out an exaggerated sigh of relief. "Thank God. Homicide would look really bad in my tenure file." I went into the kitchen for an iced tea. I got one for Chris as well and handed it to her as I flopped down on the couch. She joined me.

"And here're Cody's police reports from Colorado." She pulled a few sheets of paper out of a folder on the coffee table and handed them to me. I started reading as she opened her bottle of tea.

Let's see. Vandalism of public property, East High School. Disturbing the peace in an incident that involved a screaming match with a girlfriend and her father in Aurora, a suburb of Denver. *Nice,* I thought sarcastically. Petty theft. Picked up at a Wal-Mart with a shirt stuffed down his pants. Probation violation.

"Is he still on probation in Colorado?" I asked as Chris took a swig.

She swallowed before answering. "Yeah. Funny, that. He has to check in once a month in Denver." Here Chris took another sip from the bottle of tea and then grinned at me. "Too bad I'm thorough. I called the guy up there and asked him if he was aware that Cody no longer lives in Colorado. No, he wasn't and how long had this been going on, he asked. I told him we had a paper trail on him that said he moved to New Mexico in 2003. Well, that got him off his chair.

He's going to make some calls."

"For real? You mean we can get him picked up?"

"Hell, yes. He's been violating probation."

"So how did he check in?"

"He'd drive up there once a month and show transcripts of courses he took through Metro State College. If his probation officer was a little more attentive, he would have checked those transcripts. It's all online coursework."

"Can you arrest him for probation violation?"

"Technically, yes, but I need to go through the right channels and coordinate with Colorado law enforcement. Now given that picture, there's reasonable suspicion that he's been involved in illegal activities *here*. Seriously illegal. Mark wants to bring him in for questioning, but if we get the arrest warrants from Colorado, we can hold him for that for sure and then bring this other matter up while he's in custody."

"Can we just go get her right now? We have the address."

She looked at me, pity in her dark eyes. "You know we can't do that. We need cause to go busting into private property."

"What if I convince Megan to leave the house and we meet her somewhere? Can we do that?"

Chris smiled gently. "Yes, we can. But if we don't have a back-up in place—if we don't make sure that Cody and whatever other *cucarachas* he runs with aren't rounded up and we don't have good information—Megan's not really safe. And they'll go deeper underground. You of all people know how this goes. Now that the police are involved, we have to go by the book."

I made a disgusted noise in my throat.

"*Amiga*, we've got to do this right. If they're stockpiling, this is a federal matter, too. We're going to get Megan out. But let's take out the nest, too."

I nodded slowly. "So what exactly are you going to do?"

"I'm supposed to hear from this guy in Colorado tomorrow or Tuesday and then I'll let you know." She sat looking at me for a moment. "Which brings us back to *your* wild-ass plan." She was clearly not happy. "Kase, there's a reason that civilians aren't cops. It's because they're not trained to deal with potentially violent fucks like this guy. What is meeting with him going to accomplish?"

She had a point. But I can be really stubborn. "Normally, I'm *so* on that page with you. But Megan wants to leave him and I want to get a sense of what he's up to. Megan said that they're planning something big. Maybe he'll tell me. I'm sure gonna try to get it out of him. Besides, you just said it. The more info we get, the better."

"How do you know Megan's not setting you up?" Chris's tone was hard and flat. I hadn't thought of that but my instincts immediately said no.

"I don't think so. She didn't even know I was in town until recently. And she's been checking in regularly with Melissa, which tells me that she wants to maintain her ties to the outside world. If she had totally bought in to this shit, she wouldn't even have bothered with Melissa."

"What time on Tuesday?"

"Four. At Eight Ball."

"I have to be in court."

Shit.

"But that's in the morning. I'll make it a point to take a trip up there."

I breathed easier. "You can't be with me when I meet him."

"I won't. And you won't know where I am, so you won't be able to blow my cover. But if anything weird goes down, I'll be all over his ass faster than flies on shit." Her expression hardened. "Don't look for me. Okay?" She was in cop mode.

"Okay." I felt very small.

She reached into the file and pulled out another sheet of paper. "And now Mr. Whistler-Watkins. He's the one who was poking around the other night. He's originally from Salt Lake City and our boy has a rap sheet there. Apparently, he beat up on his sisters and mom and the Mormon elders in the ward threw his ass out." Her eyes twinkled. She was out of scary cop mode. "I called and checked."

"Chris, I so love you. I would bear your children if you wanted them."

She laughed. "Well, you won't have to worry about that. How about you just buy me dinner?"

"For a week. No, for a month." I took a drink. "So what other kind of trouble did Mr. Watkins get himself into?"

Chris looked through the paperwork. "Ah. This one you'll like. Big gun. No permit. He was pulled over for speeding near Logan and the cop found it in the car. He ran the check and discovered that Ray really shouldn't have a gun, which opened all kinds of possibilities. Sure enough, Ray had a few more illegal weapons at his house. Rifles and pistols. There's mention of white supremacist literature on the premises. He was placed on probation and jumped ship. I've got calls in to Utah and I'm just waiting for the warrant to come through."

So Watkins aka Whistler had a history of fanaticism with the right. Growing up in a Mormon household may have helped that, since most Mormons—even more mainstream believers—are required to stockpile supplies in event of apocalypse. Beating up on family members was another matter. Watkins might be unstable in and of himself or he might have learned the behavior from Daddy.

Or both. Regardless, he was messed up and he had a history of violence.

"All right," I said. "We know where Megan is. We know she's scared. We know that to a certain extent, she's a prisoner. Or at least that's what it looks like. What's next?"

Chris pursed her lips, thinking. "Like I said, we don't know for sure that Megan's telling us the truth and we need cause to go in. Now, we do have reason to pick Sorrell up and as soon as I get the go-ahead from Colorado, we'll issue an arrest warrant and take care of that. Watkins is clearly flying under the radar, given his history and run-ins with law enforcement. Plus, he's using an assumed name here," she said. "So we should be able to finagle some help out of Utah law enforcement. After all, the guy bailed. So we can easily get a warrant for him. But he could be a tip of the iceberg and we might be able to use him to figure out how extensive the movement is here."

"Maybe he'll plea bargain." I reached for my bottle of tea.

"Maybe. But from what you've told me, this *gringo* believes in martyrdom. And they might have some serious weaponry at the Edgewood place."

I thought for a moment. "Megan said there's always somebody there. Which means Cody doesn't trust her as completely as he should a true convert. Maybe she knows something and that's why he's holding on to her. If he thought she was the real white deal, he wouldn't keep her under lock and key."

Chris shrugged. "Or he might just be your basic asshole abuser and this is part of how he deals with women."

"Possibly. But Cody's into the movement. And I think he does have a little bit of a power struggle going on with Whist—Watkins. So I think the movement comes first for him right now. And I think if he could, he'd dump her but he can't right now because she's seen too much. She told me on the phone that they were planning something big but she didn't know what."

Chris ran a hand through her hair and exhaled slowly. "I'm gonna go with your instincts on this, Kase. But we still need all our ducks in a row before we go busting in. Nobody wants another Waco or Freemen. You know that."

I nodded, feeling my heart sink. A stand-off meant days of tension and people might get hurt or even killed, like what happened in the Waco conflagration. There really was no easy answer, but Chris was right. For all its flaws, it was best to negotiate stand-offs as law enforcement did with the Freemen. I wished I had superpowers. I'd just swoop in, kick ass, and fly Megan to safety *and* round up all the bad guys. "Fuck," I groaned.

Chris reached over and squeezed my shoulder. "Hey. You've

done a hell of a job gathering information in a short period of time."

"I couldn't have done it without you."

"True," she said, teasing me, "but I wouldn't even have started if you hadn't shown up." She finished off her tea. "So," she said, throwing a knowing glance at me. "You wanna take a drive to Edgewood?"

Chapter
Fifteen

CHRIS PULLED INTO the parking lot of the Allsup's convenience store from which Megan was making her calls. She scored a parking slot at the front of the building. Two pay phones stood near the store's entrance, each nestled in a graffiti-riddled shell that provided only a modicum of privacy.

We got out of her car and I went to the pay phones while she went inside. I took a black Sharpie out of the right-hand cargo pocket of my shorts. The phone closest to the store's door was the one Megan had been using. The number on its face told me that. I picked up the receiver to make sure it was working. I pretended to be looking something up in the beat-up phone book that hung in a hard plastic case from the shelf underneath the phone. Pages were missing and people had written all sorts of things on it. And I wasn't the only one with a Sharpie to visit this phone. Names and numbers were scrawled on the metal shelf and the walls of the kiosk. I noticed cuss words and dirty cartoons as well. I chose the blank left corner of the metal shelf and and wrote the number of my temporary phone and then "Kase" underneath that, which was a nickname that Megan would recognize.

What I had written took up maybe an inch-and-a-half of space. I hoped Megan found it. I didn't want to write it bigger because it might draw the wrong kind of attention. I stepped back and looked around while I waited for Chris. Edgewood had a much different feel than Albuquerque. The first town drivers came to when they emerged from the Sandias on I-40 headed east, it was unincorporated though it had a population of probably ten thousand people. The vast New Mexico plains stretched farther east to the Oklahoma and Texas borders. So in addition to the mountains, Edgewood residents were treated to flat prairie interspersed with dry, rolling hills and a near-constant wind, especially in winter and spring.

A strange philosophy permeated it. Sort of a western "don't fuck with us and we won't fuck with you" kind of ethos. It's mostly white and pretty conservative. Billboards often showed up along this section of I-40 that advertised the evils of illegal immigration and the importance of Christianity in America. I'd checked one of the official Web sites for Edgewood, and it informed me that the town's official values include individual property rights and the spirit of independence. So it was no surprise that a small group of white supremacists was based here. Looking at the small houses across the street, it occurred to me that I should find out who owned 457 Partridge Lane. I'd check with the County Assessor in the morning.

I kept scanning the immediate surroundings. Megan had to be close, since she didn't have access to a car. The neighborhood seemed run-down, an attempt at suburbia that didn't work. Poor and working-class, the two not necessarily mutually exclusive. Some of the nearby homes appeared well-maintained, edged with clean, nicely mowed front yards. Others reminded me of Cody's aunt's place, sagging on their foundations and marred by broken siding, beat-up cars, and patchy grass. The Allsup's fronted a semi-busy street off the freeway. Given the way this neighborhood looked, I suspected these pay phones got a lot of traffic because I doubted that cell phones were part of the budgets of some of these households. The air hung tired and neglected over the store and its parking lot, infused with an undercurrent of distrust.

"Ready?" Chris appeared at my elbow holding two Diet Cokes.

I followed her back to her car, a silver Pontiac Vibe, kind of an odd vehicle for her because I saw her as a truck woman, though the Vibe was pretty sporty. I got in and buckled up. She slid into the driver's side. "How about we take a little side trip and see what we can see?"

"Okay." I tried to quell my anxiety.

She backed up and exited the parking lot, turning left onto the side street closest to the phones. At the first cross street she turned right and slowed down. "That's it," she muttered, gesturing with her chin at a small white house on the left. A four-foot chain link fence surrounded the front yard and a couple of pit bulls lolled in the sun, showing only mild interest in us as we passed. Nondescript brown drapes covered the front windows and the front porch was little more than a small stoop. I caught a glimpse of a darkened interior through the screen door, which had a huge tear in the lower left-hand corner. Probably from the dogs. Three different vehicles stood in the driveway, shoved in off the street. One was a beat-up older model white Ford pick-up, another was a brown Chevy Lumina that had a right rear tire so low I wondered if it had been driven recently. And the third was Megan's blue Toyota Camry.

"Shit," I breathed. It was all I could do not to jump out of the car and go racing in there to drag Megan out. Sensing that, Chris put a hand on my arm.

"No, Kase. Not yet." She accelerated slightly and didn't take another cruise past the house, probably because she didn't want to arouse suspicion.

"All right," she said. "Here's the deal. I'm going to contact Utah tomorrow and see what we can get going with Watkins. See if you can find out who owns that place. I'll also talk to Mark about Eight Ball on Tuesday. If I can get the okay to bring Sorrell in, we'll do so. But before we do that, we need to know exactly what he's up to. Bringing him in might endanger Megan because if he doesn't trust her, chances are his friends don't either, and she's the first one they'll blame if anything happens to their noble leader. So let's see how things go on Tuesday."

I stared out the windshield, watching the lengthening shadows as we approached the mountains for the twenty-five-minute drive to the other side.

"You okay?" Chris asked quietly after a while. She took my left hand with her right, stroked the back of it with her thumb.

I sat for a minute longer before responding. "It's different, when what you research becomes so personal."

Chris didn't respond and we sat in silence for a few minutes. Chris broke it first.

"On the plus side, she's alive and probably okay physically. And if you're right, she seems to want out." Chris squeezed my hand. "We'll get her out. And we'll bring these bastards down."

"But it won't change them. And there'll be more. There're always more."

"Each one we stop is one less to deal with in the future. Don't go down this road. You're doing a good thing."

"But what if she's not done with the movement? What if she's just done with Cody?"

She shrugged. "She makes her choices. If she goes back in, that's her decision. And you might have to let her go. I know that sounds harsh."

My stomach clenched. "You're right. It'd be enabling her if I chased after her again. I guess I'll just hope that when this is over, she'll be done with it."

She squeezed my hand again. "Hang in there, *esa*. We'll get through it."

"Thanks for bringing me out here. And thanks for everything."

She smiled at me. "You're my best friend in the world. There's no way I'd let you go through this alone."

I felt a huge lump in my throat. "I love you, Chris."

"I love you back, Kase. Speaking of which, how's Little Miss Hurricane?"

She was trying to distract me because she knew how I could get all caught up in my analyses and my wheels spin and I can hit a downward spiral. But I also knew she was interested in my personal life and wanted to make sure I was okay.

I sighed heavily. "A problem."

Chris shot me a quick look. "Oh, really? In a good way or a bad way?"

"It depends on your definition of those terms." I told her what had been happening with Sage and also about the night before.

"Holy shit," Chris breathed when I had finished. "I have *got* to meet this woman. Anybody who has K.C. Fontero acting like a head case is a person of interest."

"It's not funny." I groaned and looked out my window. "I mean, she's a bit younger than I am."

"Whatever. She's thirty. You're thirty-four. Like that's such a huge difference."

"I live in Texas."

"So?" Chris glanced in her rearview mirror and then passed a slow-moving RV. She eased back into the right-hand lane. "All right, listen. Let's suppose you hook up with her."

I shot her a glare.

"No, c'mon. Just suppose. If it's going to work, distance won't matter. And if it's not, it won't. What exactly are you looking for with her?"

"I don't even know. I don't think she's the summer fling type." I adjusted my seat slightly and leaned back.

"Doesn't sound like it. And if that's all you want, then you'd better not mess with her. It's dishonest. For both of you." Chris slowed down at a curve.

"After last night, there's no way I would even try a fling. She's too—I don't know. She's a force of nature. That's the best way to describe it."

Chris started laughing. "Whoa."

"I mean, she taps into you. It's like she reads runes on your soul or some crazy shit like that. Not in a bad way. She just *is*. She lays it on the line and I get the feeling if you didn't meet her halfway, she probably wouldn't give you the time of day."

Chris was quiet for a bit. "This sounds potentially serious."

"I don't know what it is. But she moves me. And it scares the living shit out of me."

"Hey." She reached over and took my hand again. "No. No, no, no. Do not close yourself off because you had a bad experience with Melissa. Yeah, she fucked up. And yeah, you went through hell with that and maybe screwed up a little, too. But one bad experience does not a lifetime make. If Sage is everything you think she is and if she sees what a fine woman you are, there is no reason in hell not to give it a shot."

"This from a woman who isn't the marrying kind," I muttered.

"Just because I'm not doesn't mean I diss it in others. You're the marrying kind, Kase. I know that about you. I know that some day, the part of our relationship that involves sex is going to end because you'll meet *her*, whoever she is."

I opened my mouth to say something but Chris overrode it.

"Don't worry. I've always known that. So have you. And there'll be times that I'll miss that with you — no doubt. I have enjoyed that aspect of our relationship and I don't know why I got so lucky to get that with you, but it's too precious to forget. I will always have the memories and I will always be your friend, no matter how we express it."

"Dammit, Chris, I'm gonna cry." I felt tears welling up in my eyes. I wiped with my free hand. She kissed my knuckles.

"My advice? See where this goes with Sage. I think she might be really good for you. And if it lasts, there you go. If it doesn't, it's not like you haven't been there before."

"I am so lucky to have you in my life."

"Damn right. And don't you forget it."

I started laughing as we crested the rise that would take us back into Albuquerque.

WE PULLED UP in front of Sage and Jeff's. Both their vehicles were parked along the curb. Mine was still around the corner. I had bought Chris dinner as promised at Monroe's, another Mexican and New Mexican restaurant near Old Town. Chris shut the engine off and we both got out.

"Hey!" Jeff was sitting on the front porch smoking a cigar with Rob and Mike from the barbecue.

"How was your trip?" I asked as we mounted the steps.

"It was good. Way hot. I can't believe I grew up there."

"Hey, guys," I said to Rob and Mike. "This is Chris, a friend of mine."

Introductions established, Jeff asked if we wanted a beer. "Plenty left over from the party," he said, laughing.

Sage suddenly appeared at the front door. My heart stuttered.

"Hi," she said, bubbly as usual. "You must be Chris. C'mon in."

Chris shot me a look as she followed me inside. Sage was already in the kitchen rummaging in the fridge. "Beer?"

"Not for me, thanks," Chris responded. "I have to work early tomorrow. But don't let that stop you."

Sage grinned and took two Rio Grandes out. "You need one," she said to me as she popped the top and handed it over. She was right.

"And yes, I'm Chris." She shook Sage's hand.

"How about iced tea, then?" Sage asked.

"Love some."

"Cool. You want to sit down? How about out back?"

"That would be great." Chris preceded me to the back porch, where Sage and Jeff kept a few chairs. She sank gratefully into one and I took one on her left. I could hear Sage singing softly in the kitchen as she got Chris's drink.

"She's hot," Chris said softly. "You'd be an idiot not to follow up."

I glared at her.

Sage emerged, carrying a beer for herself and a big glass of tea for Chris. She handed it to her and sat down on Chris's right.

"And how was your day?" she asked both of us.

I told her briefly what had happened, including the trip to Edgewood.

"Well, I feel better about you playing cop with the real thing right here," Sage teased, throwing a grin at Chris. "Although it's a tough job, keeping an eye on K.C."

"You have no idea," Chris said innocently before she took a sip of tea.

"Hey!" I retorted, pretending to be insulted. My Austin cell phone rang. The number in the ID looked vaguely familiar. Oh, yeah. Dragon. "Excuse me, y'all. It's my tattoo contact."

"Don't mind us," Chris teased. "Wouldn't want to interrupt something like *that*."

"Whatever," I snapped good-naturedly as I stood up and headed into the mud room. "Hello?"

"Hi, K.C.? It's Dragon."

"Yeah. Thanks for calling. Listen, that situation I was telling you about is a go for Tuesday. But I was wondering if we could meet somewhere besides the shop. I don't want anyone to spot me getting worked on who might have, you know, connections."

"Oh, yeah. Totally. I get off work tomorrow at eight. I don't mind if you come to my place. I'm over on Girard and Lead. Eighteen twelve Lead. You'll know the place 'cause of the mailbox. I've got materials there."

"Excellent. Thanks. I'll see you tomorrow." We signed off and I called Melissa. She picked up on the second ring. I had to tell her what was going on with Megan and I also knew that Chris would use the time to get a read on Sage.

"Hi. I'm sorry I haven't called back. I heard from my realtor and it's a go. They're accepting my offer. We'll be able to close in a couple of weeks, maybe the first week of August."

She sounded really excited. "Wow," I said, excited for her.

"That's awesome, Meliss'. How are you doing otherwise?"

"Hanging in. I started boxing some stuff up. It feels really good."

I took a deep breath. "And speaking of good, Megan's prints aren't anywhere on the envelope or the CD."

"Oh, my God." Relief flooded her voice.

"I think either Cody or Watkins hid it there and now both want it back. I don't know if they're on the outs or not, but they've both been by."

"I'm trying really hard not to think about the fact that Megan's with a potential murderer." Melissa's voice sounded distant.

I didn't know what to say to that, so instead I quickly briefed her on my trip to Edgewood with Chris.

"Did you see her?" Melissa's voice sounded hopeful but strained.

"No." I then explained what Chris had told me about bringing Cody in and how we needed to go slowly and make sure everything was in place. She wasn't happy about it.

"I know how this goes. I know how it is with info-gathering and police work. Doesn't mean I have to like it."

"I'm not exactly thrilled myself. But I'll keep you updated, okay?"

She was quiet for a second before speaking again. "I wish I knew how to thank you."

"Hey, what's important here is making sure Megan's okay and also making sure *you're* okay. How are things at home?"

"Same as they have been for six months. Don't worry."

"Okay. I'll call you tomorrow."

"Thanks."

"And congrats again. That's great news about the house." We said our goodbyes and I hung up. I rejoined Chris and Sage on the porch, sliding into my recently vacated chair. "Okay, you can stop talking about me. I'm back."

Chris laughed. "Suspicious, aren't you?" She stood. "I have to take off. I do have to be up early and I need to get a little sleep. Wouldn't want those bad guys to kick my ass." She set her empty glass down on the little end table that stood against the back wall. "I'll talk to you in a few, Kase." She turned to Sage. "It was an absolute pleasure meeting you. I hope I see you again."

"You will," Sage said, flashing a meaningful glance at me.

"Thanks, Chris," I said as she descended the back steps. "You're a goddess."

She waved.

"Bye," Sage yelled after her.

I took a swig of beer. Sage moved into Chris's seat. I felt heat race through my veins. "So what *did* you two talk about?"

She smiled at me and I could see it even in the gloom of early nightfall. "You, of course. She's very perceptive."

"I know. I hate that about her."

"Come on," Sage said softly. She reached out and pulled on my hand. "I'm taking you home."

I followed her to Megan's and she waited while I unlocked the doors. She followed me in and locked the security door behind us before she turned on the swamp cooler. I watched her. It felt perfectly natural, having her around like this. She pushed me gently toward the bedroom. "Go lie down."

I forgot how to swallow but I managed to put my beer bottle on the shelves in the living room. I followed her into the bedroom, where I stood by the bed, sparks shooting through my stomach. Sage went into the bathroom and emerged with a bottle of lotion "Take your shirt off." She motioned to the bed. "And lie down on your stomach."

"Excuse me?" This was definitely not how I envisioned things happening between us.

She arched an eyebrow, a teasing remonstration. "You've had a rough day. I'm going to work on your back. You need to let the bad energy out. Now take your shirt off." She turned away. "I'm not looking." Her tone was gentle.

I licked my lips nervously but did as she requested.

"Bra, too," she added, back still to me.

"Geez, Sage. If you wanted to get me naked—"

"Eventually. And I can guarantee you won't be arguing with me when I do."

I almost choked on my breath but I took my bra off and stretched out on the bed, stomach down. I felt her straddle my lower back, thighs on either side of me. *Oh, my God. Why? Why must she do this to me?* The skin of her thighs brushed my sides. I heard her squeeze lotion into the palm of her hand and then she rubbed her hands together a bit, warming it. Before I was emotionally prepared, her hands met my bare back and I almost lost my mind. She started by caressing the muscles along my spine and shoulder blades then she increased the pressure, stopping a few times to add more lotion. I was caught between utter relaxation and complete arousal.

"God, that feels so good," I muttered. I heard her laugh.

"Yes, it does." She moved her hands to my lower back and kneaded carefully. "Nice art," she added, in reference to the six-inch rendition of the jackal-headed Egyptian god Anubis on my shoulder blade. He was kneeling, holding a scale. On one side was the feather of truth and on the other a heart. If a heart was lighter than the feather, that person had lived a good life and passed into all the good things the afterlife offered. If not, well, the person got stuck in the Egyptian version of hell. In my tattoo, the heart and the feather were equally balanced. "I don't think you'll need to worry," Sage continued. "Your heart is much lighter than the feather."

"You think so?" I mumbled.

"I know so."

"Your hands are amazing," I continued, not sure where the words were coming from.

"I'll bet you say that to all the girls," she said, teasing.

"Nope." I sank into the heat beneath her palms and my attraction to her. Her fingers were on my shoulders now, rubbing. Her right hand worked on my neck and the muscles in her thighs contracted against my skin as she moved above me. "Sage, you're a problem for me."

"A problem, huh? How's that?" She squeezed more lotion into her palm. Her voice was calm.

"You make me feel things." God, I sounded and felt like I was drunk.

"And that's a problem because?" Her hands moved the length of my back.

"I don't know. Shit, I don't know anything anymore."

She stopped suddenly. "K.C., why do you look for problems in the middle of solutions?" She ran her fingers through my hair. "This is about me, Sage Crandall, wanting you, K.C. Fontero. And it's about you, K.C. Fontero, wanting me, Sage Crandall. Where is the problem in that?"

I felt her lean down, felt her lips briefly on the back of my neck. "Swimming against the current is a lot harder than swimming with it." Her hands were on my shoulders. "I'm not going anywhere. I want to know you better. So let me." She pushed gently off of me. "Get some sleep. I'll see you in the morning." I grabbed my tee and put it on when she went into the bathroom to return the lotion to its rightful spot. When she emerged, I blocked her way and slid my arms around her, pulling her against me.

"Thank you," I breathed against her ear. Her arms encircled my neck. "I'm trying," I said softly.

"I know," she whispered. I felt her lips on my cheek. "It's okay to jump." She hugged me closer then released me. I followed her to the door. She turned, traced my jawline with her fingertips. "I've waited this long for you. I don't mind waiting longer." She held my gaze then turned and headed for the main house. I watched her ascend the steps.

"Good night, Sage."

She paused. "Good night, K.C." And then she went inside.

I shut the door and locked it and sat on the couch in the dark, thinking. I had dated here and there since Melissa. Nothing really serious, though. I had missed what I had with Melissa, but I wasn't sure I missed Melissa during the years away. I missed the *idea* of her more. Life hadn't been easy with her or her demons. Which isn't to suggest that I wouldn't do it again. I had fallen in love with her and I had loved her until it was done. On some levels, I loved her still. I always would. She was part of me and my past, after all. But I didn't feel for her now what I felt for her then. And what I felt for her then was nothing like what I was beginning to feel for Sage. I was different now, after all. I smiled in the dark. And Sage was completely different, too. Like nothing I'd ever experienced. *Take the path,* I heard my inner voice say. *Take it.*

It might have been an epiphany I had that night. Or it might just have been the effects of a great massage from an astounding woman. All I know is that I let go of Melissa and I let go of the years in between and it was a physical sensation, like a shedding of skin. *Abuelita* told me once years ago that opportunities and hard work are sometimes two sides of the same coin. To get to one, you need the other. I stood up and went to the bedroom. I wanted to give Sage my undivided attention and I couldn't do that just yet. Not until this thing with Megan came to some sort of conclusion.

Chapter
Sixteen

I HATED THE tattoos Dragon inked on my inner forearms, no matter that they were temporary. A small clenched fist surrounded by a Roman wreath-looking thing marked my inner left forearm, signifying white power. On my inner right he drew the number 88. Fortunately, they weren't more than an inch in size. Small enough not to attract attention from people who didn't know anything about white supremacists but just large enough to draw attention from people who had those inclinations.

He wouldn't take money so I gave him a six-pack of expensive beer instead and he was very appreciative. I was glad I hadn't gotten tatted until Monday night because I'd have made a very different impression at the County Assessor's with them, which was where I spent a good two hours Monday afternoon. The woman was very friendly and called the office up in Santa Fe since Edgewood was in the lower southwest corner of that county. I learned that 457 Partridge Lane was owned by Geraldine Hastings, Raymond's grandmother.

After a search, I discovered that she didn't actually live there. Rather, she was in assisted living in Albuquerque. That might mean a variety of things. Maybe she didn't know about Raymond's activities. Or maybe she did and didn't care, as long as the mortgage got paid. Or maybe she didn't owe anything else on the house and Ray told her he'd take care of it for her. Whatever was going on, he clearly wasn't doing a very good job by her.

Sage was busy most of the day with an installation and then dinner with friends, so I didn't see her at all. She invited me but I had to head over to Dragon's at eight and didn't leave his place until around nine. I was tired when I got back to Megan's and I didn't feel like doing anything. I turned on the TV then wandered into the kitchen for an iced tea. I checked in with Melissa. She was packing. Hillary was out of town and Melissa suspected she was at her brother's house in Santa Fe. I told her I'd check in the next day.

I let Chris know about the status of the Edgewood house that afternoon after I finished with the County Assessor. She was still waiting to hear from Colorado and Utah. I felt cranky and out of sorts so I turned off the TV and put my workout clothes on. Maybe a run would help. This area was primarily residential so I wasn't too worried about traffic. I ran in the middle of the streets for about thirty minutes, working up a good sweat. Back at Megan's, I showered, mindful of the tattoos, and pulled on a pair of boxers and a muscle tee. The edge of my irritation dulled, I headed to bed.

I HAD JUST finished eating more fresh cinnamon rolls with Sage the next morning. She had left for campus and I was sighing happily as I sat on the couch in Megan's living room, staring at the ceiling. I liked that this *thing* between us felt untapped but familiar. I liked the flirtatious tension we shared. I liked how my stomach jerked and my heart lodged in my throat when she looked at me. And I especially liked how it felt to allow myself the luxury of being in the moment with someone who moved me deeply.

I was grinning like an idiot when my phone rang. I checked the ID. "Hey, Detective *Magnifica*."

I heard Chris smile. "*Hola, chica*. Still haven't heard. But I had a talk with Mark and we want you to wear a wire at your meeting today."

My coffee cup froze on its journey to my mouth. I set the cup on the coffee table and focused on the call. "Uh—"

"Don't worry. I'll come by at three. We're trying some new stuff out and I think you'll approve."

"I'm not sure I'm down with this."

Pause. "Here's my thinking. You're going to meet with Cody anyway. So why not help build a better case against him? I'll monitor you and get the recording."

"What if I can't get anything out of him?"

"Then we don't have anything. But this is an opportunity that'll help everybody in the long run."

I stared into my cup. This was way too much like real police work and it weirded me out a little. "Chris, I thought you said that there's a reason civilians don't do stuff like this."

"You're right. I did say that. But the reality is, you're going to meet with him anyway and I would much rather be able to hear exactly what goes on than wonder whether you're okay or not."

She had a point. Even though I was meeting him in a public place in broad daylight, he might try something. I doubted it, since if he did try to start anything, he'd be on the outs with the shop. Still, you never know. That didn't make me feel much better about a wire. "I don't want to fuck anything up."

"You won't. And I'll be really close. Don't worry about that. I will not let you do this without back-up." She waited. I didn't say anything. When she spoke again, she sounded contrite. "Look, I don't want you going into this blind. I want to make sure you're okay and I can better monitor that if you have a wire."

That was an even better point. I relaxed. "Okay. I'll be here."

"Excellent." She sounded as relieved as I felt. "See you then. Bye."

"Bye." I flipped my phone closed and set it carefully on the coffee table, like it was some kind of explosive device. I sat staring at it for a while. A wire. *Whoa.* This put a whole new imperative on how my conversation with Cody would go this afternoon. *God, I hope I'm up to this.*

TUESDAY MORNING CRAWLED into Tuesday afternoon. I kept myself busy. I checked Megan's e-mail, checked my e-mail, called Grandpa, then Mom, and then checked in with my tree-hugging sister Kara. Everything seemed fine with the family. Joely was busy in Germany but I had gotten an e-mail from her and already responded. I then cleaned the house, starting with the kitchen. By the time Chris arrived, the place looked like it was ready for *Better Homes and Gardens.*

"Damn. Sage is *definitely* a good influence on you."

"Oh, no. I'm doing this for *you.*" I air-kissed her and sashayed around the living room with my dust cloth.

She laughed and handed me a car key with an automatic door clicker thing. I looked at her, bemused. "You bought me a car? Sweet! I'll clean the house more often, honey!"

"Police work is trying to get into the twenty-first century. That's your wire."

"Shut *up.*" I held it up and looked at it. "You are so shitting me."

"Nope." She handed me a carabiner. "Clip it to this and then clip it onto your belt loop. The latest fashion accessory. Plus you'll look so butch. You'll have Sage falling all over you."

I blushed and Chris grinned. She brushed past me and got herself an iced tea out of the fridge.

"So it's wireless. What's its range?" I clipped the carabiner to my belt loop.

Chris stood in the doorway to the kitchen and leaned on the wall. "It's supposed to be up to fifteen hundred feet, but it works best closer. I like within a hundred feet, but five hundred's probably okay. We're doing trial runs on a few." She took a long drink from her bottle and screwed the cap back on. "Okay, let's do some testing. Stand outside and let me see how the reception is. Try not to move around too much and make it bump against you. You don't need to worry about talking loudly or doing anything differently. Come on." She picked my cell phone up from the coffee table and handed it to me.

I followed her outside and waited as she went back to the street. A minute dragged past. My phone rang.

"Okay, *esa*. Start talking after we hang up."

"Okee dokee. Bye." I ended the call and started rambling about anything and everything in my usual speaking voice. I wandered over to the chile and tomato plants and talked to them. Then I started giving a lecture on political movements. My phone rang again.

"Nice! Pretty clear. When I hang up, finish that political stuff. That was kind of interesting."

She hung up before my retort. When she returned, we went inside and caught up a bit. She still hadn't heard anything from Colorado so there would be no arresting Cody today. Oh, well. We finished our iced teas. She was watching me.

"Ready?"

I wiped my palms nervously on my shorts. "Thanks for coming with me."

"Wouldn't miss it. Remember, try not to think of it as a microphone. That's just where you hang your car key. And don't try to figure out where I am."

"Okay." I looked at her, a little freaked.

"Don't worry. If anything happens, I've got your back."

I knew she did. But I was still nervous. We went outside and I locked up. Once in my car, I rolled down the window. Chris leaned in.

"Kase, this is your stuff. You know how they operate. You know what they need to hear to get them to talk to you. If I didn't think you were up to this, we wouldn't be having this conversation."

"Thanks."

"*Suerte*. I'll see you in a few." She squeezed my shoulder and stepped back as I pulled away from the curb. I needed to get my thoughts in order and I hoped the brief drive would help.

I arrived at Eight Ball with about ten minutes to spare. This time I drove through the alley that separated the strip mall from the residential neighborhood that backed up against it. Yep. Parking in back. Five other cars and a truck were parked here as well. I decided to walk around to the front, which took an extra couple of minutes.

A different girl was at the counter and seven people were waiting today. Three *cholo*-looking guys, a couple of white girls, one hip-hop guy, and a skinhead girl. I noticed a small swastika on the fleshy part of her left hand between thumb and index finger. She wore black jeans, combat boots, and a plain white T-shirt. She studied me when I came in. I slid into a chair and started browsing through a tattoo magazine. When I glanced up, she was still looking at me. *Poor thing,* I thought. *Get out of the movement and get a girlfriend.*

A white man about my age emerged from the back, a gauze bandage on his neck. He was wearing gangster clothes and a do-rag. One of the *cholo* guys stood up when a tattoo artist I didn't recognize joined the guy at the counter, telling him how to take care of his new ink. I figured it was Eddie, and he fit my stereotype of tattoo artists. He was a big, solid dude with a goatee and a huge mop of hair. His arms were so covered with tattoos that it looked like he was wearing a decorated long-sleeved shirt. He, too, wore black jeans but over motorcycle boots. The *cholo* who had stood up followed him into the back.

I turned my attention back to the tattoo magazine when the skinhead girl addressed me. "WP?" she asked, regarding me coolly.

I answered in my easily acquired Texas accent. "Eighty-eight."

She nodded. "You waiting for Cody?"

That almost caught me off guard. "Who wants to know?"

A faint smile touched her lips. "Recon."

Of course. Cody wouldn't walk blind into a meeting like this. He was an asshole, but he wasn't necessarily dumb. "Outside?" I offered. I unconsciously touched the key fob hanging on my belt loop, hoping Chris could hear this. Skinhead Girl got up from her chair and I followed her out into the heat. We stood in the shade in front of the building. She leaned against the brick that separated Eight Ball from the closed dry cleaner next door, scanning the parking lot.

"The pigs up his butt?" I asked quietly, not really looking at her. I instead scanned the parking lot, too, trying to look a little nervous. It wasn't hard.

"Maybe. We've had some problems." She shrugged and pulled a battered pack of Marlboros from her front jeans pocket and pulled one out. She kept her lighter in the other front pocket. I watched as she lit up. *Way to preserve the white race.* She took a drag. I tried to look at her with disapproval. She either didn't notice or ignored it.

"What are you looking for?" she asked as she exhaled smoke.

"Action. I wanna build something. I left Texas because the heat was on my home groups and I was tired of the beer and bullshit from the guys." I shrugged and leaned carefully against the glass of Eight Ball's front window. "Some land came open in the hill country down there and I thought we should look into it, but everybody found some excuse not to. So I started looking here. I'm liking the East Mountains and land is cheaper, especially in the undeveloped parts." *Not bad. I'd almost believe that.*

"What was your home group?" She put the cigarette to her lips, studying me. Testing.

"National Alliance, Dallas chapter. Last year we decided to rename and joined with a skin chapter. It didn't work out. Male ego problems. They wanted to call us the Rangerskins but we thought the name White Nationalist Front fit our goals better. It got so bad that most of us quit." I slid my hands into the pockets of my shorts and gave her a hard stare. "I want a group that doesn't have any damn problems with leadership and is looking to plant some roots." I hoped that was convincing.

She blew a stream of smoke out the left side of her mouth. "Sounds like we might be something you're looking for." She watched me. Her flat, expressionless stare creeped me out. I'd seen a look like that once before, when I was backcountry camping in Colorado a couple years ago. I was just below timberline and came face to face with a mountain lion. The cat stared at me, assessing me. I met its eyes once and quickly dropped my gaze so as not to appear that I was challenging it. Apparently, it wasn't hungry enough to pursue a dinner out of me because it slid silently into a copse of ponderosa. I was shaking so bad after that I had to sit down for a minute. Skinhead Girl had that same kind of bored, predatory glint in her eyes.

She watched a car pull into a parking slot near the Eight Ball's entrance, maybe twenty feet away. She quickly dropped the cigarette onto the sidewalk and stubbed it out under her right boot. I almost swore aloud. Megan's car. *Bastard.* I hoped Chris was getting pictures of this. Cody shut off the engine and climbed out of the driver's seat. He was dressed in jeans, work boots, and a navy tee decorated with a white skull and crossbones on the front. He stood about six feet tall. Slim but athletic.

Another white guy got out of the passenger side. He was about Cody's height and age though a bit more solidly built. I pegged him as the muscle. He wore his black jeans tucked into knee-high Doc Martens. White power fists in red decorated the black surface of his boots and his laces were also red. He wore a white T-shirt and red suspenders. Classic skin, though he needed another haircut, because stubble peppered his scalp. He wore black Ray-Bans and I noticed a few tendrils of a spider-web tattoo over the collar of his tee. The double lightning bolt of Hitler's SS guards was etched on his inner right forearm.

Cody nodded once in greeting at Skinhead Girl as he approached. She nodded back. Then he looked at me. "Sandy?"

"Yessir," I said, standing up a little straighter. Skinhead Girl's eyes narrowed. The other guy lurked in the parking lot, about ten feet from us. Keeping watch, I guessed.

"I'm Cody," he said, extending his right hand. I shook it. I saw his eyes linger on my forearms and then move quickly to my chest. "Welcome to Spictown."

"Thanks," I said, trying to sound grateful. I faced him, hoping I wasn't moving too much and smacking the key fob on my belt loop around.

"When did you get here?"

"About three months ago. It's been kinda hard trying to tap in."

Two *cholo* guys came outside to smoke. Cody moved a little farther away but didn't say anything to them. "Well, ADR has a lot going on, and we need all the help we can get. We're just about ready to do some big stuff." He sounded excited.

"Yeah?" I tried to appear interested without being over-eager.

"Yep. But you've gotta understand we can't just let anybody in. Fuckin' FBI and shit. And local cops've been in our business, too."

"Sure. I hope you check me out. Otherwise, I'd worry about you and this group. We had problems in Texas and nobody took it seriously. Some cop managed to get in, which was part of the reason we split off into another group. She'll fill you in." I motioned with my head to Skinhead Girl.

He smiled then. "I have a good feeling about you," he said, trying his flattery with me. "So what specifically are you looking for?"

"Land." I figured I'd better not dance around the topic.

His eyebrows raised. "Oh?"

"Yeah. I want a piece of land where I can bring some of my family."

"You got a husband?"

"Not yet. But I'm working on it." I gave him a meaningful stare and felt a modicum of satisfaction to see a smile work its way across his face. *Yeah, you keep thinking you've got a shot with me.*

"That's the right attitude."

The guy behind him was standing with his arms across his chest. I couldn't see his eyes behind his shades. Skinhead Girl was glaring at me. I'd obviously stepped into her territory. I bulled ahead, trying to keep my edge. "Here's the deal. I saved up a lot of money in Texas and I've been looking at twenty acres in the East Mountains. It's three miles off the main road and I have enough for a down payment. I'd like to put my vision to work but to do that, I need help. So I'm looking for investors."

His expression hardened slightly. I guessed he had a problem with pushy women. Good thing Sage wasn't here.

I eased up just a bit. "Or, alternatively, I'd be an investor in a plan like that. I'm really tired of a bunch of whiny do-nothing poor excuses for the white race. I want to work with white men who aren't afraid to act like men and white women who aren't afraid to act like women. I'm ready for the next step." I carefully folded my arms over my chest and looked up at him expectantly.

He studied me. The guy in the shades shifted his weight again. Finally, another slow smile broke across Cody's face. "I think we've got what you're looking for. And I don't think you'll need to buy anything on your own. We've already got something going in the East Mountains. How are you with guns?"

"Please," I scoffed. "I'm from Texas. And yes, I have a permit."

Skinhead Girl glared at me again. She shot a glance at Ray-Bans.

Cody nodded slowly. "I think we can help you and I think there's a place for you with us. We've got a meeting coming up."

"Sounds good. When?"

"Thursday night in Edgewood." He looked at me questioningly.

"I know where that is."

"Okay. I'll text you the address and time on Thursday. The meeting will probably be in the evening—can you make evening meetings?"

"Yeah. I'm off work at three," I lied.

"Good. You're on your own finding your way. Think of it as your first test." He grinned like a wolf. "The way the meetings work is that we'll take care of general business first and then the inner circle meets." He looked apologetic then. "It takes a while to make it into the inner circle."

"Of course." I tried to look somber.

"Okay, thanks for your time. It'll be good to see you Thursday. Rahowa."

"Eighty-eight," I responded.

He turned and walked over to Megan's car. Skinhead Girl hadn't moved from her position near Eight Ball's front window. Ray-Bans followed Cody. I decided to try to pump Skinhead Girl for more information.

"So are you in the group?"

She treated me to one of her flat, vacant stares. "Inner circle," she said, with just a trace of venom. I wondered if maybe Cody had a few women on the side. The thought pissed me off even more.

"How long did it take?" I pushed her.

"Long enough."

Ray-Bans finished talking to Cody and strode back over toward Skinhead Girl. Cody started Megan's car and pulled out of the parking space. I watched as he turned right onto Central out of the parking lot. I acknowledged Ray-Bans as well. "Thanks. I'll see you around." I went back into Eight Ball, deciding that I'd leave through the back entrance. Maybe they'd think I was getting another tattoo or hitting the bathroom. Regardless, I had a very bad feeling about each of them as individuals. Together, the two of them were downright scary. I moseyed through the shop and went down the hall toward the bathroom. Someone was using it so I pretended to be waiting. I stepped away from the door back into the cramped hallway and glanced toward the front. From this angle, I could see a part of the front door. Skinhead Girl entered the shop. That was my cue. I headed down the hallway toward the scuffed and dented gray metal back door. Someone had spray-painted "Exit" in big, red puffy letters across it. Helpful.

I pushed the door open and took barely three steps before I realized Ray-Bans was waiting for me. I turned to go back inside but Skinhead Girl was already outside pushing the door shut behind her. *Fuck. Please, Chris, be listening.*

"Let's have a little talk," Ray-Bans said quietly in a soft, deep voice.

"About what?" I asked, trying to keep panic out of my own voice.

Skinhead Girl was suddenly in my face. She was roughly my height and might have looked like Sinead O'Connor except her lips were a tad on the thin side. "Think you're somethin' else, huh?" Her breath smelled faintly of stale cigarettes.

I kept my mouth shut. I didn't want to risk pissing her off more. I heard a soft click and knew without looking that Ray-Bans had opened a switchblade. *Oh, shit.*

"What exactly do you want?" I somehow managed to keep my tone level.

"Think you can just show up and start telling us how to run our business?" She pushed me. I took a couple of steps backward. "Think you and your fuckin' down payment and fuckin' attitude can just come in here and tell us what to do? We've worked long and hard preparing and you think you can just show us the way?"

Think fast. Shit. "Look, I'm sorry if that's what you think. As far as I'm concerned, we're all working for the same goals." I put my hands up in a "whoa, there," fashion.

"You're full of shit," she rasped. I was almost to the back door. If I could just get there—

Ray-Bans grabbed my tee just below the neckline in his left hand before I even knew he was reaching. He pulled me toward him and I felt a knife blade against my cheek. *Holy shit.* He leaned in really close. "I smell a liar," he said, in a tone that he might have used to say something like "I'll take a Coke." He put a tiny bit more pressure on the knife. I felt like I was going to wet myself.

"Hey, take it easy," I said, hoping I didn't sound as godawful scared as I was. "Put the knife away." *Chris, please!*

"Cody's too soft with the ladies," he continued. "His dick gets in the way of his brain sometimes."

"Fuck you," muttered Skinhead Girl. "Be glad Cody didn't hear you say that."

"Look—" I began when the back door flew open.

"Is there a problem here, assholes?" Chris's voice was low and icy.

Jesus God, thank you, thank you, thank you.

Ray-Bans quickly released me and lowered the knife. I watched him retract the blade. Chris brushed past me, a controlled anger in her stride. She stood glaring at him in full cop mode. She was only a few inches shorter. He wavered. She slowly and deliberately reached up and pulled his glasses off his face and tossed them casually onto the asphalt.

"I asked if there was a problem."

"No." Skinhead Girl picked up the conversation. She sounded a little unnerved. Maybe it was the SIG Chris packed on her right hip.

Chris slowly turned her cop glare to her and I felt a thrill to see Skinhead Girl visibly blanch. "I don't think I asked you." Her voice was hard and cold. I'd never heard that tone from Chris and it scared me almost as much as the confrontation with the two neo-Nazis. She reached and pulled her badge off her belt and in a motion that was so fast it almost didn't register with me she had grabbed Ray-Bans by the collar of *his* shirt and shoved her badge in his face. "You see this? Get a good look. Because the next time you see it, you'll be looking *up* after I beat the living shit out of you." She shoved him backward. He stumbled a couple of steps, almost losing his balance.

"I don't know what the fuck is going on here and I could give a shit about a buncha low-life Nazi morons." She glared at Ray-Bans then Skinhead Girl and me in turn. "And I might just be irritated enough to let the owners of this fine establishment—" she gestured at Eight Ball—"know about this little situation outside the shop. You think your white power *amigos*—" she put a deliberate emphasis on the Spanish word—"would appreciate that? You losers starting crap outside Eight Ball?"

Skinhead Girl licked her lips nervously. Ray-Bans said nothing.

"I didn't think so." She turned her attention to me. "*Is* there a problem here?" She was distant and formal.

"No. Just a little misunderstanding," I said, voice shaking. I felt Skinhead Girl watching me.

Chris's eyes narrowed slightly but she was too good a cop to blow anybody's cover. To Ray-Bans and Skinhead Girl she said, "Get your stupid fucking *gringo* asses out of here. And hope you don't run into me again."

We watched as Ray-Bans quickly retrieved his sunglasses from the parking lot and followed Skinhead Girl to one of the cars parked nearby, an older Ford Mustang. Skinhead Girl got into the driver's seat and Ray-Bans took the passenger side. She gunned the engine and peeled out, whipping toward the alley. I sagged, my knees trembling. Chris pulled me into her arms.

"Jesus Christ," she said quietly. "You okay?"

"Fine, now." I was shaking. She was Chris again and I held on to her like she was a tree in a flood.

"Fuck. Kase, I am so sorry."

"For what? It's broad daylight. I didn't think they'd pull shit like this." I held on a bit longer then stepped back. "Maybe a skinhead scare tactic or something."

"I—" She stopped.

"Chris, hey." I held her hand. "I know you would've gone medieval on their asses if it wouldn't blow my cover. Do I need to remind you that you're a cop and you know what you're doing? I'm okay. A little shaken up, but okay."

She was still really upset.

"They just wanted to scare me. And it worked. But I don't think they would've tried anything else because if Cody found out, they'd be in deep shit and if Dragon or Eddie found out, all of 'em would lose their tat privileges *and* their free meeting space. Besides, I might've scored points 'cause I didn't turn them in. Not that I wouldn't like you to have the chance to open a can on their asses."

Chris started chuckling. She gave my hand a final squeeze and released it. "Dammit, Fontero. If anything happened to you, my life would not be worth living."

"I know." I smiled sweetly at her but became serious immediately. "Thanks for watching my back."

She hugged me again. "For real. You okay?"

"Yeah." I still felt shaky, but I was all right.

"Good. C'mon. I'll buy you a beer."

"Damn right you will," I teased her. "Meet you at Kelly's."

"I'm there."

She followed me to my car and waited until I got in and started driving before she went back into Eight Ball.

Chapter
Seventeen

AN HOUR LATER I pulled up in front of Sage and Jeff's. My disposable cell phone rang. I checked the number. Megan's pay phone. "Hey. How are you doing?"

"God, K.C., I am so glad you're here. I don't know what to do. He took my car and I don't know where he went. I can't get away from him. There's never enough time and there's almost always somebody watching me. I thought about telling somebody at Allsup's, but they know I'm his girlfriend and they wouldn't get involved."

"Are you ready to leave, then?"

"Yes." No hesitation. "Oh, God, I'm so fucking stupid. I can't believe—"

"Time enough for that later," I interrupted gently. "How often can you use the phone?"

"Not very. Fortunately, Timmy—one of the guys who's always around—smokes and he's addicted to PlayStation. That's all most of them do all day. So he sends me out for cigarettes and other stuff and he times me. If I'm longer than twenty minutes, he sends someone looking."

That sleazy son of a bitch. I tried to keep my voice calm. Megan needed cool heads right now. "Okay, I heard there's an ADR meeting there on Thursday."

"Yeah. That's all they've been talking about because they're also planning something big. I think they want to blow something up but I don't know what."

So they do have Armageddon fever. "Do you know what time the meeting is?"

"Eight. Timmy was talking about it yesterday."

"Will Cody be there?"

"Oh, definitely. He lives there."

Really. How convenient.

"I have to go. My time's almost up."

"All right. Now I need you to hang in there. We're working on

some stuff on this end and we'll see how things go come Thursday.
Do not do anything out of the ordinary. Promise?"

"Promise. Bye."

She hung up and I fervently hoped she got off the phone in time.
Rage crept through my veins until I felt like I honestly could
dismember each and every one of them with my bare hands. I got out
of the car and headed down the walk to Megan's. Neither Sage nor
Jeff was around so I settled in and called Mark. I got his voice-mail
and I left a message, telling him to check with Chris about the wire
and about what happened today. I automatically left my cell phone
number though he probably had it.

I went into the kitchen and started working on getting the
temporary tats off my arms now that I wouldn't need them anymore.
Chris and Mark weren't going to let me attend any kind of meeting
with white supremacists. Especially not one where guns were being
stockpiled. They'd get a real cop to infiltrate. Plus, Megan said the
meeting was at the Partridge address. She might not be able to
pretend she didn't know me. And what if that asshole Watkins was
there? He could recognize me, if he was the guy who tried to break
in. This situation was on its way to being a stake-out and sting
operation. Still, I wanted to be involved somehow. Had to be. I owed
that to Megan. The Sharpie ink was proving stubborn and I scrubbed
harder. Anything to keep me from driving to Edgewood and ripping
Cody's head off. My Austin phone rang while I was engaged at the
sink. I turned off the water and checked the ID. Chris.

"What's up? Can't get enough of me, huh?" I teased.

She gave a little laugh. "I just heard from Cody's probation
officer in Colorado and they'd sure like him to return and do some
time for skipping town without permission. APD has the go-ahead to
pick him up. *And* I called my guy in Utah and we've got the go-ahead
to pick Watkins up, too. I'm thinking we should do it Thursday at the
meeting. Have us a nice, big, New Mexico-style rodeo."

"That is the best news *ever*."

"I have to make some calls to figure out how it's gonna go down.
And no, you are not going to the meeting. Not with these guys. Not
on my watch. So get those damn things off your arms."

I looked down at the faded Sharpie tats and sighed. "Gladly. But
I have to be there in some capacity."

"Kase—"

"I know these guys are dangerous. Today proved that. But
Megan's in a freaky place right now and I think it's best for me to be
there for her. I don't have to be anywhere near the action."

"Let me think about it."

She was noncommittal but I knew Chris would make a good
decision and she would have excellent reasons, whether I agreed

with her or not. I also knew that what happened today would not play in my favor for going with them on Thursday.

"Okay," I continued carefully. "I think you'll need more than a couple of cops on this because I think they're stockpiling. Megan said that she thinks they're planning to blow something up and if they have explosives on the premises..."

"Fuck. Okay, listen. Let me consult. I know Mark's had Edgewood under surveillance for a while now and I told him about the Partridge house. He knows the address. Let's see if he thinks it makes sense to go in now or if we need to hold off. I'll let you know. Right now, I need to go home and grab some sleep, which I think you need, too."

"Thanks."

"*Esa*," she began. She paused for a bit, then continued. "Promise me you won't do anything else between now and then." She didn't have her cop tone on, but she was serious and this was her way of telling me that what had happened bothered her and that she was really worried about me.

"No, ma'am," I said meekly. I trusted her judgment.

Her voice softened. "What happened today—I can't put you at risk like that again. It scares me. And if you go running off, you could also fuck it up for Megan. Do you understand where I'm coming from on this? Did what happen today tell you something about these assholes?"

"Yeah," I admitted.

"And if anything else happened to you, I would never forgive myself. I'm serious. I can't imagine not having you around. This is bad shit. Are you hearing me?"

"Yes." I felt like a kid getting lectured.

"And I feel so bad about even suggesting that you go ahead with that meeting. Fuck, I even asked you to wear a wire. What the fuck was I thinking? I am so sorry."

I heard pain in her voice. I tried to put her at ease. "We're both adults. I was going to meet with them regardless. Think how pissed off you'd be if I didn't tell you what I was doing and all that shit went down."

She didn't respond for so long I thought the call got dropped. "Chris?"

"I cannot even think about that. Oh, my God. Please, Kase. Don't do anything for a while. Let me get some stuff figured out and we'll see where we are on Thursday." I heard her swear in Spanish before she continued with me. "I mean it. Please don't do anything for a couple of days. Please?"

"I won't. For real." I meant it.

"Good. I would never—well, if my never forgiving myself isn't reason enough, Sage would kick my ass, too." I heard a chuckle in her voice and I relaxed. "I'm on my way home now. Are you okay there?"

"Yeah. Fine. Don't worry."

"Call if you need me." Her voice had softened.

"I will. Bye." The reference to Sage made me feel sort of goofy. I hung up and examined my forearms. Though faded, the temporary tats remained visible. Ick, especially after today. Back to work. I was scrubbing at my arms when I heard a gentle knock at the door.

"K.C., it's me."

"Door's open," I yelled above the water.

Sage appeared in the kitchen doorway. "I was coming over to see if you were hungry and here you are playing in the kitchen sink."

I turned to look at her and smiled. "Damn Sharpie."

She joined me at the sink. "I have some stuff at the house that'll take care of it. Come on. You'll rub your skin off this way and you might actually need it." She grinned and reached past me to turn the water off.

I followed her and locked the outer door. I was grateful she had come by. I really wanted not to think about today for a little bit.

She sat me down on the back porch and went inside for a minute. When she returned she had a box of baking soda, a bottle of rubbing alcohol, a bottle of what looked like lotion, and a soft damp rag. She pulled a chair up next to me and poured some of the baking soda on the rag. She set to work on my right arm, talking as she did so.

"River once decided to paint his arms. He must've been about eight. Well, he used this blue paint he found in the kitchen. He pried the can open and finger-painted stripes and polka dots all over his arms. Then he started in on his legs. And holy shit, it was all over his face. When my mom got home, she about had a cow right there. I mean, he was a fucking train wreck. He looked like what everybody says the Roswell aliens looked like."

Sage looked up at me, her eyes twinkling. "Anyway, my mom got out the baking soda and rubbed him down and most of it came off. He looked like the Pillsbury Doughboy for a minute. What didn't come off with that came off with alcohol." She began rubbing again. "He screeched like a dog in heat while she was doing it. It took a couple of weeks for it to wear out of his hair so I called him Smurf for months after that. When he gets on my nerves nowadays, I'll just say 'what's that, Smurf boy?' "

I laughed. She stopped rubbing and smiled up at me. I looked down. The "88" was gone.

"Looks like the baking soda's good enough. Let me see your other arm."

I held it out to her and she got to work again, gently rubbing. I watched her, trying to sort through the flood of emotions that threatened to overcome me. She set the rag down and squeezed some lotion onto her hands. She rubbed it into my forearms. *Oh, God.*

"All right, done. Thank God. That was bad ju-ju." She stood and gathered up her cleaning materials. "So, are you hungry?"

I could only look at her and everything I was feeling must've been naked on my face because she suddenly leaned down and pressed her lips to my cheek, just out of reach of my mouth. She let her lips linger there and I closed my eyes, leaning into her kiss. She pulled away and looked at me, searching. What she saw made her grin wickedly and her whole face light up. "I still have some of that wine left. You want to help me finish off the tikka masala?"

"Please." I followed her into the house. She had already put it on the stove and it was bubbling when we entered the kitchen. She checked on the rice then retrieved plates from the cabinet.

"Where's Jeff?"

"Oh, probably at Robin's. This chick he's been dating off and on. She's one of those flaky art girls. She's nice, but he might as well try dating wind." She pointed to the cabinet where I'd find wine glasses and I removed two. The bottle of wine stood on the counter and I divided what was left between the two of us, about a half-glass each.

"He just wants to get laid and Robin puts out," Sage said matter-of-factly. She carried the plates to the table and sat down. I joined her, noticing she had the candles burning again and some soft Latin American music playing in the background. "Not that there's anything wrong with that," she said, looking at me with a cryptic expression. "But I think he actually wants something longer-term and he keeps hoping Robin will meet him on that. I told him he's wasting his time but he keeps hoping. I thought maybe he'd hit it off with Megan, but no deal. She was too busy with Cody."

"Speaking of which." And I quickly filled her in on what had happened.

"Fucking hell." She stared at me when I was finished. "Do you realize what could have happened if Chris wasn't there?" She sounded upset.

"Yes. I do. And Chris was there and it worked out and I feel like shit about it and it freaked me out." I stared at my plate and we sat in silence for a bit until I felt Sage's hand on my forearm.

"I'm sorry. I didn't mean to sound like I was berating you. I just..." She squeezed my arm gently and I looked up at her. "The thought of something happening to you is not one I ever want to contemplate. So what'd you think of Mr. Assmuncher?" She took a bite, trying to alleviate the tension.

I smiled back at her. "I can see how he could appeal to some women. And I can see that he's very good at finding weaknesses. I think I confused him. His standard lines weren't working on me."

"Hell, I have something in common with him. My standard lines aren't working on you, either." She arched an eyebrow and reached for her glass.

I chuckled. "Not true. They work all too well."

"Oh, really?" She looked at me, somewhat surprised. "So you're the strong, silent type when someone comes on to you?"

"Depends on the context. Stick around and I guess you'll find out whether I'm silent. Or strong." I took a sip of my wine. "Or both." I preferred this line of conversation to the other.

Her eyes sparkled in the candlelight and another mysterious smile played at the corners of her mouth. "So did he believe that you're a supporter of the movement?" She jumped back to Cody.

"Maybe. Maybe not. His friends obviously didn't. Still, he invited me to the next meeting. He said he'd text me the time and address on Thursday."

"Is the meeting at that house in Edgewood?"

"Yes. Megan called again and she confirmed it."

Sage stopped chewing and watched my face.

"And Chris is making some contacts to see what the police can do. She'll probably have to bring the Sheriff's Department in on it since Edgewood is in Santa Fe County. She'll let me know."

"Does Megan want to leave?"

"She said she did. It sounded pretty genuine."

Sage chewed, swallowed. "Are you going to the meeting?"

I finished the thought silently. *"Even after today?"* I shook my head. "I'll pretend I am. But at this point, Chris will either set up an arrest of sorts and get Megan out of there or she might just arrange to get Megan out." I saw concern flash in Sage's eyes but she didn't say anything. "I don't know if Chris will let me go at all on Thursday. I think I should because I think Megan might need to have me there. But Chris has the final say."

"She's good people," Sage said, reaching for her wine. "She cares about you very, very much. And if she says you shouldn't go, it's because you shouldn't go."

We talked briefly about what the Desert Rats might be up to. I told Sage what Megan had said about them planning something that might involve blowing something up.

"Figures," she said with disgust. "But if assmuncher thinks he'll get anywhere with that fuck-head Timmy as back-up, he's more of a moron than I thought. And if he's having a male ego problem with Roy, then they're about as organized as a roughneck rodeo on meth."

I stared at her, then started laughing. "That is a hell of an image. You should write books or something. The stories of your life are amazing."

She looked down, embarrassed. "Everybody's life is amazing. Even the dumb-asses."

"And there's your title." I lifted my glass in a toast.

She laughed and clinked her glass with mine. We finished off the wine and I helped her clean up. We went back to the living room and took seats on the couch, this time with cups of decaf into which Sage had put cinnamon sticks. I told her stories about my childhood in northern Arizona. My folks had moved to Tucson about five years ago, which I didn't like as much as Flagstaff, but they were tired of the snow. Both had been college professors — my dad in religious studies and my mom in anthropology.

Sage exhaled sharply. "Fontero. Of course. I thought that name was familiar. I've read your folks' stuff." She grinned. "Your mom hyphenates, though. Fontero-Skidmore."

I looked at her, surprised. "Yeah. Sounds pretentious, doesn't it?" I had slipped my Birks off and I was leaning against one arm of the couch facing Sage, who was against the other end.

"I think it sounds authoritative. Your mom wrote that cool book on trancing among Mesoamerican indigenous cultures. I spent six months in Guatemala after I finished my BA and your mom's book opened all kinds of creative energies in me. I found one of those tribes and they let me photograph one of their ceremonies. I never published those images." She stopped suddenly, looked at me. "Hey, do you think your mom would like to see them?"

I held her gaze with mine, blown away. "Oh, my God. Sage, she would *love* that. You're completely — wow."

"I've read *your* stuff, too. When Megan told me your last name I looked you up online." She smiled, sheepish. "I had been up in Idaho and reading your stuff made that shit clearer to me though it's still pretty much a load of shit." She stopped. When Sage was animated and relaxed, she cussed a lot and incorporated all kinds of colorful expressions into her speech. I found it really endearing. "So why those guys?" she asked. "Why did you get so fascinated with them?"

The quintessential question. "I don't really know. Well, that's not entirely true. I guess I've always been interested in dark and scary things — the seedy underbelly of culture. And what taps into those seedy seams more than white supremacy? Of course, they would take offense to my describing them as 'seedy,' but from my perspective, spending so much time living on hate twists you inside somehow. It takes a lot of time and energy to carry a grudge like that." I reached for my coffee cup. "And living on hate, which requires you to spew and absorb negative crap all the time, eats you up. So your energy becomes seedy. Unhealthy and nasty."

"Why sociology?"

"I don't know. I just got interested in what drives people to join movements like that. And when I give lectures, I make it clear that it could happen to anyone in a weak moment. All you need is a charismatic leader who sees your weaknesses and exploits them and maybe a vague feeling that you're getting screwed somehow. And before you know it, you're in. I work to demystify it. It's a hard life, living on hate."

Sage watched me. "That sounds kind of like what might have happened to Megan."

I nodded and turned my attention to my coffee cup.

"Your trip here—it's been tough on you in some ways. Why did you come?"

Her question took me by surprise, and not just because Melissa had asked, too. "I had to. I know how these groups work and I know what sources to access to find them. I still have connections here. It made sense for me to come. Why have knowledge like that and not use it?" I sipped my coffee. "Melissa drove down in person to ask me. It took a lot for her to do that. She could have just called or e-mailed. But she came down."

"Then it was also time for you to deal with what happened between you two," Sage said matter-of-factly.

I lifted my right shoulder in a shrug. "It was time for both of us. And maybe I felt that I wasn't the support I should have been with Megan. Maybe this is my attempt to make that up to her. I don't know. I just knew I had to come."

She sipped her coffee. Once again, I wanted to be the beverage container. I watched her and cleared my throat nervously. "Um." I stopped, wondering if maybe I should reconsider what I wanted to ask her. No. I wanted to know. "What did you mean Sunday night when you said that you had waited this long for me, so waiting a bit longer wasn't a problem?"

A slow grin made her radiant again. "Some people get weird when I talk about certain things. But you asked." She set her coffee cup down. "I went over to Megan's about two weeks after she had moved in. She was kind of messed up—I mean, not using or anything, but just kind of down—about something. So I asked her what was going on and she said that she was feeling a little bummed about her sister's ex. It was in May, a few days before her birthday. And she said that her sister's ex always remembered her birthday. Even when she—Megan—was going through bad times." Sage picked up her cup and took a drink and I hid my wince behind my own cup. I hadn't sent Megan birthday cards since I left.

"Well," Sage continued, "I had seen Melissa a few times already because she helped Megan move in but Megan didn't mention anything one way or the other about Melissa's personal life until that day I went over. I asked her about the ex and Megan's face just lit up.

She said, 'K.C. is the coolest woman on the planet. And I can't stand that she's gone.' And she told me the whole story. How you'd met Melissa and that you two were friends for a couple of years before hooking up. How you were so nice to Megan and always willing to help her with anything though you maintained good boundaries. In some ways, I think Megan considered you more of a sister than Melissa because Melissa could get so caught up in Megan's shit. I think Megan knew that on some level."

Sage was right. She adjusted her position, stretched her legs out on the couch so that her feet were between mine. I felt her body heat even though she wasn't touching me.

"I asked what your name was and Megan said 'K.C. The letter K and the letter C. Her last name's Fontero. She researches white supremacist freaks.' " Sage frowned. "Famous last words, huh?" She took another drink from her cup. "And she said that it always surprised her, that that's what you worked on because you were the sweetest, most gentle person she'd ever met. She told me that day that I would have liked you but I already knew that. As soon as she said she was bummed about Melissa's ex, I had a feeling. So I asked her questions when you came up in conversation and the more Megan told me, the more I knew that sooner or later, I'd meet you."

She stopped then, watched me for a little bit. "Does that make you uncomfortable?"

Given my experience up to that point with Sage, it made perfect sense. "No. I think I'm honored."

She raised an eyebrow. "And the day I saw your picture, I knew it was a matter of time. I had a feeling about you. I really hope that doesn't freak you out. Sometimes I say stuff and people look at me like I have six heads. But I get these feelings and they're generally never wrong. In the meantime, I looked you up online. I didn't try to contact you because the universe provides when it's ready. And maybe I wasn't going to meet you this time around. I considered that possibility. But I let it go and decided that things would happen as they would." She leaned forward and put her cup down on the coffee table before continuing. "So last week, I taught a couple of workshops and checked some stuff in the lab. I'm putting together an exhibition — did I tell you that?"

I shook my head.

"Well, you're invited. Anyway, I had just gotten home and Jeff was here and we were hanging out and Melissa came by. She had always been cordial to us but it was a little weird that she came by. She stayed out on the porch and told us that Megan was taking some summer courses out of state and that someone would be staying in her place for a little bit and she just wanted us to know so we wouldn't freak out. She said that the person coming was really nice and very responsible and wouldn't cause any problems. Jeff asked for your name and Melissa said—I will never forget this as long as I live—'K.C. Fontero. K period C period. You'll like her.' "

She stopped for a moment. "I didn't sleep that night. I could not believe what was happening. I mean, I knew there was no guarantee you'd like me. I know there's no guarantee of anything. But you were coming. And I was going to meet you. After two years of wondering what it would be like to do just that." She flushed suddenly. "Shit, that does sound crazy, doesn't it? Fuck, no wonder people think I'm from another planet. I'm sorry. I don't want to freak you out." She pulled her legs back to her side of the couch and folded her arms over her chest.

My breath compressed in my chest. *Don't analyze,* my little voice told me. *Some things are not meant for that.* "Come here," I said quietly. She looked up at me, questions in her eyes. I shook my head and reached over with my left hand so I could gently grasp her right. I pulled her toward me. She allowed me to bring her into my arms and I held on to her for dear life. She wrapped her arms around me and stretched the full length of her body along mine. She rested her head on my shoulder and I stroked her hair, lost in the feel of her, lost in what she had said and the forces that had brought me to this night, this moment.

"I'm so glad you waited," I said softly against her forehead. "Now please, just let me hold you. Two years is a lot to catch up with." She clung to me and I stroked her back, her arms, her hair, her face. We didn't say anything. We didn't need to. And I don't know when, but at some point we fell asleep like that. The last thing I remember was the feel of her against me and the stirring of a dream between us.

Chapter
Eighteen

I WOKE UP stretched out on Sage's couch, a blanket over me. Sunlight filtered through the side windows and splashed across the floor. I smelled coffee and chile and I heard Sage softly singing in the kitchen. I looked at my watch. Ten o' clock. *Holy crap.* I sat up and on cue, Sage appeared in the doorway holding a cup of coffee. "Good morning," she said, her smile as bright as the daylight. She crossed the floor and put the cup on the coffee table in front of me. "Breakfast is almost ready."

I reached for the coffee as she returned to the kitchen, singing a Sarah McLachlan song. Sage had a nice voice. I sipped and sleep began to retreat from the heavy pockets in my head. I stood and made my way to the bathroom, still carrying my coffee. When I finally made it to the kitchen my cup was almost empty. Sage was at the stove, working on omelets. I set my cup on the counter and hugged her from behind. I kissed her neck. "Good morning to you," I murmured as I traced the contour of her right ear with my lips. I grinned when I heard her gasp and moved my hands to her shoulders. I kissed the back of her head. "I thought you had to be on campus."

"Not until twelve," she said softly. "Go sit down."

"Yes, ma'am." I refilled my coffee cup and went to the dining room. Breakfast was delicious. Green chile, avocado, and havarti cheese omelets. *Papas fritas* with a little bit of ranchera sauce on each rounded breakfast out.

"So what's your schedule today?" she asked.

"Nothing. Waiting. I've done about all I can do. Chris will let me know what's happening."

"If you want to do some laundry, go ahead. We've got stuff here or Megan has detergent and dryer stuff at her place. I think it's in her closet. She does her laundry here."

"Thanks. I'd appreciate that. You need me to do anything else around here? Anything need fixing?"

She laughed, a delightful sound in the morning. "No, but I'll keep you in mind. Jeff'll probably be around to shower. He has to work tonight and he might actually sleep a bit."

I finished eating about the same time Sage did. I stood first. "Go shower. I've got this." She looked up at me, an odd expression on her face that dissolved into a grin. I smiled back. "We sure do that a lot, don't we?" I said as I collected her plate.

"What?"

"Smile. But I just can't help myself around you." I retreated to the kitchen and began cleaning up. The faint sound of water running in the bathroom floated through my consciousness. Twenty minutes later, I finished the dishes and Sage appeared in the doorway, dressed in a cute pair of baggy shorts and a loose sleeveless shirt. She wore her sport sandals, as usual. Her hair was still damp and she smelled like lavender and cloves.

"Will I see you later?"

"Absolutely. And if I'm not around, call."

"Cool." She lowered her gaze, shy all of a sudden. "I'll see you. Have a good day." And then she zipped to the front door. I went onto the front porch with my coffee and waved as she pulled away from the curb. *It's like I've known her those two years she waited. Or longer.* I went inside, shut things down, and locked up so I could go shower my own self. And then I would definitely do some laundry.

I SPENT THE rest of the morning and part of the afternoon organizing around Megan's. I washed the blankets and sheets on the bed and then started in on my own clothes. By two, the first hint of a real monsoon rain had started rolling in. I watched clouds the color of slate gather to the west. A few of them darkened and by two-thirty rain fell over the western flatlands, where a few long-extinct volcanoes jutted from the desert floor. The Hopis believe that kachina spirits bring the rains every year. If the rains don't come, the spirits are angry or sad somehow about the way the earth has been treated.

The monsoon season here comes like clockwork. Clouds gather in the late July afternoons and then massive thunderstorms pound the city for a few minutes or maybe an hour. Then they stop and catch the next wind east, dissipating like thoughts. The streets steam briefly in the New Mexico sun as they dry, but I knew that by evening rush hour, most evidence of the afternoon's rain would be completely gone. An expectant stillness clung to the afternoon heat and I knew it was time. The kachinas had finally come.

By three the clouds rolled over the city, bringing cooler air. I smelled ozone and thought I heard a distant rumbling. A few raindrops splatted onto the hard-packed earth of the back yard and I decided to watch the impending storm from the front porch of the main house. I settled into a chair with a glass of iced tea just as my Austin phone rang. The number looked vaguely familiar. I answered.

"Hello?"

"Hi. It's Mark Aragon. I was just calling to let you know that I got your message and I've talked to Chris. She should be giving you a buzz shortly. Hey, I appreciate all the work you've done and I sure hope you think about maybe consulting with us in the future." When he stopped to breathe, I jumped in.

"Well, thanks. I'll think about it. I guess now I'll just wait to hear from Chris. I know you're busy."

"I mean it. Think about it. Keep my number. Later."

"Bye." I hung up. *Consulting, huh?* It sounded interesting, but I had things to do in Texas yet. I filed the thought away for later. The thunder rumbled closer, muttering ancient incantations around the edges of the clouds. I felt the city hold its breath and I dialed nine, which I had programmed as Sage's number. It rang four times and her voice-mail picked up.

"Welcome to my — that would be Sage Crandall's — phone! I wish I wasn't doing something either completely inane or utterly compelling because I would so take your call. Please leave a message and I'll get back to you ASAP. Oh, wait for the beep. Thanks."

Her voice seeped into my skull and ran its hands along the neurons in my brain. *God help me.* I dutifully waited for the beep. "Hey, Sage's phone. I really hope what you're doing is utterly compelling rather than completely inane. I'm watching the rain move in and I wish you were here to share the moment. I've been thinking about you and I really enjoy doing that. See you later. Hope your day's good. Oh, it's K.C. That would be K period C period. Bye."

I hung up just as the clouds opened overhead. Within minutes the streets ran like rivers and the gutter overflowed with water, lawn scraps, and bits of urban remains like paper cups and stray aluminum cans. Cars had to slow, wipers working furiously to no avail. The rain thickened to hail and I fervently hoped my Subaru could withstand a true monsoon hailstorm. It looked like a winter wonderland, an inch of pea-sized hail coating sidewalks and lawns. The breeze chilled and goosebumps erupted on my calves.

Jeff's little Honda CR-X pulled up in front. He got out and sprinted toward the porch. "Woo-wee! Damn!" He laughed when he got to the top of the steps. He was drenched. "Don't need that shower after all. What's up?"

"Nothing. Hope you don't mind — Sage said I could do laundry."

"No problem. Shit! I'll shower after all. I'm freezing!" He ran inside. Out here, the temperature dropped during a storm. My theory was that in humid climates, the moisture already in the air was warm when it rained, so it helped keep the temperature relatively stable even during a thunderstorm. Which is why the rain feels warm when it falls. Out here, because there was no layer of warm moisture in the air, the rain was cold when it fell and it stayed cold until it hit the pavement. The heat from the asphalt warmed it the longer it lingered, though, which is why some of the puddles felt warm when you splashed around in them. I sighed and leaned back in my chair, delighting in the smell and feel of the rain as it lessened somewhat. My phone rang again and I checked the ID.

"Hey, Detective Incredible," I answered.

"Hiya, *chica*. I love calling you. How are you?"

"Doing better. How are you?"

"Same. Okay, here's the deal. I'm going to swing by after work and tell you what I know. That'll be around seven or so."

"I'll buy you dinner."

"*Bueno*. I'm in the mood for Il Vicino."

"Sounds good."

"I have to go. Stay dry. Later."

"Bye."

I hung up and continued to watch the rain. Twenty minutes later, it stopped and the sun tore the clouds apart. I went in to check my laundry.

"WE'RE GOING TO bring Ray and Cody in." Chris finished up her side salad and took a drink from her beer. Il Vicino brewed its own. She was drinking their pale ale, called "Pigtail Blond."

I didn't say anything.

"And I think the best way to do that is, frankly, to use Megan to do it."

I clenched my jaw, then relaxed. "That might work for Cody but not necessarily for Ray."

"Hold on. Here's what we're thinking. You're Megan's lifeline. She has your number and she's been calling you every chance she's gotten since she found out you're in town. So the next chance she has, she'll most likely call you. The odds say that."

The server took Chris's empty plate.

"Tell Megan that she needs to plan to get to the Allsup's before the meeting starts. Preferably around seven forty-five. Chances are, they're going to start coming early and some will probably hang out there most of the day. She can offer to go buy cigarettes for the meeting. That's something these guys want their women to do, right? Run errands. Make coffee. Lie down." She grimaced.

"Okay." I didn't want to think about Megan lying down for Cody. Or any of those slimy bastards, for that matter.

"Mark will be there in his personal vehicle. It's a brown Chevy Blazer, older model. Give Megan that description. I gave him a picture of Megan."

I didn't like where this was going. "Chris, I need to be there with Mark. Megan might freak."

"You will be. But a couple of these guys know what you look like, and what if they might decide to follow Megan?" She stopped and looked at me, on the way to cop mode. "Understand, Kase. I did *not* want you to be part of this. Especially after what happened yesterday." She leaned forward. "But you're right. I think you need to be there for Megan. You have a rapport with her—one that I think is better than the one with Melissa. At least for right now. So you'll be on the floor or the seat in the back. If Mark needs you to check something, he'll tell you. Okay? But you will listen to him and you will not give him any shit or argue any damn logic with him. Do you understand?"

She was now completely in cop mode and entirely serious. The server showed up and delivered two individual pizzas. I ordered another beer. Chris looked at me. "The operation is in conjunction with the Santa Fe County Sheriff's Office. I'm not going to be the arresting officer, but because of my familiarity with this case, I'm coming along." She regarded me, still deadly serious. "And I want to make sure that nothing happens to you or Megan. If you start pulling anything stupid, I will personally drag you into my vehicle and handcuff you in the backseat."

I didn't make the crack about handcuffs that popped into my head. "What time should I hook up with Mark?"

"That depends on Cody. When he text-messages you the time and location, let Mark know so he can confirm with everyone or make sure that people know what the new time and location are. At this point, we're assuming it's at eight at the Partridge Lane address. Once you have that information, ask Mark what he thinks." She took a bite of her pizza and the server delivered my beer, the "Slow Down Brown."

"Okay. Can I call you if I need to?"

Her expression softened. "You can always call me. You just need to understand that these are real people who have real weapons. These aren't just Web sites and flyers. As much as you know about them, you haven't really dealt with them."

She was right. Yesterday proved that. I nodded and ate in silence. I didn't feel so self-assured anymore. "I'm not going to the meeting, right?"

"Right. We didn't think that was necessary or a good idea. Besides, we were worried that if you showed up and Megan saw you, she might not be able to hide her recognition. And Watkins might actually recognize you from the night he tried to get in."

I took a sip of my beer. The gravity of the situation was sinking in. "What about Melissa?"

"I called her. She'll be waiting for us. She felt, as I did, that it was better for you to be there than for her. She did ask what I thought, which was interesting." Chris shrugged and took a sip of beer. "I don't think she's ever liked me much." She flashed a quick smile at me.

"She's never been sure what to make of our friendship," I said. "She trusted both of us, though. On a funny note, Megan always liked you. She once told me if she wasn't straight, she'd totally go for you." I made kissing noises.

Chris laughed, slightly embarrassed. "Great. So it was either me or the neo-Nazi. Not sure that says much about Megan's tastes."

I laughed as well. "Hey, anybody who makes a play for you has *great* taste."

She took another swallow of beer and set her glass down. "Anyway," she said, "Megan will need to make an initial statement and hopefully, we'll be able to track a few more of these fuckheads down."

Something scary occurred to me. "She'll be in danger if she does that."

"And it's up to Megan, ultimately, what she wants to do. We've got Cody and Roy on other charges. But if Megan doesn't want to follow up with them or anybody else, there's nothing anyone can do. If she does, then she'll have to think about living on somebody's shit list and changing her identity."

"They don't teach you this crap in school," I muttered.

Chris reached across the table and squeezed my hand. "You did a good thing. Your work busted up a white supremacist group that might be planning something really dangerous. And you're getting Megan out. Hopefully she'll steer clear of groups like this in the future." She let go of my hand and went back to her pizza. "Just do everything Mark says and you and Megan will be fine."

"I'm sorry."

"For what?"

"This is scary and I don't want anybody to get hurt."

"Hey." She looked at me. "It's our job. You provided the information. That's *your* job. Now it's our turn. And we're good at what we do." She picked up another piece of her pizza. "So how's Sage?"

"Amazing."

Chris lifted an eyebrow. "Oh, really?"

"No, not like that. I don't know about that yet."

"Please. From the looks of her, you've got nothing to worry

about in the biblical sense."

"I'm not really thinking about that. I'm worried about when I have to leave."

Chris chewed her pizza. "I wouldn't worry about it," she said after she swallowed.

I looked at her like she had suddenly started dancing on the table.

"*Esa*, she is so into you that if you had to go to Antarctica for a year, she'd either follow you or tell you to call her when you got back. Provided, of course, that you reciprocated." Chris looked at me over the rim of her glass.

"What are you saying?"

She put her glass down. "So you're in Texas. So she's in New Mexico. So what? If you like each other, distance can be done. And because I love you, I'm telling you that you'd be quite possibly the biggest *pendeja* on the planet if you didn't give her a chance."

"Oh, so now you're my personal matchmaker?"

She grinned. "I'm your friend. And I want the best for you. Since I'm out of the question, given my own weirdnesses, she's the next best thing. And she gives off a really good vibe. Plus, I can tell she's into you. And not just in the biblical sense."

"And you got all that from twenty minutes of talking to her?" I grumbled.

"Nope. Two. The other eighteen were just icing." She took another bite. "She's special, Kase. And so are you. Take a chance." She smiled and I smiled back.

We spent the rest of the meal talking about other things and Chris dropped me off at Megan's around nine.

"I'll be in touch tomorrow. It'll be okay." She leaned over and pecked me on the cheek. "Try to get some sleep. Call if you need to."

I got out of her car. "Thanks. See you later."

I closed the door and pulled the house key out of my pocket, holding it up for her to see. She waved and pulled away from the curb. Jeff and Sage were out for the evening. Jeff was at work, I knew. He was a bartender at O'Neill's Irish pub, which was near Central and Washington, east of their house. Sage had called around six and told me she had an art opening to go to and I was welcome to come along. I told her I was having dinner with Chris to discuss the next day's events. Sage understood and she told me she'd see me later. She also said she loved my message. I told her that I might crash early but if she felt like it, to let herself in.

I unlocked the door to Megan's. Hopefully, Megan would call soon. Either tonight or tomorrow and everything would go smoothly and nothing fucked-up would happen. I turned on the TV for background and called Melissa. She was at home organizing and packing some things. Hillary was still out of town. Melissa sounded subdued.

"You okay?" I asked.

"Fine. I guess I'm a little overwhelmed. It's been so strange but good having you around. And this stuff that's going on tomorrow has me kind of scared."

"I know. It'll be fine. These are trained professionals, after all. And Megan will be home soon."

Melissa didn't say anything at first and I heard what sounded like packing tape ripping off its spool. "At first, I wanted to go with you and wait for her. But it occurred to me that maybe that wasn't the right thing to do. Our relationship hasn't been the best. I think that maybe you're the one she needs to see first. She always looked up to you, like a mentor. And you don't have the baggage with her that I do."

I was quiet for a bit. "I appreciate that."

"Don't think it doesn't bother me that I won't be there."

"I don't think that at all. Thanks for the confidence."

She didn't say anything for a moment. "It's strange. I mean, I'm glad she'll be coming home but on the other hand, she might not be done with them. It's almost like when she was using and she'd get out of rehab and I wasn't sure how to deal with her."

That was actually a really good analogy. "One day at a time. You know that." She laughed. It was a nice sound. "You seem more relaxed. Have you been sleeping?"

"It's funny, but since Hillary's been out of town, I have slept so well. It's like..." she paused, then continued. "I know there's nothing I can do to save her and for the first time in my life, I really do feel like it's not my issue. There's something really liberating about that. And it feels really good to be packing my things. I think I might go visit my grandma in a few weeks. Maybe Megan will come."

"That's a good idea. Get out of town. Clear your head. Works for me."

Silence.

"Joke, Meliss'. My bad attempt at levity."

"Oh, I know. I was just thinking when you said that—I was thinking that Grandma talks about the cycles of life and how it's a gift to get a chance to finish what was left unfinished. I'm not going to tell you it was easy to have you here the past few days. But I wouldn't trade it for anything."

Peace washed over me. I didn't know what to say so I muddled. "Me, either. I'm glad you came to Texas," I finished lamely.

"Same here. Okay. Well." She shifted gears, probably not wanting to pick at the past too much. "I'm going to do some more packing and I'll see you tomorrow."

"Yeah. Have a good night. Bye."

"Bye."

I hung up and went into Megan's bedroom, reached onto her shelf and took her jewelry box down. I took the photograph that showed Melissa and me at Taos Pueblo out of the box. It really was a nice image. I looked at it for a long time and it was as if I was looking through a window at a tableau. It was me, but I knew it was the past, and it was done. I could only see what was happening. I couldn't hear it, smell it, taste it, or even feel it. I had a boundary now between past and present and I knew it was safe to visit the former without influencing the latter. I put the box back in its place and left the photo on the shelf.

The rest of the evening I spent watching TV in an attempt to get my mind off the events scheduled for the next day. I then started in on mundane tasks, like rinsing out my running clothes, since I had managed a workout before Chris came by. I also checked e-mail. Marla, the department secretary, had e-mailed me. Nothing going on, no worries. She hoped my trip was going well and that I was discovering lots of interesting things. *You have no idea,* I thought as I e-mailed her back to say thanks for checking in. I logged into Megan's account. Just spam again. I cleared it out and then jetted around the Web, trying to get hits on Cody or Roy/Raymond. No. No surprise, really. They probably surfed under pseudonyms. Stuff like "Odin's guy" or "Aryan battle axe." Sage would probably say that Cody's Web name was "Aryan Assmuncher."

Ten-thirty. I shut the computer down and went into the bedroom where I put on a pair of boxers and a tee. I then headed into the bathroom and completed my nightly pre-bed rituals then shut the TV off as well as the lights. Maybe I'd do some reading. It'd been a while. I got comfortable in bed and started a Tony Hillerman novel I'd brought. Three chapters in I was sound asleep.

I woke up in the dark, momentarily confused. I was on my back with Sage curled around me, her head resting on my chest between my left shoulder and my neck, her left arm stretched across my waist. Her breathing was slow and deep. She still smelled of lavender and cloves. I hadn't heard her come in, but I vaguely remembered her kissing my cheek and taking the book out of my hands. I carefully shifted my position so that I could pull her closer with my left arm. She mumbled something and snuggled closer.

The way her body felt against mine intoxicated me, like the night before. *Christ, we haven't even kissed yet.* But here I was, wanting more, missing her when she wasn't around, fascinated by her spirit and the fire that drove her. And I had just met her, though I felt more comfortable with her in that short time than I had with Melissa after we had started seeing each other. I knew it wasn't really fair to compare the two situations. After all, Sage and Melissa were two entirely different women and I wasn't who I had been seven years ago, either. I had no idea where this thing with Sage would go. All I knew, lying there in the dark with her arm around me and her head on my shoulder, was that I didn't care and I wanted in on the ride. I carefully moved and kissed the top of her head, hoping she'd feel it in her sleep.

She stirred. "Hi," she said sleepily.

"Hey," I answered softly.

"You feel amazing." She tightened her grip around my waist.

"I was thinking the same thing about you." I brushed my lips against her forehead. "Thanks for stopping by."

She giggled and I felt her hand move from my waist to my face, where her fingers stroked my right cheek. My heartbeat sped up. She moved slightly and I felt her breath and lips on my neck. *Oh, no. Not the neck. Please. I can't be held responsible for my actions if she keeps this up.* My bones started to melt. Her kisses were delicate, fluttering like butterflies along the line of my jaw to my neck and then my clavicle. I would have exploded except anything that could have blown had melted.

"Oh, God," I moaned.

I heard a smile in her response. "Hmm. I like how that sounded." She nuzzled my left earlobe and I might have had an out-of-body experience. Every muscle, every nerve ending, even my hair was aflame. "There is nothing I would rather do than make love to you right now," she whispered. Her left leg wrapped around my left leg and I wanted to tear her tee and shorts off with my teeth. "But you have a lot of work to do tomorrow and you need to have your head in the right place. Not only for Megan, but for me."

I groaned. She was right. And I had already told myself that I wouldn't give Sage my undivided attention until the situation with Megan was resolved — whatever that might mean. "Why? Why, Sage? Why do you torture me so?" I sighed plaintively.

She laughed. "You think this is easy for me? Two years? And here I am, finally, in bed with you?"

"Point taken."

"I don't want anything hanging over us. Nothing to interrupt us. Does that make sense?" She stroked my face again and she propped herself up on her right elbow. I could just make out her features in the dark.

"Yes." I covered her hand with mine, leaned into her palm. "Being with you is worth whatever wait there is." I didn't know where those words came from, but they felt and sounded so right. She leaned over and kissed me on the forehead.

"You're every dream I've had come true," she said softly. "Now get some sleep. Before I change my mind."

I laughed and wrapped myself around her, delighting in the heat of her skin, the smell of her hair, the energy she exuded. I fell asleep with the sound of her breathing in my ear and her fingers buried in my hair.

I WAS UP first for a change, so I made coffee, letting Sage sleep a bit longer. Besides, I got to watch her as she did so. I poured her a cup, and doctored it the way she liked it before carrying it into the bedroom, where I sat on the edge of the bed closest to her. She was on her stomach, head turned toward me. I kissed her right cheek and she opened her eyes.

"Good morning," I said, running my fingers through her hair with my free hand.

She smiled. "Yes, it is." She sat up and I handed her the cup of coffee. She sipped it. "Mmm. Perfect."

"So what time are you going up to Santa Fe?"

She looked at me, surprised.

"I'd go if I could," I continued. "I would love to be at one of your openings."

She looked at me shyly. "You Googled me."

"I did. Sage, your work is amazing. I wish I could go tonight. All I can tell you is that I'll call you when things settle."

"That means so much to me. And I wish I could be there for you."

"Chris wouldn't let you. She's barely letting me."

She laughed. "True. I'll probably leave here around three. The opening's at seven. Lots of chi-chi people, I'm sure, but some of my benefactors will be there and I have to go make nice."

"Absolutely." I tousled her hair. "You want a bagel? Green chile from the Co-op."

"I'd love one."

"Toasted?"

"No. Just slightly warmed." She looked at me, coy.

I felt goofy. "Don't worry about making the bed. I'll take care of it." I lingered at the doorway. "It was really, really nice having you here." *I think I'd like to make it a habit.* How I was going to do that I didn't know. But she moved me. In deep, mysterious, delightful ways. I retreated to the kitchen and worked on bagels. We ate at the table, laughing and talking.

Sage glanced at the clock on the microwave and sighed heavily. "I have to go. I have to get stuff ready."

"I know."

She stood and took her plate to the sink.

"Take some coffee for the road."

She poured another cup and I followed her to the door. Another beautiful New Mexico morning. Probably another rainstorm later on, but right now, it was a perfect day. She slipped into her Birks, which she had left at the door and turned to look at me. She reached out to me, pulled my head toward hers. She kissed my cheek and whispered in my ear. "Please be careful. Come back to me."

I kissed her forehead. "Count on it. Now go knock some benefactor's socks off." I watched her as she returned to the big house and went inside.

NOTHING LIKE WAITING for the shit to hit the fan. There's an art to waiting and I'm sorry to say that I have no talent for it. I kept both cell phones on my person at all times and I checked them obsessively to make sure they were turned on, that nothing was wrong, that the ringers were working. I refrained from calling anyone for fear I'd miss a call. I was restless but I didn't work out because I might miss a call. So I paced. And then I paced right out the door and around the block. Then I paced up to Central and back again. In the heat, as the monsoons gathered to the west again.

Like clockwork, the storms swept the city at two. I had no idea how I hadn't gone insane during that time. I was sitting on the porch of the big house again, glowering into the sheets of rain when, at long last, my disposable phone rang. I checked the number. Megan, calling from the pay phone. With a mixture of relief and trepidation, I answered.

"Hey. Is the meeting still on tonight?"

"Yes. Eight o' clock. He's started making calls. There are already people coming by. Most should get there around seven."

"Okay, here's what I need you to do. As close to seven forty-five as you can, leave. Offer to make a cigarette run and let Cody know you want to get something to drink. Offer to buy whatever for anybody who wants anything. But get out of there as close to then as you can and get to the Allsup's. You'll see a brown Chevy Trailblazer. A guy named Mark will be with the vehicle. He's big, like a football player. Dark hair. He knows what you look like so just go up to him and tell him who you are. He'll get you out of there."

Hesitation. "How will I know for sure?"

"I'll be there. I'll be in the vehicle but Mark doesn't want me to be seen and possibly recognized. Please trust me on this. I'll probably be on the back seat."

"I'm scared."

"That's okay. Just get away from the house and go to the Allsup's. Everything will be fine. Trust me, okay?"

"Okay." She did sound really scared.

"Now go on doing what you do and just let them think you're going about your business. You can do this, Megan. I know you can. You're a tough cookie."

She took a deep breath. "Okay. Brown Chevy Trailblazer. Big guy, Mark. Okay. I have to go. Thanks, K.C. I'll — I'll see you later."

She hung up. I immediately called Mark. He answered and I told him what Megan had said.

"Okay. Why don't you swing by at four and we'll get things set up and move out."

"Yessir. See you in a few." I hung up and stared out into the rain. By three it had lessened to a slow drizzle. I wondered what you were supposed to wear on a police raid. I went back to Megan's and changed into jeans and a dark blue tee. I also put my hikers on, thinking that sandals might not be a good idea.

I called Melissa. She didn't answer so I left a message telling her Megan had called me and it looked like she'd be coming home soon, I was heading out to APD, and I'd let her know what was going on as soon as I had another chance. Then I called Sage.

"Hey!" she answered. "Did she call?"

"Yeah. It's a go. I'm getting ready to go to APD right now."

Pause. "Please be careful."

"I will. You be careful going to Santa Fe. And watch out for those benefactors. Some of 'em are out for blood."

She giggled. "I'll see you tonight."

"I don't know what time we'll be done at the station. And I have no idea what state of mind Megan will be in or what she'll want to do."

"I just need to know that you're okay."

"I'll call you at least once."

"Good. I'll talk to you later," she said, relieved.

"Good luck with the show."

"I think you need more of that than me. Be safe. Bye."

"Bye." I hung up and stood staring out the door for a while. The rain had stopped and the world was in the process of drying. I made sure I had my wallet and some cash and locked up. I pulled away from the curb at three forty-five.

Chapter
Nineteen

MARK DROVE CASUALLY around the Edgewood neighborhood, canvassing it. He passed 457 Partridge once but didn't go by again. He cruised the street that Allsup's fronted and then parked at a Kroger store about a mile away and checked in with various units. I was lying across the back seat on my stomach, feeling like I was wrapped in armor. Chris and Mark had strapped me into a Kevlar vest at the police station and I now had newfound respect for law enforcement. Not only were these things heavy, but they were restrictive. You definitely had to be agile and strong to move effectively in them.

When Mark was out of earshot, Chris teased me about leaving me face-up on Sage's front porch with the vest on, stranded like a turtle on its back. I retorted that maybe that wasn't a bad idea and she just grinned and punched me in the chest to test it. She and Mark were both wearing vests as well. Mark's was under his button-down denim shirt. Chris's was over her black tee.

Cody texted me at five-ten PM but he provided a completely different address. Mark decided that Cody didn't trust me, especially after what had happened on Tuesday. So he had a couple of cops go check it out. Sure enough, the address was an abandoned house, boarded up. "Probably wanted to jump you in," Mark said, referring to the gang practice of beating the shit out of new initiates for thirty seconds. It wouldn't surprise me. Different white supremacist groups had different initiation practices for hardcore members. Given Cody's reluctance to smack Sage around, I doubted he himself would try to jump me in, but Ray probably had no compunctions about that. And neither did Skinhead Girl or Ray-Bans. I was extremely glad that Megan had called earlier and confirmed that the meeting was at the Partridge address.

"How you doin' back there?" Mark broke my train of thought.

"Never better," I answered. "But based on this vest alone, I don't think police work is in my future."

He chuckled and continued to monitor the police band and then check in via walkie-talkie to local units who were getting into position. I lifted up a tad to check my watch. Seven-fifteen. I felt sort of queasy. I had both my cell phones in easy reach and I awkwardly checked them again to make sure everything was operational.

Edgewood local police were working in conjunction with the Santa Fe County Sheriff's Office. Technically, this wasn't APD's jurisdiction but Mark's expertise with the gang unit and the fact that he had been conferring with Edgewood law enforcement about 457 Partridge for a few weeks, as well as Chris's knowledge of the case, brought them in. The New Mexico branch of the FBI even had a couple of boots on the ground, given their interest in domestic terrorism.

I hadn't actually spoken to a rep yet, but Chris said that they'd want to talk to me soon enough about my work and how I had managed to track the Desert Rats. Gus Clayton was the guy who'd contact me. Given that Megan had just recently told me that the Rats might be stockpiling and planning a possible bombing, the FBI came a little late to the party, but I was glad they were here and that everybody seemed to be cooperating. Too many times in the past, it seemed that in situations like this, law enforcement agencies didn't coordinate effectively or stepped on each other's toes and it got ugly. I hoped that didn't happen here.

I listened to Mark's cop lingo as he answered radio calls and I heard Chris's voice, cool and confident. I rarely got to see her in action and it gave me a whole new appreciation for the work that she did. "All right, we're gonna move in," Mark said. He sounded completely relaxed, like he had just said "Well, I'm gonna grab a burger." I, on the other hand, felt like I needed to puke my guts out. I shut my eyes, forcing myself to breathe as deeply as I could with the vest on. I felt the Chevy pull onto the street. *Oh God, oh God, oh God.*

Mark slowed down a few minutes later and turned left into what I assumed was the Allsup's parking lot. One of the good things about this particular store was that it seemed to function as a hang-out for lots of different people. Consequently, Mark didn't draw any attention as he sat in his vehicle ostensibly looking at an atlas. "How are you doing?" he asked without turning around.

"Well, I haven't hurled yet, so I guess that's a good sign."

He grinned. "I don't care what Gutierrez says, Fontero. You're all right."

I smiled against the fabric of the back seat. I was compulsively checking my watch now. Seven forty-five. Night would fall soon. *Shit shit shit. Come on, Megan.* Seven-fifty. *Damn damn damn. Where are you, Megan?* A male voice I didn't know called Mark's handle on the radio. I turned my head and watched him reach for the handset. "Two-five-four. Go ahead."

"We are in position. It's a full house. Target is on her way, over."

"Roger that. Two-five-four out." He slid the handset back into its holder.

"Show time. Stay down until she's here."

"Yessir," I acknowledged. *She's on her way. Megan's on her way.* Anxiety wrapped around my esophagus like vines. Mark got out of the SUV and left the driver's side door open. If I twisted my neck slightly, I could see him through the corner of the windshield, standing on the driver's side leaning on the hood. I heard him say "Hi" to somebody and I heard Megan's voice.

"K.C.?"

I sat up and opened the door behind the driver's seat. "Hey!" I got out and pulled her into a hug. She started crying.

"I'm so sorry," she kept saying as she clung to me. She felt too thin.

"Get her in," Mark said firmly but gently.

"Okay," I took her hand. "Lie down on the back seat." I helped her in then climbed in with her. Rather than stay on the seat, she hunkered on the floor behind the front passenger seat. "Hang in there." I grabbed her hand again and Mark shut the door behind me. He had parked in the spot farthest to the left of the Allsup's entrance so no one could pull up on the driver's side. He remained outside, cell phone in his hand. To casual observers, it looked like he was waiting on a call. I was sitting up in the back seat. *She's here. Megan's here.* She was staring at me. She looked more like Melissa than the last time I had seen her, though the thinness of her face made her look even older than her sister. An expression reminiscent of her second round with rehab hovered in her eyes, that boundary between hope and hopelessness.

"Welcome back, kiddo." I leaned down and kissed her on the forehead.

Mark leaned in, bracing his hands on the driver's seat. "How long before they send someone to get you?"

"Any minute now," she answered. Fear clogged her voice. What the hell had those bastards done to her?

"Who?" Mark asked.

"Usually Timmy. He's short and kinda fat. Since there's a meeting tonight, Cody will be dealing with that. It'll be Timmy or this other guy they call Boots. He wears these huge black Doc Martens with white power fists painted on the outsides in red. They go up almost to his knees. He was there tonight, so he might come. He's pretty scary."

So Ray-Bans is Boots. A guy known only by the articles of clothing he wears.

Mark reached for his handset and spoke quietly into it.

Or they might not send anyone, I thought. *Because they just might be busy over there.* I watched Mark for a bit. I was still holding on to Megan's hand, clammy in mine. *Why are we still here? Why don't we leave?*

"Company," Mark said. And then the front passenger side window exploded in a thousand shards of glass. I automatically balled into a fetal position. I heard the sharp pops of gunfire and three thunks as bullets hit the passenger side. Mark returned fire. Without thinking, I hauled Megan to my side of the car and positioned myself over her. She screamed and started crying, trying to cover her head with her hands. Her fists smacked me in the face a couple of times. Mark shouted into his headset.

"Suspects are on the move! Requesting back-up!"

Shouts and screams erupted in the parking lot. Farther away a few gunshots popped in the air. *Holy shit!*

"Stay with the vehicle!" Mark ordered. He took off running across the parking lot toward Partridge.

"Stay down," I said to Megan, trying to keep my voice calm but Jesus Christ, we had just been shot at and I had no frame of reference for that. I climbed over her and got into the driver's seat. Mark had left the keys in the ignition. One of the Allsup's clerks was standing out in front of the store shouting into a cell phone. Two people by the gas pumps were doing the same thing. I glanced out the broken window and my blood froze. Four skinheads approached the Allsup's from across the side street that intersected with Partridge. Two had baseball bats and the other two carried chains. They looked really pissed off and they were headed right for the Chevy. How had Mark missed them?

"We're about to have some more company," I said, trying to sound pleasant as I turned the key. *Good fucking God.* The clerk saw them coming and he ran inside and pulled the door shut. I rammed the Chevy into reverse and slammed my foot onto the accelerator. The skins were running now and they caught up with the Blazer and banged on it while I tried to get the vehicle into drive. Megan moaned and whimpered in the back seat. The skins got in a few good swings with their makeshift weapons.

Metal slammed against metal as a chain thunked against the driver's side and a dull thud and the tinkle of glass breaking advertised that one had smashed the right headlight. I inappropriately thought that Mark was not going to be happy about the damage to his vehicle. Megan was screaming again but I focused on getting us out of there. I rammed the gearshift into drive and accelerated. The tires screeched. The skins dodged out of the way but chased me as I roared onto the side street that Chris and I had taken

just a few days earlier. I barely avoided another car whose driver
laid on the horn and swerved into the Allsup's parking lot. I thought
I heard sirens somewhere in the distance.

Megan started sobbing and mumbling.

"Sorry, kiddo. Hang in there." *How the hell am I sounding so calm?*
Gunfire split the evening air again and too late, I realized I was
headed toward it. I glanced in the rearview mirror. The skins from
Allsup's were still running after me. It would take a few seconds to
pull a U-turn. More than enough time for them to catch up. And they
might be armed with other weapons. As if he heard me, one carrying
a baseball bat pulled a pistol out of his pocket. I saw him take aim
and fire. He missed and my peripheral vision registered a flash of
movement to the right. Mark, standing on the corner of Partridge
and this street. He gesticulated wildly at me. I accelerated directly
for him.

"Hang on, Megan!" I slammed on the brakes and Mark pulled
the passenger door open and threw himself onto the seat, directly on
the glass. His left shoulder was stained with blood.

"Fuck!" I shouted.

"Go straight!" He grabbed the handset and started barking
instructions into it. More gunfire from the asshole behind me
actually hit this time. With a dull plunk, a bullet found the tailgate. I
slammed the accelerator hard and roared down the street, hoping no
kids or dogs ran out in front of me. Mark requested more back-up to
handle the four from Allsup's.

"Turn right," he commanded. I did and drove for a block. "Right
again."

He was bringing us in from the other side. I wasn't sure this was
a good idea until I saw several police cars with flashing lights lining
both sides of the street. Several police officers trained weapons
directly at us. Mark leaned out the window and shouted, holding his
badge up. I slammed on the brakes and he got out. I turned the
engine off and put my hands up. Megan was silent. I turned to check
on her. She was rocking back and forth on the floor of the SUV.

"It's okay," I said softly. "We're surrounded by cops. We're
okay."

Four officers approached the vehicle, guns down. "Everything
all right?" A guy with the Sheriff's Department addressed me.

"We're fine. Mark's hurt."

"We're getting him help."

"Can I get out and help her?" I asked, gesturing at Megan.

"Sure."

I left the keys in the ignition and exited the SUV. I opened the
passenger door behind the driver's seat and got in so that I could
pull Megan gently up onto the seat, making sure no glass was in her

way. I hugged her and she started crying again. I felt numb, watching officers milling around, guns and rifles ready. A half-block up and to my right, I knew, was the house. I heard more sirens and a couple of ambulances pulled up on Partridge. *Please, Chris. Be okay.*

An EMT approached. She was about my age though sort of matronly in her demeanor.

"How's it going? Detective Aragon wanted us to check you over."

I managed a smile. "Nothing physical. But we've got a lot of emotional." I carefully released Megan.

The EMT wore blue gloves. I held my arms out for her. She inspected them, then went around to Megan's side and opened the door. She gently looked Megan over. "I'm going to recommend a full medical examination tonight. I think we should take her in. Just to make sure."

Megan looked at me, scared.

"Can I come with her?"

"Absolutely," the EMT said.

I got out of the car just as a tall figure approached at a fast clip. In the near-dark I barely recognized Chris. Thank God.

"Are you okay?" She strode over to me, half cop, half best friend.

"Yeah. Megan's a little fucked up. They want to take her to the hospital for a complete check-up. I'm going with her."

Chris looked at the EMT. She pulled out her badge. "Can I take them?"

The EMT nodded when she saw Chris's ID. "Sure. I'll call ahead and make sure everything's set up. Take her to Presbyterian. Go in through the emergency entrance and ask at the desk for Jenny Holcomb. She's the PA I'm going to contact."

"Thanks." To me, Chris said, "Hold on a minute. I'm going to clear this with Mark. Eventually, you're both going to have to come in for statements. But let's do this exam first."

"Okay."

"I'll be right back. And we need to get out of here. The media's arriving. But don't move until I get back," she said in her cop voice.

"No, ma'am." I watched her stride back into the group of cops. Automatically, I reached for my phone and dialed Melissa's number.

"Hello? K.C.? What's going on?"

"Hey. We're okay. Megan's here. The EMT is checking her over but we're going to go to Presbyterian for a complete workover."

"Oh, my God. She's there? With you?"

"Yeah. You want to talk to her?"

"No, not yet. There's too much I want to say. I'll meet you at the hospital."

"Okay. We'll be going into the emergency room. Ask for Jenny Holcomb, the PA."

"Are you okay?"

"Yeah," I lied. "We'll see you at the hospital." We hung up. I returned to Mark's Blazer. Megan was leaning against the back seat, a strange little smile on her face. The EMT waved at me and walked toward the house. Chris returned about five minutes later. Without a word, Megan and I followed her, my arm around her shoulders. Chris had parked her car down the block behind us. Without a word, we all got in. Megan stretched out on the back seat, drained, like she'd been running on nothing but adrenaline for months and now she could relax. I buckled up, grunting because of the vest. Chris started the engine and did a U-turn. I had never been so scared in my life. All I could do right now was try to keep breathing.

Once on the freeway, Chris took my hand and held it all the way to the hospital.

Chapter
Twenty

I SAT STARING at the television in the corner of the waiting room on the fifth floor of Presbyterian Hospital. I didn't know what was showing because it wasn't registering. Three other people occupied various chairs in the same room, which was that basic modern hospital lobby-type. Bland blue industrial carpet. Generic art on the walls. Pastels. One of the other people was a Hispanic woman with someone who was probably her son and the other was an older white guy. Chris was in with Melissa, Megan, and a couple of detectives I didn't know.

Megan was, as I suspected, malnourished and dehydrated. The docs wanted to keep her overnight for observation while they IV'd fluids into her. Megan had relaxed considerably after we arrived at the hospital. I called Melissa and stayed with Megan until Melissa arrived, on the verge of relief and freak-out. I didn't tell her anything about what had happened. She already looked a bit high-strung. She hugged me for a long time before she went to sit with Megan.

I was tired and hungry but I didn't feel like eating. I kept hearing an explosion of glass and the thud of bullets into metal. I called Sage when we got to the hospital around nine-thirty and left a message, explaining what we were doing. I figured she'd be busy in Santa Fe until late. So I sat waiting for Melissa to dismiss me. Or Chris to do it. Or something. It occurred to me that my car was still at APD.

"Ms. Fontero?"

I looked up. One of the detectives. Trim, wiry, bespectacled. He was about my height and probably a few years older than I was. "I'm Troy Bedford, with APD. This is Gus Clayton, with the FBI." I looked at the second man. This pair was like Mutt and Jeff. Gus was tall and solid. He probably stood six-four. "We'd like to get a statement from you, if you're amenable." Troy was soft-spoken and I greatly appreciated his gentle demeanor.

"Sure." I stood and followed them into an unoccupied office left open for the occasion. I sat in yet another hospital chair and for the next thirty minutes told them what had happened in Edgewood. Troy asked a few questions that helped flesh out some details. When they finished, Gus gave me his card.

"Give me a call in the next couple of days so that I can get the big picture."

I knew what he meant. I took the card and put it in the front pocket of my jeans. "Can I see Megan?"

"Sure," Gus said. He had a surprisingly light voice for such a big man.

"Ms. Fontero—" Troy started.

I waited.

"You're not leaving town any time soon, are you?"

"As much as I would love to get in my car and drive back to Austin at this very second, no. I'll be here as long as necessary, I guess."

Troy smiled but he didn't look like he was sure whether I was joking or not. I left and headed down the hall to Megan's room. Chris was just exiting.

"Hey," she said. "How are you?"

"Fucked up."

She stood looking at me. "Where do you want to go tonight?"

"Honestly, Chris, I don't know."

"I have to debrief so I'll be tied up for a bit at the station."

"My car's there," I said.

"It'll be fine." She gave me a once-over. "I'll take you back to Megan's. At least Sage and Jeff are right there if you need anything."

I wasn't sure what she said was getting through. I wanted to cry. Or yell. Maybe kick something. I buried all of it. "Let me check on Megan and Melissa."

"I'll be right here." Chris squeezed my arm as I brushed past her.

Melissa looked up at me when I came in. Megan was lying in bed, a drip attached to her left arm. She looked much better than earlier but her eyes...I had a friend who was a Vietnam War veteran. He'd get that same expression sometimes. Wary and old beyond his years. Melissa stood up and pulled me into another long hug.

"I never expected you to pull a SWAT imitation," she said, sounding worried, angry, and relieved all at the same time. She started to cry, not for the first time that night.

"Me, either. And I will *never* do that shit ever again. Count on it." I held on to her.

"Thank you," Melissa said through her tears.

"K.C." Megan's voice sounded weak.

Melissa released me and I leaned over the bed. I took Megan's proffered right hand. "You look much better. Please tell me you'll eat from now on."

She laughed. The effort seemed to wear her out. "I want to talk to you later, okay?"

"I'll be around. I can't leave 'til they're done with me. Just let me know when you're ready."

"You need some sleep," Melissa said softly. "Do−"

"Nah, I'm okay. Chris is going to take me back to Megan's. I'll deal with my car later. Sage and Jeff are right there. What about you?"

"I'm staying here."

"Good. If you need anything, call me."

"Chris gave me her number, too. She seems to think you might be kind of tired for the next couple of days."

At first I was confused until I remembered what she'd told me in the past about post-adrenaline recovery. "She's probably right. I'll catch up with you tomorrow, probably." I leaned down and kissed Megan on the forehead. "It is *so* good to have you back."

A tear slid down her cheek.

I hugged Melissa again and left. Chris stood out in the hall talking to Troy and Gus. "All right," she said to me. "Let's go." She cut her conversation short with them and walked me to the elevator. We didn't talk on the way down and I followed her silently out of the hospital to the parking lot. She unlocked and opened the passenger door of her car for me. I got in and buckled up, on autopilot as Chris settled herself in the driver's seat, buckled up, and turned the key.

"Chris, I am majorly fucked up," I announced.

She turned the car off and gave me her full attention.

"That was beyond scary. I feel pissed off, scared, freaked-out− shit, I don't know what I feel."

She kept quiet, letting me vent.

"I mean, what the fuck? Those assholes were fucking *shooting* at us! What the hell? What is *wrong* with people?"

"They got lost somewhere along the way," she said quietly. She reached over and took my hand. "You were really brave today. You scared the living shit out of me, but given what happened, you did what you had to do."

"I wish I had just gotten on the main road and kept going."

"But then Mark might've been worse off than he was. Nobody predicted that shit at Allsup's and we sure as hell didn't think there'd be so many of them at that meeting. That's police work for you. You plan and plan but there could be contingencies."

"I'm sorry, Chris. I am so sorry for all of this. You're right. The reality is a lot different than the research. I will never put you in a position like that again."

She unbuckled and leaned over to awkwardly hug me. "Hey, it

all worked out. Mark's okay. It was a cut from flying glass. Nobody else got seriously hurt, with the exception of a couple of the bad guys." She leaned back.

"Speaking of which," I said softly.

"Later. I'll tell you what's going on later. But we did get Cody and Watkins is on the run. Right now, you need to get some sleep." She buckled up again and started the engine. By the time she pulled up in front of Sage and Jeff's, we were bantering back and forth about who kicked the most ass. I felt a little better as I got out, partially because venting with Chris had helped and also because we had stopped at a Wendy's and Chris had bought me a burger. I noticed that neither Sage nor Jeff was home, as their cars were both gone though the porch light was on.

Chris noticed, too. "You all right until they get back?"

I knew Chris felt badly about not being able to stay with me. I tried to put her at ease. "Fine. Sage gave me a key to the big house. I think I'll just hang out there 'til one of them gets home." I wasn't worried about Ray coming around again. The heat was on his ass, and he wouldn't risk it.

"Okay." She held my gaze for a long moment. "I'll check in tomorrow. There's a lot of shit that needs to get sorted out, so I hope you can stick around. *Te amo, esa.*"

"I'm planning on it. And I love you back, Detective Wonder Woman." I showed Chris that I had my keys and waved. Still, she waited until I was at the front door of the big house and had opened it. She then pulled away from the curb. I went in and stood looking around, not really sure what I felt like doing.

My phone rang, surprising me. I pulled it off the waistband of my jeans and looked at it. Sage.

"Hi," I answered. "How'd it go?"

"Where are you?" She sounded concerned.

"Actually, I'm at your house. Jeff's not here and I really didn't want to be alone at Megan's. I hope that's okay."

"That is *more* than okay," she said, relief in her voice. "I'm just leaving Santa Fe. I'll be there in about an hour."

"Well, I'm not going anywhere."

"Good. I'll see you in a few. Bye." She hung up and I exhaled, feeling really drained. If I could just lie down for a couple of months and not think about anything, my life would be complete. I locked the front door and flipped the swamp cooler on before heading left through the archway into the hallway that connected the bedrooms. Jeff's was to the left and Sage's to the right. The bathroom was located between the two rooms. A spacious linen closet marked the wall between the bathroom and Jeff's room. I had never actually been in Sage's room. Maybe I should just sleep on the couch until she got home. No, I really wanted to be in a bed.

The door to her bedroom stood half-open. I entered and immediately thought, *oh, my God. Sage is really a gay man.* Her furniture looked like Ikea or some other Swedish designer who wore elegant black trousers and tailored shirts. Everything in her room broadcast smooth, clean lines with hints of industrial post-modern, expressed through things like the handles on her armoire and the wavy vertical bars of her bed's headboard and footboard. The bed itself was positioned at an angle in the corner of the room, opposite the door. A tan comforter, accented with blue and gold medallion-looking designs, decorated the mattress. She had hung several photographs around the room. Turkey, Italy, Greece. She had chosen rich earth tones for her color scheme and accented them with splashes of maroon, yellow, and blue. A large area rug that looked Turkish decorated the floor. It reached almost to the door and halfway under the bed. Six elegant candle stands stood around the room, each graced with a beeswax pillar candle. All had been used.

I found a book of matches on one of the bedside tables and fired up the candles. When I turned off the overhead light the effect was magical. "Wow," I breathed. A haven. That's what this room was. *Hell, that's what Sage is for me.* I left the candles burning, since Sage would be home soon. I took my shoes and socks off and placed them on the floor near the armoire, then slipped out of my jeans, folded them, and placed them on my shoes. I took my shirt off and removed my bra and then put my shirt back on.

I pulled the comforter back—Sage was almost as anal as Megan was about making a bed—and eased between the cool sheets. Everything smelled of Sage, vibrated with her presence, welcomed me. I relaxed, felt the day work its way out of my thoughts, felt sleep claim me. I don't know how long I dozed. It didn't seem but a minute that I had shut my eyes when I heard soft movements that registered in the part of my brain that hadn't succumbed to deeper sleep yet. I opened my eyes, relaxed but confused and rolled over.

"Hi," Sage said. She had already stacked some of her equipment near the closet door.

"So how did it go?" I sat up, moving the sheets and comforter aside, studying her in the candlelight. She wore an elegant form-fitting black dress that fell just below her knees. The neckline plunged to the tops of her breasts. It hugged everything. Every curve, every line of muscle. She had her hair tied back. I forgot anything else. "You look—damn." My heart pounded.

"Thanks," she said, laughing softly as she took her earrings out. She then pulled the tie out of her hair, describing the opening as she did so. I was caught up in the candlelight that cast shadows across her skin, across her amazing shoulders. Amazing everything. Her hair fell softly around her face, animated as she told me that she'd sold fifteen photographs out of twenty-five. She was extremely excited about that and she had met with four benefactors, which was a major plus. She was confident that two, at least, would help fund a couple of trips in the future. I sat watching her, listening to her, drinking her in. "That's awesome," I said, meaning it.

She stopped suddenly and looked at me, serious. "Do you want to talk about what happened today?" She sat down on the bed next to me and brushed my hair away from my forehead.

I shook my head. "Later." I reached for her hand. "I just really need to be near you right now."

She smiled. "I can do that." She stroked my cheek with her hand. "I got a call today from Joe Montoya."

A grin tugged the side of my mouth.

"I can't believe you did that," she said, an odd expression on her face. Sort of puzzled but relieved. And something else that I couldn't identify.

"Did what?" I said innocently.

She shook her head, smiling. "It's funny. Those are two of my favorite pictures. It took me two hours to get my equipment into that canyon. Not counting the three-hour hike into the backcountry." She sat back, looking at me. "They're the same canyon, actually. But I had to stay out there for two days to make sure I got the right light."

"They spoke to you," I said softly.

She looked at me sharply.

"The people who decorated the walls," I elaborated.

"They did. It was magical. And I wasn't sure I wanted to sell those images, but I had a feeling that the right person would buy them." She arched an eyebrow. "When—"

"Saturday afternoon. I needed to see some of your work. So I went to the gallery and I saw those two pictures and I knew that no matter what happened between us, I'd have a part of you. And I'd always treasure that."

She fell silent for a while, holding my hand. When she spoke, she raised her gaze to mine. "I told Joe to call me when those sold. I do like to know who's buying my stuff for the most part, but those in particular, I really wanted to know."

"I was going to tell you, but I totally forgot." I shrugged, sheepish.

An expression entered her eyes that I hadn't seen before. It spoke of rivers in the desert, of new trees in the wake of forest fires, and the whispers of kachina spirits on the wind. I pulled my hand gently from hers and took her face in my hands. I ran the tips of my thumbs along her cheekbones and I saw that path in her eyes again. This time, I took it. I leaned in, brought my lips to hers and felt heat race through my veins, infuse my muscles, and burn away the ghosts of my past that lingered on my bones. I felt hope enter my mouth with her tongue, felt want beneath her hands on my back, and I knew, then, what it meant to find a place in someone's heart.

Hurricane. Mystic. Nature Girl. Artist. I let myself fall into her, allowed myself to wander across her lips and journey within the circle of her arms. She welcomed me. Protected me. Drew the day's debris from my skin with the power of her kisses. I wanted to cry and laugh as I finally pulled away, staring into her eyes. "Sage," I whispered.

"Are you all right?" She said it softly. "We can wait."

"I'm more than all right. And I don't want to wait."

She stroked my face, smiling. She gently pushed me back onto the bed and pressed herself against me. I wrapped my arms around her and she kissed me again. Her fingers buried themselves in my hair, stroked my face, danced over my shoulders. I rolled over, bringing her with me. My breathing sped up, echoing my heartbeat and the throbbing between my thighs. Our kisses deepened and her mouth was more insistent on mine. Her lips tasted and felt like life itself. Her hands moved underneath my shirt and her fingers tracked lines across my back. I tore away from her kiss and ran my lips along her jaw, down her neck. She gasped and pulled me against her. I felt like I was either going to pass out or explode. Maybe both at the same time.

She grabbed the bottom of my shirt, began pulling it over my head. I helped her and she finished the job, tossing it onto the floor. She had that devilish grin going and I knew I was in for a hell of a night. I found the zipper on her dress — it ran vertically down her left side. The dress and her bra soon joined my shirt on the floor. She was wearing black silk panties. My breath caught at the sight of her nearly nude, revealed in the soft light of the candles. I could only stare, awestruck. I ran my fingers from her neck to her abdomen, tracking between her breasts. She arched into my touch.

"You're beyond beautiful." I straddled her hips and the heat emanating from her took my breath away. Leaning down, I teased her nipples with my tongue. She groaned and tangled her fingers in my hair, pulling me against her. I closed my lips around one of her nipples, sucking and pulling gently, loving how she felt between my teeth. She moaned and another surge of moisture collected between my thighs. I wanted to touch every part of her, kiss every part of her, and take as much time as possible.

I started with her face and ears, then mapped her neck and shoulders, tasting my dreams mingling with hers on her skin. She was thrusting slowly against me, then grinding. I met each of her movements, matched her rhythm as my lips explored her arms.

"You're exquisite," I murmured, my lips on her fingertips. I slowly drew her index finger into my mouth, sucked it gently and released it. She pressed her hand against my cheek and I leaned into her palm, caught up in the way her body moved with mine. Her other hand rested at the small of my back and her fingers tugged at the waistband of my underwear, breached the boundary between cloth and skin.

She quickly adjusted her angle and her mouth found one of my nipples. Her lips were like feathers and they spawned mini-tornadoes from my breasts to my clit. "K.C.," she whispered, her breath hot on my chest. "I need to feel you."

I braced myself above her and both her hands were suddenly on my hips. She pushed my underwear down. I shifted and helped her as she nipped and nuzzled my breasts. I was breathing so hard I thought I might pass out. She slid her own panties off and all I could do was bite my lip at the sight of her. She was beautiful. No, stunning. Unreal.

"What did I do right?" I whispered.

"You jumped." I felt her hand between my thighs, felt her fingertips ease through my moisture. I moaned and watched as she brought her fingers to her lips. She grinned at the taste of me, which only made the ache deep within me push harder against my bones. She kissed me again and I pulled her against me, her heat mingling with mine, her desire fueling mine. Our legs entwined and the intensity of our thrusts increased. I don't think I had ever been so wet, so completely connected to another human being. My heart jumped into my throat, my blood pounded in my ears, and nothing but Sage mattered. I lowered my lips to her shoulder, tasted sweat.

She eased her fingers between us and I shifted so she could enter and I groaned at how she felt within me. "Oh, God—Sage. What you do to me..."

"And what I'll *keep* doing to you," she teased, lips on my neck. She was thrusting, gently. Her thumb was moving against my clit and every breath I took sounded more like a gasp. "You're so damn sexy," she muttered against my lips. "The first time I saw you in person, I couldn't take my eyes off you."

I groaned again in response, wrapped around her fingers, the feel of drums deep within luring me toward a cliff.

"And you don't even realize it," she laughed softly, her breath coming in short bursts. "Everything about you." She increased her thrusts slightly, staring into my eyes. "I didn't want to put too much stock in stories about you from another person." She slowed then, gently easing me back from the precipice. "But then you stood up and shook my hand and you looked right at me." She matched the motions of her hand with her hips.

I moaned, powerless though I managed a grin. "I knew I was in for trouble. I think—oh, God," I said at a particularly delicious thrust. "I think they should name hurricanes after you."

She laughed and kissed me, drawing my tongue into her mouth and sucking it hard before she released it. "So it wasn't just me feeling something that night." She chewed gently on my neck. I had no coherent thoughts. She increased the speed of her thrusts. Her fingers plunged deep within me and the angle of her thumb on my clit took me right to an edge again. The drumbeat within me neared a crescendo.

"No," I managed. "You were just the first to do something about it." My lungs contracted and I hovered on the edge. "I'm close," I said with a gasp, meeting her thrusts, incapable of doing anything else.

"I know," she whispered, urgent. "I think I'll join you."

I held off as long as I could, staring into her eyes and then the room receded until there was nothing except the connection between us and the pounding of my blood in my skull.

"Jump," she breathed. "Jump with me."

I did and I heard a low, deep growl as I plummeted over the edge, bringing her with me somehow. I heard my name on her lips again and as I settled back to earth, I realized that the growl had been mine. I collapsed against her, shaking. Little lightning currents raced up and down my arms and legs. She held me tenderly, stroked my hair and back.

"Well, you're clearly not the silent type," she said against my ear. I heard laughter in her voice.

I chuckled. "Thanks for sticking around to find out."

She hugged me.

"I hope you stick around a bit longer," I continued tentatively. I wanted every possible second she'd give me. I had looked into the eyes of Hurricane Sage and everything changed.

She pulled my face to hers and kissed me before she answered. "There's nothing I'd rather do," she said then and I felt a molten peace settle in my veins at her words, at the expression in her eyes. I touched her lips with my fingertips, followed a line to her breasts where I coaxed her nipples to stiffen against my hand. My fingers continued their journey to her thighs and the places she wanted to share with me.

I grinned. "Hmm. Silent type? Or not?" I slid my fingers into her heat, pulled them out and brought them to my lips. The taste of her shot through me like an electrical charge. She kissed me, then pulled away.

"Why don't you find out?" she teased, as she guided my hand back to her thighs.

"I will," I murmured against her lips. Another storm brewed within me. And I welcomed it.

Chapter
Twenty-one

MELISSA STOOD LOOKING around the living room of Megan's place. I went to the fridge and got her an iced tea. She took it wordlessly, absently shaking it up before unscrewing the top.

"So Megan's going to be staying with you?" I stared at the bottle of tea in my own hand.

She nodded and took a sip.

I cleared my throat. "Good. I think that's really good. How are you doing?"

"Okay. Thank God there's no lasting physical damage." She put a slight emphasis on "physical."

"Any idea what Megan'll want to do next?"

She shrugged. "She asked for a few days to clear her head a bit. So I'm not asking. I do know she doesn't want to live in this house anymore. She was very clear about that when we left the hospital yesterday. But I'm not pushing her."

I reached out and squeezed her arm gently. "Well done."

She sighed. "I'm really trying not to fall back into my big sister nagging routine with her. I mean, she *is* an adult." She took another sip from her bottle.

"She has to find her own way, no matter how hard that is for you. And her."

"I just want her to stay away from all that racist crap." She stopped and looked at me. "So I guess you'll be leaving soon."

I thought I detected a trace of regret in her voice. "Um, that's something I need to talk to you about."

Her eyes narrowed. "What?"

"I'm..." I hesitated and glanced away, then glanced back "I'm thinking about staying on through the fall. I might be able to get an article about the Rats, in terms of group dynamics and development. That sort of thing. But also, I'll be able to hammer away on the book."

Melissa was quiet, staring at the floor. "And?"

Damn. She could still read me.

"I've missed New Mexico. And Chris. And you and Megan, actually."

She looked up at me then, skepticism on her face. "Kase, you've never been very good at hiding things. What's the other reason?"

I ran a hand through my hair and chewed my lip. "I, um, I might have met someone."

She stared at me for a long time. I didn't look away, waiting for her reaction. A slow smile edged her mouth. My whole body relaxed.

"Do I want to know who she is?" A familiar little twinkle danced in her eyes.

"You already do."

Her brow furrowed. "I know it's not Chris..." she trailed off and then inhaled sharply. "Oh, my God," she said, shock in her voice. "Sage?"

I shifted my weight nervously.

"Sage? Really?" Melissa stared at me, a mixture of disbelief and shock in her expression.

I looked at her, helpless.

Still smiling, she shook her head. "I would never have put you two together."

"Me, either," I said wryly. "Never say never, I guess."

"I'm amazed. And you think it's serious enough to warrant staying for another couple of months?"

"I won't know unless I do. And the timing is really good. I'm on sabbatical, after all. Plus, I'll be doing some research and..." my voice faded as I watched Melissa struggling not to laugh. "What?"

"You. Ever the pragmatist. What does your heart say?"

¿Qué dice tu corazón? Chris's words echoed Melissa's. And I had answered her the same way I did Melissa. "It says to stay, that Sage is someone special."

Her expression softened. "Then I'm happy for you." A shadow momentarily clouded her expression.

"Meliss' —"

"Hey, don't worry. The thought *did* cross my mind, about getting back with you. But there's too much to sort through and I like how things are between us now." She took my free hand in hers and squeezed it. "Maybe that's what guided me to Texas."

I didn't know what to say so I just stood there, holding on to her hand. How weird, talking to an ex about the possibility of a new relationship with someone else.

"Let me talk to Megan and see how she feels about you taking over the lease on her place. If she's into it, I'll call the landlord."

"Wha —"

"She's already said she doesn't want to come back here. And I know Rob would want someone *responsible* and *mature* here." Her eyes twinkled again. "Let me take care of this, okay?"

I stared at her. "I don't know what to say."

"How about 'thank you'?" She released my hand.

I smiled. "Thanks."

"You're welcome." She started moving toward the door. "Okay, I'm going home. Megan and I will be able to start moving into the new place in a couple of days. I'll let you know what's happening."

"You okay with Hillary there?"

Melissa paused at the door and looked back at me. "She's in Santa Fe until I move out."

"I'll see you later, then."

"Yes. You will." She flashed a grin and exited, shutting the door quietly behind her. I watched her walk down the walkway toward the street and this time, I felt peace.

I BRACED THE flaps of another box of Megan's books with my knee and reached for the tape. Melissa was in the bedroom, helping Megan finish up with the closet and bathroom. I heard them talking, bantering back and forth about some of Megan's goofier T-shirts.

"Hey, nothing wrong with 'Hello Kitty,' " I called from the living room as I finished up the box.

"Thank you, Kase," Megan hollered back, a giggle in her voice.

"Though I myself prefer the Powerpuff Girls," I added before I moved the box near the front door.

Megan appeared in the doorway to the bedroom suddenly. "Buttercup, right?"

I looked at her and grinned. "Of course. I could see *you* as Bubbles. Everybody thinks you're a pushover but you have a spine of steel. And you can totally kick ass."

A shadow crossed her face. "Thanks," she said softly.

"I'm going to order a pizza for dinner," Melissa interrupted as she gently eased past Megan. "Any requests?"

"Pepperoni and green chile." Megan took the phone book out of one of the boxes I hadn't sealed yet. "You're too efficient," she teased me. "Wait 'til we eat. And I'll order. Papa John's okay?"

Melissa and I voted in the affirmative and I flopped onto the couch while Megan dialed and began placing the order. She wandered into the kitchen. "You guys want anything to drink?"

"No," Melissa said. She wasn't a big fan of soft drinks and that's pretty much what Papa John's offered.

"No, thanks," I agreed. "I've got tea in the fridge."

Megan finished the order and joined Melissa and me in the living room. She sat down next to me. Melissa watched us for a bit then returned to the bedroom. I reached over and squeezed Megan's knee as I stood up. "Gotta finish these books, kiddo." I caught myself. "Shit, I'm sorry. You're not a kid anymore. I keep doing that."

She smiled. "I don't mind."

In the ten days since Megan had "rejoined the world," as Sage called it, I'd been trying to figure out how to interact with her. She wasn't ready to talk about much with regard to Cody and the Rats, and I didn't press her. She managed to provide a lot of information useful to law enforcement, but I knew she needed to do some soul-sifting about the more personal aspects of her experience. I turned back to the shelves, thinking that I needed to say a few things to her, as well. A lump formed in my throat.

"You set up an appointment with that counselor yet?" I kept my eyes on my task, which involved filling another empty box with the last of the books from her living room shelves.

"Yep. Day after tomorrow."

"Good." I heard Melissa doing something in the bedroom closet. I stopped packing and turned to look at Megan. No time like the present. "I'm really sorry," I blurted.

She looked up at me, puzzled. "For what?"

"I bailed on you, when Melissa and I broke up. I let you down. And I'm so sorry." Tears stung my eyes.

"Hey," she said as she stepped over a box and hugged me. "You were in a lot of pain and did what you thought you had to do. I should have tried to talk to you, too."

Tears slid down my cheeks. "I'm sorry," I whispered again. "I wish I could do that over, that whole leaving thing."

"Stop. It's done and you're here now." She held on to me and it was the fifty-year-old Megan, the one much too wise for her years, the one who had seen way too much before she turned eighteen. "Not like I learned much, either. Dating an asshole like that."

I laughed a little and wiped my eyes as Melissa appeared in the doorway to the bedroom. She hesitated, uncertain.

"Group hug," Megan said, reaching out to Melissa. "Come on," she pressed. "Even uptight big sisters should get in on the action."

Melissa started to say something, thought better of it, and instead joined the hug.

"There. Doesn't everyone just feel better?" Megan pulled away, smiling, and flopped onto the couch.

I wiped my eyes again, glad Melissa was crying, too. She rubbed her face with the hem of her T-shirt. "Thanks," she said softly before returning to the bedroom. I cleared my throat and continued putting books in the box I was working on. It was a start to better days. Hopefully.

"I submitted the transfer paperwork," Megan said after a few minutes.

I stopped again. She regarded me from her position on the couch, one leg drawn up underneath her. She looked so thin. Like a ghost in so many ways. But unlike when she came out of rehab, she seemed solid and grounded, somehow. "That's great news. When will you hear?"

"Pretty soon, I guess."

I put another book in the box. "There shouldn't be any problem. Your grades are great. What will you do this fall?"

"I'll take some time and go to Eugene to find a place to live." She laughed softly. "Listen to me. Assuming the U of Oregon'll let me in!"

"Of course they will," Melissa said from the doorway. "K.C.'s right. You have good grades and good recommendations."

Megan nodded slowly. "I think, though, I'll probably move in with my cousins." She stopped and I glanced at her. "I don't really want to be alone for a while." She looked over at Melissa, whose jaw tightened.

"Hey, if you're not ready for that, then don't worry about it. All in good time." I smiled at Megan then at Melissa, worried that Melissa was going to say something big-sisterly that would annoy Megan and ruin the bonding moment we'd all just shared. "Just make sure you vacuum over at Melissa's and take her shit to the cleaners and seal that tile so she knows you're not just sitting on your butt eating bon-bons and watching soaps all day while you're living with her."

Megan laughed and Melissa relaxed. She flashed a relieved expression at me. Megan got up and followed Melissa back into the bedroom. I finished with the box and looked up as the pizza delivery man appeared. Melissa raced past me to pay him and we camped out on the living room floor, the pizza box on the coffee table along with three bottles of Tazo. A picnic, Megan used to call meals like this when Melissa and I were still together. She'd get so excited, like pizza while sitting on the living room floor was the coolest thing ever. I looked at her, and she was fourteen again as she reached for a piece of pizza and threw a piece of chile at Melissa. Strange, how things changed but stayed the same somehow.

A car door slammed from the street. Melissa looked out through the wide-open front door as Chris approached.

"Hey," she announced, pulling her sunglasses off when she stepped inside.

"*Hola, mujer,*" I greeted her. "Grab a piece."

"Tempting. But I just ate. How's it going?"

"Finer than frog's hair, as Grandpa says." I stood up and went to get Chris an iced tea out of the fridge. I handed it to her and she sat down on the couch next to Megan, across from me and Melissa. She shook it up and opened it, then took a long drink.

"Okay. Would you like an update?" Chris addressed Megan, who nodded for her to continue. She then glanced over at Melissa.

"Yes, actually," she agreed.

"All right." Chris took a breath. "Those two who got injured in the raid are singing like birds, as is the gentleman Megan and K.C. know as 'Timmy.' We've got enough weapons and bomb-making stuff out of that place to get some federal charges to stick. Mr. Sorrell—" Chris glanced at Megan, who reached for another piece of pizza. "—is still being held here. Timmy says he and Watkins set up the Talbot murder but the trigger man is some drifter from northern California who has peripheral dealings with the movement. Apparently, Talbot got cold feet about what they were up to and was going to go to the cops. He didn't get the chance."

"Where is the trigger man now?" I asked, reaching for a napkin. *Fucker.*

Chris shook her head. "We've got a big net out for him. He's wanted for assault back there, so he's in a few databases. Timmy also told us that Watkins was planning to blow the courthouse here in town. That's what the 'something big' was that you kept hearing about, Megan."

"I figured it was something like that. But they never mentioned it specifically." She took a sip from her bottle. Her voice sounded tight.

Chris put a hand on her shoulder. "I can stop," she said quietly.

"No." Megan addressed Chris though she was looking at Melissa. "I need to hear it."

Chris glanced at me and continued. "No word on Watkins. Yet."

Megan's jaw clenched.

"Hey, he'll surface," I said quickly. "He's really pissed now, which actually plays in our favor because he'll make a mistake. And guys like that like to be visible in the movement."

"K.C.'s right," Chris agreed. "He'll turn up. And the heat's on now because he's wanted for federal weapons violations and plotting his own version of Oklahoma City."

I didn't say what I knew Chris was thinking. Watkins's background in an abusive household meant he probably had problems with women, which might translate into blaming Megan in particular for spilling information, though Timmy was actually the one who provided all the main details of Watkins's plans. Melissa was suddenly extremely engrossed in her pizza. Megan chewed quietly. If Watkins showed up and started messing with Megan again, I would personally start an end-times war on his ass.

"We'll get him." Chris squeezed Megan's shoulder again. She finished her tea and stood. "I have to get going."

"I do, as well." Melissa got to her feet. "Megan, do you want to come with me or—"

"I'll come with you." She stood and started cleaning off the coffee table.

I got up and glanced at my watch. Nearly eight. Sage was due back from Santa Fe in an hour and we were going to load the car for a camping trip the next day to what New Mexicans called "The Gila," a wilderness in the mid-southwestern part of the state, known for its mystical qualities and natural hot springs. I was really looking forward to it.

Chris set her empty bottle on the kitchen counter. "Oh, I ran into Gus yesterday," she said, directing the comment at me as she returned to the living room. "He wanted me to tell you thanks again for talking to him and providing copies of your notes. He said he could get you in on the consulting gig if you're interested. He'll be giving you a call in couple of days to try to tempt you." She smiled. "It'd be great if you moved back."

"What, so you can drag me along on your adventures?"

"Oh, so it's *my* fault, now?" She started laughing. "Kiss my ass, Fontero."

"Yeah, you'd like that," I retorted, smiling.

"Excuse me," Melissa interrupted. We both looked at her, sheepish. "Ladies, as much as I'd love to encourage your conversation," she teased, "I'd prefer to invite you both—and Sage as well—to a celebration at the new house on Saturday." She poked me in the arm. "Have you decided when you'll be going back to Austin?"

"Clearly after Saturday," I said, grinning.

Chris shot me a look that said *we need to talk.*

Melissa smiled. "Good. Don't worry about food or drinks. And we'll probably be able to finish up here tomorrow. Thanks."

"Sure. I'll lock up."

She turned to Chris then. "I know we haven't talked much recently, but I meant what I said at the hospital. I can't tell you how much I appreciate all you did for me and Megan. And for keeping Kase safe. It means more to me than I'll ever be able to express."

Chris looked down at her feet, then back up. Compliments made her uncomfortable. "You're welcome." She looked at the floor again.

Melissa hugged both me and Chris and stepped back. "Megan, I'll meet you at the car." Melissa headed out the door and down the walk.

"Don't worry about that," I called to Megan in the kitchen. "I'll clean up."

She joined us in the living room. "You sure?"

"Yeah. Go get some more sleep. Rent a movie. Hang out. Enjoy yourself." I gave her a big hug.

"Thanks. I'll see you in a couple of days. I think I want to talk a little more."

"Definitely. Call me and we'll grab dinner or something." I kissed her on the cheek. She'd call me, I knew. And I also knew she had a few things she wanted to say to me, as an adult. She released me and hugged Chris before following Melissa. Chris and I watched her until she reached the curb.

Chris turned to regard me. "What's up, *esa*?"

"In terms of what?" I tried to sound innocent, though I had a million different things flying through my head.

"You know exactly what I mean." She crossed her arms over her chest.

"Fuck, Chris. I have so much shit I'm trying to figure out. There's this shit with Megan, there's trying to move beyond Melissa—and it's weird, because I almost feel like I'm a co-parent for Megan. But she's not a kid anymore. But she is. It's—weird. I'm having a hard time negotiating that."

She cocked her head. "And?" Her tone told me that she was only buying part of my rambling.

I shoved my hands in my pockets. "I have to go back to Texas at some point. I have to figure out what I'm doing and check in and mundane, boring shit that comes with academic obligations. A lot of my life is there right now." I trailed off, realizing that it sounded like excuses, and that my heart wasn't in it.

She raised an eyebrow, an "oh, really?" expression. "That's not true. Most of your life has been here. Texas was an escape. You've never really settled there. So now you have a chance to come home. What are you going to do?"

I chewed on my lower lip, trying to make some sense of all the crazy things that had happened in the past couple of weeks.

She interrupted my thoughts, worry in her dark eyes. "Kase, are you running?"

"In what sense?"

"Going back to Texas—are you using that as an excuse to avoid anything deeper with Sage?"

"God, no. But I am trying to be mature. I mean, Jesus, I did take Megan's place on her lease for a bit." And there was always the possibility that Sage might think that was too forward. *Shit.*

"Have you talked to her?"

"Every damn day." I ran a hand through my hair, frustrated. "She knows I don't want to go back. Christ, I don't want to go. I miss New Mexico. I've missed it every day since I left. But I got the post-doc in Texas. And besides, Sage might think I'm being way too clingy or something. I worry about *that*, too."

"You think too much," she said, a little smile on her lips.

I shot her a "yeah, and?" look.

"Get out of your damn head." She ruffled my hair. "You do your research here for the fall semester. Then you go back to Texas to finish out the post-doc. Then you come back here. Gus could set you up with something. And Mark would definitely put in a word for you. Law enforcement uses outside consultants all the time these days, especially in terms of what *you* do." She smiled, smug. "You know I'm right. And you know you can't resist me."

I rolled my eyes. "Detective Goddess, over here."

"And I know you've already checked into this. I know how you are."

"Dammit," I muttered. "And *you* know I hate it when you're right. Okay, so American Studies at UNM might be interested in setting me up with something."

"Uh huh. As I suspected. Even in the midst of your freak-outs, you're still trying to analyze." She air-kissed me. "But it's one of the many things I love about you."

"Oh, of course," I said, smiling. "But still, whatever happens, I don't think I'll be here until next summer."

"That's plenty of time to get something here. And you can always live with me until you do. If Sage won't put up with you, I can for a bit."

"Excuse me? Put up with me?"

She punched me lightly on the shoulder. "So for real. How do you feel about her?"

I shook my head, a huge grin on my face. "It's bad, *amiga*. It's bad."

She smiled again, but it was wistful. "I'm really happy for you. I can't say I won't miss certain things between us. But I want the best for you. So don't be *estupida*."

"Well, I want the best for *you*. Since that's not me..." I grinned, leaving the statement unfinished.

"This really isn't that hard, oh great scholar. She's good for you and you know it. Yeah, you have a few things to take care of in Texas, but so what? You'll be done there soon and then—" she shrugged, a "see how it goes" motion. "Don't let the past determine your future."

"Listen to you," I said, laughing. "Are you my psychic now?"

"*Abuelita* always says, '*no espera para el pasado.*' Don't wait for the past. It's done. And Sage is—well, there isn't really a good way to describe her. But she's good for you." Chris grinned and wrapped me in a huge bear hug. "I have to run. I've got some errands to take care of and then we have to do cop stuff early tomorrow. I should be able to go Saturday. I'll call you. And don't you dare do anything insane. If there's even the remotest possibility that you are thinking insane thoughts, anything about bailing for Texas and never coming back, call me so I can smack you around and remind you to get out of your damn head. Though I suspect Sage will be better able to talk you out of anything completely *loco* like that." She grinned mischievously.

"I'm still not sure how this all is going to work," I said. I wanted it to. God, how I wanted this all to work out like Chris said. I just wasn't sure how I could make it work.

"Have some faith, Doctor Over-analysis. You've got the next five months here with Sage. Then you go finish shit up in Texas. You'll be back here in May."

I laughed again. "How can you be so sure?"

"I just am. Besides," she said, dark eyes twinkling, "*Abuelita* told me. And she is *never* wrong about matters of the heart."

"I so love her. And I love you, too. But I think all this love shit is starting to get to me."

Chris hugged me. "Because you can't really analyze it. So get over it and just *be*."

I held on to her for a while, thinking that I was the luckiest woman ever to have such cool people in my life. Yep. I had to come back to New Mexico. And somehow, I'd make that happen.

She released me. "You know you're coming back," she said, like she'd just caught my brain wave. "And I'll help you in any way you need. Though I'm sure Sage is already doing that force of nature thing. You can't resist her, either." She pinched my cheek and I blushed, which made her laugh.

"Yeah, yeah. Run along and go solve crimes and all that."

"All right. I'll talk to you later. *¡Hasta!*" She started walking back to her car.

"Chris," I called after her.

She turned, waiting.

"Thanks."

"*De nada.* Catch you in a few." She waved and continued walking.

"I'm so lucky," I said to myself as the long evening shadows stretched across the back yard. So damn lucky.

I SAT STARING into the embers, my back against a log someone had left at this campsite, probably for the express purpose of what I was doing right then. We had already pitched the tent well away from the firepit and eaten dinner. I took a sip of wine from my plastic cup and no matter what purists say about drinking wine, it tasted damn fine in that cup at that campfire, accompanied by a million

stars overhead and the crisp smell of piñon. The murmur of the Gila
River provided background music and because it was a weeknight,
we were the only ones using the campground.

Sage returned from a quick trip to the bathroom. She retrieved
her own plastic cup from the picnic table and sat down next to me,
snuggling up against my left side. "This is amazing," I said quietly.
We had spent the morning hiking up to a hot springs, where we then
spent an entirely delectable and private afternoon thoroughly
enjoying each other's company before heading back as the shadows
lengthened.

"Mmm hmm," she responded. I smelled traces of lavender in her
hair and another stirring between my thighs heated my blood.

Business first. "So," I started, nervous.

"You use that tone when you're trying to say something you're
not sure about." She stroked my hand. "What are you thinking?"

"Damn. I can't hide anything, can I?"

"Nope. But you shouldn't anyway. Unless it's a surprise party
for me." She giggled against my shoulder.

I sighed happily, then continued. "Okay, I've been thinking.
And as you know, it sometimes takes me a while to figure things
out."

She hugged me tighter.

"How would you feel if I hung out a little bit longer in New
Mexico before heading back to Texas?" I let my lips brush her
forehead. "I mean, I'd have to go back briefly to get some stuff in
order, but then I could maybe sabbatical here?"

"You have to ask?" she retorted, teasing.

"Well, I mean, it is kind of weird, maybe. We haven't known
each other all that long."

"So how are we supposed to get to know each other better if you
don't hang out a bit longer?" She started nuzzling my neck.

"Now *that* is logic I won't argue with," I said between my teeth
as her tongue worked its way down my neck.

"Rent Megan's place," she continued, murmuring against my
cheek.

I swallowed nervously. "I already did."

She stopped and pulled back to look at me, studying my eyes in
the firelight. "Oh, my God. You did. Why didn't you tell me sooner?"

"I wanted to make sure you were okay with me sticking around
for a bit. And I wanted to surprise you on this trip."

She stroked my face with her fingertips. "Am I to understand
that you're interested in seeing where things go?" She smiled
mysteriously, teasingly.

I kissed her. "Right now, they're going to go into the tent," I said
against her lips, "where I'm going to undress you very slowly."

"Do tell," she said as she pulled away then traced my jaw with her lips. "And then?" She pressed, her lips against my neck.

I took her hand. "Let me show you."

End
For now, anyway.

FORTHCOMING TITLES

published by
Quest Books

Angel Land
by Victor Banis

Late in the 21st Century, ravaged by the deadly Sept virus, the one time United States has disintegrated into The Fundamental Christian Territories, where Catholics, Baptists and Jews are registered as heretics, and gays are herded into walled ghettos: the Zones of Perversion.

Harvey Milk Walton, a runner, finds his way to the ghetto in Angel Land, oldest of the territories. A legend says that there his long ago martyred namesake will return one day to lead his people to freedom — but even to speak of freedom, of leaving the FTC, is punishable by death.

In a crumbling totalitarian society, where evil masquerades as piety, two men fall in love, and begin to dream of escape from Angel Land.

Available November 2008

State of Denial
by Andi Marquette

Albuquerque Police Detective Chris Gutierrez is not having a "Thank God It's Friday" kind of day. Not only is she on the scene of a murdered young man, buried near the Rio Grande, but she also has to put up with the other detective assigned to the case, the homophobic and sexist Dale Harper.

As if things weren't uncomfortable enough between the two detectives, they soon find out that the young victim was gay, and the trail leads Chris and Harper to another unsolved murder whose victim was also a gay youth. Soon, their suspect is a popular minister at a local mega-church who has spent years working with ex-gay groups. Enlisting the research skills, networks, and expertise of sociologist and long-time best friend K.C. Fontero, Chris works to build the case against Mumford, all too aware what mistakes in such a potentially explosive and high-profile investigation could cost her and the police department.

As Chris strives to prove the case and make an arrest before anyone else dies, she must also face her growing feelings for attorney Dayna Carson. The dangerous nature of police work and Chris's own reticence about romantic relationships are destined to collide. Struggling with her attraction to Dayna and the complexity of a difficult case, Chris is drawn into an ominous and potentially deadly game of cat-and-mouse with a man who harbors dark secrets and who will kill to protect them. Will Chris outsmart a diabolical murderer — or become another victim?

Available December 2008

OTHER QUEST PUBLICATIONS

About the Author

Andi Marquette was born in Albuquerque and grew up in Colorado. After completing a couple of academic degrees in anthropology, she returned to Albuquerque where she completed a Ph.D. in history. She fell into editing in 1993 and has been obsessed with words ever since, which may or may not be a good thing. Currently, she resides in Colorado where she edits, writes, and nurtures a fascination with New Mexico chile.

VISIT US ONLINE AT
www.regalcrest.biz

At the Regal Crest Website You'll Find

- The latest news about forthcoming titles and new releases

- Our complete backlist of romance, mystery, thriller and adventure titles

- Information about your favorite authors

- Current bestsellers

- Media tearsheets to print and take with you when you shop

Regal Crest titles are available from all progressive booksellers and online at StarCrossed Productions, (www.scp-inc.biz), or at www.amazon.com, www.bamm.com, www.barnesandnoble.com, and many others.